The Unexpected Queen

A.R. Kaufer

Courting Books Publishing

Cover image & design by: A.R. Kaufer
Edited by Emily Hoffmann
ISBN 979-8-9867469-3-7
Courting Books Publishing
First published October 6th, 2022. Second Edition.

Lisa: My friend, my muse, my sister

Kevin: My lover, my husband,
my soulmate

Chapter 1

The Unexpected Meeting

His smile is the first thing she notices about the stranger. He peruses the market at his leisure as he speaks with a few of the merchants. She admires his tan skin, contrasting her pale complexion. Even with blond hair, he appears more natural to the market than she does, as everyone else is bronze. He brushes his hair back when a breeze sweeps through. Blushing at the sight, Sera turns her attention back to the young boy at her side, who is dressed in ripped pants, a loose shirt, and sandals too small for him.

She shakes her head in disappointment. "Kye, you know better! Why were you caught stealing?"

"We… we were hungry, Miss Sera," he admits, keeping his head down in shame.

"Then you know to come and see me." She hands him a slip of paper. "Deliver this message to the doctor. Bring me his response, and I will pay you. Deal?"

"Yes, Miss Sera. Thank you!" A smile on his face, he runs off to deliver it.

She sighs as she rearranges some of the produce at her stall. Glancing over, she pretends not to notice the stranger as he continues speaking with the merchants. She watches in confusion when one of them points in her direction. Turning away, she's smoothing her black hair down when the stranger clears his throat to get her attention.

"How may I help you today?" she asks as she gives him a polite smile, trying not to stare at his dirty, mismatched clothing.

"I am…um—" He clears his throat again. "Apologies. I am Dankin. I was told to see you for work?"

Sera studies him a moment and looks into his bright blue eyes, honest face, and unkempt hair. She takes a breath, thinking it over as she admires how well-built he is, then blushes as she meets his gaze. "What sort of work can you do?"

When he smiles at her, her stomach flutters. "I am physically fit and capable of any work you may require. I assure you, I am up for the task."

"Physical labor? Repairs? Various odd jobs?"

"Yes, I can do whatever you need. I only ask for room and board in exchange. I have nowhere to stay, and I was told you could help."

Kye approaches and catches her attention. "Excuse me a moment." She steps over to Kye to speak quietly with him. Upon receiving his response, she gives him a gold coin and two pieces of fruit, before giving her attention back to the stranger. "I don't need any harvesters at the moment, but the estate is in need of repairs." She notices his empty hands. "Do you have any other clothes?"

"No. The ship I was on was attacked by pirates and destroyed. I was the only one to get away. I—I lost everything." Looking down with emotion caught in his throat, he implores her. "Will you please help me?" He meets her gaze.

As she debates what to do, she takes a breath and looks at him with pity. "Yes, I will hire you. We'll have to get you clothing before l take you to the estate. It's almost time to break for lunch. We'll go then."

"I appreciate the opportunity. Thank you, Sera."

"That's Miss Sera, to my workers," she corrects.

"Of course. Apologies, Miss Sera."

She rearranges a few pieces of produce while waiting for her relief. Smiling when another worker arrives, she gestures to Dankin. "Hi'tob'a, good timing. This is Dankin, our newest worker. Dankin, Hi'tob'a. He's a permanent worker and has been with us for many years."

"Nice to meet you," Dankin says as he looks up to meet Hi'to'ba's eyes.

At six feet and two inches tall, Hi'tob'a towers over him. "You as well," he replies, looking him over with distrust. He brushes a piece of lint off his white cotton work shirt.

"Hi'tob'a, I may be a little late returning from lunch since I will be showing him around," she explains.

"Yes, Miss Sera. That is fine. Thank you for letting me know."

"Dankin, this way," she says and gestures for him to follow. They walk through the market, where Dankin admires the booths and buildings. He notices the curve of the roofs, the exposed wood siding, and how nestled together they are, barely room for a small alley in between a few of the buildings.

"The village is nice."

They arrive at the clothing merchant. Stepping inside, she's grateful they aren't busy.

"Miss Sera, what can I do for you today?" Kea'nda asks as she approaches her. The shop owner is dressed in a grey and blue hanfu, her sash tight to accentuate her thin waist. The skirt flows down her long legs, the hem riding her ankles. Her chestnut brown hair is pulled up tight, with a gold fan and white orchid pinned in.

"Kea'nda, this is our newest worker, Dankin. He needs two work outfits, sleep clothes, one dress outfit, and um," Sera blushes, "… necessities."

"Of course, Miss Sera, whatever he needs."

Sera turns back to Dankin. "I'll browse while she gets you taken care of."

"Thank you," he says, flashing her a smile, causing her stomach to flutter again.

Looking over the hanfu gowns, she runs her fingers along the silk displayed in vibrant colors with layers and sashes before giving her attention to the fancy gowns, made for the upcoming ball. Admiring a pink and white gown, she imagines arriving at the ball in a carriage, dancing the night away.

Blushing and growing warm when she realizes she was humming her favorite song, she looks around, grateful to be the only one in the room. She glances up when Kea'nda approaches her.

"He has an outfit to wear today. I'll make the necessary alterations to the other garments and have them delivered to you this afternoon, tomorrow morning at the latest. He discarded his old clothing."

"Thank you, Kea'nda. Put it on my tab, please."

"Um, about that, Miss Sera—"

"Yes?" she asks, shame washing over her.

"Nothing, we can discuss it later," Kea'nda offers when Dankin walks in.

"Thank you." Sera sighs in relief before turning her attention to him, studying him in his new clothes. Dressed in khaki pants with a simple short sleeve, grey shirt, and work shoes, she can't help but notice how handsome he is. "Are you ready to go to the estate?" she asks.

"Yes, Miss Sera."

Dankin follows her out the door, leaving the village and strolling along the beach. The sand is pink with the turquoise water crashing on the shore. She walks to the water, cupping her hand and scooping some out. Curious, he watches her trail her fingers along the surface and wonders what she is thinking about. She smiles at him as she returns to his side.

"Even growing up here, I never tire of the ocean. It's my favorite place," she says. "The water is so comforting." He returns her smile.

* * *

When they arrive at the estate, Dankin's jaw drops at the sheer size. "This is incredible! How many acres?"

"Fifteen. Now—"

"How many rooms?" he asks, looking at the manor. The exterior is dark brown with black shutters and roof.

Sera laughs softly. "Okay, it was built over a hundred years ago. It's two stories tall. It has twelve bedrooms, four parlors, eight washtoires, a kitchen, a dining room, and a basement. There are servants' quarters in a small cottage behind the estate, and workers' quarters by the orchard. My room is upstairs in the manor so I may aid the mistress and her family any time, day or night."

"It's incredible."

"It is the Dahvaene estate."

"What? As in Tsuji Dahvaene?" Dankin asks.

"Yes. You've heard of him?"

"I have," he replies with a gruff voice, clearing his throat. "Apologies. I am parched. Please, continue."

"We grow koko'appuru here. It's a special hybrid of pineapples and coconuts. We are the only orchard that grows them."

"On the island?"

"Anywhere. I created them myself a few years ago," she says with pride.

"Most impressive. That's what you were selling back at the market?"

"Yes. We grow a variety of fruits and vegetables to sell, in addition to the koko'appuru." She leads him into the grand foyer, where he stares in wonder at the dark wood trim and paneled walls, crystal chandeliers, and marble floors. He continues to admire the room as she leads him to the stairs. "I run the day-to-day affairs of the estate while overseeing the orchard and market stall." Once upstairs, she stops in front of a carved mahogany door and turns the knob, gesturing him inside as she opens the door.

"This is very nice," he comments, taking in the mahogany floors, the fireplace, the marble mantle, the canopy bed, and small chaise.

"You will stay in here, temporarily," Sera says.

"Planning to get rid of me already?" He chuckles until she gives him a serious look. "Apologies, Miss Sera."

"Our workers' quarters are currently full as we are in the middle of harvesting. A few seasonal workers come here from the mainland. Once the current season ends, you will then move to those quarters." She looks him up and down. "Assuming you are still here, that is."

"I see. Thank you."

"Please, freshen up," she offers as she gestures to the washtoire, "while I see to lunch. Come back down the stairs we used, make a right at the bottom, and that will lead you to the kitchen. After lunch, I will show you what is in need of repair."

"Thank you, Miss Sera, for your kindness and trust in me."

She swallows hard. "We'll see how this goes."

He gives her a small smile before he goes to the washtoire. She goes downstairs to prepare lunch, getting the tray out and fixing three plates which she then carries to the main quarters. Balancing the tray, she knocks softly. The door opens to a woman with dark brown hair, coated in make-up, and draped in fancy robes. She sighs at the sight of her, stepping back.

"Sera, come in," she says as she opens the door further.

Sera steps inside, narrowing her eyes as she tries to see. The curtains are pulled shut, with a few lamps giving some illumination. The room has crimson walls, a high ceiling, ebony wood floor and trim, with a large bed against one wall, and a smaller bed against the other. As Sera steps in, she walks towards the small table where she places the tray each meal. "How is everyone feeling?" she asks as she sets it down.

Rae'lin shakes her head. "As well as can be expected."

"Does Na'ito have an appetite?"

"He says he does, so we'll see. Any word on the doctor?"

"He will be here at two o'clock."

"Oh, thank goodness."

"We have someone to do repairs now. All he asks is room and board in exchange for the work."

"Very good."

"I will return to my duties, unless you require anything else of me, mistress?" Sera asks.

"No, Sera, you are dismissed."

She gives a small bow before returning to the kitchen. When Dankin walks in, she's fixing up two plates. She gestures him over to the small table in the corner. Setting the plates down, he lets out a low chuckle as he looks over their meal of fish and rice with salad.

"It looks good. Thank you," Dankin says, taking a bite.

As she eats, she tries not to stare at him. Blushing when he catches her, she lowers her gaze. "So, um, where are you from?"

"Somewhere far away. After we were attacked, I'm not sure how long I swam before I arrived here."

"Were you traveling with anyone?" Sera asks.

"Thankfully, no."

"Do you have any family?" She regrets asking when anger flashes across his face. "I apologize, that was too forward."

"It's all right. I had a family but lost them in the war," he explains, taking a drink and avoiding her gaze.

"I'm very sorry for your loss."

Hearing her sincerity, he gives her a smile with sorrow in his eyes. "Thank you for that."

After lunch, he washes dishes as she wipes down the table and counters. They go outside, where she walks him around and points out various areas in need of repair. She gestures to the shed to the left of the orchard. "That should have everything you need. If not, please see me so I may attend to it. If I am not here, find Ti'ako or Hi'tob'a. They will aid you however you need."

"Yes, Miss Sera. Thank you."

"I will return to the market. Please, do not wander around inside. See to your tasks, and if you finish before I return, you may rest in your quarters." She looks up, covering her eyes with her hand. "Also, stay hydrated. I do not wish to find you passed out when I return."

"I will. Thank you for your concern," Dankin says.

* * *

She arrives at the market and helps Hi'tob'a with an unexpected afternoon rush. Sighing in relief when the last customer walks away, she smiles at Hi'tob'a. "Where did that come from?"

Letting out a laugh, he shakes his head. "Apparently, they are having an event at the promenade. Many mainlanders came today."

"We may get busy again, then. Will you return to the estate so we may restock?" she asks.

"Yes, Miss Sera, at once." He promptly leaves.

"Afternoon, Sera. Hmm, what are we selling that's good today?"

She is arranging what few pieces are left when she tenses at his voice. She sucks in her breath before facing him, forcing a smile. "Everything from the orchard is good. What can I get for you, sir?"

"I don't want anything from the orchard," he says as he leans on the counter. "What I want comes from the manor," he teases as he stares at her intently.

Her face goes flush as she drops her gaze. "Sir, please—"

"Oh, stop with the fake humility. I know you want me just as badly. You hide by lowering your face, but I saw it in your eyes."

She fights down the vomit threatening to rise in her throat. "Sir, I know you are a good, wealthy man. I am sure there is someone out there—"

"What will it take, to get you to my estate?" Fury'am'a asks boldly, standing up straight.

Fighting her unease, she takes a breath. "I apologize, but that is most improper as we are not even courting."

"Because you reject my advances! I will speak to the mistress. I am sure she and I will work out an agreement. I need a wife, and you are the right age for childbearing." Staring at her mouth, he smiles. "It doesn't hurt that you are also beautiful. Are your lips as delicious as they look?"

She turns away to hide her anger and shame when he grabs her arm. "Sir—"

"You do not turn your back on me!"

"My apologies." She cries out in pain and shock when he slaps her across the face. Looking around for help, she sees the merchants are busy with their own stalls.

"You will do better!" he spits out as he walks off. She hangs her head, gently rubbing her face as her shame worms through her.

"Miss Sera, I'm back," Hi'tob'a says before unloading the cart.

"Thank you," she says, wiping her tears and helping him refill the booth. "Are you okay?"

"I'm fine. Please, return to the estate."

"Yes, Miss Sera." Hi'tob'a says, leaving the cart behind.

* * *

The market begins to empty, and she is relieved to finish the day. There is only half a bushel left, so she takes it over to Kye and his friends, who are grateful for the food. Kye reaches for the fruit when he sees the mark on her cheek. "Miss Sera! What happened to you?"

She brings her hand to her face. "I'm clumsy, is all," she says as she laughs softly. "Please, enjoy your fruit."

"Thank you, Miss Sera." He studies her face once more, before the boys dig into the bushel.

Sera starts her walk back to the estate. Along the way, she parks the cart and stops at the beach where she slips out of her dress, already wearing her suit underneath. Diving in, she lets her shame and anger flow out as she swims. She dries in the sun and dresses, then returns with her cart to the estate. Ti'ako approaches and takes it from her.

"Thank you."

"Yes, Miss Sera."

Upstairs, she changes gowns and freshens her make-up, covering the bruise on her face. She's cooking supper when Dankin walks in.

"Evening, Miss Sera. I've completed all of the repairs."

She looks up in surprise. "Already?"

He nods. "I told you I am quite capable."

"Apparently." Seeing the worry on his face, she gives him a reassuring smile. "I have other jobs for you."

"Thank you," he says with relief.

She sets his plate down before taking three more and placing them on the tray. "I will be right back. Please, go ahead and eat, as I'm sure you're famished after all of the work you've done." She goes to the main quarters, knocking softly. Rae'lin opens the door and lets her in. Sera sets the tray on the table, then turns to her. "Did the doctor come by?"

"Yes," Rae'lin answers, shaking her head. "They still don't know what is wrong with Na'ito. They know it is some sort of blood disease, but not what it is exactly. He gave him another dose of medicine to help ease his pain.”

Fighting her sorrow at the words, Sera takes a breath. “I'm sorry. I wish there was something I could do.”

“Well, for starters, you could've told me Lord Fury'am'a is interested in you!” Rae'lin beams.

“Mistress?” Sera asks, gently touching along her tender cheek. “You couldn't possibly be thinking of making an agreement with him, could you?” She shudders at the thought.

“He did send a message to me, asking to meet so we can discuss an agreement for you. Now, how long has this been going on? He is one of the wealthiest suitors here. You and I would both benefit.”

“He is a horrible—” she tries.

Rae'lin grabs her arm and throws her to the ground. “Stop and listen, you wretch!” She kneels beside her as Sera hides her face. “I will not abide such insolence!”

“I'm sorry, mistress.”

“Leave now. We will discuss this later.”

“Yes, mistress,” Sera says as she gets to her feet and flees the room. She goes into the kitchen, leaning over the sink as she composes herself, her heart pounding in fear at the thought of becoming betrothed to Fury'am'a. Dankin gently grips her arm, causing her to jump.

“Miss Sera, are you all right?” he asks.

“I'm fine,” she whispers as she brings her hand up, fixing her hair. “Please, retire for the evening.”

“I haven't eaten. I was waiting for you,” he admits.

She looks over and sees the two plates on the table. “Thank you. That's fine.” Once seated, Sera shifts uncomfortably. “I'm not used to eating with someone.” She gives him a small smile. “How long do you plan on staying?”

“As long as you'll have me, I guess.”

She frowns at his vague response. “Were your clothes delivered?”

“Yes. I've put them up already. I will repay you for those.”

“I know you will. Whenever you can, I'm not worried about it.” She sighs as she looks down. “Everything else I have to worry about.”

“Sera?”

She meets his gaze. “Sorry.”

“Are you all right?” he asks, genuine concern in his voice.

She gives a small nod, examining her plate as she eats. "I am, but thank you for asking."

He studies her face, curious about her milky complexion as he admires her long black hair cascading down her shoulders and back. He smiles at her when her bright blue eyes meet his. "Apologies, Miss Sera."

She lets out a quiet laugh. "You aren't the first person to stare."

"Still, I am sorry. I didn't mean to—"

She shakes her head. "It's okay. Everyone else here is so dark and bronze, while my skin is as white as mountain snow." She sighs. "Not that I've ever seen snow. Only in paintings."

He smiles at her, unable to help staring at her mouth. "Your lips are as red as any rubies I've ever seen."

She gasps softly, blushing as she hangs her head. "Thank you," she manages. A few strands of hair fall over her face. His hand reaches to brush it back when she recoils from him. "Please, don't touch me!" she cries out, jumping to her feet.

He stands up and takes a step back. "I'm sorry. What did I do?"

"Please, finish your meal and clean this up. I am retiring for the evening. My quarters are directly across from yours, should you require anything."

"Sera—"

Ignoring him and running to her quarters, she rushes to lock the door behind her. It takes a few moments for her heart to stop pounding. *What was he thinking? Reaching for me like that?* She takes a breath and goes to the washtoire to get ready for the night, then she climbs into bed. Sighing, she picks up a book from her nightstand, hoping to distract herself from the day she's had.

Her thoughts are racing as she thinks of his hand coming towards her. *He was only trying to help. He doesn't know. I have to give him the benefit of the doubt, as he seems sincere in his intentions, though I know absolutely nothing about him! How long is he staying? What is his true purpose here?* She puts the book back, falling asleep without any answers.

* * *

Sera is awakened by someone knocking quietly at her door. Sitting up, she stretches and looks at the clock, seeing it's a little past two. She gets into her robe and slippers before opening the door.

"Dankin, what do you need?" She yawns and wipes sleep from her eyes.

"I apologize for waking you. I had bad dreams. Do you have tea?"

"Follow me."

They go into the kitchen, where she puts the kettle on. He gets down two cups and saucers while she gets the tea. They sit in awkward silence while their tea steeps until Dankin speaks up.

"Thank you for making this. I am sorry for the inconvenience."

"You're welcome. It's no trouble. I am used to being awakened all hours of the night," she says, taking another sip of tea.

He starts to ask but thinks better of it. "I heard there is a festival coming up?"

"Yes. We are honoring the goddess Amphit'ran. She blesses us with fish from the ocean, so we have a celebration each year in her honor. It's a week of feasting, dancing, and ends with releasing floating lanterns. It's a few weeks away."

"It sounds fun. Is it?"

"Oh, I wouldn't know. I've never been," she says with a shrug.

"Why not?"

"I have too much responsibility. My obligations are here, to the estate and people within. Not to have fun."

"Perhaps we could go, if only for an hour?" he inquires.

She sighs, thinking it over. "We'll see." She finishes her tea, looking up as he takes her cup with his and washes them. "Thank you. Please, get some sleep now."

"You as well, Miss Sera."

She watches him leave. *Me? At the festival? I highly doubt it.* She brings her hair around, running her fingers through it, laughing quietly at the thought. *The mistress would not permit it. I shouldn't even ask, it will only upset her.* She sighs and gets up from the table. *No, I can't possibly go.*

* * *

Her alarm wakes her, and she yawns as she silences it. She slips into a pink and grey hanfu before walking over to knock on Dankin's door. He opens it, dressed only in pajama bottoms. Biting her lip as she eyes his muscular build, she quickly lowers her gaze to hide how deep she is blushing. "Um, apologies. I was seeing if you were awake yet."

"As you see, I am." He grins at her when she meets his gaze. "I will get dressed and be down momentarily."

"Thank you." She goes downstairs to prepare breakfast, takes the tray in, and returns to the kitchen, grateful to avoid any interactions with the mistress. As she fixes their plates, Dankin walks in. Seeing he is dressed in his work clothes, Sera nods in approval. He pours himself a cup of coffee, then they sit and eat as an uncomfortable silence passes by.

"Are you upset with me?" he asks bluntly.

Her breath catches in her throat as she nearly drops her fork. She looks at him. "No. Why would you possibly think that?"

"You were being quiet and didn't look at me."

"I'm used to eating by myself, in silence. Apologies. Um, after we eat, will you help me prepare the bushels for going to the market?"

"Of course, Miss Sera."

"Thank you."

He gathers the dishes to wash as she wipes off the table. They go outside, and she leads him to the cart. He follows her into the orchard, lifts the bushels, and places them onto it. "Will four be enough?" Dankin asks.

"Hmm. We had a small rush yesterday. Go ahead and add two more, please."

"Are you okay to get these to the market?" he asks as he finishes loading the cart.

"Would you help me?" Sera asks, thinking perhaps if she spends some time with him, she can finally learn something about him.

"Yes, Miss Sera." He lifts the handles, pushing the cart as she leads the way. As they stroll along the ocean path, she moves across the sand, cupping her hand in the water. He smiles as he watches her, quickly looking away when she glances up at him. She joins him back on the path as they near the market.

"We would put yesterday's fruit here, if we had any, so we can sell it first," she explains as she sets up the stall. Sera sighs when Fury'am'a approaches, forcing a smile as she faces him. "Good morning, sir. How may I help you today?"

He returns her smile as he takes her all in. "Well, you know what I want. Are you sure you aren't interested?"

Studying the lines in his face, she swallows hard. She notes his salt and pepper mustache and his noble dress, matching his status. "I am quite all right, but thank you."

"Hmm, I can be persuasive, you know."

"I'm sure you can, sir. Now, did you wish to make a purchase today?"

"Is that not what I'm trying to do? What's your price?" he asks as he smirks at her.

"The fruit—"

"No, Sera. How much for you?"

Her face goes flush as she looks down, adjusting her already straight gown. "Sir Fury'am'a, I know you jest. However, could we focus on a market transaction, please?" She glances over when Dankin steps up beside her.

Fury'am'a scoffs. "Who said that was in jest? I know you need the money." He smiles then as he sees the shame wash over her. "Oh, yes. I know all about your… situation."

Dankin sees Sera's face is red and her eyes are watering. "Miss Sera, is everything all right here?"

Fury'am'a looks at him with disdain. "And who is this?"

"No one," she answers quickly. "Another worker, who is returning to the estate." She gives Dankin a begging look. Reluctantly, he turns to leave.

"And how are you paying him? Under the table? Or perhaps… between the sheets?" Fury'am'a laughs as her face grows redder.

Unable to resist, Dankin spins around, his fist hitting Fury'am'a in the nose. He falls to the ground, gripping his face in his hands. Sera stifles a laugh as she runs over, kneeling beside him. "Please, sir. I am so sorry! What do you need?"

Yanking his elbow away from her, he slowly gets to his feet. He pulls out a kerchief and wipes his face. "Nothing today." He grins at her, blood in and around his mouth. Her stomach turns at the sight. "I'll get what I need from you, soon enough," he yells as he storms off.

She sighs as she turns to Dankin. "Why did you do that?"

"I was defending your honor. What's wrong?"

"He is a nobleman. This will only end in trouble," Sera says, shaking her head.

"I am sorry, I didn't know. I heard what he said and couldn't stop myself. I had to defend you."

"Dankin, he and I have been dancing around this for years. I can handle myself. Please, return to the estate. I am sure we will be dealing with this soon enough."

"Yes, Miss Sera."

He's surprised when she smiles at him. "Even so, thank you," she says.

He returns her smile before leaving the market. She glances around, grateful the market isn't busy yet. No one else seemed to take notice of the altercation. She says a quick prayer nothing will come of it before returning to her stall. As the morning goes on, she remains upbeat, trying to think positive. Her smile disappears as the magistrate approaches her stall.

"Miss Sera, morning."

"Miya, how are you?" She studies her black robes, trimmed in gold embroidery. The sleeves are long, tapering and billowing at the wrists. Gold embroidered knots run over the shoulders, with gold trim along the hems.

"I'm doing well." She straightens a tassel.

"What can I help you with?"

"I'm afraid I am here on official business," Miya says.

"Fury'am'a?"

"Yes."

Sera swallows hard. "How bad is it?" she asks.

"He will not press charges, nor pursue the matter further, if you agree to pay him one thousand gold in compensation."

Sera shakes her head, afraid of what is to come. "I do not have that." She looks at Miya, hopeful. "He slapped me yesterday."

"Did you press charges? Are there witnesses?"

"No," she murmurs.

"Then my hands are tied," Miya replies.

"What will happen, since I do not have the gold he is asking for?"

"He offers an alternative payment solution."

Sera gasps softly in fear. "What is he asking for?"

"If you will dine with him tomorrow at six, at his estate, he will consider the matter closed. If not, the man who hit him will be forced to spend twenty days in the stocks. It is your choice."

Sera hangs her head when she realizes there really is no choice. "Please, inform him I will see him tomorrow evening for supper," she says, biting back tears and trembling at the thought.

"Then the matter will be closed." Miya clears her throat. "Sera, I am sorry."

She collects herself before meeting her gaze. "Thank you."

"No, you misunderstand. I am sorry to pile this on you, however, there is the matter of your stall."

"What? What are you talking about?" she asks, suddenly confused.

"We have not received this year's taxes."

"She said she—" Sera shakes her head. "I apologize. You will get them soon, I promise."

"If they are not paid by next week, your stall will be forfeit."

"I understand." Sera's heart races in her chest as she watches Miya leave. Trying to calm herself down, she takes a deep breath before she turns her attention back to her stall. She smiles when she sees Hi'tob'a approaching, happy to see a familiar face.

"Good day, Miss Sera. Has it been busy?"

"A little steady, is all. I will return shortly."

"Of course."

* * *

Dankin comes in to find Sera in the kitchen, preparing lunch. "Sera, are you all right?"

Refusing to look at him, she focuses on the food she is preparing. "I'm fine. Lunch will be ready soon," she says as she is moving quickly to finish.

"Sera—"

"What?" she asks as she gathers three plates and places them on the tray, loading them with food.

"Did something happen because of me?"

"I need to deliver this. We'll talk in a moment." She carries the tray, still not meeting his steely gaze, and hurries to the main quarters. He plates food for the two of them and sets them down. His fingers drum on the table as he waits for her to return. "It has been taken care of," she says as they sit down.

"How?" he asks, curious.

Fighting back tears, she lowers her fork. "He asked for a thousand gold, which I do not have." She sighs. "So, I am having supper with him tomorrow night."

"What? There must be something I can—"

"Otherwise, they would lock you in the stocks for twenty days."

"I'll do it."

Her fork falls to the table as she looks at him in shock. "What?"

"This is my fault. I will make the restitution. Who do I speak with?"

"You can't."

"I'll be fine."

"No, I mean, you literally can't. You officially work for the Dahvaene estate, carrying the name and representing the family. For you to go into the stocks would bring shame upon this house. I will take care of it."

"I am truly sorry. Please, how can I make this up to you?" he asks sincerely.

"You can't. Don't worry about it, it's just supper. I'll be fine."

He grows concerned when he realizes she is trembling. "Sera?"

"He scares me," she admits, her voice quivering. "He is a noble, and I cannot refuse him. I have done my best to keep him at bay, but now I do not have a choice."

"What do you mean?" Dankin asks.

"If he asks for my hand in marriage."

"What?"

"I have refused other offers, refused advances. I do not court anyone, as my life belongs to this estate. I am cursed to never leave here. I know this. If he asks for my hand—" She shakes her head. "I don't know what I'll do."

"Please, do not take this the wrong way, because you know how I feel about him, but surely it would not be all bad? You would be a wealthy noblewoman, raised in stature, wearing fancy gowns, hosting parties, living the high life—"

"I don't care about any of that!" she cries out. "My duty, my obligation, my very life is dedicated to this house and family. No matter what, I can never marry, nor can I ever leave." She wipes her tears. "It's how it is. I have served as long as I can remember." Sighing, she picks up her fork to resume eating. "I will figure it out. I am sorry for putting this on you."

"Given that I caused this, you owe no apology. I would give anything to make it right."

"It will be okay." She finishes her meal. "I need to return to the market, to relieve Hi'tob'a.

"Would you like me to accompany you?"

She clears her throat, glancing down as a small pain tugs at her heart. "I am fine, but thank you. If you would go to the orchard, I believe there is a fence in need of mending."

"Yes, Miss Sera. After I clean this up, I will tend to that."

"Thank you." She gives him a reassuring smile before leaving the estate.

* * *

Once at the market, she is grateful to see it calmer than the previous day. They remain steady, with Hi'tob'a staying to help until the last customer. When they close up the stall, Sera takes a few remaining pieces over to Kye and his friends, who are standing nearby.

"Please, eat," she insists.

"Thank you, Miss Sera!" Kye responds as they attack the fruit.

She laughs as she takes the empty bushel to her stall and places it on the cart. "If you will return this to the estate, I will be there shortly."

"Yes, Miss Sera," Hi'tob'a replies.

Walking to the beach, her mind nags at her about all of the things that could go wrong at her dinner with Fury'am'a. She sits on the shore, pushing the worries away as she watches the waves flow in and out. A shadow falls over her, startling her. She looks up.

"Dankin? Why are you here?"

"Hi'tob'a returned to the estate by himself. I was worried about you. I apologize, if that's too forward."

"No, it's okay. It's nice to know someone worries over me."

He sits beside her. "Do you have no one?"

She looks down as her fingers trail over her arm. "Not really."

"I'm sorry."

"It's okay, I'm used to it." She gives him a sad smile before looking back to the water. "I love watching the waves, hearing the water crash on the shore. It's the only time I have peace. The world disappears around me. It's my favorite place."

"I have loved the ocean for as long as I can remember," Dankin says as he looks at the water's surface with longing.

She pulls out her pocket-watch. "I need to return to the estate. My duties call."

"I'll accompany you back, if you'll have me."

"Yes, thank you."

He helps her up. They walk in silence along the shore, sneaking an occasional glance at each other until they arrive at the estate. Once inside the kitchen, he gets down plates as she prepares supper.

"What are we having?" he asks, chopping onions and mushrooms.

"It's a basic plate with beef and sauce smothered over vegetables, and a side of rice."

"It smells good," he says as he inhales the flavors.

"Thanks." She fills the plates, putting them on the tray and carrying them to the main quarters. Rae'lin opens the door and gestures her in. She watches as Sera sets the tray on the table.

"How are they today?" Sera asks.

In the large bed is a man in his fifties, grey hair, and scarred all over. In the smaller bed on the opposite side of the room, is a boy of fourteen, pale and trembling as the blood illness consumes him.

"The same as every day, I'm afraid. Sera, Fury'am'a sent me a message that you are having supper with him tomorrow evening. I cannot tell you how delighted I am to hear this."

"I know I am needed here, so I will not stay long—"

"You will stay as long as he wants, doing whatever he asks of you. Do you understand me? You know what he could do for both of us. This is the best news we've had in a long time."

"Mistress, please—"

"Sera, do not argue with me."

"Apologies, mistress. I will do as you ask." She bows and hesitates before asking her question. "Mistress, why were the taxes not paid on the stall? I gave you the gold—"

Rae'lin slaps her, but before she can say another word, a weak man's voice calls out.

"Sera?"

She approaches the large bed and bows before him, ignoring the sting on her cheek. "Good evening, sir. I am sorry if we disturbed you."

"It's all right. What are you two discussing?"

Forcing a smile on her face, Sera answers. "A potential suitor."

"I know Rae'lin is thinking of us, but I want you to marry when you are ready, when you love someone. I know the idea seems foreign to you, but not everything is about duty or obligations."

"I appreciate that, but I will always put this family first."

He chuckles softly. "Stubborn, to a fault. You and I are so alike. Thank you for all you do for this family, taking care of our every need." He looks over when Rae'lin clears her throat. "Do you need something?"

"No," she quickly replies.

"Good. Now leave Sera in peace. She has enough to deal with."

Sera bows to him. "Thank you." She gives him a small smile before walking for the door. Rae'lin grabs her arm, pulling her out of earshot. Sera looks at Rae'lin as her grip tightens.

"You will go tomorrow, you will do whatever he asks, and you will not embarrass us. Do you understand?"

"Yes, Mistress. Has he paid you—"

Rae'lin slams her against the door. She looks over to be sure Tsuji didn't see or hear them. "Do not question me!" she says through gritted teeth.

"Apologies, mistress."

"You are dismissed."

Sera joins Dankin and stares at her plate, looking up when he clears his throat. "Did you say something?" she asks.

"I asked if you're all right."

"Just worrying about tomorrow. I'm sorry, I'll be fine." She finishes her meal, looking up as he reaches for her hand. He takes her plate instead. "Will you sleep tonight?" she asks as he's washing the dishes.

He turns to her, surprised by the concern in her voice. "I will, but will you?"

She laughs softly. "Yes. If you can't sleep, wake me. We'll have tea."

He returns the laugh. "That sounds good." He resumes washing the plate in his hand.

"I am retiring for the evening. Good night, Dankin."

"You as well, Miss Sera."

She goes upstairs and into the washtoire to shower. Standing under the hot water, she cries as she releases her fears and worries. I will not let this control me. I will be okay, I know I will. No matter what happens tomorrow, I will trust in the plans the goddess has for me. After washing her hair and drying off, she changes into her pajamas. Staring at the ceiling, she pulls the blanket up and says a quiet prayer over her supper with Fury'am'a.

* * *

The nightmare fades as she jerks awake. She gets to her feet, puts on her slippers and robe, and goes to the kitchen to put the kettle on.

"Couldn't sleep?"

She looks over as Dankin walks in. "Oh, I slept."

Realizing what she means, he stops in his tracks. "Nightmare?"

"I guess that's something we have in common." She gets down two cups then adds water to the tea. She carries them to the table, smiling as he takes his cup.

"Thank you."

"You're very welcome," she says, drinking her tea.

"Will you tell me about your nightmare?" he asks, wanting to stroke her arm and reassure her but worries how she would react.

"It's one I've had as long as I can remember. I'm locked in the basement, crying out for help. No one can hear me, or no one cares." Shrugging her shoulders, she takes another sip.

"I'm sorry. That sounds horrible."

"Oh, you have no idea," she says with a shudder.

He clears his throat. "What will you have me do today?"

"If you'll help me at the market, I would appreciate it."

"Of course. I mended the fence and added extra bolts so it shouldn't come loose again. Can I ask how it was damaged?"

She laughs. "The neighbor's cow got loose and rammed into it." She finishes her tea, smiling as he takes her cup. "Thank you, Dankin."

"Of course. I'll see you in a few hours."

Chapter 2

Dinner with Death

Sera glances over at the clock. "Really? Five minutes before my alarm would go off? Oh, well. At least I slept," she says to herself in exasperation. She lies back, wondering what it would feel like to be wrapped in Dankin's strong arms. Pulled from her thoughts when her alarm finally goes off, she silences it, pulls herself off the bed, and dresses in a grey hanfu gown. She styles her hair into a side braid, making sure she is proper. She walks across the hall and knocks softly. Dankin opens the door, fully dressed.

"Morning, Miss Sera."

"Morning."

"Shall we?"

They go downstairs, where he sets the table and helps her cook breakfast. She loads up the tray, then carries it to the main quarters. She leaves quickly, sighing in relief she did not see the mistress. When she walks into the kitchen, she sees Dankin has their breakfast set up at the table. He stands when she approaches.

"Dankin?"

"Apologies," he says. "Is it not customary for the man to stand when the woman walks in?"

"Learning about our customs?"

"I did some reading last night, yes," he admits as they sit down.

"It is custom. However, for our status, not necessary."

"I see. Thank you."

"May I ask what you did before coming here?"

He swallows hard, thinking on his answer. "I was a court jester," he says with a grin.

Closing her eyes, she shakes her head. "Dankin—"

"I'm sorry." He chuckles softly. "I can't help it."

"I would appreciate straight answers from you."

"Yes, Miss Sera. Apologies," he says, taking the dishes.

She goes to the mirror in the small interior hallway, fiddling with her braid. Looking up, she catches Dankin staring at her. She faces him. "Do you need something?"

His skin warming with embarrassment, he turns to the sink and continues washing dishes. "Um, apologies."

Feeling bold, she approaches him. "Dankin?"

"I like your hair that way," he confesses.

Her cheeks go flush, and she lowers her gaze. "Thank you for that. Are we ready?"

"Yes, Miss Sera."

They walk to the orchard, where they prepare the cart and take it to the market. "This is what you do every single day?" he asks.

"For as long as I can remember. I was born here, and as soon as I was old enough, I began to fix meals, load up the cart, work the stall, oversee the housekeeping."

"What happened to your fam—" His words die in his throat at the sight of Fury'am'a waiting at her booth. Dankin's hands clench in anger.

She looks at him as she takes the cart. "Return to the estate."

"Sera—"

"Now!" she commands. He turns and sulks off, unhappy to leave her with him. She forces a smile as she approaches Fury'am'a. "Apologies, sir, that we are not yet open—"

"Save it," he snaps.

"I am sorry. Have I done something to offend you?"

"Well, for starters, I see he still works for you."

She thinks carefully how to respond. "He is indebted to us. We cannot simply release him."

"Oh, that I understand." He gives her a knowing smile. Her stomach churns at the sight.

"How can I help you?"

"I am just confirming we are on for supper tonight."

"Of course," she replies.

"Unless you have the gold," he offers with a chuckle.

"And if I did?"

His chuckle grows into laughter. "That would be the day!" Calming himself down, he looks her over. "Hmm, I don't like the braid. You will wear your hair in a more… attractive manner for this evening."

"Of course, sir."

"Dinner is at six." He leans down, his breath warm on her face. "If you are even a minute late, I will send the guards for both of you," he threatens.

"I will be there, on time, I promise."

He scoffs as he walks off. Heart pounding in her ears, she takes a breath. She turns her attention back to her booth and begins setting it up. To her dismay, she stays busy as the day flies by. She returns to the estate at lunch, surprised to see Dankin cooking.

"I wanted to help, since I know you are unhappy with me."

"Why would you think that?"

"Because you sent me away," he responds, obviously unhappy.

"To protect you from him. He has more power than you realize."

He scoffs. "I'm not afraid of him."

She walks to his side and clasps his hand. "You should be." Studying her hand in his, he grins at her. She blushes as she pulls away. "Thank you for cooking." Dipping a spoon into the dish, she has a taste. "This is very good."

"I'm glad you like it. It will be ready in a minute."

Before they sit down to eat, Sera fixes the tray for the mistress and carries it into the other room. She sets it on the table and almost makes it out the door when Rae'lin calls to her. "Sera?"

"Yes, mistress?" she offers as she looks at her.

"What are you wearing tonight?"

"My best gown, the blue one. I will be proper, I assure you."

"Wear this," Rae'lin instructs, going to her closet. Sera looks over as Rae'lin pulls a gown off the rack. A gasp escapes her lips, and she stumbles back in surprise when Rae'lin holds up a red, strapless gown with a sweetheart cut. The skirt is floor length with a slit up to the hip. She shoves the gown into Sera's arms, getting out red gloves and silver heels, piling them on.

"But mistress—" Sera starts, unable to believe what she is holding.

"Don't! You will not argue. Wear this gown or so help me, goddess…"

"Yes, mistress."

"Good girl. You are dismissed!"

Sera gives a small bow, then runs upstairs with the clothing. She places everything in her closet before joining Dankin in the kitchen, her appetite diminished. Sitting at the table, she pushes her food around with her fork. Dankin sighs, causing her to look at him.

"Are you all right?" she asks.

"Seems I should be asking you that."

"I'm okay," she says, making herself eat to reassure him.

"Sera—"

"Really, I'm okay now." She takes another bite. "Would you help the others in the orchard this afternoon?"

"Whatever you need," he says as he gathers dishes.

"I am closing the stall at four today, so I have time to clean up before…" she clears her throat, "before supper with him. Thank you again for cooking lunch. It was delicious."

"You're welcome."

* * *

She returns to the market, worry gnawing at her as the afternoon goes by. At four, she loads the remaining bushel onto her cart, not seeing Kye or his friends.

"I'll take that."

She turns, surprised. "Mr. Hi'ro'ta." She gives a small bow. "How are you this afternoon?"

"Quite well."

She reaches for the bushel when he gets to it before she does. "Apparently, my daughter loves these. Pregnancy craving, I believe."

"Congratulations!"

"Thank you."

"I'm glad she enjoys them so." Sera smiles at him.

"She insisted I have to try them, as well." He lays the gold coins on the counter. "I'll return your basket tomorrow."

"Oh, at your convenience, sir."

"Thank you."

She loads the empty bushels onto the cart, pockets the gold coins, and leaves the market. Looking over as she walks by the beach, she is overwhelmed with the desire to swim. Sighing at the thought, she realizes she has to get everything taken care of.

* * *

As she drops the cart off at the orchard, she catches sight of Dankin working with the others, his hair damp with sweat. Her heart quickens at the sight.

Once inside the manor, she finds Chi'yo and asks her to prepare the evening meal for the mistress, since she will not be around for their usual supper time. Upstairs, Sera showers and dries off. Stepping into her room, she's surprised to see Rae'lin waiting for her. "Mistress, can I help you?"

"I am making sure you look proper for this evening. Get dressed, then I will do something with that hair."

Sera slips on the gown and examines herself in the mirror. She shakes her head at how revealing it is, wishing desperately to be in one of her hanfu gowns instead. Rae'lin walks up behind her, handing her the gloves.

"Make sure they fit," she commands. Sera slips them on, silently looking herself over. "Perfect fit. His lordship will be pleased. We will all benefit from this supper." She looks at the vanity. "Sit, now," Rae'lin commands.

"Yes, mistress," Sera says quietly as she obeys.

Rae'lin pulls on her hair, folding it while thinking how best to fix it. She looks her over, shaking her head. "This is a blessing, you know. To have his lordship interested in… someone like you."

"Yes, mistress," Sera says again, clenching her hands in her lap.

"You will do whatever he asks, you will not embarrass us, and if this does not work out, do not bother coming back here! I will not tolerate insubordination nor shame. Do you understand me?"

"I will do as you ask, I promise."

Rae'lin puts Sera's hair up, adding her kanzashi, a gold fan pinned in. She checks again, looking her over to ensure everything is how she wants it. Sera slips on the heels and walks around the room as she adjusts to wearing them. She removes her gloves, placing them by her bag on the vanity so she can apply her make-up, then places it in her bag before slipping the gloves back on. She stands up, facing Rae'lin.

"Oh, yes. He will be most enamored with you." Rae'lin smiles as she leaves the room, counting the gold in her head she is sure to come after their dinner.

Sera looks herself over once more before hanging her head as fear and worry threaten to consume her. "I can do this," she assures herself, wiping her eyes. "Tears won't help me now." She straightens up, taking a breath as she steps into the hallway. Dankin is near the top of the stairs, his shirt slung over his shoulder as sweat glistens on his torso. He pauses, his hand gripping the rail before he approaches her.

"Sera?" he asks, nearly breathless at the sight.

"Do you need something?" she asks.

"Apologies. I was taken back at how lovely you look."

"Thank you. It's not what I want to wear, but the mistress demands it. She insists I must agree to whatever he wants tonight, or—" She takes a breath, shaking her head.

"What do you mean?"

As she closes the door, she sees the clock on her nightstand and worries over the possibility of being late. "I need to go now," she says as she turns to him.

He takes her hand as she passes, her breath catching in her throat. "Please, be safe," he says, pushing down his own worry.

Looking down, she runs her fingers over his hand. "Thank you," she says. Reluctantly, he releases her hand, angry with himself as she leaves. The heat of the day clings to her as she steps outside. She approaches the stable to get her horse ready.

"Miss Sera?"

Startled, she turns around. "Hi'roso, how are you?"

"I am well. The mistress instructed I take you in the carriage."

Surprised, she follows him to the white carriage, adorned with gold vines and red interior. He helps her inside before pulling himself into the driver's seat. She admires the view of the palm trees and beach as they travel along the road.

* * *

They arrive at the estate of Fury'am'a Kaneiko. Sera utters a quiet prayer for the night to be over and that everything goes smoothly. The carriage stops outside the main entrance. Looking out the window, Sera's breath catches in her throat at the sheer size of the manor. It is the closest to a castle she has ever seen, built with white stone and adorned with blue towers. Hi'roso opens the door, taking her hand to help her exit the carriage. She thanks him before walking up the steps to the front door and ringing the bell.

The door opens to a young woman wearing a black sheath gown trimmed with white lace on the collar and a lace apron around her waist. "Sera?" she asks.

"Yes," Sera replies, nodding.

"Please, come in," the woman says as she opens the door fully and gestures her into the grand foyer. The room is white marble with grey accents, dark wood furniture and bookshelves, and a twin set of stairs leading up to the second level. The woman leads Sera to a sitting parlor. "I apologize, but his meeting ran over. He will be with you shortly. Can I get you anything?"

"No, but thank you." Sera sits, fidgeting with her hands on her lap. Her worry begins to consume her, forcing her to take a breath and repeat her silent prayer. She stands up to greet him when he walks in a few minutes later.

"Sir Fury'am'a," she says, bowing and lowering her eyes to hide her fear.

He smiles as he looks her up and down. "Hmm, Sera, that gown is exquisite."

"Thank you, mi'lord."

He approaches her, crooking his arm. She laces her arm through his, confused when he leads her upstairs. They arrive at his private quarters, where he gently pushes her inside. A small table with two chairs has been set up, along with wine and candles. He pulls out her chair. As he's helping her into her seat, his fingers brush along her neck and exposed shoulder. Swallowing the lump in her throat, she removes her gloves and places them in her bag, placing it on her lap. He smiles as wine and food are served, then gestures the servants out.

Sera's heart races when she realizes it is just the two of them in his bedroom. She takes a quick look, seeing where the only door is, in case she needs to make a quick escape. Realizing he is speaking to her, she gives him her attention.

"I believe you will enjoy this vintage. It is nearly four hundred years old."

"Why so special?"

"Because this is a very special night."

Her skin grows flush as she tries to keep herself from trembling. Holding her glass up, he follows suit. "To new friends," she toasts.

He chuckles at her words, drinking his wine while she only takes a sip. "Oh, my dear, by the end of tonight, you and I will be much more than that." His eyes trail along the cut of the gown.

"Thank you for this nice supper," she offers, embarrassed by the way he is staring at her.

"You are most welcome, my dear. I have been waiting for this for a long time. I have already spoken with Mrs. Dahvaene."

Her heart sinks. "About what?" she asks, though she already knows the answer.

He laughs. "What else?" She keeps her eyes fixed on her hands in her lap, unable to speak. He continues. "She has agreed to give me your hand in marriage, but unfortunately, you have to agree to it. What is your answer?"

"Please, I…" Her mind races, trying to figure out what to say. "Could I have a day to think it over?"

He stands up, towering over her. "Do not make me call the guards on your worker. I will have him imprisoned."

She gasps at the thought of Dankin in the town square, humiliated and hurt. "I kept the agreement, having supper with you—"

He laughs. "Did you really believe it was as simple as that? I may not be mayor, but I hold much influence on this island. I assure you, it will be done. Now, what is your answer?"

"If I say no?"

"I'll call in the debt, burying the Dahvaene family so deep, they will never be free. What will little Na'ito do without his medicine? Who will take care of Tsuji while Rae'lin is too busy slaving here? How will any of them survive?"

"You are heartless!"

He slaps her across the face, the sting bringing tears to her eyes. "You will not disrespect me, little one!"

Fear flows into her veins as she hears Rae'lin's threats echoing in her head. "I'm sorry, I—"

Sighing, he waves his hand. "Go to the washtoire. You are a mess!"

She rushes to the adjoining room. Her reflection in the mirror is one she does not recognize. She adjusts her hair and fixes her make-up. Trembling at what will happen if she refuses, she cups cool water in her hands and drinks some in. After checking her reflection once more, she steps out to see Fury'am'a is back in his chair, drinking his wine.

"My apologies," she says as she resumes her seat at the table.

He studies her a moment. "Were you foolish enough to think I want to marry you for love?" He laughs. "I need children to pass my wealth to, and it doesn't hurt that you are so beautiful," he says. "We will make a beautiful family." He reaches across the table and trails his fingers down her arm, smiling at the raised bumps on her flesh.

"Please, don't do this," she begs.

"I will do as I please. Now, you are trying my patience! What is your answer?" he demands.

Realizing she has no choice, her eyes close in shame. "Yes, I will marry you." Her head drops at her words.

A smirk spreads across his face. He grabs her arm, pulling her to her feet in one quick motion. Before she can protest, he picks her up and carries her towards the bed. "Hmm, let us celebrate, shall we?"

She struggles in his arms, fear ravaging her at the sight of the bed. "No, I'm not ready for this. Please, don't—"

He drops her on the bed, smiling, then turns her over so she is half standing, half laying on her stomach. His hands tremble in anticipation as he opens the fasteners on the back of her gown. She knows she should fight back, but she is frozen in place, unable to move or think. She cries out when he suddenly lands on top of her, the weight of his body almost crushing her. Her scream echoes across the room and two guards rush in, shocked at the sight. They run over and pull Fury'am'a off. He falls to the floor, dead.

"What happened?" she asks as she pulls her gown back up, struggling with the fasteners.

"We should be asking you that!" one of them yells.

She stares down at Fury'am'a's lifeless body, not able to comprehend what has happened. "I… I agreed to marry him," she starts, "He carried me to the bed, he was about to—" She is too ashamed to finish the sentence. "I don't know what happened, he just collapsed on me!" The other guard rushes out, calling for the doctor. She looks up when the guard who remained behind holds her arms and binds her in irons behind her back. "I did nothing wrong!"

"We shall see."

He pushes her into the chair, standing over her as they wait. She stares at the floor, still not comprehending all that is happening around her. This can't be happening. Please, somebody, do something. I can't… I didn't do anything!

The minutes tick by slowly until the doctor finally arrives. He kneels beside the body as he performs his assessment and takes a few blood samples.

"My initial diagnosis? Cardiac arrest. I will run his blood and examine his heart to be sure," he explains to the guard.

Sera begs to be let go once the doctor has given his assessment.

"No, you are going to the prison until you are cleared or convicted," the guard states plainly. They all watch as two men come in with a gurney, loading up the corpse and carrying him out.

"There are no eye hematomas, no redness or sores around his mouth. I assure you, I am most certain it was a simple heart attack," the doctor says, looking at Sera with pity.

"Even so, she will go to prison until her trial in the morning," the guard states.

"No, please!" she tries again as the guard drags her from the chair. He escorts her out and takes her down to the prison. Locked in a cell by herself, she buries her face in her hands, wondering how her night went from bad to worse so quickly. She lays on the cot, unable to fall asleep without the image of Fury'am'a's face haunting her. After several hours, she gives in to the fear and exhaustion, passing out.

* * *

She comes to when the guard bangs on the cell bars, looking over and seeing the tray in his hand. "Please, I have to go. I have my duties to take care of!" she begs as she stands up and approaches him.

"We sent word, and Mrs. Dahvaene said you are banished from the estate."

"What?" she cries out. "No, please, tell her I did nothing wrong!"

He slides the tray through the opening. "Prisoner, eat this."

She glances down at the tray, her stomach churning at the sight of oats and burnt toast. She turns away. "No, thank you."

"Fine," he snaps, whisking the tray away.

Struggling to keep all composure, she sits on the cot before she gives in and weeps into her hands, her uncertain future looming over her. The shadows in her cell grow long when she looks up to see the guard approaching.

"They are ready for you at court. Approach the bars, hands behind you. Once cuffed, you will step forward. Now!" he barks.

"Please, could I have a jacket or something? I need to be covered. Plus, my dress is filthy. I cannot go into court looking like this. Please?"

"No," he states without emotion.

She does as he instructs. Once her wrists are bound, he opens the cell and escorts her to the tribunal, his grip tight on her arm. At the courthouse, a large crowd has gathered, watching in curiosity.

Sera searches in vain for the mistress, if nothing else to see a familiar face. Once inside, the guard walks her to the defendant table, sitting her down and removing her irons. Again, she searches the room. She cries out in surprise when the guard grabs her wrists and chains her to the table. The judge walks in. Sera looks down in shame at her appearance.

"Good morning. We are here to discuss the death of Fury'am'a Kaneiko. Doctor, do you have your results?"

Standing up at the prosecutor's table, he lifts the paperwork in his hand. "I do."

"Defendant, stand. State your name and place of residence for the court." Sera does as he instructs. "Now, address the court and tell us what happened last night."

Sera takes a moment to think. "Fury'am'a invited me to dine with him. During supper, he asked me to marry him. I agreed." She looks down and explains what happened, leaving out what he was intending to do to her. "He wanted to celebrate when he collapsed on me, dead."

When she has finished, the judge nods at her and looks back at the prosecutor's table. "Doctor?"

"She is correct," he says as he stands. "I had previously discussed with him his heart condition, and all tests were negative for any poison or foreign contaminants. He died of natural coronary failure."

"Defendant, you are cleared in this matter," the judge claims, banging his gavel. The guard walks over to undo her bindings. "There is one other matter, since you agreed to marry him," the judge continues, "and because of the manner in which he died, traumatizing at it was, you are legally entitled to compensation. I order his estate to pay you one thousand gold pieces, by end of today."

Sera gasps in surprise, clasping her hands. She looks over when a man stands up, dressed in a suit with a leather briefcase. Years of experience reflect in his eyes, contrasting his youthful appearance.

"I am Fury'am'a's barrister, representing his estate. We will pay her."

"She will need to sign for it. Sera, where shall we have him deliver it?" the judge inquires.

"She will be at the Dahvaene estate."

Sera looks for the sound of the voice, shocked to see Rae'lin in the doorway. "Mistress?"

Rae'lin raises her hand to silence her then looks at the barrister. "Send the money to my estate, and she will be there to sign for it."

"Yes, madam." The judge bangs his gavel again. "This tribunal is dismissed."

Sera walks to Rae'lin. "But I thought—"

"I almost didn't come. When I heard, I was so angry. I believed you had hurt him to escape marrying him," Rae'lin says, leaning close to Sera and speaking quietly. "But I was wrong." She clears her throat. "I would like for you to return to the estate and resume your duties." She hesitates before adding, "Please."

Sera knows it is as close to an apology as she will get. "Yes, mistress."

"Good girl."

Rae'lin removes her cape and wraps around Sera's shoulders. "Thank you."

"I can't have you seen like this out on the street," Rae'lin says as she guides Sera away from the courthouse, then they climb into the carriage. Silence settles between them during the ride until Rae'lin breaks it.

"I must say, that man you hired is a good choice. Dakin?"

"Dankin, mistress."

"What kind of name is that?" She laughs, lurching slightly as the carriage rolls over a bump. "Anyway, he cooked breakfast for us this morning. He did a fine job. Wherever did you find him?"

"He found us," Sera admits. "I am sorry about last night."

"Oh, no. You agreed to marry him. You did everything you were supposed to. What happened was not your fault. Oh, this gold is sent from the goddess herself! This will help me so much."

"We owe the clothing merchant, the doctor, taxes —"

"Yes, yes. I know. We will take care of what we can." They pull up to the estate. "Hi'tob'a is running the stall today. Why don't you clean up and rest, after what you just endured?"

"Really?" Sera fails to hide her surprise at Rae'lin's words.

Rae'lin laughs. "What? I'm not completely without compassion, am I?"

"No, of course not," she responds, wondering what Rae'lin's ulterior motive is.

"Take the day to yourself. You will resume your duties tomorrow. Dankin can continue cooking as Chi'yo is overseeing the household affairs."

"Thank you, mistress."

"Just stay close by, so you can sign for my gold."

Sera's hands clench as Rae'lin's true motive is exposed. "Of course."

Once the carriage stops, Rae'lin exits first. Sera steps out after her, grateful to see the manor. Once inside, she rushes upstairs and removes the gown. A fire burns in the hearth and without thinking, she throws the dress in, setting it ablaze.

She steps into the shower, crying as the water washes her fear and shame away. Falling to her knees, she weeps as the memory of him collapsing on top of her plays over in her mind. She lies down in the tub for what feels like hours as she collects herself. When the tears finally subside, she stands up to rinse off, puts on fresh clothes, and sits on the bed with her knees to her chest. Someone knocking at the door startles her. Thinking it's Rae'lin needing her signature, she says to come in.

"Sera?" Dankin asks as he enters. "Are you all right?"

She stands up and jumps into his arms, gripping him tightly. She pulls back, blushing. "I'm sorry. After everything I went through—"

"It's okay. No one will tell me anything. What happened?" He looks down when he realizes she is trembling. He takes her into his arms and holds her tight. "Shh. It's okay. Whatever happened, you're home now. I'm so grateful you're safe."

"Thank you." She relishes his comfort and the safety of his arms. Reluctantly, she pulls back to wipe her tears. "I needed that." She looks over when she hears the bell ringing. "Please, wait here. I'll be right back." When she goes downstairs, Rae'lin gestures her over. Sera signs for the delivery, taking the coin pouch, and handing it off to Rae'lin, who immediately disappears with it.

Sera returns to Dankin. "I need to get out of here. Will you come and swim with me?"

"Yes."

They change into their suits and meet in the orchard. As they walk towards the water, Sera breathes a little easier. "The mistress was most pleased with your cooking."

"I'm glad." He chuckles. "She stared at me the whole time."

"Really? I apologize. Taking care of her husband and son, she doesn't get out much."

"I see that."

"Could we—could we swim for a while, then I'll tell you what happened as we dry in the sun?" she asks, removing her gown. She's wearing a pale blue traditional swimsuit, with sleeves that come to her elbows and shorts, with a small skirt that stops a few inches above the knees.

"That's fine," Dankin says.

He removes his shirt and shoes, laying them with their towels. They go into the water. Unable to help himself, he stares at her as she swims, impressed at how good she is. They swim together and play in the water. After a while, she gets tired, walks back to the shore, and sits on her towel. He sits beside her.

She takes a breath, thinking over what to tell him. "We ate dinner in his chambers. I was so nervous the whole time. He um… he dropped dead of a heart attack."

"What?" Dankin shakes his head in shock.

"His guards came in, thinking I had killed him. They detained me while waiting for the doctor to examine him. I was arrested last night then cleared at trial today."

"By the goddess! Of all things to happen last night, that was the last thing I would've expected."

"How do you think I feel?" Sera asks, pushing down her anger and fear at what she endured.

"I am so sorry." He takes a chance, tracing his fingers over her hand, grateful she does not pull away.

"Oh, Dankin, no. I mean it, that dinner with him was going to happen eventually. You may have been a catalyst, but I assure you, you did not cause this."

"I'm grateful you are all right. When we couldn't find you this morning, I was worried. I went to the kitchen and fixed breakfast. The mistress came in, asking who I am then she asked me where you were. I told her I had not seen you. She smiled, saying that was probably a good thing. She took the tray and left without further explanation. A messenger arrived a short while later, but when I inquired, her only response was a dirty look."

"That's typical of her." Sera sighs. "The mistress thinks she can marry me off, find a man to pay for me." She shakes her head. "I know she won't give up now just because Fury'am'a is dead."

"Can I ask, how much does she think she would get for you?"

"She hasn't said a figure, but I believe she thinks around four to five thousand gold, as I am pure and vibrant." She says these last words in a mocking tone. "That is how she describes me for potential suitors."

They sit in silence for a while, only the sound of the waves crashing on the shore filling the space between them.

"Dankin, thank you for being a good friend. I didn't realize how much I needed one of those."

"You are welcome, Miss Sera. Same goes for you."

"Please, call me Sera."

He smiles in response. "Yes, Sera. Thank you."

"You know, when I was a child, all I wanted was to be a dancer. Instead, I have spent my life here, in servitude to the household. Now, talking of being married off and starting a new life…" she holds back tears. "I don't want to think of it."

"I'm sorry. Is there anything I can do to help?"

"You don't have five thousand gold, by chance?" She laughs, turning serious at the surprised look on his face. "I am truly sorry. I don't know what I was thinking. That was inappropriate."

He takes a breath. "It's okay. I would not buy you, Sera."

Shaking her head, she lets out a nervous laugh. "It seems that's what I am, a commodity for sale. It is my lot in life."

"Sera—"

"It's okay."

"I only wish I could help." He leans towards her as he says it and clasps her hand tightly in his. She flinches but does not remove her hand.

"I know. You already are by being here. Thank you for that." The sun is low in the sky now, the day almost over. She turns and gives him a sad smile. "Let's return to the estate, shall we?"

* * *

Back at the manor, she showers again, crying as she thinks of the night before, of being imprisoned, unsure of her future. *I could've been hanged for that. I could've*— She shakes her head. *I can't think like that. I'm okay, I'm alive and safe.* Drying off, she stares at the mirror, looking herself over. *What is my place in this world? Where do I belong? I may have grown up here, but this is not my home. Will I ever have one of those? A place where I am loved, where I am wanted for who I am, not what I can do? I wish I had a different life, a better one.* She climbs into bed, thinking about Dankin. *He is kind and handsome, but I don't have a chance with him. The mistress would never approve.* When she closes her eyes, she is back in his arms, and she smiles at his warmth.

Chapter 3

Tea, Scones… and a New Suitor?

Sera is finishing breakfast with Dankin when Chi'yo walks in. "Miss Sera, the mistress is asking for you."

"Thank you." She looks at Dankin in confusion before leaving the kitchen. She walks to the main quarters and knocks softly. Rae'lin opens the door, smiling at the sight.

"Sera, we are going to the mainland today."

"For what, mistress?"

"I have arranged for us to have tea with a young duke, who is most eager to meet you."

"Please, I'm not ready—"

"Sera, what have I said? You know we need this. They need this," she says, gesturing over to the beds. "His pension is running out, and Na'ito is only getting worse. What will we do then?"

"You could work—"

Rae'lin gasps. "Don't you dare!" she huffs, offended at the notion. "I work all day, tending to them."

Sera nearly rolls her eyes but catches herself. "Apologies, mistress. When do we leave?"

"We will board the nine o'clock ferry, so hurry up and get ready." She goes to her closet, fingering through her gowns. She hands Sera a pale blue hanfu with silver accents. "Wear this with the silver heels I gave you."

Taking the gown, she bows. "Yes, mistress." Blinded by tears, she runs upstairs and collapses onto her bed.

Dankin grows concerned when she doesn't return to finish her meal. He picks up her plate and carries it to her room. "Sera?" he asks, knocking on her door.

When she doesn't respond, he lets himself in. She's on the bed, curled up over the gown, and crying into her pillow.

"I'm sorry to intrude," Dankin says as he walks in.

She looks up. "Please, don't look at me. It's embarrassing!"

He walks to her. "Sera, you need to eat."

"She's making me meet a potential suitor today, a young duke."

The plate nearly slips from his hand. "What? I don't understand."

She sits up, looking at him as she wipes her tears. "What do you mean?"

"You are a servant here. Why would a duke—"

"Sera!" They look over as Rae'lin walks in. "This is most inappropriate," she cries out. "Why is there a man in your room?"

He holds up her meal. "I was only bringing her—"

Rae'lin snatches the plate. "I don't care. Get out!" she commands.

"Yes, mistress, my apologies," he says, looking back to Sera. She nods, and he quickly leaves the room.

"I am glad I came up here. I was coming to help you get ready." She looks down, as if only just realizing she is holding a plate. "He's right, though. You do need to eat. I don't need you passing out and embarrassing me."

Reluctantly, Sera finishes her meal then sets the plate on her nightstand. She gets to her feet, taking the gown with her. Rae'lin follows her to help her dress and fix her hair.

"He will be most impressed with you."

"I am not a noble, so why would a nobleman be interested in me?" Sera asks, Dankin's question lingering in her mind.

"Our name carries much weight, even on the mainland. Knowing you created this famous fruit, how… unique looking you are, we have attracted the attention of the right people."

"I see," she says, noticing how Rae'lin is dressed. "Mistress, is that a new gown?"

"I couldn't look poor entertaining the duke, could I? As soon as I received his response yesterday afternoon, I went straight to the shop. Thankfully, Kea'nda had exactly what I needed."

"We received this gold—"

"To do as I please! Don't fret. While I was in town, I paid off some of your debt and paid the doctor, in addition to the gowns I purchased. Now, we need to finish getting you ready. It's an hour ride on the ferry, so we need to leave soon."

"Mistress, why are you doing this? Business is very good right now, our next crop will be ready, and—"

"Sera, stop pestering me," Rae'lin says, waving her hand at her. "I will marry you off, then all of our problems will be solved. I will finally be free of you and your nonsense."

Her eyes close to hide her pain at such words. "Yes, mistress."

Rae'lin looks Sera over once more before they leave the room. Dankin is waiting for her by the front door. Sera smiles at him as he admires her in her gown. "Miss Sera, what would you have me do while you are away?"

"Please, continue to help in the orchard."

"Be safe," he says, returning her smile.

* * *

Sera and Rae'lin ride in the carriage to the harbor. Boarding the ferry, they are grateful for a pleasant day out at sea. Rae'lin looks her over. "You look… nice in that color."

"It is a beautiful gown. Thank you for letting me borrow it."

"It's yours."

"Really?" Sera asks, surprised by her kindness.

"Yes, as I could not wear it now."

"Of course," she responds, her heart heavy again.

A carriage is waiting for them when they arrive at H'ondo, the mainland. A servant approaches. "Mrs. Dahvaene?"

"Yes," Rae'lin replies.

The servant bows. Sera admires her black kom'ono with pink and white accents. Her hair is pulled behind in a tight bun with small silver fans pinned in.

"I am here to escort you."

"Thank you," Rae'lin says, climbing into the black and gold carriage. Sera follows behind. They ride in silence, with Sera ignoring the servant practically staring at her. They pull up, and Rae'lin squeezes Sera's hand at the sight. Sera smiles in return, hiding her fear and anger. Stepping out of the carriage, Sera's breath escapes at the sight of the duke's vast chateau.

She admires the rose bushes and white marble pillars, black shutters with dark blue accents, a grey marble exterior, and the gold trim along the roof. She looks at Rae'lin, who is also taking it all in. The duke steps out to greet them.

He approaches Sera. He is shorter than her, wearing blue and black dressing gowns, with dark, thick rimmed glasses. He takes her hand, kissing it as he gives a small bow. "Duke Abi'ko, at your service."

"Dear duke, it is a pleasure to meet you," Sera replies, smiling as she gives him a full bow. "Your home is lovely."

"Thank you." He turns to Rae'lin. "Madam."

"Duke," she offers, bowing. "Thank you for hosting us today. It is a pleasure."

Eyeing Sera, he gives Rae'lin a smile. "Hopefully, the pleasure will be all mine. Now, we have refreshments arranged inside. Please," he gestures. He holds Sera's hand as he leads them into the house. They go into a large parlor, where a high tea is set up on a beautiful, long, dark wood table. The room is covered with espresso paneling with white marble floors. A black chandelier hangs above the table. Duke Abi'ko helps Sera into her seat before sitting beside her.

"Thank you, mi'lord."

He smiles as he surveys her gown before meeting her gaze. "May I ask, how did you come up with this custom fruit that you sell?"

"It is a long story. I'd rather hear about you." Sera smiles at him.

"Of course! A good subject, no doubt." He laughs. "I am on the council, where we keep the peace and pass the laws for the mainland. Your island falls under our jurisdiction, but as your mayor runs things so well, we rarely need to intervene." He looks at Rae'lin. "Is it too early to discuss business?" His voice is calm, only betrayed by the eagerness in his eyes.

Rae'lin lets out a gentle laugh, placing her hand on his arm. "Oh, dear duke, it's never too early for that."

"Hmm, a woman after my own heart. Too bad you are already spoken for."

She blushes, feigning humility. "Oh, thank you."

"Now, I would offer twelve hundred gold—"

"Only twelve hundred?" Rae'lin interrupts. "Surely, you see how young and beautiful she is."

"Well, even so, she is a little… old for my preference."

"But she is pure, she keeps house, and she is an amazing cook."

"I believe fifteen hundred is as high as I would go. Especially after that… unfortunate business with Lord Fury'am'a."

Rae'lin clears her throat, taking a drink. "News of that has already reached here?" she asks, attempting to hide her surprise.

"Yes, and ultimately, that sort of scandal can be costly. She has depreciated because of that."

Sera's jaw clenches, angry at being treated as nothing more than property. She takes a breath, thinking of swimming with Dankin and smiling, before clearing her head to focus on her current situation.

"I apologize, Duke Ab'iko. I will not accept less than four thousand gold for her. I assure you, she is worth every coin."

He chuckles, taking a bite of his cinnamon scone. "Tell me, why do you believe she is so valuable?"

"You have eaten our fruit, have you not?"

"I have, it is very good. Now, are you saying the agreement would also be an investment? If I pay you four thousand for her, I will get a portion of the profits?"

"We could discuss—"

Sera laughs. "What profits?" she blurts out, bringing her hand to her mouth, shocked to have said it.

"Sera!" Rae'lin exclaims.

The duke quickly stands up. "Well, I guess that answers that. This has been a pleasant morning, but I am quite through with you both. I see no need to continue wasting my time. Good day!" He tosses his napkin on the table and walks out.

"What is wrong with you?" Rae'lin asks, her face contorted with anger.

"I didn't mean to—"

"This was our best chance, your best chance! What will we do now?"

"It'll be okay. You know I will do everything to keep the estate going," Sera assures her.

"What? What will you do? Please, tell me your grand scheme."

"I don't know. It will be okay—"

"Sera, just stop! You are giving me a headache. I do not wish to hear any of your nonsense." Rae'lin storms from the room.

Sera finishes her tea, eating a pastry to help stifle the laughter threatening to erupt. She feels bad for how things went but is delighted to see the mistress put in her place. When she is finished, she gets to her feet and goes outside, expecting Rae'lin to be waiting in the carriage for her, but she is nowhere to be found.

"I apologize. The woman you came with already left," a servant says when she sees Sera looking lost.

"Thank you." Frustrated, Sera makes her way to the harbor, realizing when she arrives that she has no money for a ticket. Desperation creeping in, she looks at the people waiting for the ferry as she searches the crowd for Rae'lin. She paces as she tries to think of a plan.

"Sera, are you all right?"

She looks up as Mr. Hi'ro'ta approaches her. "Sir," she says with a bow. "I am okay, but I was separated from the mistress, and I have no money to buy a ticket."

"Here," he says, offering her his own. "I am in no hurry to get home, as the misses has a list of things for me to do once I return." He chuckles.

"Sir, thank you. See me at my stall tomorrow, so I may repay you."

"Not necessary. Your fruit was worth it. My daughter nearly ate half the bushel herself, though I guess that is expected when eating for two."

"Still, thank you," she says again.

"Better hurry," he suggests, smiling as she turns and runs for the ferry.

She manages to board just as it's about to depart. She gets her ticket stamped before putting it in her bag as she finds a seat. Anger flows through her veins as she thinks about how the morning went, being told she has depreciated then being abandoned by Rae'lin.

* * *

Sighing in relief once she steps off the ferry, she rushes to the estate, wanting to clean up and put the morning behind her. Dankin is loading up a bushel when he sees her approaching. Wiping the sweat from his brow, he sets it down and catches up to her.

"How did it go?" he asks with genuine concern.

"Not good," she answers, pushing down her tears. "The duke would only go as high as fifteen hundred for me. The mistress was so angry that she left me on the mainland."

"What? How did you get back?"

"A customer of mine was waiting for the ferry, and he gave me his ticket." She shakes her head. "I need to clean up." She watches the sweat dripping down his face. "Will you clean up and join me to cook lunch?" she asks, wanting to spend time with him after the morning she's had.

"Of course."

She runs inside and showers before meeting Dankin in the kitchen. His damp hair is clinging to his forehead. Without thinking, she reaches up and brushes it out of his eyes. She blushes when he looks at her affectionately.

"Apologies," she says. She cooks the meat as he steams the rice. "What am I going to do?" she whispers to herself.

Dankin takes her hand. "Sera, I could—"

"Sera? Are you here?" Dankin immediately drops her hand as he steps back, working the food on the stove. Rae'lin walks in. "Good, you did make it back. I need you to—"

Sera turns on her heel. "After you left me!"

"Sera—"

"I am sick of being treated as your property, and you will not sell me. I will continue in my duties around the estate, but I am putting my foot down. I would rather walk into the ocean, never to return, than be with any of these suitors!" Sera declares.

"I understand it's frustrating. You know our laws and customs, but you are not my property. I am not selling you—"

"You were literally discussing price right in front of me. I have depreciated? Really? This is still my life, and I will maintain some control over it!"

Rae'lin's eyes go wide. "Fine, for now. Keep us above water, and I will not bring up marriage again. Deal?"

"Yes, mistress."

"I need you to take care of a few things tomorrow while you are at the market." Rae'lin hands her a list before quickly leaving the room.

Dankin walks up to Sera. "What does she mean, above water?"

Speaking quietly, she looks up at him while she slips the paper into her pocket. "She is struggling, financially. That is why she's desperate to sell me off. Please, do not mention this to anyone. We do not speak of it."

"I understand. Thank you for trusting me with that." He sees the weariness in her eyes.

She finishes cooking then loads up the tray. She sighs at the thought of dealing with the mistress again. Dankin picks up the tray. "May I?" he offers.

She looks at him in surprise. "Really?"

"I don't mind."

"Thank you. Do me a favor, though. Take it in and leave. Do not stare, and do not ask questions."

"I won't," he assures her, confusion written on his face.

She gets their plates ready, setting them on the table then waiting for him to return. She stands up, thinking something is wrong until he finally walks back in. "What took so long?"

"I helped rearrange Na'ito's pillows."

"Thank you," she says as they sit.

"Can I ask you about them?"

"Yes, you can. What do you know about Tsuji?"

"He was a hunter—"

"No, a fisherman, before the war that is. Wherever did you hear he was a hunter?"

"Oh, just one of those things." He laughs. "So, a fisherman then served in the war?"

"Yes. He lost his left leg below the knee, to a cannon ball. It's a miracle he survived with so many explosions on the field. Now he is bedridden. The mistress spends her days caring for him and their son, Na'ito, who is battling an unknown blood disease. Every gold piece from this estate goes to their care."

"I see." He clears his throat. "Sera, I have a confession to make."

"Dankin?"

"I wasn't just rearranging his pillows. The mistress and I had a little talk, about you."

Sera's heart quickens. "What about me?"

"She has given me permission to court you, if you'll have me."

Sera jumps to her feet. "What? How? I don't—"

He stands up, taking her hand and folding between both of his. "Does it matter?"

"Yes! Because unless you handed her five thousand gold, I don't see how it's possible."

"We came to… an agreement. Will you court me? Please?"

She turns away, going to the sink, and looking out the window. Her skin is flush as she thinks on the possibility. "I don't know how to respond. I usually don't because—" she hangs her head. She glances at him, seeing concern for her, thinking on how kind he has been. "Yes, I will court you."

"Really?" he asks, perking up at her words.

She approaches him, smiling. "Yes, really. If you'll promise you are okay with taking things slow?"

"I promise."

"We will keep it professional during the day, is that understood?"

"Of course, Miss Sera." He smiles with a wink. She laughs as he wraps her in his arms. "There we are. Isn't that better?"

"After the day I've had? Yes, it is." She lays her head against his chest, his heartbeat thumping against her ear in a soothing rhythm.

"Please, let's finish eating." He helps her into her seat before sitting beside her.

She takes a breath before looking at him. "I do have to show you something. If you don't wish to court after seeing them, I will understand."

"Sera?" he asks. She brings her hand to her head, pulling her hair back. She blushes as he examines her pointed ears. He reaches his hand up but stops himself. "Can I?" She nods. He brings his hand to her ear, gingerly feeling around. "Are you embarrassed by these?"

"I am. It's another reason I haven't courted before."

"They're beautiful."

"Really?

He smiles at her. "What? I mean it," he says, his hand lowering down to cup her cheek before returning to his meal.

Blushing, she pulls her hair back down as relief floods her. "Thank you." Once they finish eating, she reaches for his plate, but he takes hers, instead.

"Sera, I will take care of dishes. Get some rest after the day you've had."

"A nap? I—Thank you." She steps up and kisses his cheek. A giggle escapes her when she sees him blush. "I am sorry. Was that too forward?"

"No, Sera. It was perfect, like you."

She goes upstairs, changing into a nightgown. Thinking on how different things might be, her worries gnaw at her. *What if Rae'lin changes her mind? Or someone else offers her gold for me? I am excited to be with him, but with so many unknowns still ahead for u, it scares me. If we get married, not much here will change.* She giggles. *What is wrong with me? Here I am, asking him to take it slow, and I'm thinking of marriage?*

* * *

She wakes up when someone is knocking. "Sera, I fixed supper. Are you hungry?"

"Yes, Dankin. I'll be down in a minute. Thank you." Stretching, she gets out of bed and slips on her gown. She sees it's just five o'clock. She goes down to the kitchen, smiling as he hands her a plate.

"I've already taken a tray in for the family."

"Thank you. I—why have you helped so much today?"

"I feel bad for what you went through. I also want to show you I'm more than just good-looking muscle." He smirks at her. She laughs, not believing yet that this could be real. He makes up his plate then sits with her. "Now, I haven't... courted in a while, and I am still learning your customs. Do not hesitate to correct me or point something out while we are starting out."

"I appreciate that. Thank you." She looks down, studying the veins on the back of her hand. "Can I ask about the agreement?"

His breath sucks in. "I'd appreciate it, if you didn't."

"Just one thing?"

"All right," he offers, worry in his voice.

"Is it..." She clears her throat. "Is the agreement just for us to court or..." She looks away.

"Sera, I mean it. We are taking things slow, and you do not have to do anything you do not want to. I don't know what previous agreements you have had, nor do I care to know, as it is not my business. It is an open agreement, to be changed or amended as we go on. Any further changes require your permission."

"What? Why?" she asks, looking up at him.

"Because it is wrong how you have been treated. A relationship should be based on mutual feelings and respect, not about heaps of gold."

She smiles at him in surprise. "Thank you. I—I'm not used to having someone who cares for me. It's a wonderful feeling."

"Wonderful?"

"Like you," she says as she smiles at him.

"Let's finish eating and get into bed."

"Dankin!"

He laughs. "I meant let's clean up and turn in. I didn't mean—Sera!" They laugh together. Once the kitchen is spotless, he offers his arm and escorts her upstairs. She stops outside her door.

"Thank you for today," she says.

"Sera, can I kiss your forehead?"

She smiles, blushing. "Yes."

He leans forward, pulling her into his arms as his lips gently brush across her skin. She bites her lip when she looks at him, imagining his lips on hers.

"I'll see you in the morning," he says as he pulls away from her.

"Until then," she replies, watching him go into his quarters. As she's thinking of the future ahead, she changes and tucks herself into bed. *He's so warm and gentle. I never knew being held could feel so wonderful, so safe. Still, I have to wonder what kind of agreement did they create? The mistress only cares about gold, and I know he doesn't have any. I— She collects herself. He obviously cares for me. I can't worry over it now.*

* * *

She's pulled from her sleep when the doorknob rattles. She gets to her feet as someone is knocking.

"Why is this door locked?" Rae'lin demands.

Sera opens the door, gesturing her inside. "I would think that would make you happy, knowing there is a man across the hall." She yawns.

Rae'lin smiles at her. "Of course. Are you and he courting? Tell me everything," she demands. "You didn't refuse him, did you?"

"No, I didn't refuse. What kind of agreement did you make?"

"You needn't worry over the details. A man of his word, not telling you. Good. Sera, just be happy, and don't ask any questions. Can you do that?"

"But I don't understand—"

"Sera!"

"Yes, mistress. Apologies."

"If he asks for your hand in marriage, you will accept. Do you understand me?"

Sera raises her head to argue but decides against it after seeing the look of determination on Rae'lin's face. "Yes, mistress. I will accept."

Rae'lin sighs in relief. "Oh, thank the goddess! After the lord, then the duke, this is the blessing we have been waiting for." She laughs when she sees Sera is clearly confused. "Now, get some sleep. I can't have you embarrassing me in front of your customers."

"Yes, mistress." Sera's curiosity only grows as she wonders about their agreement.

* * *

Sera returns to the kitchen, deep in thought. As Dankin steps up beside her, she meets his gaze.

"I'm sorry. Did you say something?" she asks.

"I asked if you're all right?"

"Fine," she replies, giving him a reassuring smile and sitting at the table.

"Sera?"

"Hmm, yes, Dankin?"

"Something is wrong. Talk to me." He watches her intently, taking a drink of his coffee.

"I just—I have to wonder what kind of agreement you could've made with her. The only thing the mistress cares about more than herself is gold." She shakes her head. "I'm sorry. I know I shouldn't be questioning it."

"It's okay. You would be curious. You'll know everything soon enough, I promise."

"Thank you. Now, will you help me at the market today? Friday is our busiest day."

"Of course." They clean up and go to the orchard.

Sera is loading up the cart when Rae'lin approaches her. "Sera, what are you doing?"

"We are going to the market."

"Dankin, apologies, you do not have to work for us—"

Dankin shoots Rae'lin a warning look. "We are not discussing that."

"Yes, Dankin."

"Just because we are courting, doesn't mean anything else has to change," Sera says.

"Dankin?" Rae'lin asks. He nods at her. "If you insist." She goes into the house.

Sera rolls the cart over and reaches for a bushel. Dankin gently grips her arm. "Sera, I've got these."

"Thank you." She watches him load them on before they head for the market. As they're strolling along the shore, he sees her looking over the water.

"I would like to swim after supper, if you want," he suggests.

"That sounds really nice."

* * *

He helps her set up the booth and prepare for the morning rush. She smiles at him. "People love having this with their breakfast."

They get through the rush, finally able to catch their breath once it dies down. "Here comes Hi'tob'a," Dankin points out.

"Good. We'll go prepare lunch."

"Morning Dankin, Miss Sera."

"Morning. We've already had one rush. We will hurry back," Sera assures him.

"Take your time. I'll be fine," Hi'tob'a replies.

"Thank you." Dankin takes her hand, walking with her to the estate. He notices her glancing at the ocean. "Want to swim now?" he teases.

She laughs. "We will, soon enough."

* * *

She smiles as he chops vegetables while she cooks the meat. He brings the board over, adding the vegetables. His scent invades her nostrils, coffee mixed with sea air. She smiles at him as she finishes cooking, and he steps back while she prepares the tray. Her skin is flush as she leaves the kitchen. She goes in, setting the tray down, and starting for the door when Rae'lin blocks her path.

"How can I help, mistress?"

"So far, he has fulfilled his end of the agreement. I just want to be sure you will, too."

"Well, he hasn't asked me to marry him yet. I mean, it is only our first day—" she cries out when Rae'lin slaps her face.

"I don't appreciate that kind of attitude from you. Now, adjust yourself before he sees you like this!"

"Yes, mistress." Sera runs from the room, stopping in the hallway to check herself in the oval mirror hanging on the wall. Pushing down her tears, she runs her fingers over her cheek. In the kitchen, she sits beside Dankin, keeping her head down.

"Sera, are you all right?"

"Fine," she answers quietly, making herself eat. She quickly wipes her tears and clears her throat.

"Look at me," he commands. Not thinking, she raises her head. He jumps to his feet. "Who did that to you?"

"The mistress. I deserved it, for speaking to her the way I did."

"Sera—"

"Please, it's okay."

"No, it certainly is not!" He turns to walk out when she grabs his hand.

"Dankin, please, I am begging you. Let this go, for me?"

He wants to argue, but the fear in her eyes stops him. "If it happens again, I will not stand idly by." He sits back down.

* * *

At the market, Dankin has Sera laughing as they wait on customers. When she sees Mr. Hi'ro'ta approaching, she removes three gold coins.

"Good afternoon, sir."

"Afternoon, Sera. I see you made it back, safe and sound."

"Thanks to you," she says, offering him the gold.

He holds up his hand. "I meant it, when I said you need not reimburse me. I am here for fruit, not gold." He holds up the empty bushel.

She places the coins back in the box. "Thank you. What will you have?"

Dankin prepares the bushel as she figures out the total. Mr. Hi'ro'ta gives her the gold, taking his fruit. "Everything looks great."

"Thank you for your business." She smiles at him. Once he's gone, she turns to Dankin. "As you probably figured, he's the one who gave me the ticket. His daughter is a little younger than me and, apparently, she loves our fruit."

Dankin chuckles. "I see that, as much as he bought."

The afternoon goes by, and they are finally able to close the stall for the day. Dankin loads up the empty bushels while she moves the coins from the box into a purse, then places it in her pocket. They are returning to the estate when she stops at the beach. He watches her cup water in her hand. She walks back to him.

"You really love the ocean, don't you?"

She blushes. "I do."

* * *

They are almost to the estate when she hears someone calling out. She stops as Dankin continues toward the orchard. She turns back to see her neighbor waving his arms and pointing.

"What's that—" Sera starts to ask. Before she can finish, an angry cow is plowing right for her. Closing her eyes, she braces for impact when Dankin shoves her out of the way. He's knocked off his feet as the cow smashes into him before running off. Sera sits up in a daze, rushing to Dankin once she realizes he's not moving. Her skin is cold as she kneels beside him and begins looking him over.

"Dankin? Where are you hurt?" she asks, near panic at the sight of him crumpled on the ground.

"I'm okay." Sitting up, he groans in pain. "I'll be sore, but I'm okay. Help me to my quarters?"

Sighing in relief, she gets him up with his arm around her shoulder as she helps him into the house. "What do you need?"

"To soak," he answers.

She gets him into his washtoire, sitting him on the edge of the tub. Looking at him in concern, she starts the tap. "What can I do?"

"I'll be okay on my own."

"You don't need help?" she asks.

"I thought we were taking this slow." He grins at her, raising his eyebrows.

She laughs. "I'll give you privacy, but I will be right out here if you need me." She bends down to kiss his forehead. "Thank you for saving me."

As soon as she's gone, he strips down and slides into the hot water. He brings his hand to his ribs, wincing in pain. Concentrating as he whispers in a strange language, he keeps his eyes closed as a blue light sparks from his hand, running through his ribs and mending them. He sighs in relief when he heals.

"Dankin, are you all right?" Sera asks through the door.

He sits up, trying to remember if she locked the door on her way out. "Yes, I'll be out in a moment. Unless you want to come in here and help bathe me," he teases.

"Inappropriate!" She groans audibly but joins in when she hears him laugh. "Don't rush. I just wanted to check on you."

"Thanks." He lies back, letting the water soothe his tired body. He pulls the drain, steps out, and dries off. Once he's dressed, he opens the door and smiles at the concern on her face. "What? Worried about me?"

"Dankin, it's not funny. You could've been killed!"

"I'm all right, as you see. Though I am tired now."

She takes him to the bed, where she helps him lie down and covers him with the blanket. "Rest. I'll bring you supper shortly."

"Sera—"

"Don't argue. Please, take it easy for me?"

"Yes, Miss Sera." She laughs when he winks at her.

She goes downstairs and cooks supper. She takes his meal up, happy to see him eat. "I have to see to the others. I'll come and check on you shortly."

"Thank you."

She goes into the kitchen and carries the tray to the main quarters. Rae'lin is sitting by the bed, holding Tsuji's hand. Sera sets the tray down and walks over. Tsuji is in a deep sleep.

"Is something wrong?" she asks.

"Nothing that concerns you," Rae'lin snaps.

"Mistress—"

Rae'lin jumps to her feet, slapping her. "What have I said about that? You do not question me."

"I was only trying to help. I'm sorry." She quickly bows and runs from the room. Looking over her plate, she makes herself eat. She goes upstairs to check on Dankin. He is sitting up and reading. The book falls from his hand at the sight of her.

"Sera, what happened to your face?"

She turns away, bringing her hand to her cheek. "It's nothing—" before she can finish, he jumps from the bed and runs downstairs. She stands frozen for a few moments, fearing what Dankin will say, and the retaliation the mistress will inflict on her. When she hears raised voices, she goes after him. She approaches the main quarters and stops in the doorway.

"Well, I don't appreciate how you are handling the merchandise! Lay another hand on her, and our agreement will be void," Dankin growls.

Anger and hurt flow from Sera's heart as she runs from the house. Her feet lead her to the beach, where she sits on the shore, watching as the waves crash before her. She buries her face in her knees, no longer fighting the tears as they flow.

"Sera?"

She doesn't look up. "Just go."

"What's wrong?"

She looks at him as she gets to her feet. "Seriously? You're worried about your merchandise? I thought you were better than the other men here! How could you?" she cries out, burying her face in her hands.

He takes a deep breath. "Sera, I asked her not to hit you because you do not deserve to be treated as such. She scoffed at me. I had to speak in her language, using words she would understand. I hated saying it. Believe me when I tell you, I do not think of you as merchandise. You are not my property, nor a thing to buy. I'm sorry you have ever been treated as such."

"Really?" she asks, looking at him.

"Really. I would never treat you that way." He leans forward, but she quickly steps back.

"I'm sorry."

"For what?"

"For wanting to take things slow. You are the man, so you should be making these decisions."

"Sera, no. We are in this together. I told you, I will do nothing without your consent first, and I mean that."

"Thank you. I'm sorry for what I said. You aren't like the other men here. Forgive me?" she asks, approaching him.

"Of course," he says, taking her hand and kissing her palm.

"Can we return to the estate? I need to clean up and get ready to turn in." She pulls away, giving him a small smile.

He holds out his arm, confused when she doesn't take it. "What's wrong?"

"You were just nearly killed. How are you all right?" she asks, looking him over.

"It wasn't that bad. I was able to move out of the way."

"But I saw you—"

"From where you were, I'm sure it looked bad. As you see, I'm fine."

"Okay." She resigns herself in order to avoid an argument. She takes his hand, smiling at him as they return to the estate, both thinking over the incident with the cow. They stop outside her room, where she leans up and kisses his cheek. "Thank you for saving me, for protecting me. In more ways than one."

He smiles at her, staring at her lips. "You are most welcome. I'll see you in the morning."

"Until then." She goes into her room, changes, and climbs into bed, thinking of the cow. *He was right in the way. I saw him get hit. How did he—no. I have to trust him, to stop questioning him. I will do better about this. He may be the key to my freedom, to a better life. He is worth taking a chance on, despite how little I know about him.*

* * *

Sera wakes up, the scream dying in her throat. Seeing it's just past midnight, she gets on her robe and slippers before going downstairs to put the kettle on. She's adding the water when Dankin steps in.

"Are you all right?"

She looks at him. "Nightmares about angry cows."

He chuckles. "Sorry. I shouldn't laugh."

"Do you want a cup of tea?"

"Please." He gets down the cups as the water is boiling. They make up their tea. "Can I ask, about your life here?" he asks once they are sitting.

"Please, ask anything," she offers, hoping he will open up as well.

"What has your life been like?"

"I told you everything I do here."

"Even as a child?" he asks in disbelief.

"Yes. The mistress taught me at an early age, and I have spent my life in servitude here. I dreamed of running away, of being free. I never thought it would be possible."

"It's a shame you never had a childhood." He takes a drink. "You said you were cursed to stay here?"

"Well, not a real curse, obviously." She laughs. "Those aren't real. I just—it's how I feel, that I will never leave here. With Na'ito's blood disease, his medicine is very expensive. It's why the mistress has worried so over the finances. It's why she was trying to sell me off." She looks in his eyes, hopeful he may discuss the agreement with her.

"I see. Thank you for trusting me as you have been."

"You are the first person I've trusted like this," she admits. Pain flashes across his face. "Dankin, are you all right?"

He chuckles, taking her hand. "I'm fine. Must be a remnant from my encounter with the cow."

"Do you need to stay in today and take it easy?" she asks in concern.

"No, I'll be fine. Do you run the stall on Saturdays?"

"Only from eight to eleven. Then I prepare lunch, see to the house, make sure laundry and housekeeping is being completed, check the orchard, and whatever else is required of me."

"You really don't get a day off, do you?"

"No, but Sunday is a bit of a break since I only cook the meals. Hi'tob'a runs the stall while Chiyo oversees the household."

"I am sorry, for the life you've had."

"It wasn't all bad. I learned how to use a sword, learned to follow the stars if I was ever lost, read adventures and legends, dreaming of traveling the world and seeing new things. I would read in the evenings by the fire and sometimes in bed. That was my second favorite thing to do, after swimming in the ocean. What about you? What has your life been like?" she asks, taking the chance.

"I was in the war and lost my family," he answers abruptly as he gets to his feet.

"Dankin, please—" she pleads.

He takes her cup with his, washing them off and hanging them to dry. He leaves without another word.

Hanging her head, she wipes her tears. *It just seems wrong. He knows everything about me, and I know almost nothing about him. He is a private person, and I have to accept that. But I'm starting to fall for him, and I don't want to lose him. It scares me beyond words, caring for someone like this.* She goes to her room, sitting on the edge of her bed and pushing down her tears. *He didn't mean it. I upset him, so it's okay. I won't push him again.* She lies awake in bed as she wonders why he is so private.

Chapter 4

The Mistress

The next morning, Sera and Dankin walk to the market together. She says nothing as he pushes the cart. He knows why she is being quiet but is unsure how to fix the gap between them. He glances over, but she keeps her eyes fixed on the ground as they make their way.

"You're mad at me," he states with no emotion.

"No," she responds quietly.

"Why didn't you wake me then?"

"I didn't want to bother you."

He stops, taking her hand. "Sera, I'm sorry about last night. All you did was ask a question. You didn't deserve that from me."

"Thank you."

"So, Saturday is a short but busy day?" he asks as they resume walking to the market.

"Yes, because of the mainlanders. They come on the weekend to buy Piscantur exclusives, like my fruit or Ri'coa's meat. He runs the farm nearby. He has a special breed of cow that produces the most tender meat. It's considered a delicacy. He owns the cow that came after us yesterday."

"I see. Have we eaten that?"

"No, it's for special occasions. I was thinking of making some tonight."

"As revenge?"

She doubles over with laughter before composing herself. "I wanted us to have a special supper, to celebrate officially courting."

He smiles at her. "I would say that qualifies as a special occasion."

They set up and run the stall, staying steady until eleven. Once they are able to close up, she gathers the coins while he loads the empty bushels.

* * *

Sera knocks softly on the door to the main quarters.

Rae'lin opens it, surprised to see her. "Sera, what do you want?"

"It's Saturday, mistress. We can go over the books."

"I am handling that now."

"But the debts—"

Rae'lin slaps her. "If you tell Dankin about this, you will regret it. Until this transaction is complete, you are mine. Do you understand?"

"Yes, mistress. But what about the books?"

"Child, you will never learn."

Sera cries out when Rae'lin grabs her arm and drags her inside.

$* * *$

Dankin walks in, freshly showered and confused when he doesn't see Sera in the kitchen. "Sera?" he calls out, knocking on her door.

"Dankin? Um, tonight's not a good night. I'll see you tomorrow." She sniffles.

He turns the knob, worried when he finds it locked. "Sera, what is going on?"

"Nothing. I—I just don't feel very well. Chi'yo will see to your dinner, or you can cook. I'll see you in the morning."

"Sera, you sound terrible! Let me in, please?" Thinking over what could be wrong, he worries she is hurt or sick.

She cries into her pillow before calming herself. "Goodnight, Dankin."

Leaning against the door, he debates how to proceed. "Goodnight, then." He's turning away when he hears her sobbing. "Sera, let me in!" he begs.

"I can't," she replies softly.

"What do you mean?"

"The mistress commanded I not see you tonight." He rams his shoulder into the door, forcing it open. He's shocked at the sight of her lying on her stomach, with nothing but a wet towel covering her back. She grabs the blanket, quickly covering herself. "Dankin! What are you doing? I don't want you to see me like this!"

He walks over and yanks the towel off, then gasps at the sight. The marks on her back turn his stomach. "What did she do to you?" he asks, his voice seething with anger.

"She whipped me for questioning her."

"Sera—"

"If you say anything, you will only make this worse. Please, go for supper then turn in," she pleads.

He takes the towel into the washtoire, running it under cool water, then dabbing her back. He covers her with it. "No, Sera. This I will not stand for. Stay here and rest. I'll return in a moment."

He goes downstairs and pounds on the door. Rae'lin opens it, surprised to see him.

"Dankin, what are you doing?" She looks over, seeing her husband and son both asleep.

"How could you do that to her?" he demands.

She steps out into the hallway and shuts the door behind her. "This is how I run my household. You have no right to question me, nor to question how I do things."

"I will take her from you, and you will not see one gold piece."

"What? No, you can't—"

"I told you what would happen if you laid another hand on her!" he snarls.

"Please," she begs, "the gold isn't for me, it's for them." She nods towards her room. "I won't hurt her again, I promise."

"Fine," he spits out, going back upstairs. He stands outside her room, trying to calm his anger. When he hears Sera crying, he goes inside and sits on the edge of the bed. He places his hand on her arm. "I'm here, Sera. You aren't alone."

"Thank you," she says, giving in to her pain and exhaustion.

He looks down when he realizes she passed out, his heart aching at the thought of her enduring such pain. Knowing she will be free of Rae'lin soon enough keeps his anger at bay. He pulls the blanket up, smoothing it over. He kisses her forehead then gets a chair and stays by her side as she sleeps.

Chi'yo comes in with dinner. "Sorry, Mister Dankin. I did not know you were here. Would you like me to bring you a meal?"

"No, that's okay. Thank you."

"Very good." She gives a small nod before returning to the kitchen.

"Sera, can you eat?"

"Hmm," she moans. "I'll try." She whimpers as she attempts to sit up. "I can't. The pain is too much."

"Here," he says, handing her the bread. "At least eat this."

"All right," she relents, taking the bread. She eats it quickly. "Thank you."

"I'll be right back." He puts the plate on her nightstand then runs to his quarters. He returns a moment later with a small pouch in his hand, takes the towel, and goes into the washtoire. Returning to her, he dabs the towel on her back again before picking up her plate.

"Did you speak to the mistress?"

"I did. She will not lay another hand on you. If she does, you tell me. Understood?"

"Yes, sir."

His eyes close. "Sera—"

"Sorry, a habit." She yawns. "I need more sleep."

"I really wish you would eat more."

"Maybe later."

"All right." While she sleeps, he eats her meal then goes downstairs. He gets a fresh plate before heading back up. Watching her sleep, his anger flows through him at what Rae'lin did to her.

"Dankin?"

He sits up. "I'm right here, Sera. What do you need?"

"I need," she takes a breath, "to use the washtoire. I'm not dressed, and I need help. Would you fetch Chi'yo?"

"I will wrap a robe around you and help you over. Would that be all right?"

"Yes, please."

He gets her robe off the hook, turning away as he helps her get it on. She whimpers softly as he helps her to her feet. He walks her to the door then waits for her. When she steps out, she is grateful as he helps her back into bed. "It's not proper for me to be here, is it?" he asks.

"No," she answers softly, "but I don't want you to go."

"Sera, I'm not going anywhere." He takes her hand and kisses her palm. "Will you try to eat?"

"Yes," she answers, adjusting her pillows to sit up. He lifts up the plate and holds it for her, happy to see her eat every bite. "Thank you for helping me."

"You're welcome. Now, will you get more rest? I think you'll feel better if you do." He brushes her hair away from her forehead, before kissing it gently.

"I will. The pain is easing, at least. Will you stay with me, at least until I fall asleep?" Sera asks.

"I promise."

She smiles at him as he covers her up, then he stays by her side all night.

* * *

"Dankin, what are you doing in Sera's room? Again?"

He faces Rae'lin, trying to keep his voice down as Sera sleeps. "After what you did to her, I had to stay and help her. She could barely walk because of you!"

"Maybe next time she won't question me," Rae'lin says with a smirk.

He stares her down. "There won't be a next time," he snarls. "You know what I will do. Now, what do you want?"

"I wanted to see how she is. Regardless of how she treated me," she looks up when he scoffs, "she is my daughter. I have a right to know how she is."

"Wait, what do you mean she's your daughter?" He stares at her, incredulous.

"She's Sera Dahvaene. I thought you knew this? Why else would you offer—"

He looks over when Sera groans. He grabs Rae'lin's arm and drags her into the hallway. "What did we say about the agreement?"

"It was an accident. Seriously, you didn't know who she is?"

He shakes his head. "I thought she was your servant! The way you treat her, the way she behaves. What have you done to your own child? Treated her this way in her own home?"

"I raised her to be proper, respectful, and hardworking, not lazy or decadent. There is nothing wrong with how I raised her."

"You made your own child your slave!" Dankin cries out. "I was already disgusted with how you treat her, but this? What is wrong with you?"

"Well, but—" she sputters, "who are you to say these things? This isn't your household to run. I've had to make choices, make sacrifices for my family. What would you know about that?"

"I don't. At least, not since I lost my family in the war."

Her eyes go wide. "I didn't know. Wait, how old are you?"

"Enough of this. I need to check on Sera." He shoots Rae'lin a look as he goes into Sera's room, brazenly shutting the door in her face. He walks over to see Sera sitting up. "How do you feel?" he asks in concern.

"Sore, but better. What was that all about?" she asks.

"Your mother wanted to check on you."

Sera scoffs. "I don't believe that."

He sits on the edge of the bed, taking her hand. "Why not?"

"I am not allowed to call her my mother, nor does she treat me as her daughter. The only reason she would check on me is to be sure I will be up to my tasks."

He shakes his head in disgust. "She really did raise you as a servant in your own home, didn't she?"

"She did."

"Why didn't you tell me who you are?"

"What do you mean?" Sera asks.

"I just found out you're a Dahvaene!"

"I thought you knew. When you were asking about work, didn't the merchants tell you who I am?"

"They mostly gestured over to you or said to see Miss Sera."

"I'm sorry. I didn't hide it from you or lie. I assumed you knew. Why are you upset by this?"

"Your father—" he starts, catching himself. "I can't. I need air."

"Dankin, please. What is going on?" she asks, watching as he runs from the room. She hangs her head, confused as to why he would be so angry. Grabbing clean clothes on her way to the washtoire, she gets a shower. The hot water helps soothe her back as she cries, worrying over their courtship. She goes downstairs, growing concerned when she doesn't find him in the kitchen or orchard. Praying he hasn't left for good, she goes to the beach, relieved to see him sitting on the bench.

He jumps to his feet at the sight of her. "Sera! You are supposed to be taking it easy today. What are you doing out of bed?"

"I had to find you, find out what I did wrong."

"You did nothing wrong! I made the assumption you were a servant, and that is my fault."

"I don't understand. What difference does it make?"

He takes her hand and helps her sit down, kissing her palm before folding it between his own. "It doesn't matter. I'm sorry I got upset, especially since you did nothing wrong. However, I do have a question."

"Please, ask."

"If you aren't a servant indebted to her—"

"Why do I stay?" she asks. He nods. "Part of it is the law. I cannot leave until I reach the age of twenty-five, unless my parent releases me or I get married. Also, they are my family. Regardless of how I feel about her, I love my father and brother. I don't want to leave them. It's another reason I thought I would never marry, as I can't bear the thought of being away from them."

"I can understand."

"Before he was wounded in the war, my father and I were very close. He was the one who taught me how to use a sword, how to defend myself. He was away at sea for months at a time, but when he was home, we would read together and play games.

"I don't really know my brother, as he has been battling this blood disease most of his life. He sleeps night and day. We've spoken with several doctors, taken him to various clinics, even on the mainland, but no one can diagnose what is wrong with him. Now the money is running out. If we can't afford his medicine," her breath hitches, "he won't make it. I work so hard to make sure he never runs out."

"It's not fair to have so much put on you."

"Fair or not, it's what I've dealt with my whole life." She looks out over the water. "I used to dream of walking into the ocean, becoming part of the sea, and never returning."

"The ocean is full of splendor." He takes a breath before looking at her. "You need to rest. Will you let me help you back?"

"Please," she replies, as he helps her stand. She wraps her arm around his waist. "I'm sorry you have to see me like this."

"Why are you apologizing for something that is not your fault?" he asks as they make their way back to the estate.

"Because it's not proper."

"I don't care. I want to help you, and that is more important than any customs, I assure you."

"Thank you."

* * *

Rae'lin walks up to them as they enter the grand foyer.

"Where have you been?" she demands. "Chi'yo prepared our breakfast, but you know I much prefer your cooking. If you are able to stand and walk, you are able to cook."

Dankin helps Sera to the sofa, sitting her down before turning back to face Rae'lin. "This ends, here and now! You will stop treating her as one of your servants. You may ask her to help or to perform various tasks, but you will no longer command it. I do not know why you hate her so, why you treat her this way, but I have had enough! I have not been here that long, and I am already fed up with it. I do not know how she has tolerated this her entire life."

"Dankin—"

"No, Rae'lin. Treat her like this again, and I will keep my promise. Is that really what you want?"

"No," she responds, humiliated.

"Good. Then we are in agreement." He walks to Sera, getting her to her feet and helping her into bed. Bringing his hand up slowly, he gently strokes through her hair. "How do you feel?"

"Tired, but I think it did a little good for me to walk in the fresh air."

"For now, rest. I am going to help Chi'yo make lunch. I'll be back shortly."

"Thank you."

He kisses her forehead before walking out. He goes into the kitchen. Chi'yo is happy to have him help her prepare the meals. He takes the tray, curious to see Rae'lin's reaction. She opens the door, her eyes wide at the sight of him.

"Dankin?"

"I will be helping today while your daughter is recovering from what you did to her." He carries the tray to the table then faces her. "Anything you would like to say to me?"

"Plenty," she mutters under her breath. "No, not as long as our agreement stands," she says to him.

"It does."

"How can you possibly afford this?"

He laughs, meeting her gaze. "Why would you think I can't?"

"You look like a peasant who works at an orchard."

"Looks can be deceiving. Take yourself, for instance. To any other man, you appear as a beautiful woman. All I see is your bitter ugliness, twisted and disturbed. I will be more than happy to take your daughter from here."

"So why don't you go now?"

"I told you, I can't. Not until the full moon."

He leaves the room and returns to the kitchen. Fixing up two plates, he takes them to Sera's room. She sits up to eat with him.

"How is it?" he asks when she takes a bite.

"It's good. I can tell you helped. Chi'yo is a good cook, but she relies a little too much on spice for her flavor instead of the food itself."

Dankin laughs. "I basically told her that, only politely."

"How did she react?"

"She gave me a dirty look." They laugh. "Are you still in pain?" he asks.

"Only a little. Not as much as I expected."

Relief sweeps across his face. He thinks for a moment. "Has your mother been like that your entire life?"

"Yes, though I don't know why. I have done everything she has ever asked of me, tried being the best daughter I could. Nothing I do is good enough."

"For her, but I assure you, to me, you are more than enough. You are fantastic at everything you do."

"Do you mean that?" she asks in disbelief.

"I do. You are beautiful, in the water and out, a great cook, and a wonderful merchant to your customers. I haven't seen you be bad at anything."

Blushing, she lowers her gaze. "Thank you," she says.

"Sera, look at me." He smiles when her eyes meet his. "You are beautiful. You know that, right?"

"Thank you. My beauty wasn't enough for the duke," she adds.

"Well, I'm glad didn't work out. I like this agreement much better, don't you?"

She smiles at him. "Yes, I do. I still don't see how it's possible, and I'm not asking you to tell me. It's just, when we first met, I thought you were handsome, but I knew she would never let me be with someone of your status." She traces her fingers over his arm. "I'm still confused about that."

"I understand. As I said, you will know everything soon enough. Now, a week from tomorrow begins the festival. I plan on taking you every night, if you'll let me."

She laughs. "You are very excited for the Festival of Lights, aren't you?"

"I am."

"Yes, we will go."

"I'm glad to hear that." He takes her plate with his. "I'll take these downstairs. Be right back." He smiles at her before leaving.

She pulls her blanket up, looking over when Rae'lin walks in. "Mistress, can I be of service?"

"Probably not in your current state," Rae'lin quips.

"What do you want?"

"Has he told you his plans for you?"

"What are you talking about?" Sera asks.

"Hmm, I see he hasn't." She approaches, sitting on the edge of the bed. "Let me say, with this agreement, I will come out ahead."

"Mistress—"

"Sera, I have been burdened by you long enough."

"Burdened?"

"Please. To have a daughter who looks like…" she gestures her all over, "this?" Rae'lin gets to her feet. "Rest today, as you will resume your duties tomorrow. I don't care what he says. You still belong to me. Is that understood?"

"Yes, mistress," Sera replies.

"Good." She storms out.

Sera wipes her tears, not seeing Dankin come in. "I'm a burden?" she quietly asks.

"Never! Who—" Dankin's eyes go wide when she looks at him. "The mistress was here?"

"Yes," she answers as she hangs her head.

"Sera, you have never been a burden. She is a horrible woman who is jealous of you. She looks like every other woman here, while you are beautiful and unique," he says as he takes her hand.

Her head snaps up at his words. "Really?"

"Yes, my little sea nymph. Really."

She giggles. "What did you call me?"

He scoots closer to her, kissing her forehead. He looks into her eyes while his fingers are caressing her cheek. "My little sea nymph."

"Really?"

"What? The way you swim, are you telling me you aren't one?"

"Maybe I am," she teases with a wink. "I think we can swim tomorrow after supper."

"Do you swim every day?" Dankin asks.

"I try to. It really is my happiest time. Well, it was before I met you," she admits, roses rising in her cheeks.

"Sera!" He chuckles softly. "Now, you need to get more rest."

"I don't know why she called me that."

"Honestly, I think all that time in a dark room caring for her husband and son is taking its toll on her."

"You're probably right. She has been a lot moodier lately, and I don't really know why. I thought it was the financial situation, but even that is steadily improving, while she hasn't." He helps her lie down. "Thank you."

"Get some sleep. I'm right here if you need anything."

"Would you—never mind. It's too improper."

"Sera?"

"Would you lay with me? On top of the blanket, I mean? I don't want to be alone right now. Not after what she's done to me."

He shuts the door, climbs into bed, and pulls her into his arms. "I'm right here, Sera. Is this all right?"

"Yes, thank you." She snuggles into him, falling asleep.

He looks at her intently, brushing his fingers through her hair. *I know you'll be angry and confused when I tell you the truth, but it's worth it to free you from the life you have lead here. You are destined for something greater, and I know you are almost ready for it. The full moon is approaching, and the timing isn't what I want, but I know it will work out. I am taking it slow because you asked me to, but I have fallen so hard for you. I don't know how much longer I can keep it in.*

* * *

As she sleeps through the afternoon, he quietly tells her how beautiful she is and how much she means to him. She opens her eyes and smiles at him. "I'm feeling a lot better. Could we swim after supper?"

"Are you sure?" He laughs when she nods. "Yes, my sea nymph, we will go swimming."

"That sounds really nice."

He helps her downstairs, where she insists on helping with supper. They cook together, then he picks up the tray. She tries to argue, but he is out the door. He smiles at the look on Rae'lin's face as he takes the tray over and sets down before facing her.

"How dare you call her a burden?"

"I'm simply speaking the truth."

"You wouldn't know the truth if it slapped you."

"What do you know? As you said, you haven't been here that long."

"In that time, I've seen the real you."

"Has she seen the real you?" she scoffs. "I don't know who you really are, nor how you are able to afford this, but I wonder what she will think when she finds out you aren't simply a peasant trying to make his way in the world. I wish I could see the look on her face!"

"The way I have things planned, it will be one of joy and gratitude. Neither of which you are capable of feeling."

"I wouldn't hold my breath if I were you." She looks up when he laughs. "What?"

"Nothing, mistress. Enjoy your meal." He returns to the kitchen, sitting with Sera as they eat.

* * *

They walk to the beach, arms linked, and smiling as they talk about the upcoming festival. She lays out their towels then slips out of her dress and shoes. She dives into the water, laughing as she splashes and swims. He laughs with her.

"I was right, you are a sea nymph!"

"I didn't plan on swimming like this, but my back is nearly healed already." She smiles at him. "I've loved the water as long as I can remember. The first time I came here, I was only two or three. Apparently, I took right to it, and I swam on my first try."

"You were made for the water," he says.

"Sometimes, it feels that way. The water calms me, body and soul." She sighs as the sun is sinking towards the horizon. "We should get back. It will turn cool once the sun is gone."

* * *

Upon returning to the estate, Rae'lin is waiting in the foyer. "I need to speak with you." Sera and Dankin walk forward. "Just Sera," she clarifies.

Dankin kisses Sera's forehead, shooting Rae'lin a warning look as he goes upstairs. Sera follows her into the parlor. "Is everything all right, mistress?" she asks, clasping her hands tight.

"What are you doing tomorrow?" Rae'lin asks, sitting on the sofa. She's in a black and silver robe with her hair pulled up in a tight bun.

"What I always do, setting up the booth and selling produce."

"All right."

"Did you need something?"

Rae'lin studies her a moment. "Do you love him?"

She steps back. "I—I don't know. We haven't known each other that long, and I'm not sure where this will end up." Her shoulders slump. "You're worried about your agreement, aren't you?"

Rae'lin approaches her. "You do have a way of screwing things up," she says nonchalantly.

"Don't worry. You'll get everything you deserve!"

Rae'lin's hand is up in a flash and strikes Sera on the back, sending her crumpling to the floor. Rae'lin smiles when Sera whimpers in pain. "No fresh wounds for him to see, right?" She chuckles, leaning down. "Tell him about this, and I will tell him where you were when Fury'am'a died. Exactly where you were."

Sera looks up at her with fear in her eyes. "You wouldn't—"

Rae'lin laughs. "Try me."

As Sera attempts to stand, Rae'lin strikes her down again.

"Why are you hurting me? What have I done to you?" Her tears fall fast as she braces herself for Rae'lin's next fit of anger.

She scoffs. "You question me, you embarrass me. Your father was asking all sorts of questions about you and Dankin, wanting to be sure you are actually happy. What did I ever do to wind up with a thing like you?"

Kneeling on the floor, the vomit threatens to rise as pain radiates through her entire body. She takes small breaths, calming herself through the pain as she tries again to stand. She's had enough. "I would ask the same about you!" Sera cries out. Rae'lin's arm crashes down on her back, sending her sprawling to the floor. Nearly passing out from pain, she unleashes her stomach contents.

"Clean this up, now," Rae'lin demands as she's leaving the parlor.

Sera gets to her knees, her body trembling in pain. She goes to the small washtoire next door to get a towel and clean up the floor before tossing the towel into the hamper. Gripping the rail, she drags herself upstairs, fixing a bath, and crying the entire time she soaks.

"Sera?" Dankin knocks on her bedroom door.

"Give me a moment," she calls out from the washtoire. Slipping on a pink and white hanfu, she fixes her hair and make-up before facing him.

"I just wanted to make sure you're okay."

"I'm fine. I had fun swimming with you." She smiles at him. He brings his hand towards her face when she flinches and steps back. "I'm sorry," she says, hanging her head. "Please, I didn't mean—"

He takes her hands and kisses them both. "Sera, I'm not upset or offended. I wish you had never been hurt in the first place."

She looks in his eyes, her heart racing as her skin is flush all over. "Dankin—" she tries as he brings her to him with his hands on her back. Pulling away, she grips the doorframe to stay upright.

"Sera, I'm so sorry! Is your back still bothering you?" he asks, confused.

"A little. It's easing," she says as she takes deep breaths, praying for the pain to stop.

He sighs. "I'm sorry."

She lets go, facing him as she takes his hand. "I'm okay. It was just a moment, but I'm fine now." She smiles to hide her pain.

"I never want to hurt you."

"I know. I want to show you something. Come with me," she says, squeezing his hand. She hopes going for a short walk will help ease her pain, or at the very least, take her mind off of it. They go downstairs and away from the manor, arriving at a hilltop that overlooks the valley. "Isn't it a beautiful sight?"

"Yes, it is."

She looks at him, blushing when she realizes she is the sight he is admiring. He smiles at her. "Sera, may I kiss you?"

Her breath sucks in. "Yes." He leans in, his lips on hers as he kisses her softly. Her mouth opens slightly at the feel. She brings her hand up, gripping his hair as his mouth devours hers. Her heart pounds in her ears as her skin is flush. She pulls back, smiling at him. "My first kiss. Thank you."

He chuckles softly at her reaction. "You are most welcome," he replies, gently wrapping her in his arms. "This doesn't hurt, does it?"

"No, it's fine." She nuzzles into his chest, holding him tightly as his arms are around her waist. They stand together in silence, the only witness to their bliss are the stars flickering in the heavens above. She looks up at him. "Can I have another kiss?"

"Always."

She leans up, holding him tightly as their lips meet again. He takes her hand, walking her to the manor and up to her quarters. They say nothing as they walk, reflecting on their first kiss.

She lingers in her doorway. "Good night, Dankin."

"Good night, my little sea nymph."

Blushing, she slips into her room and shuts the door. Her skin is still warm as she thinks of their kiss. Is this real? My first kiss under a sky full of stars? It was more amazing than I could have imagined! I think I am falling in love with him.

* * *

Sera wakes up as the pain rolls over her. Clenching the blanket with both hands, her pain ebbs and flows. She sits up and leans over the bed, gasping for air. Making it to her feet, she's going for the door when she collapses to her knees. Taking a moment to collect herself, she makes herself stand and knocks on Dankin's door.

"Sera, what's wrong?" he asks, rubbing his eyes. She collapses in his arms. Bringing her inside, he kneels to the floor, easing her down.

"My back—" she tries as her tears are rolling down.

"I'm sorry," he says, rolling her over and lifting her gown. A gasp escapes him at the sight of her bruises. "These are fresh, Sera!" He takes her into the washtoire, sitting her on the edge of the tub. Mixing together a batch of salt and water, he applies it to a small towel. He rubs the mixture gently over her back. "Is this helping?"

"Yes. I'm sorry to bother you."

"It's no bother. Will you tell me about it?"

"Please, don't," she begs, looking up at him. "Let it go?"

"What else did she do to you?"

"She said horrible things. I lost my temper, so it's what I deserve," she explains as she wipes her tears.

"No, Sera, she has no right to put her hands on you," he says, rage flowing through his veins. "It seems my threats have fallen upon deaf ears. I will take care of this."

"Please, give her one more chance?"

He wants to argue, until he sees the look on her face. "I won't say anything," he answers.

"Thank you."

He grabs a clean towel and dries off her back. "I apologize for lifting your gown. I know it's not proper—"

"It's all right. You helped me, so thank you. I woke up in pain and unable to breathe. I don't know what you did, but I feel much better already."

"That's what matters. Will you sleep now?"

"I will."

He helps her back to her room and into her bed. "Until morning."

She smiles as she watches him leave, grateful to have someone who cares for her so.

* * *

An hour later, she jolts awake. She sighs, realizing she's okay and was having a bad dream. Standing up, she's surprised to have no pain. Downstairs, she puts the kettle on.

"Sera."

She turns, seeing Rae'lin. "Mistress, I am making a cup of tea. Would you like one?"

"That would be nice. We need to have a little chat, girl to girl."

Sera turns back to the kettle to hide her fear. She prepares the tea, setting the table as it steeps and putting out a few scones and pastries.

Rae'lin takes a sip of her tea. "Sera, are you prepared to fulfill the duties of a wife?"

"How do you mean?" They drink their tea and discuss what married life is like. "Dankin and I are not even close to getting engaged. May I ask why we are discussing this now?"

"Because whenever the time does come, and believe me, it will whether with him or someone else, you need to be prepared. I do not wish to open the door to a humiliated husband returning you to me!"

Sera doesn't attempt to hide her hurt. "Mistress, please, how can you think so little of me? Why do you think this?"

"Because it would not surprise me," she admits bluntly.

Sera gets to her feet. "Whatever you are worried about, is not going to happen. I assure you, if I get the chance to escape this nightmare, I will gladly take it!"

Rae'lin jumps up and grabs her arm. "Do I need to teach you again?"

"What is going on?"

They turn as Dankin walks in. Rae'lin immediately releases Sera. "Just a disagreement, I assure you."

"Sera, did she hurt you?" Dankin asks.

"Not this time," she answers.

Dankin steps up to Rae'lin. "I have never hit a woman, but there is always a first time for everything. If I catch you with her like that again, there will be no warning. Am I clear?"

"Yes, Dankin," she says as she hurries from the room. Sera sits at the table, keeping her head low.

Looking her over to be sure she's not hurt, he sits beside her. "Sera, what's wrong?"

"I'm humiliated for what she said about me. She... she's worried about..." She shakes her head. "She's worried whenever I do get married, my husband will try and return me because he will be unhappy with me."

"I am so sorry." He grows concerned as he sees tears falling down her cheeks. He wipes them away. "It's all right. That won't happen." He squeezes her hand. "Has she always put her hands on you?"

Sera sighs, not in the mood to discuss her past. "When I was a child, it was more grabbing me to toss me where she wanted me. Only as I entered my teenage years did she get more physical. She hadn't in a while, but I guess everything with the lord and the duke were too much for her. She blames me for what happened to them."

"The lord?"

"Fury'am'a."

"Why does she blame you?"

She traces her finger over the lip of her teacup. "I'd like to get more sleep."

He decides not to press. "All right." They wash and dry the dishes before he takes her upstairs. "May I give you another kiss?"

She smiles at him. "Yes, please." Leaning down and kissing her softly, his hand caresses along her arm. She moans quietly, blushing as she pulls back. "I'm sorry."

"Sera, it's all right. Get more sleep. I'll see you in the morning." One last goodnight kiss, then she watches him go into his quarters.

I love him. She bites her lip and grows warm at the realization, giggling softly as she goes inside and shuts the door.

Chapter 5

Uncharted Waters

When Sera takes the breakfast tray into the main quarters the next morning, she freezes at the sight of Rae'lin.

"Sera, is something wrong?"

"Mistress, have you looked in the mirror this morning?" Sera asks as she hurries to set the tray down.

"I have not. Why?" She goes into the washtoire, bringing her hands up in shock. She gingerly runs her fingers over her swollen, purple face. She storms up to Sera. "What is this? What did you do to me?"

"I didn't do anything! I'll send for the doctor to—"

"No! No one can see me like this. I will clean up and take some medicine. I'm sure it's just some type of infection. Feed them while I shower."

"Yes, mistress."

Sera picks up a plate and sits beside her father. She helps him eat, growing concerned when he barely touches his food and immediately falls back to sleep. Looking at Na'ito, she sees he is also sound asleep. She leaves the plates, knowing Rae'lin will feed them when she gets out, and returns to the kitchen, laughing about how Rae'lin looks.

"What's funny?" Dankin asks as she walks in.

"Nothing," she answers, though she can't help letting one more giggle escape her lips.

* * *

Their morning breezes by as they are steady with customers. "Miss Ka'iko, how are you?" Sera greets one of her regulars.

"I am well, thank you," she replies as she peruses the fruit on display. "Sera, you have the best fruit on the island. I will take my usual."

"We appreciate that, and thank you for your business," Sera says as she wraps the fruit.

"I would like to stop by and visit your mother soon."

"Today would be a fine day for that," she says, handing the package to her as Dankin takes the coins. "I'm sure she'd be glad to see you."

When Hi'tob'a arrives at eleven, Sera and Dankin return to the estate for lunch. Rae'lin nearly knocks the tray from Sera's hands when she comes in to deliver their food.

"Do you think you're funny? Telling Miss Ka'iko to come see me today?"

"I am sorry. She asked if she could, and we had been so busy I forgot—" she tries, setting the tray on the table.

"Worthless!" Rae'lin knocks her to the floor. "When will you ever learn?"

"You look a little better," Sera says, standing up.

"Don't try that with me. Now, what did you do to me? Was it in my food or drink?"

"I swear to the goddess, I had nothing to do with this!"

Rae'lin grabs her arm, jerking her forward. "Liar!"

"Let me go!" Sera cries out. She looks at Rae'lin, stifling a laugh. "You… um… you look purple again."

Rae'lin shoves her to the ground. "I need to lie down. Feed them both," she commands.

"Yes, mistress." She watches her leave the room then gets a plate, taking it to her father's bedside. "Hello, father. Will you eat for me?"

"I will. What is wrong with your mother?"

"I'm not sure. Personally, I believe it's karma." She helps him eat, a question nagging at her mind. "Would you be all right if I ever married and left?"

"Sera, it's what I want for you. I've always wanted you to be your own person, to have your own life, away from here."

"I don't want to leave, though. My place, my duty—"

"Your entire life has been spent caring for us. I want you to have a life of your own. Are you and your suitor discussing marriage?"

"No, not yet. I care deeply for him, but I don't really know what I want."

"Ah, yes. A battle as old as time, the heart versus the brain. When the time comes, you'll make the right choice."

She smiles and leans over to place a gentle kiss on his forehead, whispering a thank you. She takes the other plate to Na'ito, gently waking him. "Will you eat for me?"

"Hmm, what time is it?"

"Time for lunch."

"Where is mother?"

"She had to lie down, she's… not feeling well."

"Okay." He takes the plate, feeding himself. "Thank you."

She gathers the empty plates, taking the tray, and leaving the one plate of food for Rae'lin.

"I'll check on you both before heading back to the market."

"Actually, would you bring your suitor in here before you leave? I would like to meet him."

"Of course."

She returns to the kitchen. Dankin stands up, concerned. "Is everything all right?"

"Yes. I was helping Tsuji and Na'ito."

"Because the mistress looks like a blueberry?"

"How do you know that?"

"I went to use the washtoire in the hall as she was passing by. She was quite embarrassed that I saw her." He chuckles softly, looking over when Sera groans as she sits. "Sera, did she hurt you?"

"Can we eat?" she asks quietly.

He gets the plates from the warmer and sets them on the table. "Sera?" he tries again.

She studies her plate, pushing her food around with her fork. "I'm okay. I just want to eat and return to the market."

"All right."

She finishes eating and reaches for his plate. He stands up, taking her dishes with his to the sink. "Dankin—"

"I've got these."

"Thank you." She smiles at him. "Oh, my father would like to meet you." She watches him straighten up, dropping a dish in the sink. "Dankin?"

"I can't."

"Why not?"

His hands clench as he turns away. "I've seen him before."

"What? Where?" Sera asks, walking up to him. "Why didn't you tell me?"

"It doesn't matter."

She puts her hand on his arm, gasping when he jerks away. "Dankin, please—" she tries again. He looks at her, shakes his head, and goes outside. With a heavy heart, she returns to her father's bedside and apologizes for her suitor's absence, saying he has already returned to the market. As she's leaving the room, she nearly runs into Rae'lin.

"How are you feeling, mistress?"

"A little better. Sera, may I say, that gown is lovely on you."

"Thank you," she responds, wondering what Rae'lin could possibly want from her. "We are returning to the market."

"All right. Take care."

"Yes, mistress." She walks away, confused by her sudden kindness. Going outside, she finds Dankin leaning against the fence with his arms crossed. Taking a chance, she approaches him. "We don't have to talk about it, but I would appreciate it if you would escort me back to the market. We need to load up a few bushels to take with us."

Dankin sighs. "Sera, it's not going to work." He sees the pain and fear in her eyes as she stumbles back. "Wait, Sera—"

"If you're going to go, then please do so. I do not wish to drag this out." She turns away to hide her tears. "At least tell me what I did wrong before you go."

He walks over and takes her hand. "Sera, I didn't mean us."

Struggling to form the words, she looks at him in confusion. "I—what?"

He points over. "I was talking about the cart." She sees the back wheel has broken off.

Looking down, she sucks in her breath. "Oh, I am so embarrassed now." He gently squeezes her hand and brings it up, kissing her palm. She looks at him with tears in her eyes.

"Sera, it's okay." He takes her into his arms. "Why are you trembling?"

"Please," she looks down, "I was scared of what the mistress would do if she thought I broke your agreement."

"You have nothing to worry about, I assure you. I should've worded it differently. I never meant for you to think I was leaving. I am truly sorry."

"No, I am, for prying and pushing you to tell me about your past. I should be more patient."

"You didn't do anything wrong. Let's just forget about this." He kisses the top of her head and nods towards the broken wheel. "Now, what are we going to do about this cart?"

She walks over to kneel beside the cart and examine the wheel. "The axle looks okay, I think it's just the wheel itself that's broken." She goes to the shed and returns with a new wheel and some tools. He watches her remove the broken wheel, replace it, and return the tools to the shed. When she is by his side again, she admires her work. "Good as new."

"You never cease to amaze me," he says with a smile.

* * *

They return to discover a long line at the stall and rush to help Hi'tob'a, unloading as people order. Sera sighs in relief when the line dies down and sends Hi'tob'a back to the orchard for the rest of the day. She and Dankin fall into a steady rhythm together as customers come and go.

"When will the next crop of koko'appuru be ready?" he asks during a lull in customers.

"After the festival."

They run out of produce to sell around three o'clock. "Should we close early and go for a swim?" he asks, smiling when she blushes. "I know you wear your suit under your dress."

"Am I that predictable?"

"So much so, that I have my swim-shorts on."

She laughs. "Yes, we'll go swimming." They load the empty bushels onto the cart and stroll to the beach. He leans it aside as she gets two towels out of her bag. They go into the water, drawing nearer to each other as they splash and swim. "Could we—" she clears her throat. "Could we kiss in the water?"

He smiles as he pulls her to him, his kiss starting soft and growing in intensity as her hand caresses his chest. She pulls back, smiling at him. "How was that?" he asks.

She giggles as she looks down. "Wonderful, like you." Looking over, she sees the sun is getting low. "We need to return and start supper." She gasps when he takes her in his arms, kissing her again before he takes her hand and leads her back to shore.

They sit on their towels, drying in the heat of the sun before dressing. "The mistress would never forgive me if she knew I did this. She thinks it is inappropriate."

"Swimming with me?"

"Swimming."

"Really?"

"Yes. Even though my suit covers most of me, she thinks it is neither feminine nor appropriate."

"That red dress —" Dankin tries, shifting uncomfortably. "Didn't she pick that out?"

Sera laughs as she slips her gown on over her suit, shakes the sand from their towels before rolling them up, and puts them into her bag. "Of course. She was… um… showing off the goods." She stores the bag on her cart. "Swimming is just another thing she would take from me, so I've managed to keep it from her."

"I'm glad you have. I see how happy it makes you. You deserve this, after everything you have been through," he says sincerely.

* * *

Once at the estate, they clean up and cook supper. Sera sighs before taking the tray in.

"Mistress, you look much better."

"I feel better. Thank you."

She sets the tray down. "Do you need anything else?"

"Come here."

Palms sweating, Sera approaches. "Yes, mistress?"

"Perhaps I have been too hard on you. After all, it's not your fault you were born looking the way you do. Regardless of my own opinion, men do seem to find you attractive. I have to ask, has Dankin seen your ears?"

She blushes. "He has. He thinks they're beautiful."

Rae'lin laughs. "Really?"

"Yes."

"How are the two of you doing?"

"We are doing well," she answers, wishing to be dismissed. "Was there anything else?"

Rae'lin steps toward her, bringing her hand up. Sera flinches. "Sera, why are you afraid?"

"Apologies."

She brings her hand up to Sera's face, looking her over and brushing her hair back to look at her ears. She pulls her hand down, watching as Sera's hair drapes back around her shoulders. "Well, as long as he stays interested, that is the most important thing. Do not screw this up. Do you understand?"

"Yes, mistress. May I go now?"

"Sera! Are you that desperate to get away from me?"

"No, but he is waiting to have supper with me."

"Of course. I didn't think of that. Now, I cannot divulge any details regarding our agreement, but I will say this. He is more important than you realize."

"Yes, mistress."

"Dismissed."

Without bowing, Sera runs from the room. She joins Dankin in the kitchen. He gets their plates then sits with her. "Everything okay?" he asks, concerned.

"Yes. The mistress was making sure you are still happy with me," she explains.

"If she only knew," he says with a chuckle. "Now, are you happy with me? After what happened earlier—"

"No."

"Sera?" he asks, his heart quickening.

"Oh, that's not what I meant!" She laughs. "No, what happened earlier wasn't your fault. To answer your question, I am very happy with you. I told you before what a great friend you are and how happy I am to be courting you."

"I'm glad to hear that. Are you excited about the upcoming festival? I know I am."

She laughs softly. "Yes, I am, too. Have you been to a festival before?"

"We've had a few ourselves."

"What's it like, where you're from?"

He thinks a moment. "It's beautiful. We haven't had much damage from the war, but the tension and fear is thick in the realm. Our war has raged on far too long. Honestly, it's one of the reasons I had to get away."

"I understand. When my father left for the war, we didn't know if or when he would return. The way he did…" She looks down.

"You think it would've been better if he hadn't returned, but had been killed in battle?"

"Yes," she admits with shame. "Only because I know he suffers so. He is in constant pain and has to endure night terrors. I feel sorry for him." She looks at Dankin. "Can I ask, or will you get mad at me again?"

He hesitates before answering. "I apologize. I wasn't mad at you. During the war, your father killed someone I knew."

"I'm terribly sorry to hear that." She traces her fingers over his arm. "I want to ask, but I'm afraid of the answer."

"Sera?"

"I'm just curious, but why are you with me? What is your ultimate goal?"

"You think I would hurt you for revenge? I promise you, that is not my intention. I meant it when I said I never want to hurt you. I didn't even know you were a Dahvaene when we began courting."

"I know you've said that. I still worry. Please, don't take it personally against you."

"How else should I take it?" he huffs, getting to his feet.

She looks at him. "I'm not meaning to upset you. Can't you understand my concern?"

"You're right. I would probably at least wonder the same thing. As far as my goal with you? Right now, just taking it slow like you asked."

"Thank you for that." She scoffs as she thinks of Rae'lin. "I know the mistress isn't happy about it. If she had her way, we would wed tomorrow."

"That's not necessarily a bad thing, is it?"

"Dankin!" She jumps to her feet.

"I'm sorry," he offers, stepping towards her. "We're talking about taking it slow, and I practically propose. I only meant that we get along so well, and I… I care for you greatly."

"I know you do, even saving my life. I'm sorry."

"It's all right. Let's finish eating then get ready to turn in."

Sitting down, she keeps her head hung. "I—I didn't mean to upset you. I know you wouldn't hurt me. I'm sorry I thought that."

"Look at me." She raises her head. He leans forward to plant a gentle kiss on her cheek. "Sera, it's okay. We're okay."

She smiles in return as they finish in the kitchen. Upstairs, standing out the door to her quarters, she looks in his eyes. "You know, you asked me if every day was the same, and I said yes. That was true, until I looked up and saw a stranger wandering around the market."

"Oh? What did he look like?" he asks playfully.

Roses fill her cheeks. "Blond and handsome, with piercing blue eyes and the perfect smile. You could see the honesty on his face and tell he was a hard worker. I had no idea he would come in and turn everything upside down," she teases back.

He smiles at her as he leans in and kisses her forehead. "I would say the same about you, the woman with the heart of gold. You took quite the chance with me." He takes her hand, kissing her palm. "Good night, sea nymph."

"Good night, Dankin." She goes into her room, smiling at the thought of kissing him in the water. She bites her lip as she changes for bed. She lies down, closes her eyes, and grows flush as she thinks of his lips on hers.

* * *

Sera wakes up, covered in a cold sweat. She sits up and wipes her forehead. Disgusted with how she feels, she takes a shower and slips into fresh pajamas. Walking across the hall, she knocks softly.

"Sera, what's wrong?" Dankin asks with a yawn.

"I had a nightmare. Would you like to have a cup of tea?"

"Of course." He gets his slippers on and follows her down. Watching her put the kettle on, he says nothing as the water is heating up. He gets two cups. Once the water is ready, she fixes them up and sits with Dankin at the table. "Was it a bad one?" he asks when he notices her wet hair.

"It was. I was back in the basement, screaming for help. I had to get a shower. I felt the grime and dust from being down there."

"It sounds awful. I can't imagine."

"I'm sorry I woke you up."

"I want you to. I did it first, remember?" He laughs softly. "I owed you one."

"Thank you." When they've finished their tea, he takes her hand and leads her back upstairs. "Could I have a hug?" she asks, standing in front of her door.

He pulls her into his arms and relishes the feel of her. He kisses the top of her head. "Please, get some sleep without bad dreams."

She steps back, looking at him. "I'll try."

"Can I give you a goodnight kiss?" Dankin asks.

"Please."

She steps forward as he leans in, their lips meeting. She grips his arms. He breaks the kiss, smiling as she gasps in air. "Now sleep, my little sea nymph."

* * *

Dankin wakes up, smiling as he looks at the clock, and gets to his feet, going to the washtoire. Turning on the shower, he strips down before stepping in. He closes his eyes as the water rains down on him. His hand rests on the wall as he leans over, standing under the water for ten minutes before shutting it off and drying himself. He sits on the bed, putting his work shoes on.

She is absolutely beautiful. How the mistress can be so cruel to her own daughter, is beyond me. She has something incredible, and she treats her like her slave. Sera will be free of her soon enough and start living the life she is meant for. He smiles at the thought while he walks to her room. He's about to knock when she opens the door. His heart speeds up when she smiles at him.

"Morning."

He returns her smile. "Morning, my sea nymph. Did you sleep better?"

"Thanks to you." She takes his hand. They cook breakfast, then she sets up the tray. She takes it in, giving Rae'lin a small smile. "You look well today, mistress."

"I am much better. Thank you."

Sera bows and walks out, grateful to avoid an altercation. She returns to Dankin in the kitchen. "So far, so good."

"Glad to hear it. We'll load up the cart and leave shortly."

She studies his face, wanting to ask but not upset him. She looks down, watching her fork tap on the edge of her plate. "Dankin, can I ask? Who did you lose to my father?"

"Someone I knew," he replies brusquely.

Pushing down her anger at his vague response, she bites her tongue. "I know that, but—" she shakes her head. "Never mind. I guess it's not important."

"Not important?" he scoffs. "What does that mean?"

Her eyes go wide. "No, please, I didn't mean that whoever you lost wasn't important! I—" She looks down as she bites back the tears. "Please, forgive me?"

"Fine. Are we ready to go?"

She gathers dishes and carries them to the sink. She sets them in, leaning over, and turning on the tap. Dankin watches her cup water in her hand, gently rubbing it over her face. She looks up when he is standing beside her.

"I'm sorry," she whispers.

"No, I am. You were simply asking a question. I will tell you everything in time. Please, for now, will you trust me?"

"I will. I won't ask again."

"Thank you. Now, is today going to be like yesterday?" he asks, kissing the top of her head.

She laughs softly. "I hope so. Apparently, word of my koko'appuru is spreading, and the islanders are coming here to try it."

They load up the cart and go to the market, where they set up the stall and stay busy until lunch. They greet Hi'tob'a when he arrives, bringing a cart full.

"Morning, Miss Sera."

"Hi'tob'a." Sera looks at Dankin. "Will you stay with him while I go fix lunch?"

"Yes, I'll stay," Dankin replies.

"Thank you. I will bring you a meal." She kisses his cheek, takes the empty cart, and returns to the estate. She fixes up lunch and delivers it to the mistress.

"Sera, how are you?"

Surprised by the kindness in Rae'lin's tone, she collects herself. "We have been quite busy at the stall today."

"That's good to hear. Are you excited for the festival next week?"

Sera's eyes go wide. "Am I allowed to go?"

"Yes, I will allow it. I know Dankin wishes to take you."

She starts to ask, quickly biting her tongue. "Thank you."

"Have you kissed yet?"

Looking down, she blushes. "Yes, mistress."

"Good, things are moving as they should. You haven't embarrassed yourself or upset him, have you?"

She clears her throat. "No, mistress."

Rae'lin walks over. "Sera, you know you are a terrible liar. What have you done?"

"Nothing—" she tries, when Rae'lin slaps her.

"What did you do?" she yells.

"I only asked him questions about who he is, where he's from. It was a misunderstanding, and he wasn't upset after. I swear it!"

"Do not let that happen again. He is our ticket to everything. Do not screw this up, do you hear me?"

"Yes, mistress," Sera says with a bow and runs from the room. She hurries to her room to cover the new bruise on her face with make-up. She knows Dankin will be furious if he sees it.

As she starts to leave, her stomach grumbles, reminding her that she promised to bring lunch back to Dankin and Hi'tob'a. She quickly packages the food, loads it onto the cart with additional bushels of produce, and heads back to the market. They are grateful to see her. She sighs when the last customer walks away. "Was it like this the whole time?"

Dankin chuckles. "On and off. Good timing!" He looks down when her stomach grumbles. "Sera, are you all right?"

"Fine," she replies, taking the remaining fruit and restocking the stall. Dankin and Hi'tob'a take turns eating when there are lulls. She is grateful when the afternoon is a little slower. "Nice to be able to catch our breath."

Dankin laughs. "I guess people are already starting to arrive for next week's festival?"

"I didn't think of that. Of course, there are merchants, nobles, and others who would come from the mainland and even some of the other islands. The rest of the week should be pretty steady."

He looks down when her stomach grumbles again. "Sera, did you eat lunch?"

"I um, I forgot. I'll be okay until supper. We'll be leaving shortly, anyway."

He debates asking but decides to let it go for the time being. There is less than a bushel left as Sera closes up the booth. She gestures to Kye. He and his friends walk over, happy when Sera divides up the fruit among them.

"Thank you, Miss Sera!" Kye smiles at her, eating greedily.

She smiles at them. "You are welcome. Now, stay out of trouble. You all should be able to find some work with the upcoming festival." The kids all nod their thanks then run off to ask the local merchants for work. "They should be in school during the day," she explains to Dankin.

"Are they all orphans?"

"A few. Kye's father died when he was a baby, and his mother is in about the same shape as my father. He has no other family. He begs and does odd jobs to keep them with food and shelter. I help how I can, but we've had enough problems of our own."

"It's nice what you do for them."

"I wish I could do more. Now, are we ready to head back?"

"Yes, because you need to eat. If your stomach gets any louder, I think you will attract a whale here!"

She laughs as they gather the empty bushels and load up the carts. Dankin stops in the kitchen, getting a drink of water. He stops in place at the sight of food on the stove then looks at Sera. "Why didn't you eat earlier?"

She takes the old food and dumps it in the composter out back. She walks in, placing the pans in the sink. "I forgot. I'm going to clean up and start supper."

* * *

She's cutting vegetables when Dankin walks in.

"It smells good," he says.

"It will be ready soon."

"Good, because I hear how hungry you are." He goes to the skillet, working the fish and rice. He turns back to her, starting to ask but sees she is trying to concentrate. He sighs, turning down the heat and helping her plate the food. Sera looks at him when she is reaching for the tray. Grabbing her hand, he pulls her to him. "Why is your face bruised?"

"It was an accident—" she tries as she lowers her head.

"Sera, we talked about this. Was it the mistress?"

"Yes," she admits. "Don't—" she says as he grabs the tray and leaves the kitchen. She follows behind him as he enters the chambers without knocking. Rae'lin runs over as he sets the tray down.

He stares at Rae'lin intensely. "What did I say about that?" he asks, gesturing to Sera. "We have an agreement, but if you continue in this manner, I will happily back out. Is that what you want? Do you want me to leave you with nothing?"

Sera gasps at his words, tears forming in her eyes. *He would leave us? And I am nothing? I thought he cared for me!* Her hands clench in anger as she runs from the room.

"Please," Rae'lin begs.

"No, I have been kind and given you patience. Do I need to speak to you the way you speak to her? Will that get through to you?"

She falls to her knees before him. "I beg your forgiveness." Her head snaps up when he laughs heartily.

"No. You will beg for hers, or you will get nothing. I mean it. You will beg her the way you are begging me. Otherwise, I will keep my promise."

"I can't," she says, standing up. "She doesn't deserve—"

"She doesn't deserve how you have treated her!" he shoots back. "Now, you will beg her with everything you have, or I will leave you empty handed. The choice is yours." He looks over, only now realizing Sera is gone.

"Fine!" she hisses. "Bring her here."

Dankin walks out and goes to the kitchen, not finding her. "Sera?" he calls out, walking through the house and orchard.

"I believe she went to the beach," Hi'tob'a responds.

"Thank you."

Dankin rushes to the shore, seeing her dress and shoes on the bench. He strips down to his shorts and dives in. His anger grows when he finds her so far from shore.

"Sera! What are you doing all the way out here?"

She doesn't face him. "I thought you cared about me."

He swims to her, taking her hand and leading her to shore. He stops once their feet are touching sand. "I do care for you. What's wrong?"

She looks at him. "You would leave us? You would leave her with nothing?" She looks down. "I'm nothing to you?" she asks quietly.

"No!" He takes a breath and grips her hands. "Sera, I threatened her that if she touched you again, I would take you away from here, and she would get nothing from me. Not a single gold piece. I meant that I would take you and leave her with nothing."

"Really?" she asks, staring into his eyes.

"I swear it. You don't mean nothing to me." He studies her face while his hand is caressing her cheek. "You mean everything to me," he says before he leans in and kisses her fiercely. He pulls back. "Sera, I love you." With bated breath, he waits for her response.

I care for you, but I'm so confused about my feelings. She thinks of her time with him, how he has cared for her, showing her kindness and compassion, defending and saving her. "I love you, too."

He smiles at her as his mouth crashes on hers, fire in their kiss, and is surprised when she pulls away. "What's wrong?"

"I'm sorry. This isn't proper—"

Chuckling softly, he leads her towards the shore. "Come, you still need to eat."

"We both do." They dry in the sun and dress, then return to the estate. Standing in the doorway, he kisses her again. They look over when Rae'lin clears her throat at the sight of them.

"Don't you have something to say?" Dankin asks Rae'lin.

She walks over, looking at them and smiling when she sees Sera's hand held tightly in his. She kneels before Sera, her head bowed, ready to play her part. "I am sorry for how I've treated you."

"Answer me honestly, please."

"Of course," Rae'lin answers, smiling at her.

"Do you mean this, or is it only because you are worried about getting nothing from him?"

She looks at Dankin, who gives a small nod. "We need the money he is promising, for your father and brother. Is that not enough reason?"

"Fine. I do not know what will happen between us, as he and I are still taking this slow. Whatever happens, know this; I am no longer your property. Whether he and I marry then run the orchard, or he and I stop courting, I am not your slave anymore!" she cries out. She steps up to her. "You will never lay another hand on me, call me a burden, or treat me as lesser."

Rae'lin looks at Dankin as a smug smile plays across her lips. "Did you know she was in bed with Fury'am'a when he died?" she asks as she stands up.

Sera's face grows red as her stomach turns. "Mistress!" She quickly turns to Dankin. "It's not—"

He looks from Sera to Rae'lin. "The agreement is off!" he snaps as he storms out.

"How could you?" Sera cries out, knocking Rae'lin off her feet. "Dankin?" she yells after him. "Dankin, please, talk to me!" she begs when she sees him in the orchard. She runs to him and takes his hand in hers. "Hear me out."

He pulls away. "Is it true?" he demands.

"Not the way you think! Please?" She takes his hand again, leading him to the bench. They sit. "He carried me to his bed, but before he could… before he could hurt me, he died. Then I was accused of his death."

"Why did you not tell me this detail before?"

"I was too ashamed," she admits, pulling away and clasping her hands together. "The mistress made me go, and she told me I had to do whatever he said. Even so, I told him no, even begged him. He didn't listen. When I felt him collapse on me, I was terrified of what he was doing, until I realized he wasn't moving." She looks at him. "If you want to leave, I'll understand."

Dankin takes her hand and kisses her palm. "Will you forgive my anger?"

"You had every right! I'm the one who was deceitful, and I'm sorry for that."

"I'll stay, if you're sure you want me to."

"Dankin, I love you."

"I love you," he says, leaning down and kissing her. He pulls away when she gasps. "Sera?"

"In my anger, I—I knocked Rae'lin down!" She looks up as he is laughing. "What is funny?"

"Because it is no less than she deserves. Come, let's go speak with her." Once in her chambers, Dankin wraps his arm around Sera. Rae'lin looks at them, her smile spreading at the sight of Sera nestled in with Dankin. "Sera and I are still courting. I will honor our agreement."

"I will not," she says, walking over.

"What?" Sera asks, growing cold at her words.

"Sera, leave us!" Rae'lin commands. Sera looks at Dankin with fear in her eyes.

"It'll be all right, Sera. I'll be with you in just a moment," he assures her.

Reluctantly, Sera leaves the two of them alone. Rae'lin smiles at Dankin. "As I predicted, I see now that I have the upper hand."

He scoffs. "How so?"

"You are in love, aren't you? I don't know how things work where you come from, but here, she is mine until her twenty-fifth birthday or until I release her for marriage. If you want her, you will pay dearly for her."

"We agreed—"

"Yes. Now I want more. Much more. It's that simple."

"How much?" Dankin asks. Rae'lin smiles as she leans in, whispering in his ear. He pulls back, shock on his face. "You are out of your mind."

"Maybe I am, but that doesn't change the facts. I can have you removed from the property, banish you from ever seeing her again. I can do anything I please."

"Fine. We will have a formal agreement written up in the morning, signed and witnessed. It will include a clause that if you hurt her again, I will then have her as my own, and you will receive nothing from me."

"Agreed. Until then, I am done with you!"

His hands clench as he turns on his heel, leaving the room. He finds Sera in the kitchen. She gets the plates out of the warmer. "Will you eat with me?" she asks as she sets the table.

"I will," he answers as they sit. "She will not hurt you again. We have an agreement."

"I won't ask the details, only—"

"You're safe now. That's what matters."

"Thank you," she says, taking a bite. "I'm sorry you had to do that. I never wanted you involved. Please, do not think that's why I brought you here."

"Even if you had, I am happy to free you from this life."

She looks at him with surprise on her face. "You mean that, don't you?"

"I do. When I approached you, looking for work, I was attracted from the start. I was struck by your beauty, and I apologize if that is being forward, but it's the truth. I didn't expect us to end up here." Taking her hand, he kisses the back then works his way to the palm, before folding it between his. "My little sea nymph."

She giggles as she squeezes his hand. "Thank you, Dankin." They clean up and head upstairs. Stopping outside her room, she looks at him. "I don't know what you are giving up for me, but I promise that I will somehow pay you back. Whatever you need or require, I will give it."

"Anything?" he teases.

She blushes, worried until he lets out a small laugh. "Dankin, that is most improper," she says as she laughs with him.

He kisses her forehead. "You have nothing to worry about, nor do you owe me anything. I swear it to you."

"Thank you."

"I love you, my little sea nymph."

She smiles at him. "I love you, too." She goes into her room, lying in bed and thinking of her future, a real future. Changing into pajamas, she climbs into bed and falls asleep, dreaming of kissing him in the ocean.

* * *

Sera wakes to someone knocking on her door. She smiles, walking over. "Dankin, do you want tea?" she asks, opening the door.

She yelps in surprise when Rae'lin pushes the door open, forcing her back.

"Mistress—" she tries. Rae'lin grabs her arm, dragging her downstairs. She takes her into the parlor, tossing her onto the floor. "What are you doing?"

"Once he has this official agreement made up, I will not be allowed to lay a finger on you. Otherwise, he has the right to take you from here." She smiles at her. "So, I am letting out any remaining frustrations I have with you while I still have the chance."

"What are—" The words die in her throat as Rae'lin's hand strikes her face. Sera brings her hands up, attempting to protect herself from the brutal assault.

"If you tell him I did this, you will both regret it. I will have him banished from the estate and lock you back up in the basement!" Once Rae'lin is finished, she leaves Sera weeping on the floor.

Sera's cheeks are hot with tears against the cool marble floor. As she lies there, unable to move for the pain, she closes her eyes, and thinks of fleeing the estate, never coming back. I couldn't, though. I love my father and brother too much to leave them. They need me here. Eventually, she finds the strength to lift herself off the floor and return to her room. Devastated and alone, she prays for the morning light to come and bring an end to her pain.

Chapter 6

Koy'lei

Sera wakes up, groaning with every movement. She manages to get to her feet, nearly falling back onto the bed before she makes it to the mirror and looks herself over. *Every inch of me is covered with bruises. I will never be able to hide this. What do I do?* Sitting on the edge of the bathtub and holding her head in her hands, she looks over when she hears Dankin's voice.

"Sera? Are you in here?" She stands up and tiptoes her way to the linen closet. She slips inside right before he enters. "Sera?" He looks around before stepping out.

Peering through a crack in the linen closet, she watches him leave. Waiting a moment before leaving the washtoire, she listens to his footsteps going down the stairs. She quickly dresses, wearing a long sleeve and ankle length hanfu. Then she goes into the washtoire, putting on her make-up as best she can. She stretches her arms and legs, stifling the groans of pain as she does so. Dankin walks into her bedroom as she steps out from the washtoire.

"There you are! Where were you?" he asks, walking over.

She smiles at him. "I ran downstairs for a moment." She clears her throat. "I guess we missed each other. Shall we?" She takes his hand and leads him to the kitchen.

"I'll need a pen, paper, and one of your staff as a witness to the agreement."

"Okay. I'll get you everything you need." She goes into the parlor, retrieving a pen and paper. She brings it to him. He sits at the table, drafting up the agreement as she cooks breakfast. "I think Hi'tob'a would be a good witness. He is a permanent resident of the estate, plus he is known for his hard work and honesty," Sera suggests.

Dankin agrees. Setting the tray on the table, Sera is thankful the mistress is nowhere to be seen. She hurries back to the kitchen, seeing Dankin fixing their plates. They sit and eat together. He washes dishes while she finds

Hi'tob'a. Once she's explained the situation, he happily agrees. Dankin gets the agreement, looking at Sera.

"This shouldn't take very long. Please, wait here."

"What? Why can't I be in there?" she asks. "It's about the both of us, so we should be there together."

"I think it's best with the mistress, if you aren't."

Sera thinks for a moment. "You're right. I'll finish in here then go to the orchard."

"I'll meet you there shortly." He kisses her forehead before leaving with Hi'tob'a.

Sera finishes cleaning the kitchen and goes to the orchard, curious to know how the agreement is going. She picks up the first bushel, nearly falling to her knees in pain. She grips the cart to keep herself standing.

"Miss Sera! Are you okay?"

"Yes, Ti'ako. Will you help me?"

"Of course." He smiles at her as he loads up the cart.

"Thank you," she says. He gives a small bow before leaving her. She leans against the cart, waiting for Dankin. Her mind is racing as she worries over the agreement. Reassuring herself that everything will work out, she sighs in relief when Dankin approaches her. "Ready?" she asks.

"Yes. The agreement is final. I have the master copy, and she will never hurt you again."

"Thank you," she says softly. "I never would've thought that possible."

He stops, looking at her. "Sera, I mean it. If she lays another hand on you, I don't care what she says, what threats she makes, come to me. It will be taken care of."

"If she does anything else, I will tell you," she answers honestly.

* * *

They set up the booth and have a steady day. Dankin notices Sera groan from time to time and watches her lean over the counter. Hi'tob'a brings a full cart and takes the empty one back, instructing Chi'yo to cook lunch. Dankin gets a meal for himself and Sera from the eatery in the market, hurrying back. They take turns eating and waiting on customers. As they stroll to the estate, they sneak glances at each other.

"Sera, are you all right?"

She sighs. "I have something I need to show you. We'll stop at the beach."

Once on the shore, she takes him over to a private cove. She takes his hand and traces her fingers over the lines in his palm. "Please, don't be angry. I waited until after the agreement, since you know she can never hurt me again. I didn't want to—"

"What is going on?" he demands.

She starts pulling up her sleeve. At the sight of bruises, he gently takes her arm and pulls the sleeve up, doing the same with the other arm. "She did this last night, saying she could since there was no official agreement in place." She gasps when he spins her around, pulling her gown up to her knees. She grabs the gown back down. "Dankin!"

"Is there anywhere on you not bruised?" he asks as her head goes down. "Not even your face?"

"No, they're everywhere," she admits. "I was afraid if I you saw me like this before the agreement, you would go after her. I couldn't take the chance she would keep her word and banish you from me. We both need this agreement, for me to be free of her and for us to continue courting. That is what you want, isn't it?"

He takes a breath as he pushes down his anger. "It is." He looks at her. "Wait a minute. Were you hiding from me this morning?"

She sucks in her breath. "Yes." She meets his gaze. "I had to! I didn't want to, but I knew you couldn't see me like this. I couldn't risk jeopardizing everything."

"I understand why you did it, but it does not ease my anger any."

"I'm so sorry."

"No, Sera, I'm not angry at you. I should've seen this coming. I'm sorry I didn't protect you." He brings her hand up and kisses it softly. "Thank you for opening up and showing me this."

"I don't want to keep any secrets from you."

"Neither do I."

"Dankin, everything about you is a secret." She smiles at him. "That's okay. It makes you handsome and mysterious."

He chuckles as he kisses her gently. "Now, let's return. We'll get supper taken care of, then I have something I think will help."

* * *

Sera sits on the edge of her tub as Dankin draws a bath for her. When the water is ready, he hands her a small pouch filled with fragrant bath salts.

"These will help ease your pain."

"I appreciate that." She pours them in before standing up. "I'll say good night, if you're okay with that. I know I will fall asleep after this bath."

He chuckles, kissing her forehead. "Of course. You need the rest. I'll see you in the morning. Sleep well, sea nymph."

"You, too. Thank you for the salts." She kisses him softly, then watches him leave and locks the bedroom door behind him. In the washtoire, she strips down and climbs into the hot, steaming bath. The scent of the salts fills her nostrils and reminds her of the ocean on a hot day, soothing her weary mind and aching body. Her eyes close as she lies back, letting her cares and pain melt away. She jerks forward when she nearly falls asleep and lets out a laugh as she stands to unplug the drain.

Relaxed from the wonderful bath, she is out before her head even hits the pillow.

* * *

In the morning, Sera picks out her gown for the day and goes into the washtoire to change. At the sight of herself in the mirror, she freezes. The gown falls from her hand as she walks closer, staring at her reflection. There isn't a single bruise in sight. She clears her head, gets dressed, then rushes to Dankin's room. She pounds on the door.

He opens it immediately. "What's wrong?"

She brings her arm up to show him. "I have no bruises!"

He smiles. "Then the salts did their job."

"What? What are you talking about?"

"They're a rare salt from the mines found on Isle Soge'umm'ul. They are supposed to have incredible healing powers."

"Wait, is that how you survived the cow?"

"Yes," he admits. "That was the last of them, but I would say it was worth it."

"Dankin, thank you." She leans up and kisses him suddenly, then pulls back, flustered. "I'm sorry. That was too forward—" Her words die off as his mouth consumes hers, his hands caressing over her arms. She pulls back again, smiling at him. "Thank you, koy'lei."

"What does that mean?"

"In my native tongue, it means 'beloved.' Is that okay for me to call you?" she asks, studying his face.

"I like it."

Her smile grows. "Now, shall we eat?"

They fix breakfast and take the tray in together to present a united front. Rae'lin is troubled when they enter. Sera decides to be bold.

"How are you this morning?" she asks.

"I am well. Yourself?"

Sera looks at Dankin, smiling, then back at Rae'lin. "Couldn't be better. We will be leaving shortly for the market."

"Would you send for the doctor? Your brother was coughing up blood again last night," she asks as she picks up a plate.

Shocked to hear Rae'lin call him her brother for once, she steps back. She collects herself quickly. "Of course."

Sera sends a worker for the doctor. After eating, she and Dankin start walking for the market. He looks at her when she sighs.

"What's wrong?" he asks.

"I would give anything for my brother to be better. The life he has isn't much of a life, not when it's spent in bed and being jabbed at by doctors all day. I wish I could do more."

"I'm sorry. I do, too."

She smiles at him. "Thank you."

* * *

Arriving at the market, her smile grows at seeing the lanterns hung up. "They are starting to decorate already. Saturday is a boat parade with the fishermen. Then Monday will start the booths, dances, music, and food. Mistress has given me permission—" she catches herself. "Apologies. It's a habit, and I know I do not have to answer to her any longer, thanks to you."

They finish setting up the booth and stay busy throughout the day. She sends Kye to the estate to ask Chi'yo to take care of lunch and supper. When he returns with a cart full of fruit, Sera gives him five gold pieces and some food, thanking him for the help.

She leans against the counter as the last customer walks away, laughing at the sight of empty baskets all around her. "Well, I guess it was a good day! We will sell out tomorrow, too. I can already tell. The orchard workers will have more collected over the weekend, ready for our out-of-town guests next week."

They load up the empty bushels and return to the estate. "We need food," he says, taking her to the kitchen. "We were so busy, we forgot."

She cooks up rice and fish, then takes their plates and surprises him by leading him upstairs and out onto the balcony terrace. "I almost forgot this was here. I don't like to eat out here by myself, so I never really use it."

"It's a nice view of the orchard from up here." When he looks at her, he sees sorrow in her eyes. "What's wrong?"

"I wonder what the future holds." She takes a breath, looking at him. "I don't mean us. Please, don't think I'm rushing—"

"That's exactly what I think," he says, his tone serious.

"But—" she starts, when he breaks into a laugh. She gives him a teasing nudge on the arm. "That's mean! I thought you meant it. No, being free of her, no longer under her thumb. Knowing I can still help here and be with my family but not her servant. It doesn't seem real. Thank you."

"You are most welcome. Now, can I kiss you out here or is it improper?"

She giggles as she looks at him. "Yes, you may kiss me." He brings his hand up, cupping her face as his lips find hers. With his tongue, he gently presses her mouth open, then reaches his hand back to grip her head as his kiss grows in hunger. When at last he breaks the kiss, she gasps in air. "You're so good at that."

He lets out a small chuckle. "So are you."

"Thank you, koy'lei." She yawns and stretches. "Let's get through tomorrow, then we may actually have a weekend together. How does that sound?"

"Hmm, are we spending it in your quarters?"

"Dankin!" she cries out, getting to her feet and turning away while he rolls with laughter. "That is neither funny nor appropriate. How dare you?" she asks.

He rushes to her, apologizing. "I'm sorry—" he stops when she starts laughing.

"Got you back," she says with a grin.

"My little sea nymph, what am I going to do with you? Perhaps I will throw you into the ocean!"

"No!" she cries out as he picks her up. He puts her back down, kissing her as she laughs. She yawns again.

"Let's retire for the evening," Dankin says.

They gather dishes, and he takes them downstairs while she gets ready for bed. When he returns upstairs, she is in her robe and slippers, waiting in her doorway for him. He walks over and pulls her up to him, wrapped tightly in his arms.

"Dankin, I'm so glad I met you."

"Sera, you have no idea. Now, get some sleep," he says, his fingers gently rubbing over her ear.

She blushes at the sensation. "Yes, koy'lei." She pulls away, slowly releasing his hand. She goes inside, shuts the door, and leans against it. Her skin is flush as her heart is racing. "Oh, I love him," she says, going to her bed. "I want to marry him." Shocked by her own admission, her face grows flush. *Take it slow, Sera.* As she crawls into bed, her thoughts are of Dankin and his amazing kisses.

* * *

Dankin wakes up, stretching and getting into his work clothes. A smile crosses his face as he thinks of Sera in his arms the night before. *With me, that is where you belong. Last night with you was wonderful. After all I've been through, I never thought I would feel this way about someone, but you are so incredible beyond words. I am curious about the future, as well. Our future, together.*

He goes to her door and knocks softly, smiling when she opens it. His eyes go wide at the sight of her in a pale blue hanfu with white and silver accents, lotus blossoms embroidered on it.

"Sera, you look lovely."

"Thank you. This is one of my favorites."

"What the occasion?"

Playfully, she shrugs her shoulders. "Breakfast with you."

* * *

Once everything is prepared, Dankin offers to take the breakfast tray in for Sera. When he returns to the kitchen to eat with her, she is pouring his coffee.

"How is everyone this morning?" Sera asks. She smiles as they sit together.

Dankin looks down a moment before meeting her gaze. "Right now, okay. Your father is having some issues, and your mother said your brother is getting worse. The doctor says Na'ito may only have a few months. I'm sorry."

"We knew it could happen. It's a miracle he has held on this long. They didn't think he'd make it to ten, but at fourteen, he's been holding his own. I hate to lose him, but I know he will be free of his suffering." Her breath hitches in her throat. "Excuse me," she says, running from the room. She goes into the small washtoire and splashes cool water on her face as she wipes her tears. The tears continue to flow as she grips the counter, hanging her head.

"Sera?"

"Um, I'll be out in a moment."

"Can I help?"

She opens the door. "How?"

He grabs her hand and envelops her in his arms as he strokes her hair. She weeps into his chest. "It's all right. I'm sorry you have to deal with this. No one that young should perish. It's not right."

Once she is calm enough, they finish their meal and prepare to head into town. The market is busy, and Sera is grateful for the distraction to take her mind off her brother. She gestures Kye over.

"Would you help us run the stall today?"

"Yes, Miss Sera. Thank you!"

The day flies by, same as the day before, with rarely a break from the stream of customers. Dankin grows concerned as he watches Sera lean over the counter.

"Are you all right?" he asks.

"I don't feel well," she admits.

"Come on. Let's get you home." He turns to Kye. "Can you load up the cart and bring it to the estate?"

"Yes, Mister Dankin."

He reaches into his pocket, digging out some gold coins and handing them to Kye. "Thank you for your help today."

"Any time!" he says, loading up the cart.

Dankin helps Sera from the booth. They are almost to the estate when she collapses against him. He picks her up and carries her inside. Getting her on the couch in the parlor, he brings his hand to her forehead.

"My sea nymph, you are burning up!" Chi'yo comes rushing in with another staff member, and Dankin sends them to fetch the doctor while he sits with Sera. "How do you feel?"

She shakes her head. "Awful. I'm hot and cold, and my stomach hurts."

"When's the last time you were sick?" Dankin asks.

"I don't remember. I don't get sick very often."

"Just take it easy now. The doctor will be here soon." He holds her hand, concerned at how cold it is, compared to her forehead. He lays the throw blanket over her and stays by her side as they wait for the doctor. His hand caresses her arm as he comforts her.

Chi'yo returns and makes introductions. Dankin steps back to give the doctor room to do an examination. He steps up to Sera, pulling up his medical bag. Dankin paces with worry but stops when the doctor approaches him.

"She'll be all right," he says. "She has a simple bug. I gave her medicine, and she needs to rest and stay hydrated. If she is still like this at this time tomorrow, send for me."

"Thank you, Doctor Ma'ipe." Dankin returns to her side while Chi'yo sees the doctor out. "Sera, do you want to stay here or go to your room?" he asks.

"My room, but I don't think I can walk up there."

He scoops her into his arms and carries her to bed. As she gets comfortable under the covers, he brings a chair over to her bedside. "I'll stay here tonight."

"No, you need sleep, too."

"I'll sleep when you're better."

"Dankin—"

"I'll sleep fine in this chair, I promise. Do you need anything?"

"Just you."

"I'll be right here, whatever you need."

"Thank you, koy'lei." She turns on her side. "I do feel a little better already."

"Good. Now, sleep."

She looks at him. "Promise me you will sleep, too?"

"I will," he assures her, pulling the blanket off the back of the chair and covering up. He watches her eyes flutter shut as she dozes off. When he's sure she's asleep, he leans down and speaks softly in her ear, the foreign words rolling off his tongue as a blue light sparks from his fingertips and flows into her. Then he leans back in the chair, his task complete, and falls asleep, exhausted.

* * *

"Dankin?"

He jerks awake, jumping to his feet. "What's wrong?"

"I feel better, but I'm really tired. Would you fix breakfast and take some in for my family as well?"

"Of course. I'll be back shortly." He kisses her forehead, relieved she is no longer burning up.

When he returns a short while later, he is carrying two plates. He hands one to Sera, who is now sitting up in bed, and he sits again in the chair beside her to eat.

"How do you feel?" he asks.

"Much better. I would like to go to the parade."

He smiles, happy to hear it, and they finish eating. She gets out a gown and looks at him.

"Do you need help?" He grins at her.

"Dankin!"

He laughs as he walks to the door. "I'm kidding! I'll give you privacy."

"Thank you." As soon as the door shuts behind him, she changes into the pale pink hanfu with white embroidered roses and silver layers. She fixes her hair, pinning in a silver shell. She opens the door, smiling at him.

* * *

They go to the harbor, surprised at the crowd already accumulating near the water. He holds her hand tightly as they maneuver through the people. They get to the front, watching as the boats begin sailing by. Admiring the sail boats, she smiles up at him before turning back to the parade. Some of the boats are decorated to look like pirate ships, while others are adorned in silver or gold, contrasting their dark hulls. She laughs at one with a blue dragon on the bow. He holds her to him as they watch, her back nestled against his firm torso. Gripped in his strong arms, she has never felt safer. When the parade ends, the crowd shrinks away.

"I want to take you somewhere while we're here," he says. "Are you up for that?"

"Yes." She says nothing as he leads her through the streets, stopping in front of the clothing merchant. "Why are we here?"

"Next Friday is the ball and lantern release. I want to buy you a gown for that. Please, get it in your favorite color. It's important, as you'll see soon enough."

"We're—We're going to the ball? How?" she asks, her eyes lighting up with excitement.

He smiles at her. "I got us tickets. You do want to go, don't you?"

"Yes, thank you! I assume you're getting something, too?"

"What? Is there something wrong with my work clothes?" He smirks at her.

Laughing, she shakes her head as she walks around. Kea'nda, the shop owner, approaches them.

"Hello, Miss Sera. Are you here for your mother's gowns?"

"She's here for a gown herself," Dankin answers. "To wear to the ball Friday. It is my treat, whatever she wants."

Kea'nda gasps in surprise. "How did you manage to get tickets? It's nearly impossible!"

Dankin smiles. "I know the right people."

"I see. So, you both need an outfit?"

"Please," Sera replies.

"Ka'eto! You have a customer."

Ka'eto walks in, dressed in all black in his fine suit with his tailor's tape draped around his neck. "How may I help?"

"Dankin, this is my husband Ka'eto. He is our best tailor for fine menswear."

"Nice to meet you," Dankin says, shaking his hand.

"You as well. Follow me," he gestures for Dankin to follow him then walks into the adjacent room.

Dankin smiles at Sera. "I'm next door if you need me."

"Yes, koy'lei." She smiles at him before giving her attention to Kea'nda. "Now, for Friday?"

"Yes, Miss Sera. Let's pick out what you want." They sit at the table, going over fabrics and patterns. Running her fingers over the fine silk, she realizes she has never worn anything so fancy. She decides on her gown, her smile growing at the thought of dancing with him. They look up as Dankin walks in. "Finished already?" Kea'nda asks.

"Yes. How are things going here?"

"We just finished ourselves," Sera answers.

"Let's settle up then return to the estate." He pays the tab, with Kea'nda promising their outfits will be delivered in a timely manner. As they walk towards the beach, Dankin reaches for Sera's hand. He's confused when she pulls away and looks at him, her hand on her hip.

"What's wrong?" he asks.

"Nothing," she says, sighing as she walks ahead of him. He catches up to her.

"Sera?"

"How did you pay for that?"

"I need you to trust me. I swear to you that this time next week, you will know everything. Please?"

She thinks a moment before taking his hand. "You mean it? Everything?"

"I swear."

"Then yes, I'll continue to trust you. After everything you have done for me, it's the least I can do in return."

"Thank you." Unease flashes over her face. "Sera?"

"Just—" She takes a breath. "No, it's okay. Let's return to the estate."

"You can ask one question, and I will answer it."

She thinks a moment before meeting his gaze. "Do you know how to dance?"

Relief washes over him as he laughs softly. "Yes, believe it or not, I do."

"Great!"

* * *

They arrive at the estate, going inside and fixing lunch. Sera is still daydreaming of dancing when she takes the lunch tray in and checks on her brother.

"How are you feeling?" Sera asks.

He's trembling and pale, cold to the touch. "I'm okay."

"I wish I could do something to help you."

"It's all right," he replies weakly.

"Rest now." She gives him a reassuring smile before going back to the kitchen. She sits with Dankin, her heart in her stomach. She makes herself eat. "I think I need to lay down."

"Are you still sick?" he asks, his voice thick with concern.

"No. I'm okay, just tired. Please, finish your lunch."

"I'll come check on you shortly."

"Okay."

She goes to her room and lies on the bed. *Why does my brother have to be sick? It's not fair, he's just a child, and he doesn't deserve this. Please, goddess, give me a chance. Let there be something I can do to save him. I swear, I'll do anything.* She cries into her pillow before falling asleep.

* * *

Sera walks into the kitchen, smiling at the sight of Dankin. He is standing over the stove, cooking supper and humming. He looks at her, returning her smile. "How do you feel?" His expression changes when he sees her eyes are red.

"I'm all right," she assures him.

She takes the tray in and sets on the table, looking over when Rae'lin approaches. She is dressed in black and silver robes, with her hair pulled up and adorned with silver flowers.

"Sera, is it true? Are you and Dankin really going to the ball?"

"How did you hear about that?"

"Kea'nda delivered my gowns earlier, and she was very excited about yours."

"Yes, we are going."

"This is incredible. I was wondering," she runs her fingers across her neck, "do you suppose he could get me a ticket?"

Sera scoffs, catching herself, and turning it into a cough. "I'm sorry. No, he can't."

"How do you know if you don't—"

"Sorry," she says, walking out. She leans against the wall to calm her pounding heart before rushing to Dankin to tell him what happened. "My mother had the nerve to ask for a ticket to the ball."

"Do you want me to—"

"Oh, no." She laughs. "I already told her you couldn't. After everything she has done to me, that is the last thing she should get right now."

"I don't blame you." He takes a bite and looks over when she sighs. "What's wrong?"

"Even so, she does spend every day taking care of my father and brother. I do pity her for the life she lives."

"She chose this life."

"How?"

"Don't get me wrong, I pity her as well, but she could step out and do something for herself from time to time. It's as though she would rather sit in a darkened room and lament her situation, crying the victim, than live her life. Your father and brother basically sleep twenty hours a day. She could do something in that time. She could go to the beach, walk the market, engage with people. She chooses to sit in that room, day in and day out."

"You're right, although I suppose I'm not much better."

"What? You were forced into this life, given no choice from the time you could walk. You cannot possibly compare yourself to her. Why do you think that?"

"I guess because sometimes I have pitied my life, crying over it, and praying for a better one. I have a roof over my head, food every meal, I should just be grateful."

"She raised you to think like that. I assure you, your life here should've been so much better than what you had."

"Thank you. It has gotten better." She smiles at him.

He takes her hand. "What are we doing tomorrow?"

"I will leave Chi'yo in charge, and we will have the day together. Would you like to visit the mainland?"

"That would be nice." He thinks a moment before looking at her. "Does your father still want to meet me?"

"He does. You don't have to—"

"No, it's okay. Just, let's not bring up what I told you, about the war?"

"All right."

Holding hands, they go to the main chambers. Sera's heart races as she worries how this meeting will go. Rae'lin steps back in surprise at the sight of them.

"What do you want?"

"Father asked to meet my suitor."

"I doubt—"

"Rae'lin, bring them over," Tsuji commands.

"Yes, husband." She walks them over, angry when he gestures her away.

"So, you are the young man who has captured my daughter's heart?"

"Yes, sir. I am Dankin. It's an honor to meet you."

"You have an unusual appearance about you. Where are you from?" Tsuji asks.

"Somewhere far away."

Tsuji looks at Sera. "Is he always so vague?"

She laughs. "You get used to it. I assure you, he has been honorable and kind with me, protecting me and helping me."

"Then you have my blessing, for whatever the future may hold."

She takes Tsuji's hand, gently squeezing it. "Thank you, father. Now rest."

"I will."

They go into the parlor and sit down. Dankin brings her hand up, kissing her palm. "Sera, are you all right?"

"Yes. I never thought he would give his blessing, but that's because he knew Rae'lin was trying to marry me off for gold, instead of love." She looks at him, flush. "I'm so sorry. I know we haven't discussed that yet."

He chuckles. "Sera, it's all right. I know what you're saying. Now, you asked me if I know how to dance. I know a few, but I don't believe I know the dances of your island. Would you teach me one?"

"Yes." She walks over to the gramophone and plays a slow song. She takes his left hand, placing it on her waist. She takes his right hand and places it on her shoulder. "This is a basic dance. It's the most common one." They dance about the parlor, his smile growing as their bodies move to the melody. She gasps when he pulls her in closer, holding her tight.

"You are the first person I've ever danced with," she admits as the song ends.

"What? You're so good at it."

"Thank you." She walks over and shuts the gramophone off. "I only ever wanted to be a dancer. There is a school on the mainland, and I used to dream of being accepted there, leaving this life to dance. I couldn't imagine it now. They would sometimes come to the town square to perform their dances for us. I learned what I could by watching them, wishing desperately I was part of their troupe. I'm not complaining, at least I never went hungry or slept in the rain, like some of the children here."

"We don't always get what we want, but life still has a way of giving us what we need."

She smiles at him. "I like how you put that."

He sits on the sofa, looking up at her. "Would you dance for me?"

She smiles and nods, then goes to the closet to retrieve her golden fan. She plays a different song. Her hips sway as her feet glide, her body moving to the music. She teases with the fan, daring and bold then shy again. She turns the gramophone off once the song ends.

"You are a beautiful dancer. I could watch you dance all night."

"Thank you." She places the fan in the closet before walking up to him. They walk upstairs, where she takes both of his hands. "Dankin, I don't know what our future has in store for us, but it's already been wonderful."

Smiling, he leans down and kisses her. "With you, it certainly has. Sleep well, my little sea nymph."

"Good night, koy'lei."

Chapter 7

A Rose for Love

"You seem awfully happy," Dankin says, watching her look out across the water. They are on the ferry heading to the mainland, drinking tea as they enjoy the ocean breeze.

"I'm just looking forward to our day together," she admits with a smile.

He admires her in the pale pink and blue hanfu, contrasting her raven hair. He smiles when her eyes meet his, lowering, and staring at her lips.

"Where do you want to start?" she asks.

"I'm sorry?"

"Follow me," she says with a knowing smile as they depart from the ferry. Walking along the promenade, Dankin is impressed with the elegant shops lining either side of the street. As they come around a corner, he suddenly scoops Sera up and jumps back when a horse and carriage nearly runs them over. He holds her a moment as she collects herself. "That was too close!"

They arrive at the university, four stories with dark brown, curved roofs. and a white exterior. Dankin takes in the pagoda style of architecture.

"It's impressive," he comments.

"It has the most amazing library! Chi'yo would bring me books from here when she came to visit her son. He's a barrister here on the mainland."

They walk around, admiring various works of art, statues, and of course, books. They come upon a painting of a woman walking out of the sea, the waves forming her gown.

"Who is that?" Dankin asks.

"The goddess Amphit'ran, the one we are celebrating this week. She is goddess of the sea, providing us with gifts of food and water. We honor her in return."

"How many gods and goddesses are there?"

"Five goddesses and two gods. Amphit'ran is our main goddess." She lists off the others, explaining each one. "Freyj'us is my favorite," she concludes.

"Goddess of love?"

Sera blushes, looking down. "Yes."

"Why do you do that?"

She meets his gaze. "Do what?"

"Embarrass like that? Looking down as you blush? You have no reason to feel like that, not with me."

"It's part of our custom. Does it bother you?"

"No, but I want you to feel comfortable with me," he says as his hand brushes through her hair.

"I do."

"All right. Where to next?" he asks, taking her hand. Leaving the university, they head back to the city center.

"There is a temple I've always wanted to see," she says with excitement as she leads him there.

"How many times have you visited the mainland?"

"This is my third time." She looks up when he stops walking. "What's wrong?"

"Only three times?"

She takes his hand, continuing forward. "The mistress does not care for the mainland, since she prefers the quiet and safety of our island. I was not allowed to come here without her."

"I see. Why did you come before?"

"The first time was to accompany her as we searched for a doctor to help Na'ito. I was eleven at the time. Then we came recently, as you know, to meet the duke."

"Right. Hopefully, this time will be much better."

She smiles at him. "It already is." They arrive at the temple. He admires the pagoda, separated into three stories. "We don't build individual temples, instead we have this one with shrines inside. You may approach whichever shrine you need, to pay tribute, to light a candle, or to pray." They go inside.

"Are you doing any of those?"

"Yes. I want to pray to Aesculap'eir."

"I beg your pardon?"

She laughs. "She is the goddess of healing. I want to pay tribute and pray over my brother."

"Of course."

She leads him to the statue of a beautiful woman, holding a staff with a serpent dragon wrapped around. Dankin stays back as she pays her respect.

"Any others?"

She blushes. "I am leaving tribute to Freyj'us."

"Then I will, too." They walk over, waiting for a pilgrim to finish.

"I wonder how far they came?" Sera asks, nodding towards the woman at the shrine.

"What do you mean?"

"See her dress? She is not from here. She must have family or know someone on the island."

Dankin's fingers brush over Sera's cheek. She starts to look down, remembering he wants her to be comfortable, and looks at him instead. "This is the main hall, where the seven shrines are attended to. This one is called ami'dado." Once the pilgrim steps away, Dankin escorts Sera to the shrine. They lay gold coins on the plate. She reaches into her bag and pulls out a small, dried, pink rose.

"What is that?" he asks, confused.

"This is a flower I found the day we met. I hung it up in my room to dry."

He smiles at her. "Really?"

"Yes. I had hoped to pay tribute here for you coming into my life. Even if I didn't know at the time where we would end up." She lays the rose on the plate, then looks at him as she is flush. She leans up, but instead she clears her throat and takes his hand. "Are we ready for lunch?"

"Of course."

They leave the temple and walk to the main part of the village. The shops are all indoor, and a fountain with a statue of Amphit'ran is in the center. Going into a small eatery, she admires the dark wood floors and walls as they walk past the large fireplace. She's grateful they aren't busy yet. They're seated at a booth in the back with a small, crystal chandelier overhead.

"This is nice." Sera says as they look over the menu and order their meal. "I'm not used to this," she admits.

"If you haven't been here, how do you know about these places?" Dankin asks.

"I've read about the mainland for years, learning where everything is, planning to come one day."

"You have been an excellent tour guide."

She laughs. "Thank you."

Their meals arrive, steamed fish with rice cooked in hibiscus water, served with a white cheese pasta. They enjoy every bite. He pays once they have finished, then they walk back outside, rejoining the bustle of people.

"Well, tour guide, where to next?" he asks playfully.

She laughs as she squeezes his hand. "I've been saving this one for last."

"Now you have piqued my curiosity."

They walk for a while before arriving at the botanical garden. She beams at the beautiful roses, hibiscus, and white lilies lining the path.

"We have a few of these flowers back home, but I have heard this park has over five hundred varieties," she says.

"Let's see them all, shall we?"

They walk in, where she gasps at the sight of such splendor and beauty. The flowers are in gardens and paths along the walk. She leans down, running her fingers over a red rose. "I believe these are my favorite." When he doesn't respond, she looks at him. "You're not bored, are you?"

"Absolutely not. Like you, I am taking it all in. These are the most incredible flowers I have ever seen."

"They're beautiful," she says wistfully.

"What's wrong?"

"I haven't had a red rose in a long time. Tsuji used to bring me a few when he came here to sell some of his wares. He could get more coin here for his treasures than our little village." She pushes down the memory as she smiles at him. "I think there is one area you will really like."

"Why is that?"

"You'll see." Her smile grows as she leads him down the path. They begin to walk underground, with small lights along the path, guiding their way to an underground grotto. "Well?" she asks.

His breath sucks in at the sight of so many underwater plants and flowers. "You're right."

They walk around the pool, admiring the water lilies and lotus flowers. "I've waited my whole life to see this," she admits, looking at him. "Being here with you makes it special."

"Thank you for sharing this with me." Noticing they are the only two people down there, he pulls her to him and kisses her. Seeing the love in her eyes, he smiles. "I love you," he says softly.

"I love you, too," she replies before kissing him again. "I'm ready to head back if you are."

They walk around a little longer then head for the harbor. While they stand at the pier waiting for the ferry to arrive, she gently runs her finger across his hand. "Thank you," she says at last.

"For what?"

She leans up and kisses his cheek. "For giving me the perfect day."

"My little sea nymph, it was perfect for us both."

They drink a hot chamomile tea and enjoy each other's company on the ride back to the island. They arrive at the estate and fix supper. Dankin plates their food while Sera takes the tray in, her perfect day cut short when Rae'lin approaches her as Sera is setting it down.

"Did you two have fun today?" Rae'lin asks.

"We did. It was a nice day."

"You really do love him, don't you?"

"I do," she admits. "He loves me in return. I've never been this happy in my entire life."

"Well, you do have a glow about you. He must be doing something right. I'm glad you are in love, but I hope you're being careful."

"Careful about what?" Sera asks, naïve to what Rae'lin is suggesting.

"I loathe to think what would happen if he left you. Could you imagine?" she asks, smirking. "And how scandalous it would be."

Refusing to answer, Sera takes a breath and quickly leaves the room. She walks into the kitchen, where Dankin has their food and drinks on a tray.

"Where are we going?" Sera asks.

Only answering with a smile, he walks past her and leads her upstairs to the terrace, where the sun is starting to sink below the horizon. "Well?"

"Oh, it's beautiful. Thank you."

They eat their meal, talking about their day at the mainland. Once they've finished, he stands up and takes her hand. He pulls her to him, away from the table, and slow dances with her. They sway to the sound of the waves crashing on the shore as the stars above flicker. She holds him tight, pushing down Rae'lin's hurtful words. He pulls back, studying her face before lowering down and kissing her.

"You know how much I love you, right?" he whispers in her ear.

She nods, her head resting against his chest as she fights back the tears. "I do. I love you, too."

He hugs her then releases her so they can take the dishes downstairs. He walks her to her room, kissing her outside her door. "Good night, sea nymph."

She giggles softly. "Same to you, koy'lei." She goes to bed, thinking on their perfect day and wishing every day could be as good.

* * *

"Sera, I've decided watching you suffer is worth more to me than every gold coin on the island. I will not honor the agreement, and he will be banished!"

"Mistress, no, please! What do you want? I'll do anything!"

She laughs heartily. "All I want is to see you miserable, to see you suffering, as I have been since the day you were born."

* * *

"No!" Sera cries out, nearly falling off the bed, but she catches herself and sits up. Her face is flush, her hands clammy, and her heart is pounding in her ears. She goes into the washtoire, getting a shower and into fresh pajamas. She sits on the edge of the tub, crying softly into her hands. Calming herself down, she cleans her face and climbs back into bed, reassuring herself it was just a nightmare, that everything is okay.

* * *

In the morning, when Dankin opens the door to her, she pushes her way inside and takes him in her arms, holding him tight.

"Sera, not that I'm not enjoying this, but what's wrong?"

"Nothing, I just needed to hold you."

"All right." He squeezes her tight, kissing the top of her head. She looks up at him when she kisses him, her lips devouring his. "Sera, this is improper in my quarters. I don't want you to feel—" She kisses him again, her grip tightening on him as though she never wants to let go.

"I'm sorry," she says, stepping back. "I couldn't help myself. I needed this, needed you."

He traces his fingers along her jawline. "Whatever my little sea nymph needs. Now, let's go cook breakfast before we get into trouble with the mistress," he teases with a wink. He grows concerned when tears stream down her cheeks.

She falls into his arms again. "Just hold me, please? I had a bad dream last night."

"I'm right here. How bad was your nightmare?" He looks down when she shakes her head. "All right, you don't have to tell me. I'm right here, Sera. You're okay." He wipes her tears and kisses her. "Now, shall we?"

"Yes, thank you for your comfort. I'm sorry I needed it."

"Don't apologize, it's okay." He takes her downstairs, smiling when he makes her laugh as they cook. She takes the tray in, setting it down and promptly leaving, then smiles at Dankin as they eat together.

* * *

"Are you feeling better? After this morning?" he asks as they walk to the market.

"I am. Thank you. Did you sleep well last night?"

He chuckles softly. "I practically passed out. The walking and fresh air did me in."

"It was nice."

"I know you didn't seem too keen on the idea at first, but are you getting excited for the festival?"

"I am." Sera is shocked by the size of the crowd already milling about. "I did not expect this so early, since the festival doesn't even start until this afternoon." They arrive at their stall, smiling at the sight. "You guys, it looks great!" Hi'tob'a and Kye had arrived earlier to hang up flower garlands and lanterns.

"Thank you, Miss Sera," Kye says, beaming with pride.

Dankin smiles as he hands Kye a few gold coins. "How is your mother?"

"The same, Mister Dankin. Thank you."

"Will you be helping us today?" Dankin asks.

"Of course!" He looks over the crowd. "You'll definitely need it today."

"I wonder why so many people are already here?" Sera asks.

"Oh, they're saying the queen is attending the festival," Kye explains.

"Really? She hasn't left the palace since losing her husband in the war," Sera says, looking at Dankin.

He shrugs. "Who knows?"

"They said this year will be different, that they have dragons of light and will set off fireworks. It's supposed to be very exciting," Kye exclaims as his eyes light up at the thought.

Sera laughs and tosses her hair back, ready to serve her first customer. They work all day, relieved when the last piece sells. At three, she pays Kye and closes the booth so she and Dankin can return to the estate to freshen up before the festival. Sera meets Dankin in the hall wearing a lavender hanfu gown with silver and white layers. He's in black slacks with a matching yuka'mono jacket and pale blue shirt.

"Where did you get this?" Sera asks.

"Rae'lin gave me some of your father's clothes. I hope it's okay for me to wear?"

"It is. It looks nice on you… different."

"Do I not stick out already?"

"You are the only person here with hair the color of the sun."

He laughs. "I like that description."

* * *

Returning for the festival, the village is buzzing with travelers and fair goers, dressed in everything from common work clothes to gowns of silk and expensive robes. Sera's smile grows at the sight of the dragons dancing around the crowd. She and Dankin smile at each other as the smell of smoked meats and fresh baked breads invade their senses.

They walk around the booths to admire the artwork, crafts, jewelry, and leatherwork. They make a few purchases before stopping to eat, getting a basket of fish and chips then sitting down to enjoy it. She laughs as Dankin picks up the fish and looks it over.

"This is different," he comments.

"Apparently, it's something from the mainland. Instead of the way I usually cook the fish, they fry it in a type of oil."

He takes a bite. "This is fantastic!"

She laughs, eating her piece with a fork. "Yes, it is." She laughs harder as he continues to eat with his hands. "Dankin! Do you not have manners?"

"Apologies, Miss Sera." He winks at her, picking up his fork and eating.

They finish and continue to walk around the festival, watching the dance troupe from the mainland perform a hu'lua dance. Sera explains to Dankin that the dance they are performing tells the story of Ak'ki, who fell in love with Amphit'ran, but was killed by the god Kra'tyr because he felt Amphit'ran belonged to him. As the sun goes down, the hanging lanterns illuminate.

"Those are beautiful," she comments.

"Like you," he whispers before kissing her softly. He pulls back when she looks down. "What's wrong?"

"We are in public—"

"Of course, your customs. I apologize."

She raises her head slightly, looking at him. "It's okay. Are you ready to return for the evening?"

"Let's stop by the beach and have a quiet moment, without the crowd."

"Yes," she agrees. They walk away from the lights and music, arriving at her favorite spot on the beach by the small private cove.

"Dankin, can I kiss you?"

He smiles in surprise, leaning down until his lips are pressed on hers. "Sera, you never have to ask."

"My koy'lei, thank you." She kisses him again. "I love you."

"Sera, I love you. Let's turn in, as it looks like we have a busy week ahead of us!"

"I'm looking forward to Friday," she admits, taking his hand as he escorts her back to the estate.

"Speaking of which, our clothes should be delivered tomorrow."

"I can't wait!" She laughs. "I've never been to a ball before. How did you get us in?"

"I know the earl who is running it."

She doesn't ask anymore, walking upstairs with him. "Goodnight, Dankin."

He kisses her again. "Good night, my little sea nymph."

She giggles as she goes into her room. She changes for bed, her heart racing as she thinks of his kiss, of being in his arms. Thinking of the upcoming ball, she lies in bed and hums the song from their first dance together.

* * *

Dankin wakes up, stretching. *I can't wait until I reach over, and you are with me. Waking up with you beside me is what I long for the most. For now, I will settle with kissing you first thing.* He gets to his feet, dressing and knocking on her door. As soon as she opens it, he grabs her arm, pulls her to him, and kisses her passionately.

"Dankin!" she laughs. "What has gotten into you this morning?"

"Just the excitement of the festival, I guess."

"Now, can you behave yourself, or do you need to stay in this morning?"

He laughs. "I will behave, I promise." He kisses the top of her head.

"Really?"

He lets go, taking her hand. "Really."

They eat breakfast and go to the market, quickly setting up. Kye helps until they sell out of produce around four. Sera pays Kye as he loads up the empty bushels.

"How is your mother?" she asks.

"Good days and bad," he answers. "Thank you for the gold."

"Thank you for helping. I think soon I may be able to hire you on, permanently," Sera says, flashing a look at Dankin before turning her attention back to Kye. "If that's what you want."

"Oh, yes!"

"The deal is, you will have to go to school, too."

"Yes, Miss Sera."

Dankin and Sera return to the estate, cleaning up and going to the festival. They watch the dragons weaving through the crowd while they eat fish with rice and enjoy the fireworks once the sun has gone down.

"Those are fantastic," Dankin exclaims in awe.

"You've never seen fireworks?" she asks.

"No."

"We use them for festivals, wedding celebrations, and holidays." She looks over, yawning. "I'm ready for bed."

"I'll join you."

She shoots him a look until she sees the grin spreading on his face. "Is this you behaving, Mister Dankin?"

He laughs. "No. Come on." They return to the estate. She stops him at the bottom of the stairs. "What's wrong?" he asks.

"I'm going to check on them," she says, nodding towards the main quarters. "I'll see you in the morning."

"All right." He kisses her before running upstairs.

Sera goes into the room, ignoring Rae'lin as she approaches her brother. "How are you feeling?"

"Not bad today. How is the festival?" Na'ito asks, giving her a small smile.

"It's really nice. I wish you could go."

"Maybe one day."

She bites back the tears. "I'm sure you will. Do you need anything before I turn in?"

"No, I'm good."

She leans down, hugging him. She goes to Tsuji. "How are you?" she asks.

"All right. I had some spurts of pain earlier, but your mother gave me medicine, and it seems to have helped. Go on to bed, I know you've had a busy day."

"Yes, father." She kisses his forehead before leaving and going upstairs. She leans against her door, crying over her brother. She wants to knock on Dankin's door, have him take her into his arms, and comfort her. Instead, she takes a breath and goes into her own quarters. As she changes for bed, she pictures her brother at the festival, trying new foods, and watching the dragons.

Chapter 8

The Unexpected Gift

Friday arrives quickly, and they close the booth early to prepare for the ball. Sera's gown had arrived a few days prior, and she had been unable to stop looking at it since, taking it out of her closet and admiring it any chance she got. Her excitement grows as she takes it out again, finally putting it on for the ball. With a towel carefully draped around herself to protect the gown, she applies her make-up and fixes her hair, adding in kanzashi, a pink orchid with a silver fan, for the final touch.

Pleased with how she looks, Sera runs her fingers over her dress. The gown is silver, with tulle sleeves and silver-white roses trailing from the bust to the hem of the skirt. She slips on her silver shoes and walks to the door. Dankin is waiting for her when she opens it. He is in a navy-blue suit, with matching embroidery on the jacket and tie, wearing a navy-blue button up shirt and silver tie. She smiles at the sight.

"This is different," she says.

"It's customary for the ball, or so I was told." His breath sucks in at the sight of her in her silver gown.

She laughs, taking his hand. "You look wonderful."

"So do you." He kisses her softly. "Are we ready?"

She sighs. "My mother asked us to stop in, so they can see us dressed up. We don't have to—"

"It'll be fine."

They go downstairs. Rae'lin opens the door. "Oh, my. You both look great. Are you excited?" she asks, looking at Dankin.

Dankin looks at Sera before turning back to Rae'lin. "We are. I tried to get another ticket but was unable to. I apologize."

"It's all right," she says, her voice thick with disappointment. "You have fun tonight," she says with envy.

"Oh, I promise you, her life will never be the same," he says, smiling at Sera. She blushes, looking down.

Her father's voice calls out from across the room. "Can I see my beautiful daughter?"

Dankin walks her to Tsuji. "Evening, sir."

He takes in the sight of them, tears welling up in his eyes. "Your mother is right, you both look great."

"Thank you, father," Sera says, leaning down and kissing his forehead.

"Enjoy yourselves."

"We will," Sera says as they head for the door.

When they step outside, Sera is surprised to see the carriage waiting for them. She looks at Dankin.

"Rae'lin gave us permission," he explains. "She didn't want us to look poorly walking up to the ball."

"Of course. She values appearances."

"Are you complaining?"

"Oh, no. I wasn't really looking forward to walking there in these shoes!" She laughs.

He helps her into the carriage, then climbs up behind her. Sitting beside her, he folds her hand between his. "Are you nervous?"

"A little. I've never been to anything like this before."

"I have. You'll be fine. You have nothing to worry about. Just do as I do."

"That helps, thank you." She looks up at him. "Since we have to be proper at the ball—" Before she can finish, his mouth devours hers. She pulls back, gasping in air. "Koy'lei!"

"Is that not what you wanted?" he teases.

She looks down, squeezing his hand. "It was."

He brings his other hand up, gently raising her head. "Sera?"

"I know. I'm trying."

"Thank you."

They pull up to the manor. A footman approaches, opening the door and helping her out. "Good evening, madam."

"Evening," she responds. Dankin steps down, lacing her arm through his. They go up the steps, and he hands over their invitations.

The man checks his clipboard, finding Dankin's name on the list and marking it. "Please, have a nice time."

"Thank you," Dankin says as he leads Sera inside, where she nearly stops at the sight of the crystal chandeliers, beautiful lanterns, and silver candelabras. Gold leaf trim with silver vines adorn the marble columns. Despite the size of the ballroom, there is hardly any walking room with so many guests.

Dankin keeps her moving, taking her further in. She admires the ladies in decadent gowns, some in silk dress robes while others are in fancier ruffle gowns she doesn't recognize. Dankin and Sera step back as a low horn blows, announcing the arrival of Queen Kery'oto. She is dressed in a red silk kom'ono with pink and white flowers embroidered along the bodice. As she's walking by, Sera catches her eye. The queen approaches her, looking at her intently.

"What is your name?"

"Sera, Your Majesty," she responds with a bow.

The queen takes her hand, looking it over. "Not make-up?" she asks quietly, surprised by Sera's pale complexion. "Where are you from?"

"Right here, on this island."

She looks Sera up and down. "You are quite beautiful."

"Thank you, Your Majesty." Sera bows again. The queen nods and continues on towards her table, greeting people as she goes. Sera sighs in relief and looks up at Dankin. "That was unexpected," she says, her heart still racing.

"I agree." Finding their table, they sit down, surrounded by noblewomen and noblemen she doesn't know. Her stomach lurches when Duke Ab'iko sits beside her.

"Evening, Sera."

She takes a breath, avoiding Dankin as she smiles at the duke. "Evening, mi'lord. How are you?"

"I am well. I was quite surprised when I saw your name on the list."

"This is Dankin, my suitor. He acquired the tickets."

"I see. Pleasure to meet you," the duke says, giving a small nod.

"You as well, your lordship."

Once supper is served, the duke continues their conversation. "How is your mother, Sera?"

"She is well. She attends to her husband and son all day."

"Yes, I am sorry to hear that. She seems like an… interesting woman."

Sera takes a breath when he turns to the person next to him and begins talking about current events in the court. She gives Dankin a small smile. The plates are removed as the music begins to play. Watching as the dance floor begins to fill, Dankin stands up and offers Sera his hand. She follows him out, nervous about dancing in front of so many people. Her nerves ease as she relaxes in his arms. They move about the floor gracefully as the night wears on. During a pause between songs, he catches her yawning.

"Tired already?" he asks.

"It's been a busy week. I'm okay. I need a little break, though." Admiring the dessert table, she smiles at him. "Everything over there looks so good," she says as he walks her back to their seats.

He lets out a quiet chuckle. "Sit and rest, and I'll get us some." He caresses her cheek before he walks over to fix them each a plate. She looks over when she realizes the duke is staring at her.

"Are you having a good time, your lordship?"

"I am," he responds, leaning over. "Perhaps it was hasty of me to toss you aside so easily. If Dankin himself is courting you… Tell your mother, whatever Dankin is paying, I will double it."

Swallowing her shock at his offer, she gives a small shake of her head. "I apologize, but a binding agreement has already been made."

He chuckles, looking over at Dankin, who is speaking with a young countess at the dessert table. "Smart of him," Ab'iko says as he turns his attention back to Sera. "He knew that once us nobles saw you together, it would only raise your stature. I knew I had heard the name before. It doesn't seem real. Still, I never imagined someone like him would—well, anyway."

She looks at him, troubled, but doesn't push. "I apologize."

"Not necessary," he says, getting to his feet. "Excuse me."

What does he mean, he's heard the name? Who is Dankin really? I—No, I have to stop this. Dankin asked me to trust him and promised he would tell me everything soon. Smiling when Dankin sits beside her, her eyes go wide at the slice of cake.

"We're sharing this, right?"

"If you want," he answers, feeding her a bite.

"Hmm, this is very rich." Once the cake is gone, she takes his hand. "Are we going to the lantern celebration?"

"Yes. That should be starting soon. Let's head out." He gets to his feet, taking her hand. They leave the manor and walk towards the shore. Above them, the paper lanterns float through the sky, each one with a red flower painted on the side and giving off a soft yellow hue. Only a few dot the sky at first, then hundreds are drifting overhead.

"Oh, it's so pretty. This has been a wonderful week." Sera sighs. "It's a shame it has to end."

"Who says it does?"

"What do you mean?" Sera asks.

"I have a gift for you," Dankin says. He kisses her softly before walking with her to one of the docks. They look out at the water, illuminated by the near full moon overhead and the lanterns floating by. "Sera, I know we are supposed to be taking this slow, but this time with you has made me the happiest I have ever been. You mean everything to me, and I cannot bear the thought of facing another day without you in my arms." He gets to one knee, pulling out an eternity band of small ocean pearls. "Will you marry me?"

Her hands fly to her mouth as she gasps in surprise. She takes a moment, thinking back on her time with him—of him protecting and defending her, holding her as she wept, comforting her, saving her very life. Suddenly, there is no doubt in her mind. She knows in her heart, being with him is where she is meant to be.

"Yes."

He jumps to his feet, takes her in his arms, and kisses her fiercely. "Do you swear on this ring, here and now, that you will marry me?"

"I do," she says, smiling up at him.

He slips the ring on her finger. Once it's in place, she watches in disbelief as it glows blue, tightening as the light fades. Her breath catches in her throat as her body goes tense. Dankin holds her up, caressing her face.

"I know. It's going to hurt. I'm sorry."

"What—" she tries but her legs suddenly give out. He eases her down and kneels beside her as he holds her hand. She watches as her gown begins to shrink, revealing her legs. Her shoes flatten as they merge with her feet and turn them silver. Watching in horror, silver scales are climbing up her legs, burning as they grow. Desperately, she tries to keep her legs apart as they fuse together, but she's unable to stop it. Crying out in pain, her back arches while the gown continues forming silver scales which reflect in the moonlight. "I—please!" she cries.

"It's almost over," he says, kissing her hand.

"What is happening?" she asks, falling on her back and crying out again. "My legs. I can't feel them. What—" her breath hitches in her throat. She pulls up what's left of the gown, watching as her waist narrows. Her chest tightens as the silver scales climb up her stomach, and thin slits form along her ribcage, creating gills. She gasps for air, sobbing as she drops the fabric in shock. "What did you do to me?" she cries out before losing consciousness.

Dankin watches as her transformation completes before scooping her into his arms. He walks towards the water before diving in, ready to take her to their home.

* * *

"Hmm," Sera groans, rolling onto her back. "Did I drink last night?" She looks up when Dankin chuckles.

He's sitting on the edge of the bed, studying her face. "No, Sera."

"Oh, everything feels… off. What happened?" she asks as she's looking around the room. "Where are we?" The room is decorated in pink, white, and silver colors. The trim and floor are white marble. She looks at Dankin as she realizes they are on a large, soft bed.

"We're home," he answers, kissing her.

She smiles, looking at the ring on her hand. "Oh, right. We're engaged!"

"Yes, my little sea nymph."

She leans on her arms, struggling to get upright. "What's wrong with my legs?" she asks, pulling the blanket off. A silver tail rests where her legs should be. She cries out, bringing her hands to her face as the shock washes over her.

"It's okay," he reassures her. "You changed last night. Do you remember?"

"The dock, after you proposed. I thought that was a nightmare."

"No, Sera." He takes her arm, helping her out of bed. She realizes they are swimming as he takes her to the mirror. She can only stare in horror at the sight of her tail. Examining herself in the mirror, she sees her gown falls just below her waist. She lifts her gown slightly and sees the pectoral fins on either side where her tail meets her stomach. She quickly releases the gown. Her breath sucks in at the sight of the creature staring back at her from the mirror, unrecognizable and more than she can bear.

"What did you do to me?" she demands. His bright blue tail suddenly catches her eye. "What are you? Who are you?"

"Well, I told you I would answer your questions. Shall we talk?"

She closes her eyes. "This isn't real. I'm going to wake up at the estate, in my bedroom, as a human, and everything will be fine. This isn't real," she assures herself. When she attempts to move her legs, her tail reacts with a swish. She cries out, gripping his arm. "Oh, goddess. This is real, isn't it?"

"It is. Please, give this a chance? Give me a chance? I promise you will be happy here."

"You took me from my home, from my family, and turned me into this… this disgusting thing! How could I possibly be happy here? Take me back, now!" she demands. "Change me back," she begs.

"There is no going back. It's binding, remember?"

She thinks of the agreement. "What did you give her?

"Sera—"

"You said you would answer my questions."

"Ten thousand gold."

If not for the fact he was holding her up, she would've collapsed to the floor in shock. "What?"

"It was worth it."

"You bought me from her?" she asks, her anger rising.

"Sera, you know I had to make an agreement. Why does this anger you so?"

"You told me you wouldn't buy me! I thought you bartered with something else…"

"Please, look at it like this, I didn't buy you, but I bought your freedom."

"And turned me into this! I went from a slave of the estate to a slave of the ocean. How is this freedom?"

"You are free of Rae'lin, free of your duties to her and her household, no longer having to work from sunrise to sunset."

"I don't want this. Please, take me back."

"You promised to marry me."

Sera scoffs. "That certainly isn't happening now!"

"Yes, it is. Tonight."

"You can't make me go through with that."

"I'm not, you are."

Her eyes narrow in confusion. "What are you talking about?"

He raises her hand, showing her the ring. "You swore on this that you will marry me, and the ring will bind you to your promise."

Her eyes go wide in horror. "Take it off!" she screams, clawing at her hand.

"Sera, stop," he commands.

She looks at him with fear in her eyes. "Wait, you… you said we're getting married tonight? Does that mean—" Her head goes down as she panics at the thought.

"We won't do anything as husband and wife until you are ready. I swear it to you."

"I need to sit down."

He swims her over to the bed and sits beside her. "I know it's a lot to take in, but give this a chance? That's all I am asking of you."

"How could you do this to me? I thought you loved me."

"I do, and that's why I had to. We couldn't very well be together with you on land and me in the ocean, could we?"

"Why not stay a human?"

"I'm needed here."

"I'm needed at the estate!" she screams. "Please, take me back!"

"They will be fine without you." Regret floods him as she cries into her hands. "Sera, I didn't mean it like that. I was trying to reassure you, that with the compensation they can hire additional help."

"I can't live like this! Please, please, change me back," she sobs.

He pulls her to him, holding her as she cries. "I'm sorry, Sera, but I need you here. I need you with me."

"I won't marry you!" She pushes him away. "I don't care what you say about this ring. I will fight it with every piece of me I can, fighting until I am utterly spent."

"I'll make you a deal."

"No more deals. It's how I got stuck here in the first place." She hangs her head.

"I'll heal your brother."

Frozen in place, she thinks on his words before meeting his gaze. "Say that again."

"I will heal your brother."

"If you have the power to, why haven't you already?"

"I wanted to. Please, don't think me heartless. I am not supposed to interfere with land-dwellers." She scoffs at him. "I made an exception for you, as you will understand soon enough. Marry me tonight of your own free will, without protest, and be my equal, become my partner. Continue being with me as you have, loving and kind. If you do, we will go to the estate tomorrow. You can say goodbye to your family, and I will heal your brother.

"What… what all do I have to do? Willing bride?" she asks, her panic rising again as she thinks of Fury'am'a on top of her.

"Sera, I don't mean what you're thinking. Please, push that aside. I only mean, say I do and honor our vows."

"How can I trust that?"

He raises her hand, running his finger over her ring. "I swear here and now upon this ring, I will heal your brother tomorrow, if you do as I ask." For a moment, the ring shimmers blue.

She wants to pull her hand away, to scream and fight back. I asked for a chance to save Na'ito. I swore I would do anything I could. I'll pay the price.

"Yes, I will marry you tonight," she resigns herself, lowering her head. "I will do whatever is necessary for my family."

He gently raises her head to meet his gaze. "Sera, I love you so much."

"No, you don't. If you did, you wouldn't hurt me this way."

"You know how much I love you."

"I fell in love with Dankin, the human who was kind, loyal, and protective of me. Not the monster who is forcing me to bend to his will!" Anger flashes across his face, causing her to recoil in fear. "I'm sorry, but this is too much. I can't—" She cries into her hands.

He holds her tightly. "You can, and you will. You'll see. Please, trust me?"

"I don't really have a choice, do I?" she whispers.

"We need to eat. We'll go to the great hall—"

"No, please. I don't mean that I won't eat, but I'm not ready to… to go out like this. Please, don't make me."

"It's all right. I'll have lunch brought in."

"Lunch?"

"Apparently, the transformation took its toll on you. It's almost noon." Dankin swims out of the room. In his absence, Sera's mind begins to replay the events of the last few days. He returns a few minutes later, wearing a black dress shirt with a gold leaf crown upon his head.

"How did the nobles know who you were last night? What is your role here?" she asks.

"You honestly don't know?" He's surprised when she shakes her head. He sits beside her and gently takes her hand. "I am King Dankin. Tonight, you will become my queen."

"I—I thought you were a peasant? I don't understand. Do they know… what you are?"

"They have heard of King Dankin, but they know only that my kingdom is a great distance away. I have had to travel on land before, out of necessity."

"Who was running the kingdom while you were gone?"

"My younger brother, Da'vae. He is the Crown Prince. He will be excited to meet you. He never thought I would remarry. Honestly, neither of us ever thought I would."

"You've been married before?"

"I had a wife and three daughters, but I lost them in the war with the sirens."

"I'm sorry."

He looks down, his voice just above a whisper. "It was my daughter, El'ena, who your father killed."

"He would never!"

"I guess he thought she was a siren. They look similar to us and are known for luring men off their ships with their song."

"They drown them?"

"No. They kiss them, transforming them into sirens. Maren, the siren queen, has waged war with men and my people for as long as I can remember. She has wiped many of us out, and we need to rebuild our numbers."

"Is that why you came looking for me?"

"To a degree. I will tell you about that tomorrow." He looks over when someone knocks. "For now, we will eat." A young mermaid enters, carrying two plates to them. Sera stares at her orange tail as she swims out of the room.

"After we eat, I'll show you how to swim."

She swallows hard, glancing down at her own scaly tail before quickly looking back up. "I can't even think about it right now."

"Then don't. Eat your food and spend time with me."

"Okay," she says, staring down at the sushi on her plate. She lets out a small laugh. "Of course, fish. Is this what you eat for every meal?" she asks as she eats with her hands. "Now I see why you used your hands so much when we ate!"

"Not for every meal, and I know how to use proper utensils." He smiles at her, grateful to hear her laughing. They finish eating, and he hands the plates off to a staff member waiting outside the door. He returns to her and offers his hand. "Come with me."

Closing her eyes, she turns away. "Please—"

"You need to learn how to swim, so you can get around the palace on your own. Let me teach you?"

"Will you take me to the mirror, first?" She takes his hand, and he leads her to the door where the mirror is. She forces herself to study her silver tail. Slowly, and with her eyes closed, she brings her hand to her hip, tracing it down the scales.

"Are you all right?"

"I will be. I still need a little time for this." She opens her eyes, watching her tail in the mirror. When she tries to step forward, her tail jerks in response. Gripping him tighter, a small gasp escapes her lips.

"Sera?"

"Please," she begs, "I need a moment. I wanted to see my tail move."

"Why?"

Embarrassed, she hangs her head. "It's—never mind," she says as her face goes flush.

"Are you okay?"

"Yes. I'm ready to learn."

He wraps his arm around her waist. "Let's go out into the open ocean, where we can have room and privacy for me to teach you."

They leave the room, with Dankin guiding her through the palace. She admires the white marble everywhere, with high ceilings and… windows?

"Dankin? There are windows?"

He laughs. "Wouldn't want to wake up to a shark sleeping beside you, would you?"

She gasps. "No!" She continues taking everything in. "It's beautiful down here."

Dankin smiles, praying she stays happy. They leave the palace and head towards the ocean floor. She laughs as a school of fish swims by.

He sits her on a rock. "Does this hurt?"

"No, it's fine."

"Okay. For starters, I know you'll want to use your arms, like this." He swims like they did as humans, his arms going up and around. "That will only slow you down. Watch." He raises his arms, pulling himself up then folding them down to his sides as his tail propels him around. "You can also do this, if it's more comfortable." He clasps his hands together, holding them in front as he swims back to her. "Do you want to try?"

"I can't really… feel my tail."

"Try to move it."

Closing her eyes, she moves her tail as though she were bending her knees. Her eyes fly open as her tail folds slowly in. "Oh, okay."

"That's good."

"Can I swim with you first?"

"Of course." He holds her hand, pulling her from the rock and swimming slowly along the bottom. As she focuses on moving her tail, she suddenly cries out in pain.

"What's wrong?"

"It hurts!"

She grimaces as he lowers them down to sit on the ocean floor. "Let's take a break. You might be working it too hard. I'm going to be honest, you are the first human I've ever turned into a mermaid. Let me see if I can help." He speaks softly in a language she doesn't understand. A streak of blue light emerges from his hand and pours into her, causing her back to arch as the pain eases. "Did that help?"

"Yes. What did you do?"

"I healed you. Please, tell me anything you feel or need. I don't want you to suffer."

Grateful to hear such concern in his voice, she smiles at him. "You really care for me, don't you?"

"Sera, I love you. I truly mean that." He leans forward and kisses her, but she doesn't respond to his touch. Disappointment floods his face. "What's wrong?"

"I'm sorry, I'm still angry." She looks down. "Please, help my brother. Don't punish him because of me!"

"It's okay. Sera, I promised I would heal him, and I meant that, too. I know this is a lot to take in. Do you want to try again?"

"Yes, please."

He pulls her up, swimming with her. Letting go of his hand, she swims on her own. Her hands lead as her tail propels her. "Good job!" he beams as she swims back to him.

"It feels so… weird!"

"I can imagine."

"How?"

"The first time I used my legs."

"Oh, I didn't think of that." They swim side by side. "That probably was weird."

"Let's return to the palace. We'll get ready for supper then the wedding. There is a reception after. Will you be up for that?"

Thinking of her brother, she nods. "I will."

As they're swimming to the palace, he checks on her from time to time as she swims on her own. He takes her to her room and swims with her to the closet. "These are the gowns you can wear," he says as he opens the door.

She laughs. "They're so short, they look like hanfu shirts."

"If you are wearing one when I turn you human, it will grow into a dress. Opposite of what happened last night."

"I see. Wait, is that why you told me to wear my favorite color?"

"Yes. Your tail is absolutely beautiful."

She blushes. "Um, thank you." She picks out a pink and lavender hanfu, glancing at him. "Could I have some privacy, please?"

"Of course. I'll change and come back."

"Thank you." As soon as he's gone, she removes her gown and studies herself in the mirror, tracing her fingers over her waistline where here tail meets her stomach. She sees the scales covering her chest and stomach, then lowers her hand. Her fingers trail along the cool scales, watching as they react to her touch. She gently grips her tail, feeling the slight pressure. Running her fingers over her pelvic fin causes her to let out a gasp. "Oh."

Dankin swims in on her, and she pulls the gown up and slips it on. "I was… I—" She hangs her head, embarrassed.

"I'm sorry," he says quickly, "I didn't know you weren't dressed yet." He swims to her, taking her hand and guiding it along his tail. "Feels the same, right?"

"Yes," she says, meeting his gaze. "I'm still trying to get used to it. I'm not ready to touch my… my ribs."

"Your gills?"

She nods. "It's too weird,"

"It's really not, Sera."

"If I leave the water, will I suffocate like a fish?"

"Why would you ask a question like that?" Dankin asks, concerned.

"I'm just trying to learn about... about what I am now."

"Of course. I'm sorry. Ask anything you want."

"Can we go to supper? I'm ready to eat."

"Tell me you're okay."

She pulls away from him and clasps her hands. "I don't know."

"Come here," he says, pulling her into his arms. He takes her to the bed, holding her on his lap. "I know it's a lot. I thought about telling you or trying to talk to you about it, but I figured it would be easier if you could see it for yourself."

"You knew I would say no."

"Okay, I thought that was a possibility, yes." He gently turns her head, studying her face. He gives her a small smile as his fingers run through her hair. "Are you okay?"

"I am now. I—" she glances down a moment before looking at him. "Can I?" she asks, bringing her hand to his chest. Unsure what she is asking, he takes the chance and nods. She grips the bottom of his shirt and lifts it up, her fingers trailing gingerly over his gills. "Does that hurt?"

"No, but it's a weird sensation."

She pulls her hand back as she lowers his shirt. "Thank you."

"Now, can we eat?"

"I don't know. Can you?" she teases.

He laughs, pulling her up with him. Holding her hand, he leads her over to the closet. "You can't wear a crown until your coronation, but you can wear one of these," he says, getting out a silver circlet with pearls and diamonds. "May I?" Once she nods, he slips it on her. "Beautiful."

"Thank you," she says, leaning up and kissing his cheek. He stares at her lips, but she immediately looks down. "Please, I'm not ready. I will be for the ceremony, I promise."

"It's okay. Let's eat. I'm sure swimming made you hungry."

They swim to the great hall. Once inside, her breath catches in her throat at the sight of so many merpeople. He leads her to the front table as everyone watches in a revered silence. As they sit down, everyone goes back about their business. Two beautiful, young mermaids approach.

"Majesty," they say, bowing to Dankin.

"Sera, once you are crowned, they will be your handmaids."

"I see," she says, looking them over.

"I am Fai'mi," says the blonde mermaid with a teal-colored tail. "It's an honor to meet you."

"And I am Ava'lei," says the mermaid with strawberry blonde hair, her tail blue with black scales forming a stripe down the side.

"I am pleased to meet you both. May I ask, what are your duties?"

"We are here to serve you," Fai'mi says.

She looks at Dankin. "Really?"

"This is not like the estate, I assure you."

She sighs. "We'll see." She turns back to the mermaids. "Thank you." Dankin nods to the two mermaids, dismissing them. They give a small bow and swim off. Shaking her head, Sera looks at Dankin. "Servants? Really?" she asks again.

"They help you get ready and will aid you in your duty as queen, but they are not slaves nor servants. It is an honorable position, to aid the queen."

"If I don't want them?" she asks.

"Sera, be reasonable—"

"Fine," she says as a merman places a plate in front of her. It has crab and fish with sea lettuce, plus a few other pieces she doesn't quite recognize. She eats quietly, observing the others around her. After a long silence, she looks at Dankin. "How long until… until the wedding?"

"Two hours. Would you like to see more of the palace?"

"I need to rest," she says as she finishes her meal.

"That's understandable." They return to the room she woke up in. "These are your quarters for now. Once we are wed, we will—"

"No.

He sighs. "Sera, please, do not argue with me about this. You promised, remember?"

Closing her eyes, she rolls her head back and lets out a sigh. "Fine." Once in the room, she shuts and locks the door. She swims to the bed and sinks down onto it. Burying her face into her pillow, she screams and cries until she falls asleep.

Chapter 9

The Grotto

Sera wakes up, staring at the ceiling as she realizes she is still, in fact, underwater. She groans in frustration.

"Feel better?"

She jumps at his voice, pulling herself to sit up. "What are you doing in here?" she demands.

"I was worried, with the sounds coming from here."

She lies back down. "What do you care?"

He sits on the edge of the bed and takes her hand. "Are you okay?"

"No," she quietly admits. "I'm not ready to… to share a room with you."

"Just because we share a room, it doesn't mean anything. It's to keep up appearances, as you are adapting."

"Really?"

"Yes."

"I'll try. That's all I can say right now." She sits up, trailing her fingers over his arm. "Will you kiss me?"

He smiles before gripping the back of her head, his mouth suddenly on hers. She wraps her arms around him and holds him tight. "Sera?" he asks, concerned when she pulls back and cries into her hands.

"I'm sorry. I really am trying. Please, don't punish my brother for this. Please…" she pleads.

"Sera, take a breath." She shoots him an angry look with her hand trailing along her side. "You know what I mean. Everything is okay." He holds her as he strokes her hair. "Why are you so upset? You can be honest. I will heal your brother as promised."

"It's too much! I wasn't meant for this. Please, I can't do this."

"Yes, you can, Sera. You can marry me tonight, and everything will be okay. What do you need? Are you in pain?"

"Everything feels off, I feel… wrong. I don't know what it is."

"Come with me," he says, swimming up. She clings to him. He wraps his arm around her, leading her from the palace. They swim to a grotto on a small island. A sand bar separates a small pool from the ocean, with a waterfall cascading off to the side. Trees and brush line the border that leads to a small beach. "This is private, so we can be ourselves here."

"Please, turn me back? If only for a few minutes?"

"I will tomorrow when we go and see your family."

"Dankin, please, I can't do this!"

"Here, this will help." They swim up to the sand bar, where he lifts her over and places her in the pool. "Relax."

"It's so warm!" she says, soaking.

"There's a natural vent underneath. Is this helping?"

"Oh, it really is! Thank you." Out of habit, she takes a breath. "Wait, I can still breathe? I mean, I was sort of underwater, but I guess because it's what I'm used to?"

"As merpeople, we have gills to move water through our bodies, giving us oxygen under the water. Once above water or out of water, our lungs will take over. It's a little harder on the body, but you'll get used to it."

He climbs over and takes her into his arms. For a while they don't speak. They rest together in the warmth of the pool, until finally she looks at him. "What was it like for you, the first time you became human?"

"It was painful and a little scary, watching my tail split and turn into legs. I felt like I was walking on pins and needles at first. After that, my transformations were faster and easier."

"Will it hurt when I turn back human?"

"It shouldn't, but I really can't say for sure. I'm sorry."

"It's worth it, so I can see my family one last time."

"Is that part of what's bothering you? That it will be the last time?" he asks as he strokes along her cheek and neck.

"It is. So many changes at once, with no warning or preparation. Transforming into," she gestures down at her tail, "this, leaving my home and my family, becoming a queen. I really am trying, but it's all so overwhelming."

"I know, and I'm sorry for that. I will do what I can to help you. We need to return to the palace. Are you all right?"

"I will be," she says, following him back over the sandbar.

"This water feels colder now, doesn't it?"

She laughs. "It really does. How often can we come here?"

"As often as you want, I promise." He smiles and takes her hand as they swim towards the palace. Once they arrive at the palace, he leaves her at her quarters. "Fai'mi and Ava'lei will be here shortly to escort you to the chapel."

"I'll be ready, I promise."

He kisses her hand. "I love you, Sera."

"I love you, too." She closes the door, then buries her face in her hands. *How will I get through this? I haven't even accepted what he's done to me, and now I have to marry him? I tried today, tried to love him. I know it's there... but I feel so alone. I hate what he's done to me.* Clenching her hands, she pummels her tail and cries out in frustration.

I have to stop this. I have to get ready. Regardless of my feelings about all of this, I have to marry him, and I have to do it of my own free will. If this will save my brother's life, it will be worth it.

In the closet, she finds a white hanfu with silver embroidery and layers. She slips it on, admiring it as she looks herself over. After looking through the drawers, she removes the circlet then pins the white and silver flowers she finds into her hair. Still adjusting to her tail, she swims to the door, opening it to find the two mermaids waiting for her.

"Ready to go to the chapel?"

"Yes, Ava'lei. Thank you." She follows behind them, unsure of what is ahead. "What will the ceremony be like?"

"Oh, it's very pretty," Fai'mi says.

"And short," Ava'lei adds, laughing.

They arrive at the chapel. Her handmaids open the doors and gesture her inside.

"Not how I envisioned walking down the aisle," Sera murmurs to herself. Clearing her head, she makes herself ready to get through the ceremony so she can see her family again. Dankin smiles as she swims up to him, then he takes her hands. The priestess is dressed in silver robes with a pearl circlet covering a sheer silver veil. She has pink hair and a red tail. Sera tries not to stare.

"The love in our hearts can no more be measured than the grains of sand in our ocean. As such, when two hearts come together, the love between them is immeasurable. We are gathered here today to celebrate such a love, between Dankin and—" she looks at Sera, embarrassed to have forgotten her name.

"Sereia," she answers quietly. Dankin gives Sera a look but says nothing.

"Dankin and Sereia, you are joining together in matrimony, to be husband and wife. Do you have the rings?"

Sera looks at him as he pulls out two rings. "Yes, I have them."

"Dankin, place the ring on the tip of her finger." He does as instructed. "Repeat after me; I, Dankin, take you Sereia, to be my wife. I will love, honor, cherish and support you, always." He repeats the vows, sliding the ring on. Sera watches as it merges with the pearl band. Dankin hands her his ring. She holds it over his finger, repeating the vows. "Now, under the protection of Calyp'seidon, I hereby proclaim you are married. You may kiss your bride."

Sera leans up, closing her eyes as his lips meet hers, kissing her with all the love he has in his heart. As she kisses him, she gives in to her feelings and holds him tight. She pulls back. He's relieved at the smile on her face.

"Now, for Sereia's coronation." The priestess picks up the crown, adorned with diamonds and pearls, that had been resting on the pedestal behind her. She holds it above Sera's head. "With this crown, I bestow upon you the title and rank of Queen, Majesty over the Realm. Do you accept this title and the responsibilities thereof?"

"I do," Sera answers.

She lowers the crown. "I present to you, His Majesty, King Dankin and his wife, Her Grace, Queen Sereia." The merpeople break into applause as they rise, then bow to their new queen.

Dankin leads Sera from the chapel and into a small room. "We will rest here a moment while everyone else goes to the ballroom. It is customary for us to make a grand entrance."

"I see." She looks away, torn between her love for him and anger for what's he's turned her into.

"You are a beautiful bride."

"Thank you."

"Sera, will you look at me?" She does. "Why didn't you tell me your name is Sereia?" Dankin asks.

"I didn't think of it. My brother had a hard time pronouncing it and called me Sera, which just kind of stuck. It's what I've gone by for as long as I can remember. Everyone on the island called me that, once they heard him saying it."

"What does it mean?"

"Treasure of the sea. Why?"

"Nothing," he answers, smiling at her as he thinks of what it means in his own language, pondering if it is merely a coincidence. "It's a beautiful name."

"How long do we have to stay for the reception?"

"We'll leave when you want."

"I'm sorry, I didn't mean to sound sharp." She sighs, studying his face. "I think a good night's sleep will help me feel better."

"We won't stay long."

"No, it's a celebration. I understand. From what you've told me, your kingdom is long due for one."

"Yes, our kingdom is." He turns when the door opens.

"Majesty, Grace, they are ready for you," a merman with black hair and a grey tail says, opening the door fully and gesturing for them to follow.

"Thank you." Dankin offers his hand to Sera. "Shall we?"

"Yes," she answers, rising with him. Dankin takes her into the ballroom, where she admires the gold and silver accents on the black marble. White ribbons are draped from column to column, tied in bows. She looks out the window and watches the schools of fish swim by. "It's beautiful."

They sit at the main table at the front of the room, elevated on a platform above the other tables. "What's wrong?" he asks when she looks around.

She laughs. "No cake?"

"I'm sorry. We can get some tomorrow at the market."

"Really?"

"Yes. I'm not just taking you there to say goodbye. We will spend some time on land together."

"That will be nice. I'm worried, though."

"That you will fight tooth and nail not to come back here?"

"Yes," she admits in a soft tone. "I don't want it to come to that, but after becoming human again, I don't know how I'll feel."

"I admit, I hadn't thought of that. I am only offering, so please do not get upset. Do you want to stay here while I go and heal your brother?"

"No, it's worth everything to see him healed and say goodbye."

"Very well."

"I will come back with you, I promise."

"I trust you," he says, squeezing her hand. The celebration begins, and they meet various members of court. Knowing she will never remember all of the titles and names, Sera admires their fancy attire as Dankin speaks with them. Once they have finished eating, she lets him guide her on the dance floor, not sure how to move her tail like his. "Sera, you are doing fine," he whispers in her ear.

"That obvious I was worried?"

"Yes," he answers with a chuckle. "It's okay." He gasps when her tail wraps around his. "Sera, what are you doing?"

She pulls back. "I'm sorry. What's wrong?"

He gently grips her arms and brings her back to him. "That…" he sighs. He leans forward, his mouth an inch from her ear. "Wrapping tails indicates that you are ready."

She buries her face on his shoulder as her body is flush with humiliation. "I… I didn't know."

"It's all right. Please, look at me?" Once his eyes meet hers, he sees her weariness. "Are you ready to turn in?"

"I am."

They leave the ballroom, bidding goodnight to those they pass on their way and receiving congratulations. He takes her to her room. "Let's get you a few things for now, then we'll have everything else moved in."

"Where is your brother? Why haven't I met him yet?" she asks as they swim into her quarters.

"From what I hear, he encountered some sirens. He is still pursuing them, so he is unaware I have returned. He should be back in the next day or so."

"Okay."

She gets out some clothing and nightgowns. They swim next door, to the royal chambers. He opens the ornate door, gesturing her in first. The grandness of the room catches her by surprise. The walls are black and gold, contrasting the white marble floor. A black and white bed are up against the wall to the left, with a matching dresser and chest to the side. She swims over to examine the dresser. "It's beautiful." Opening the drawer, she finds it empty. She looks at him, confused.

"I haven't used this room since… not in a long time."

"I'm sorry for your loss."

"I'll have the staff bring over some of the clothing from the other room, so you will have everything you need." He leads her over to the closet and opens the doors.

"This is huge!" she gushes, swimming inside. The right side has a few of Dankin's shirts with a few dresses to the left. They hang up the clothing she had brought over. She turns to him, bringing her hand up to cup his face. "You mean it, though? That we will only sleep tonight?"

"I will not touch you like that without your consent. I mean it. Do you trust me?"

"I feel like I shouldn't," she admits, looking at her tail then giving him a small smile, "but I will." He gives her privacy in the closet to change for bed. A few moments later, she swims out, wearing a white cotton nightgown. "What's wrong?" she asks when she sees sadness in his eyes. Her mouth opens in surprise at the realization. "This was your wife's nightgown, wasn't it?"

"It's okay. I gave you her clothes because I want you to have them."

"Still, I wouldn't have worn it tonight."

"Sera, really, it's not a big deal."

Hearing the pain in his voice, she decides not to argue. "Are we turning in now?"

"We are."

She swims to the bed and lies down. As she looks over the room, she is still amazed at the sheer size of it. "This is the biggest room I've ever slept in."

"Do you like it?"

"Yes, it's beautiful." She faces him. "I know I'm still adapting and trying not to be overwhelmed. Thank you for your patience with me."

"It's the least I can do for the woman saving our kingdom."

"What?" she asks, sitting up. "What does that mean?"

"I only meant, since you are our queen."

"What aren't you telling me?"

"We still have a lot to discuss. Let's get some rest, see your family tomorrow, then I will tell you everything."

"All right," she says, turning away from him.

"Sera, can I hold you?"

She closes her eyes. "Of course," she answers, clenching her hands in anger. *I know I swore I would do anything for my brother, and I know I love Dankin, but this is too much. I'm not ready for so much change at once.*

* * *

Sera wakes up, realizing she's alone in bed. She sits up and looks around the room. Dankin is in the doorway, speaking to a guard. Sera waits until he comes back to her, staying under the covers.

"Is everything all right?" she asks.

"Yes. Are we getting ready for breakfast?"

"Could we eat on the island? Not because I want to rush, but since it's my last day there, and I want to enjoy all of it."

"Yes, that's fine. Get dressed, and we'll go."

Feeling self-conscious, she pulls the blanket higher. "I…" She looks away.

"I'll wait for you in the hall."

As soon as he's gone, she swims to the closet and pulls out a pale blue gown with pink and white layers. She changes then pins a silver and sapphire crown into her hair. Dankin swims inside, admiring her.

"Ready?" she asks, trying to hide her excitement.

He chuckles, seeing right through. "Yes, let's go."

Noticing the sword on his hip, she says nothing as he leads her out. They leave the palace and swim for the island. As they get close to shore, they surface. Making sure it's just the two of them, he takes her into his arms.

"I trust you."

"What?"

"Turning me human."

"Right, well, here goes." He leans forward and kisses her as his magic flows between them. He walks to the shore, smiling at her legs as her gown reaches her ankles.

"Well?"

"It didn't hurt."

"I'm glad." They sit on a bench to let the sun dry them off. She admires his dark blue pants with black dress shirt and a gold crown. Once dry, they go into the market to buy tea and pastries. People stare at them, shocked to see Sera and Dankin with royal crowns upon their heads.

Kye's voice rings in her ears as he runs up to her. "Miss Sera, what happened to you? Where have you been?"

Sera hesitates as she thinks on her answer. "Kye, I am married now. This is my husband, King Dankin."

"What?" he asks admiring the crowns they are both wearing. "Your Majesties," he offers with a bow.

"Good morning, Kye," Dankin responds. "I was hoping we would see you." He hands him a coin purse. "Consider this a bonus for all your help."

Kye takes the purse, smiling at the weight of it. "Thank you! I will take this home right now." He bows again before running off.

"A bonus?" Sera asks.

"A thousand gold to help his family."

"You are generous. Thank you."

They eat their pastries as they walk about the market. Sera looks at Dankin with pain in her eyes.

"Ready to see your family?" he asks.

"Yes and no."

"Sera, I'm sorry—"

"It's okay. This is how it has to be, I know. Doesn't make saying goodbye any easier. I am grateful that you are doing this for me, for them."

They walk to the estate, listening to the waves crash on the shore and enjoying the warmth of the sunshine. Chi'yo runs out to meet them and wraps Sera in a hug.

"Apologies," she says, pulling back. "I've been so worried!" Her eyes go wide at the sight of their crowns. "Miss Sera?"

"Chi'yo, this is my husband, King Dankin."

Losing her color, she fans herself. "Really?"

"Yes, really."

Chi'yo bows to them. "How can I help, Your Majesty?"

"No, Chi'yo. Please, nothing has changed. We are going to see my family before returning to our kingdom."

"Of course. Please, come in." They follow her inside. She bows again before returning to the kitchen.

Sera takes Dankin's hand as they walk down the hall. At the door of the main quarters, she knocks softly. Rae'lin opens the door then gestures them in.

"I wondered how everything went. Did you—" she stops, staring at Sera's crown. Sera smiles as Rae'lin looks at Dankin in shock. "Who are you really?" she demands.

"I am King Dankin, and this is my wife, Her Grace, Queen Sera."

Rae'lin looks at them, studying them both. "I see. What happened the night of the ball?"

"He proposed to me at the lantern festival."

"I knew he was going to do that. What happened after?"

"He took me straight to his kingdom so we could marry. I apologize if I had you worried—"

"I was only worried about when I would see my end of the arrangement," she interrupts. "It was delivered last night, so that's what matters."

Sera looks at Dankin. "I'm going to see my father if you wish to visit with Na'ito."

"Of course."

She walks to her father's bedside and takes his hand. "Is my daughter really a queen?" he asks, giving her hand a gentle squeeze.

She smiles at him. "I am."

"Oh, wonderful news! I am sure you will do great things, for land and for sea. It's everything you deserve and more. You know that, right?"

"What do you mean?"

"It's why I named you Sereia, my treasure from the sea. You were the most beautiful baby I had ever seen. I knew at once you deserved a special name."

"Thank you, Father. How are you feeling?"

"Weak, tired, but a little better now that I know you are where you are meant to be."

"I'm sorry. Can I do anything?"

"All I want is for you to go live your life. Will you do that for me?" Tsuji asks.

"Yes, Father." She watches him fall back to sleep then kisses his brow. "I love you."

When Rae'lin leaves to use the washtoire, Sera walks over to Dankin and Na'ito. She listens as Dankin speaks quietly. She focuses on his words as the blue light flows from him and into Na'ito. She's amazed at how quickly his color comes back. Dankin gives her a small nod as he slumps into the chair by the bed. Rae'lin steps back into the room. Sera calls her over as Na'ito's color is back and the trembling stops.

At the urgency in Sera's voice, she rushes to Na'ito's side. "What's wrong?"

"He… he looks better! Was the doctor here today?"

"No. He hasn't been here in two days." Rae'lin leans over, studying his face and placing her palm on his forehead. "He's not cold anymore!" She watches in shock as he opens his eyes and sits up. "Na'ito? How do you feel?'

"I'm tired, but I feel much better."

"I'll send for the doctor. We have to be sure you're okay now," Rae'lin says.

Sera chokes back her tears, taking Dankin's hand and holding it tightly. "Thank you," she mouths to him.

He smiles at her before turning his attention to Rae'lin. "What will you do now, with the boy well?"

"I don't know. I still can't believe this is possible." She takes a breath. "I will help him catch up in his studies so he may go to school. I still have to care for Tsuji, but now I have a future with my son to look forward to. Oh, thank the goddess!"

Sera sits on the edge of the bed. "Na'ito, it's time for me to leave."

"What do you mean?"

"I'm married, and I am a queen. We have a kingdom to run, so I don't know when or if I'll ever return."

"You can't leave! I'm better now, and we have so much to catch up on," he cries as his strength is returning.

"I know. I'm sorry, but I have to. Just know, I will think about you every single day."

He looks at Rae'lin. "Mother, do something."

She sighs. "Na'ito, we all have our duties. Hers is to her husband and their kingdom. Please, do not create a scene."

"Yes, mother." He looks at Sera. "My sister, the queen. Who could've seen this coming?"

She leans down, kissing his forehead. "I know you will grow up to be a wonderful, compassionate young man. I'm sorry I won't be here to see it."

He hangs his head and wipes his tears away. "It's okay. I know we'll see each other again."

She gets to her feet and helps Dankin up. "We are returning to our kingdom now. Goodbye, everyone," she says, quickly turning away to hide her tears. She clears her throat, wiping her eyes.

Rae'lin walks them out, looking at Dankin with curiosity as he relies on Sera to help him walk. "Did you do that?"

"I have no idea what you mean," he answers as they approach the door. "I can only pray you treat him better than you ever did her."

"I love my son," she exclaims.

"Yes, we know," Dankin scoffs, looking at Sera with pity.

They walk out the door, and Sera knows it may be the last time she sets foot there. As they leave the manor, they pass Hi'tob'a in the orchard, and she says a tearful goodbye to him as well. Dankin pushes down the guilt as he watches her taking everything in for the last time. He wraps his arm around her as they walk the path to the shore. Once at the beach, Sera pulls away, pacing as she struggles with her emotions.

"Sera?"

She looks at him. "I am coming with you, I promise. I just need a moment for... for everything."

He walks to her and wraps her in his arms. "I know it's a lot to take in. I'm sorry."

"Thank you for that." She pulls away and sits on the sand, running her fingers through it and taking in the sun. He sits next to her.

"There's no rush, I mean that."

Running her fingers over his arm, she takes his hand. "Thank you for your patience with me and for saving my brother."

"I made you a promise and kept it."

"I see." She sighs as she thinks about asking him to heal her father, but her fear is too great. If he refuses, she is unsure she could forgive him. She considers taking the chance, when she looks at him and realizes how weary he is. Guilt floods through her when she realizes the toll using his magic takes on him. She decides she will ask later, when he has had a chance to recover. "I guess there's no point in putting it off any longer. I'm afraid the longer I sit here, the less likely I will come willingly."

He stands up, pulling her with him. He kisses her softly. "Are you ready to begin your duties as queen?"

"I am," she answers, resolve on her face and in her heart. They walk into the water. He scoops her up, carrying her the rest of the way in. As soon as they are submerged, they are in their merperson form. Looking down at her tail, she's relieved to not be as disgusted or horrified by it. They're swimming for the palace when a group of sirens approach.

"I am your king. You will let us pass, unharmed!" Dankin commands, pushing Sera behind him as he unsheathes his sword. She grips his shirt, watching the sirens as fear floods her.

The siren closest to him laughs. "We aren't afraid of you. You may have won this round, but Maren's power now rivals yours. Soon enough, your kingdom will be no more!"

Sera looks over his shoulder, studying the koi markings and coloring of the sirens' tails. They are wearing matching black, short kom'onos with a silver obi tied around. Their bright red hair and white skin fascinate her, but she is most surprised by their pointed ears, similar to her own. Examining the siren's upraised hand, Sera sees the webbed fingers with claws extending out, grateful hers aren't like theirs. She cries out when she's grabbed from behind.

Dankin rushes over as the siren yanks Sera's gown off, placing her claws at her chest. "One move, and I will rip her heart out," she growls.

"What do you want?" he demands.

"To continue as we have been, destroying your people! You deserve to die for what you've done to us."

"I don't know what Maren has told you—"

"She told us the truth. We know it was your father who desecrated our previous queen. He tried to destroy our kingdom!"

"Lies!" Dankin cries out. "She is filling your head with nonsense. I don't want war. I want us to live together in peace. She attacked us first."

The siren scoffs. "We know that's not true." Her claws dig into Sera's chest. "Now, you get to watch your precious queen die!"

Sera cries out as blood floats upward from the wounds when the siren digs in deeper. Dankin rushes to them, grabbing Sera away as his sword runs through the siren. He pulls Sera to him, holding her with one arm as he defends them with the other. "I will do the same to any of you that come after us!"

"Sister!" a siren calls out, watching in sorrow as the wounded siren dissolves into sea foam. "You will pay for that," she cries out as they swim off.

Dankin sinks to the ocean floor, laying his sword beside him. He places his hand on Sera's chest.

"What are you doing?" she asks.

"Sera, I'm healing you." She watches as the blue light flows into her, healing her wounds. "How do you feel?" he asks. He looks over, seeing her gown has floated down nearby. He picks it up and helps her get it back on.

"I'm okay. Once we return to the palace, will you tell me everything?"

"I will. Come on." He sheaths his sword, carrying her in his arms to the palace.

She pulls away as they approach. "I'm okay to swim. I don't want your people thinking I'm weak."

"They wouldn't, not if they found out you survived a siren attack." Once inside, they go to their quarters. Sera removes her dress and crown, sets them on the nightstand, and gets into bed, pulling the blanket over herself.

"Are you sure you're okay?" he asks, sitting on the edge of the bed.

"I need to rest, then we can talk."

"I'll be back shortly."

"Dankin, you look as though you could pass out. You need to rest, too," she says with concern in her voice.

"I will. I need to check on a few things."

"I know, a kingdom to run. I'm sorry."

"No, Sera. It's okay." He kisses her forehead. "I won't be long."

She sighs when he swims out, leaving the door open behind him. She slips over to shut it, when she hears two guards talking as they patrol the hallway.

"So, he found someone to break the curse?"

"Yes, apparently she was a land-dweller, and her name is Sereia."

"Wait, a land-dweller named Sereia was turned into a mermaid? You're pulling my tail," the guard says with a laugh.

"No, I mean it."

"How ironic," he says with a chuckle. "His Majesty cut it awfully close."

"Still, he found a woman to marry him and break the curse. That's what is important."

"For now. We will have to continue being vigilant, as our numbers are so few."

Sera quietly shuts the door. Swimming to the window, she leans her head against it when, to her surprise, it pops open. Forcing it the rest of the way, she swims out then shuts it behind her.

*He never loved me? He was only using me! I'll return to the island, there must be someone who can help me. I can't believe he—*She cries out when she's scooped up into a net. "No!" she yells as she desperately tries to get free. The net rises up to the deck of a ship.

"Well, boys, check out our catch of the day!"

"Let me go!" she demands.

The man steps closer, dressed in black breeches and a pale blue shirt. He laughs at her. "Oh, no. Mermaid tail is a rare delicacy on the mainland. We were on our way to Isle Ky'oto to trade, when we saw you swimming along. We are merchants who trade in treasures from the ocean, whether it be fish or mermaids, pearls, rare gems." He grabs the net, pulling her across the deck. The net opens, spilling her out. She lands hard on the wood deck with a thud, her arms sprawled out.

She looks at him in fear. "Please, don't hurt me!" she begs.

"Oh, we won't. We'll sell you. Then whatever happens to you, happens."

Looking around as she tries to come up with a plan for escape, she begins gasping, hoping he will take pity and throw her overboard. "I… air… I need… air! I need… water… please!" She clutches her hand to her throat, feigning suffocating.

He laughs as he scoops her up and carries her inside the cabin. She sees a large tank of water with dead fish along the bottom. He tosses her inside. "There you go."

Gasping as the cold water encloses around her, she beats her palm against the glass as he covers the tank. She begs him to release her.

As soon as he steps out, she pushes on the lid. Trying with all her might, she manages to get the lid to budge slightly. She smiles as she continues pushing it aside, open enough for her to lift her head out. Suddenly, men are yelling as metal clangs, followed by loud thuds. She lowers her head back down as she sinks into the tank when a man walks in. She's surprised when the lid is pushed off the tank, landing with a crash on the floor. He reaches for her, pulling her up and out of the tank.

"Please, stop!" she begs.

"Sera, it's me. You're safe now."

She looks at Dankin in surprise then holds him tightly, shivering and clinging to him. "I'm so sorry!"

"What happened? Were you taken from the palace?"

She hangs her head. "No, I left of my own accord. I was heading for the island when they caught me."

"What? Why did you leave?"

Her teeth chatter. "Please, I'm so cold. Help me get warm?"

"Sera, close your eyes and keep them closed until I tell you to open them." She squeezes her eyes shut, burying her face in his chest. He holds her to him as he steps onto the deck, ignoring the sight around him as he climbs over the rail and dives in, transforming as he falls into the water. "Now you can open them."

They look over when they hear shouting. He sees a merchant who had fallen off the ship. Dankin takes Sera under the water, the merchant following them. Dankin and Sera look in shock behind him. The merchant looks at them in confusion before turning around to see a siren approaching him with her arms open. Before he can swim away, she pulls him to her and kisses him. His clothes melt away as his skin turns white. His legs fuse together, growing scales with the koi markings as his short brown hair grows out and turns red. Dankin looks at Sera.

"We need to go while they are both distracted." He swims with her to the grotto and gets her into the warm water. "Is this better?"

"Yes, thank you."

"Why did you leave?"

She takes a breath. "Please, give me a moment. After all of that…"

"Let me know when you're ready to talk." He squeezes her to reassure her and strokes her hair as she gets warm, relieved when she finally stops shivering.

"I went to close the door, and I heard two guards talking about a curse… about you using me to free your kingdom."

"Sera—"

"No, you said so last night. You said I saved your people. It makes sense to me now. I know they were speaking the truth. You used me, didn't you?"

"No, Sera. I came looking for a bride to break the curse, that is true. Then I fell in love with you. You have to know that's the truth."

"Right now, I don't know what's true."

"I'll start from the beginning. Our goddess, Calyp'seidon, created merpeople after a ship wrecked in a terrible storm. She saved the people, turning them into merpeople. She only asked that they worship her in return. They built up this kingdom and lived in peace. Calyp'seidon's sister, Athe'nus, was jealous of her sister's followers. She kidnapped some, transforming them into sirens. Still, we lived in peace for many centuries. Then, three hundred years ago, war broke out. Maren and I are bound by the laws of the sea, however, her sirens attack and kill my people any chance they get. I have been trying to stop the war."

"How could your father have caused it, if it started three hundred years ago?"

"Because it's part of our blessing from Calyp'seidon, that we are immortal."

"What? So how old are you?"

"I am only eighty-seven. Young compared to many others."

"The sirens murdered your wife and daughters?"

"My wife and two of my daughters."

"Right, my father."

"He was not a fisherman, Sera. That was his cover and a means to make his wealth, but he was a siren hunter. I don't know if it was an accident, or if he thought she was a siren, but he killed my daughter."

Sera pulls away. "And you took me from him as revenge?"

"No, Sera. You know I didn't know who you were."

"So you claim."

He sighs. "I swear to you, I didn't know. Please, believe that."

Clasping her hands together, she looks down. "I don't know who you are or what you want with me. I don't know anything anymore."

"Everything I am telling you is the truth. I swear it to you."

"We wouldn't be together if you weren't trying to stop the curse, would we? Tell me I'm wrong."

"No, you're right."

She dives over the sandbar, returning to the sea. Dankin quickly follows. "Sera!" he calls out, chasing her and grabbing her hand. He lets go when she gives him a look, pain and fear reflecting in her eyes. "Please, talk to me."

"There's nothing you can say. You never loved me but only used me!"

"Like you used me to heal your brother?"

Her mouth opens in surprise. Seeing the hurt on her face, he immediately regrets it. "I didn't even know you could help him when you made the deal!" She stops swimming, sinking to the ocean floor. Dankin swims to her, staying back to give her space.

"Just leave me here," she says. "Let the sirens have me."

"Sera, please, you can't give up. You saved this kingdom, saved your brother… saved me." Her head snaps up, confusion in her eyes. "Sera, after losing my wife, I never thought I could, or would, love again." He swallows hard, emotion catching in his throat. "I didn't see how it could happen. Yes, I came to the island to find a woman to love me, to marry me because of the curse. I didn't plan on falling in love with you at first sight."

"I don't believe you."

"Sera—"

"Let me go. Prove your love to me by releasing me!"

"You know I can't do that. You are just looking for a way out."

She turns away. "Take me back to the palace then."

"Sera—"

"Now!" she commands, refusing to look at him. Taking off his shirt, he wraps it around her. Looking down, she hadn't even realized she had been so exposed. Her fear of the merchants had consumed her thoughts. She buttons up the shirt, reluctantly accepting his hand, then says nothing on the way to the palace. Once inside, she goes to the smaller quarters next door. "I need to be alone," she says, shutting and locking the door. She swims to the bed and lies down, remembering what it was like to wake up there for the first time. She was so confused when she couldn't move her legs, confused about what had happened to her.

He risked his life for mine, pushing me out of the way. He cared for me and defended me after the mistress hurt me. Did he do that out of love for me or to make me fall in love with him? I don't know what I believe.

Burying her face in her hands to muffle her screaming, she lets everything out. Dankin leans against the door, his heart aching as he listens to her frustration and pain.

"I love you, Sera. I really do. Please, believe me," he pleads. He reaches up to knock, then thinks better of it, swimming next door instead.

* * *

Sera wakes up, stretching as she starts to stand. Crying out in shock, she sinks to the floor. She remembers what had happened to her as she folds her tail under, running her fingers over her scales.

"How could he make me a monster? You don't do that to someone you love." She weeps, lying on the floor until the tears run out. Sighing, she sits up as she realizes she has no choice. *I have nowhere to go. I must accept my role, my new life. Otherwise, I am no better than the mistress, spending all day in my room as I wallow in self-pity*. When she swims next door, she goes inside without knocking. Dankin is surprised to see her.

"How do you feel?"

"Better," she answers, refusing to look at him. "What do you need from me?"

He swims to her. "What do you mean?"

"As queen, for the kingdom. What do you need?"

"For now, we need to eat. It's time for supper. Then Ava'lei and Fai'mi can assist you with your duties."

"How do I address you, once we are out of quarters? Do I address you as Your Majesty?"

"Well, I am partial to koy'lei."

Scoffing, she looks at him. "That ship has sailed."

"Sera, please, don't say that."

"I will be your queen, be your wife, but I will never be your lover."

"Sera, please, give this time. I will prove to you how much I love you. You will see, I have only ever been honest about my feelings for you."

"It's not possible, but what choice do I have?" She swims to the closet to change then pins a gold and sapphire crown in her hair. "Are we going to supper now?"

Realizing there is no emotion in her voice, her movements are cold and reserved, he rushes to her. He raises her head, forcing her to meet his gaze. "Sera, I love you."

"So you say," she responds as she swims away from him and towards the great hall. He catches up to her and holds her hand so they can swim in together.

As they eat, she looks at him. "What will you be doing as my handmaids are working with me?"

"My brother has returned, so I will go check on him and get an update."

"I see." She looks over when her handmaids approach.

"Your Grace," they say together with a bow.

"His Majesty has asked us to take you on a tour of the palace, to educate you on the everyday affairs of the kingdom and the history of our people."

"That is fine, Fai'mi. Thank you." Without a word to Dankin, she follows them from the great hall. She catches Ava'lei looking at her.

"If I may, you are... unique looking, Your Grace," she says, embarrassed to have been caught staring.

"Thank you. I think." They all laugh.

"Now, would you like us to start from the beginning or is there anything particular you wish to learn about?"

"I'm not really sure."

Fai'mi laughs. "Ava'lei, lets head for the vault. We can tell her your favorite story about the sea witch on the way there."

"The vault?" Sera inquires.

"It's where the kingdom houses its wealth and treasures. It's probably the most secure room in the palace. Follow us."

"And the sea witch?" Sera asks with piqued curiosity.

"She is said to be the most beautiful and most powerful siren. She is able to ensnare even the strongest of minds, trick the most cunning of all. None can refuse or resist her charms."

"Where does she live?"

Fai'mi laughs. "Oh, she's not real. She's a myth they tell us, to keep us here in the safety of the palace. Well, before the war at least. Now, we know better than to leave."

"I see. How did you become my handmaids?"

"We went through training and received the highest marks. We worked hard to achieve this position, and we are most honored to serve you."

They arrive at the vault, where two guards are at their post. Sera admires their polished armor, bright blue with gold seaweed trailing down the chest plate. At the sight of the queen, they open the door. Sera follows her handmaids inside, staring in amazement.

"This has been collected over the centuries," Ava'lei explains. "Gold, jewels, crowns, anything we can sell or trade with. Since we have basically been trapped because of the war, most of the treasure just sits here."

"Who do you trade with?"

"Other merpeople clans, some who live in kingdoms like ours. There are a few wild clans who live in the open sea."

"I can't imagine that," Sera says.

"Neither could I," adds Fai'mi. "To not have the protection and safety of the palace walls? We also trade with land-dwellers sometimes."

"Cos!" Ava'lei exclaims. "We do not even know if that is true."

She looks at Sera, suddenly timid. "Has… has his Majesty been on land?" she asks.

"Yes," Sera confirms.

"Wow," Fai'mi whispers, her mouth agape. "Apologies. We are both fascinated by land-dwellers."

Sera says nothing, not wishing to discuss the life she already misses greatly. "Where to next?" she asks, yawning.

"Your Grace, are you all right?" Ava'lei asks, trying to mask her concern.

"I believe I am ready to retire. I had a busy morning."

"We'll escort you to your quarters. Tomorrow morning after breakfast we can continue."

Sera nods, grateful for their kindness, and follows them out of the vault. Once Ava'lei and Fai'mi have gone, she takes a nightgown from the closet and goes to the quarters she stayed in her first night. She is lying in bed when Dankin swims in.

"Why are you in here?"

"I need some space tonight." She looks at him when he sits on the edge of the bed. "Really?"

"What's wrong? Why won't you sleep in our room?"

"Our room," she scoffs as she sits up. "Nothing here is mine, not even the clothing. I need to rest now."

He pauses, unsure how to proceed. "Sera, can I kiss your forehead?"

"You are the king and will do whatever you please," she comments as her fingers trail over the blanket covering her tail.

"Fine," he snaps, swimming from the room.

She sighs. *That was rude of me. He did at least ask, instead of just grabbing me and kissing me.* She pulls up from the bed and swims to the royal chambers. Dankin turns to her in surprise.

"I'm sorry," she offers.

He swims up to her. "If you need space tonight, take it. I know how hard today was for you."

"Thank you. I'll see you in the great hall for breakfast?"

"Until then."

She gives him a small smile before returning to her room. Lying on the bed and thinking of how her brother looked as he was healed, she smiles at the thought, knowing everything she is going through is worth it to save him. Her eyes close as her hands clench in anger. *No. I have to stop being so angry. My brother has a future now. He will live the life I never did. That is worth everything to me.* While she sleeps, she dreams of walking on the beach with the sun warming her face.

* * *

Sera wakes up, watching the lights turn on. Laughing at the ingenuity, she realizes they are on timers to resemble daylight. She swims to the closet and changes into a pale blue hanfu, pinning in a small diamond and sapphire crown, then joins Dankin in the great hall for breakfast.

"I'm sorry. Am I late?"

He chuckles. "No, I get up early to see to things before breakfast. How did you sleep? Any nightmares?"

"No, I slept fine."

"Are you all right?"

She looks at him, seeing concern on his face, hearing it in his voice. "I am," she answers, as her plate is set before her. Sighing at the sight, she hangs her head, worrying Dankin until he hears her laughing. "Fish, again?"

"I'm sorry. We normally try to have a better variety, but with the war, we don't venture out unless it's necessary."

"But you took me to the grotto and the island?"

"It was necessary for you. I mean it, Sera. I love you, and I only want you to be happy here." He takes her hand, kissing her palm. "It's what I want more than anything else."

Unsure how to respond, she gives her attention to her meal, glancing at him occasionally. "I enjoy learning with the girls," she says, breaking the silence.

"I'm glad."

"Tell me about the sea witch."

"Ah, what did they say?"

"That she's a myth. I'm curious to hear more."

"There's not much to tell, I'm afraid. I'm sure they told you how beautiful she is, how powerful?"

"They did."

"It's said she lives out east, past our grotto. Any hapless mermaid caught in her path will succumb to her magic. Supposedly, she is not only immortal, but unable to be killed by any mermaid or merman, though many have tried."

As they finish their meal, her handmaids approach, bowing. "Are you ready to learn more, Your Grace?" Ava'lei asks.

"I am," Sera says, squeezing Dankin's hand before joining them as they tour the palace.

"This kingdom is over five thousand years old. The royal line that King Dankin is part of has been ruling over this kingdom from the beginning. His great-grandfather built up this kingdom and was considered a hard, but fair ruler. There is almost no crime and no poverty. Everyone has a purpose, working towards good of the kingdom or the merpeople. You won't find a better merdom in the ocean," Fai'mi explains.

"Merdom?" Sera asks, stifling a laugh.

"Merpeople kingdom," Ava'lei replies.

"What happened to Dankin's family? His parents and grandparents, I mean?"

Ava'lei takes a moment. "He has lost his entire family in the war with the sirens."

Sera shakes her head, biting back tears. "All of them?"

"Yes," Fai'mi answers, solemn.

"Um, let's continue the tour," Sera says to break up the melancholy.

They take her to various rooms and offices, instructing her on the roles of the council, the royals, and the court.

"Now, when you say court, is that the nobles or you do mean tribunals?" Sera asks.

"Court is the nobles. Our tribunal is almost non-existent. If there is a serious offense, the king or his commander will make the judgment," Ava'lei explains.

"What was the last serious offense?"

"Hmm. I will have to inquire. It was before our time, that's how long it has been."

"That's good, right?"

"Yes, Your Grace. Now, is there anything in particular you would like to see?" Fai'mi asks.

"Is there a throne room?"

"Of course!" Ava'lei answers.

Sera follows them into a room with a high ceiling and marble columns. Sera swims up to the thrones, looking them over. They are gold with blue trim, adorned with silver tentacles on the legs and arms.

"You may sit, Your Grace," Fai'mi offers.

Sera puts her hand on the arm of the throne, pulling herself up and sitting. She looks at the girls. "Do I look like a queen?"

They nod and smile before bowing to her. "You do," Ava'lei exclaims.

"Thank you." She swims over to them. "Let's continue our tour."

Her handmaids teach her the history of their people, leading her through a long passage lined with marble statues, explaining who they are. After a few hours of touring and lessons, Ava'lei and Fai'mi lead her back to the great hall for lunch.

Sera sits with Dankin, sighing at the fish on her plate. She eats without complaining.

"How are you enjoying it so far? Are you learning a lot?"

"I am. How is your brother?"

"He's fine. He'll join us for supper tonight."

"I'm eager to meet him."

"Oh, believe me, the feeling is mutual."

She laughs. "Really?"

"Yes. Now, eat your fish. I know it's your favorite." He laughs when she sticks her tongue out. She continues eating her meal, then takes his hand.

"Are you all right?" he asks.

"Can we stay together for the rest of the day?" She sees the surprise on his face. She leans up and plants a soft kiss on his lips.

"Sera, what changed from yesterday?"

"I realized you did what you had to, in order to save your people. You've lost so much, and…" She takes a breath. "Last week, I was in bed and praying for any chance to save my brother. We both had to do things for the people we love. I will give you the benefit of the doubt and be your wife, if you'll have me."

"I will," he answers, smiling at her. "I need to see to a few things, but you can accompany me."

She squeezes his hand. They swim about the palace as he checks on supplies, the armory, and the treasury. He takes her back to their room.

"What are we doing in here?"

He smiles as he pulls her to him, kissing her. "What are we doing?"

Snuggling into his chest, she giggles. "Dankin!"

"Are we not married?"

She turns serious, looking up at him. "Please—"

"I'm sorry. We will take our time, celebrating our union when you are ready. Do not feel rushed because of me."

"Thank you. I'm sorry I'm not much of a wife right now."

"Sera, I changed you into a mermaid and brought you here. I assure you, I understand."

She looks at him and kisses him softly. "I do enjoy that."

He chuckles, his fingers running through her hair. "So do I." His mouth meets hers, his hand gripping her back as he holds her to him. He floats over to the bed, sitting and holding her on his lap. She starts to pull away. "I was just getting us comfortable. Please, don't think—"

"It's okay. I trust you."

"Even now?"

"Hmm. Maybe I shouldn't," she teases.

"Sera!"

She laughs, kissing him again. "You know I trust you."

"Now, how are you feeling? From becoming a mermaid, I mean? Any pain?"

"No. I can't seem to get warm, though. I keep thinking I'll get used to the water, but it still chills me so."

"Do you want your grotto?"

"Could we? I know you have things to take care of—"

"Right now, I need to take care of my wife."

They swim out, leaving the palace and going to the grotto. He helps her over the sand bar, climbing in behind her. He holds her to him, as she eases in his arms.

"Why didn't you tell me you were still cold?"

"I thought I needed time, that I would adjust. I didn't mean to keep it from you."

"You didn't. Is there anything else I can do to help?"

"No. I don't have any pain. I couldn't get warm, was all."

"I worry about you. We are both learning from this."

"It's okay. Will you tell me about the curse?"

"What do you mean?"

"I've heard mention of it, but not what the curse itself was."

"I had to find a woman who would marry me for love, not my wealth, my station, or my power, but for love, before the next full moon. Obviously, all of the mermaids know who I am. I couldn't try with any of them. That's why I came to the island, hoping to find someone. When they pointed you out to me, as someone who could help, I never envisioned being here with you."

"Why not?"

"I thought you were far too beautiful for me."

She snuggles closer to him as she traces her fingers over his arm. "Did you really think that?"

"I did."

"But you're so handsome." She giggles.

"Sera, really?"

"It's the truth. I noticed right away but tried not to pay too much attention because I never thought it would be allowed."

"You should've seen Rae'lin's face when I made my offer. She laughed, certain I was joking."

"How did you convince her to trust you?"

"I told her a little of who I am. Please, don't be mad."

"About what?"

"In order for her to agree to let me court you…" he looks away, swallowing hard. "I had to pay a deposit."

"What?"

"Sera, please. I had to, in order to convince her. Between telling her about some of my life in the court and the gold, she believed me, begrudgingly."

"You paid a deposit for me?" she quietly asks as her face flushes in humiliation. "Then you bought me outright."

"No, I told you I would never buy you, and I meant that. I did what I had to, per your customs, to be with you. I never saw it as buying you."

She sighs, pulling away. "It doesn't matter. I'm here now, right?"

"Please, let's not argue. Work with me like you have today. I need you—"

She looks at him. "What do you need from me?"

"Just your love. That's all. I'm not asking for anything you don't want to give. Please, Sera? I love you, so much."

"I love you, too," she replies quietly. "Though sometimes it's harder to admit than others."

He pulls her to him and caresses her face. "Can I kiss my wife?" She nods, moaning softly as their lips touch, and his hand grips the back of her head. He pulls back. "Now, are you ready to meet my brother?"

"I am."

"Please, don't keep this from me again. If you need to get warm, I will bring you here any time. I mean that."

"Thank you."

"Anything for my sea nymph." He smiles and helps her back into the ocean, leading her to the palace.

* * *

"Anything?" she asks once they arrive.

"What's on your mind?"

"No, it's too dangerous."

"Sera?"

"I want to know how my brother is doing. I was going to ask if we could send a scout or something—"

"Say no more. I have a network, including on the island. I will inquire about your family."

"Thank you. I know you healed him, but I still worry."

"I understand."

* * *

They change for supper and enter the great hall. Dankin's brother, with the same blond hair but a bright green tail, swims over to greet them.

"Da'vae, this is Sera."

"Nice to meet you," he says.

"You as well," she says with a smile.

He looks her up and down. "Well, she looks nothing like your first wife."

"Da'vae!" Dankin hits his shoulder. "That is inappropriate. You know better."

"Yes, brother. Sorry, Sera."

"For what?" She looks at Dankin. "It's the truth, isn't it? I don't look like anyone here."

"That's not true," he says with a laugh.

"That is enough, Da'vae!" Dankin sighs. "Please, can we have a nice, quiet supper together?"

"Yes," Da'vae responds. "Apologies. I tell you what, we'll eat together tomorrow. Enjoy the rest of your night." He looks Sera over once more before swimming away.

They look up when their meal is set before them. Sera smiles at the shrimp and lettuce on her plate.

"Can I join you tonight?" she asks quietly, taking Dankin's hand.

His eyes go wide. "Really?"

She leans in, her mouth on his ear. "To sleep." She pulls back, smiling at him.

He laughs. "Of course."

"Thank you."

"You're my wife. Why are you thanking me?"

"I know we haven't exactly seen eye to eye on some things. I want to make that up to you."

"You don't owe me anything. You saved us from the curse, remember? You've had to adjust, so I understand. Now, are you sure we'll just be sleeping?" He smiles as her cheeks grow red. "Sera, I'm only teasing."

"I know."

* * *

Before turning in, he takes her to the library to show her books that the merpeople created specifically for being in the water. "You can learn anything you need in here, from our history to our culture."

"I will definitely be spending a few days in here."

He laughs. "That's good to know. If I can't find you, I'll come to the library."

She spends a few minutes perusing the shelves and reading some of the titles. "Can we turn in now? I'm tired."

"Yes." He escorts her to their quarters.

Sera looks through the closet to find a nightgown. "Who makes these clothes?" she asks when Dankin swims in to change.

"We have a seamstress. As you see, my magic affects our clothes when we transform."

"I can't get over that. You basically let me pick my own tail color."

"As soon as I saw the gown, I knew you were going to be gorgeous. The silver tail with your black hair is a beautiful contrast."

"Wait, will my tail change colors?"

He laughs at the thought. "No, for the first transformation, the tail gets its color from the clothes the person is wearing. Then it stays that color."

She looks down, tracing her hand over her waist. "It still doesn't seem real, though." She looks at him, removing her gown.

"Sera?"

She laughs. "No. I don't want to do this while I'm alone."

"Do what—" he starts, when she traces her fingers over the gills on her ribcage. "Well?"

"It's so weird! I still breathe through my mouth, too."

"You will, out of habit, but as I've said, we do have lungs. They also filter water, that's why it's a little harder to breathe on land. What else are you trying to get used to?"

"Everything."

"What do you mean?"

"My tail feels… heavy at times, like it doesn't want to respond. I have to make myself move it, and—" she looks up at him, "sometimes it hurts after I've been swimming around."

His shoulders fall. "Sera, why didn't you tell me?"

"Because you have enough to carry, worrying about your people."

"Our people, Your Grace."

"Yes, our people. Still, you know what I mean."

"When you say it doesn't want to respond, does it feel like dead weight?"

"Yes! I couldn't think of how to describe it."

"When that happens, tell me."

"Why?"

"I'll show you an exercise that will help." He sees the confusion on her face. "The first time I transformed back, after being a human, I had the same issue."

"Really?"

"Yes. It didn't take long for me to fix. It should work for you, too."

"All right." She yawns. "For now, I'm turning in. I know it's still early, but—"

"You've had a busy day. Come on."

He dims the lights. "How do those work?" she asks, as they swim onto the bed together. "Lights underwater?"

He explains the hydroelectric process they use. Dankin looks down at her. "You sure you're okay to have me in bed with you?"

"I am," she says.

"Can I hold you?"

"Yes," she answers as she scoots back. He pulls her to him, wrapping his arm over her. "I know it's been a lot for me, but I really hope you know how grateful I am. You saved me from the mistress, saved my brother. Thank you for everything you've done for me."

"I would do anything for the woman I love."

Chapter 10

Grief Comes in the Morning

"How do you feel?" Dankin asks when Sera is coming out of the closet, dressed for the day.

"Better. I'm not as cold and—"

"But you're still cold?"

"A little."

He swims to her and wraps his arms around her. "Let me help."

"Hmm. Thank you," she says, holding him. "Can we go to the beach sometime? Or is it too dangerous?"

"Sera—"

"I miss laying on the sand with the sun on my face."

"There is a beach on the same island as our grotto. We can lay out there."

"Perfect!"

* * *

They are eating breakfast in the great hall when her handmaids approach, bowing to them.

"Morning, girls. More learning today?" Dankin asks.

Ava'lei smiles. "Yes. She is learning quickly."

"So I've heard," he replies.

"We will leave you to eat," Fai'mi says.

"I'll meet you in the library."

"Yes, Your Grace, until then," Fai'mi says. They both bow, then swim away.

"Are you enjoying learning with them?" Dankin asks.

"I am. We're still learning history, so I haven't really learned my duties yet. When do you need me?"

"I always need you."

"I meant to help oversee the kingdom, as your queen," she says.

He chuckles. "Of course. Whenever you are ready. Do not rush."

"Thank you." She looks at him, sighing and fiddling with her hair.

"What's wrong?"

"I'm done eating, but my tail—" she looks over when she realizes she can be heard. She leans in. "It doesn't feel right."

"The hall will clear out in a few minutes, then I'll help you."

"It's embarrassing."

"Why? It's not your fault."

No, it's yours—she stops herself, taking a breath. "I know," she replies. "Still, I can't help the way I feel about it."

"When you're feeling like this, do you get angry?"

"Yes," she admits, hanging her head. "When you said it wasn't my fault, I was thinking that it's yours." She looks up at him. "I'm so sorry. I wish you could've found a noble or—"

"Sera, stop. Regardless of status, you literally became a mermaid and left your home. I am trying to help, if you'll let me."

"Why are you angry?" she asks, clasping her hands.

"I'm not." He sighs when she gives him a look. "I'm angry with myself," he admits.

"Because of what you did to me?"

"Sera!"

"I didn't mean—" She realizes she's being stared at. "Please, escort me out of here."

"I'm sure you'll do fine on your own," he growls, swimming away.

She keeps her head down, ignoring the looks. As time goes on, the hall empties out. She looks up when her handmaids swim to her.

"Your Grace," they both say with a bow.

"I apologize that I left you waiting."

Ava'lei swims closer. "If I may, are you all right?"

"No," she admits, burying her head in her hands.

"Shall we get His Majesty?" Fai'mi offers.

"Absolutely not!"

"Apologies, Your Grace."

"No, I'm sorry. You're both trying to help.

"What do you need?" Ava'lei asks, looking at her in concern.

Sera stares at her hands. "Will you take me out to the ocean? I need to swim there."

They look at each other. "We aren't supposed to leave—"

"Please?" she begs, looking at Ava'lei. "I need your help. I… I have an issue with my tail. I need you to take me there."

"Yes, Your Grace." She and Fai'mi each grab an arm, helping her from the hall. They swim from the protection of the walls, staying close by. "We do not venture further."

"That's fine. Would you take me to that rock over there?" Sera gestures. They swim her to it, helping her settle.

"May I ask what's wrong?" Ava'lei inquires.

"I need a moment, then I'll be okay."

"Would you like some privacy? We can turn away but stay close."

"That would be great. Thank you." She watches them swim towards the palace. Looking down at her tail, she groans in frustration when there is no movement. She pounds her fists on her tail, quietly crying to herself when she feels nothing from it. "This isn't happening!"

"Sera, stop!"

She looks over, seeing Dankin swimming to her. Her hands clench as she hangs her head. "Go away!" she begs.

He kneels before her, taking her hand. "I never should've left you like this. I'm sorry."

"You say you are, but you don't mean it. Not the way you treat me."

"After what you said—"

She glares at him. "This is not my fault!" she cries out. "It's yours. I was right to think that."

"You're hurting, you're angry, and you're taking it out on your tail and on me. Let me help you."

"I asked for your help! You left me."

"Sera—"

"No. What do you want from me? I am trying!" She buries her face in her hands. "Why won't it move?" she asks.

"Because you're trying too hard."

Her head jerks up. "What?"

"The more you try, the heavier it feels?"

"Yes," she admits.

"Take a break from it, and swim with me."

"I can't swim!" she cries out.

He sighs. "Hold onto me while I swim. Will you do that?"

"It won't do any good."

"Do you know that for a fact?"

"No, but—"

"Then quit acting like this. You are a queen, remember?"

"Only because you made me one," she scoffs.

Dankin swims back, turning away. He thinks on his words before facing her. "You have the choice in this. You can sit there and rot, or you can try."

"You would leave me here?"

"What will it take for you to stop thinking the worst of me? Why do you feel like this?"

She looks down, tracing her fingers over her hand. "Because you abandoned me in the hall, knowing I could only sit there by myself."

"Sera, what do you want?" He frowns when she shoots him an angry look. "I mean, as a mermaid. Do you want to be able to swim on your own so you can take on your responsibilities as queen?"

"I want to be free of you," she admits.

Pain flows through his chest. "I hurt you that badly?"

She nods her head before burying her face in her hands. "I literally could do nothing but sit there. How could you leave me like that?"

"I was angry and hurt. Even so, I never should've left you. How can I make this up to you?"

"I'm so tired and frustrated that I can't even think properly," she admits, looking at him. "I need to rest."

"I know, and you will, after we work with your tail."

"Okay. What do I need to do?"

"Take my hands."

She shakes her head as she reaches up for him. He pulls her from the rock, releasing one hand and swimming with her. "Now, focus. Don't try to move your tail. Don't try to swim. Just move your body with me."

She does as he says, her body curving and floating along. Her tail begins to move on its own, going up and down as she begins to swim with him. "It's working," she says, squeezing his hand. "I'm sorry."

"I am, too."

"I've wasted today, haven't I? I have so much to learn—"

"It's okay. Ease into everything. Don't push yourself."

"I can't help it. My whole life has been one of work, of tasks and duties. I can't take a sick day, can't take it easy."

"You aren't. You're adapting to the changes to your body and your life."

"Can I try on my own?"

"All right." He releases her, backing away. She swims around, enjoying the movement instead of focusing on her tail. She sees the smile on his face as he watches her.

"What?"

"You know how beautiful you are!"

She giggles, looking away. "Thank you, koy'lei."

His smile grows at his nickname. He swims up to her, gripping the back of her head and kissing her fiercely. "My little sea nymph," he says, pulling back. "Hmm, what you do to me."

"Dankin!" she blushes. "They can see us."

"Handmaids, you are dismissed."

Sera watches as her handmaids swim into the palace. "And what do you think we're going to do out here in the open sea?" Sera asks.

He chuckles. "Swim and enjoy this time together."

"Can we go to the grotto?"

He takes her hand and leads her to the small island. "I thought you might like this, first." He picks her up, carrying her onto the shore. "What?" he asks when she laughs in delight.

"How quickly and easily you transform like that. It's incredible."

"Give it time, and one day, you will, too."

"Wait, what?"

"I told you I go on land from time to time. Did you not think you would go with me?"

"But you made me say goodbye to my family."

"For now. We won't travel as long as we are in jeopardy from the sirens. If we can end the war, you can travel with me."

"Really?" she asks, disbelief in her eyes.

"Sera, I mean that." He is lying next to her on the sand as his tail returns. "Now, enjoy the beach."

She laughs. "Yes, Dankin. Thank you. I've missed this." She relaxes as the sun warms her and moans in happiness when her tail moves on the hot sand.

"Are you all right?"

She blushes, biting her lip. "I'm fine," she manages.

"What happened?" He leans over her on his elbow and looks down at her. "Sera?"

"Kiss me, please?" He eases down, kissing her softly as she grips his head. His hand trails down her neck and arm, down to her tail. She sucks in air. "Dankin—" she tries, as he kisses her again. She grips him tighter, losing herself in his kiss, in his arms, in his heart.

"I love you, Sera."

She studies his face, trailing her fingers over his jawline. "I love you, too." She gasps in surprise when she turns human. "Dankin?"

"I was waiting for you to believe me, then I would do this. You can't stay this way, I'm sorry. If you want to walk the beach and swim like this for a while, we can."

"Oh, please?"

He gets to his feet, helping her up. She holds his arm with both hands as they walk around the beach. She picks up shells and traces lines in the sand. He takes her into the water, watching as she kicks her legs and swims with him.

"It's time to go back, isn't it?" she asks, her eyes closing as her tail is forming. "I see."

"I'm sorry. Is this what you want from time to time? Or is it too painful a reminder?"

"For now, it's painful. Give me time, and I will want to do this again. I know I will. I enjoyed my day with you, my koy'lei."

"I did with you, my sea nymph."

* * *

They return to the palace, where she sees her handmaids waiting for her inside the main entrance. "Did you wait this whole time?"

"Apologies," Ava'lei says, "but we were worried about you, Your Grace."

"Thank you. I'm okay, now. I am still adjusting, and sometimes it's harder than I want to admit."

"We want to help, if we can," Fai'mi offers.

"I appreciate you both. For now, we are going to supper. I will study with you tomorrow, I promise."

"Your Grace," they say with a bow before swimming away.

"They are very sweet. I am lucky to have them." She looks up at Dankin. "Can I ask?"

"Go ahead."

"What happened to your wife's handmaids?" She regrets asking when she sees the pain on his face.

"They… perished with her."

"I'm sorry. I shouldn't have asked."

"No, I want you to ask about anything. I mean that. This is your home, your kingdom."

"Thank you. Supper?"

"What do you think we're having?"

She laughs as he takes her hand, swimming with her to the great hall. She gasps at the sight before her. "Shark?"

He laughs. "My brother caught one."

"Hmm," she studies her plate, unsure, "I don't know if I can eat this or not."

Dankin chuckles, eating his shark. "It's a bit… chewy, but it has a very good flavor."

"All right."

She tries a bite, instantly regretting it. "Oh, no. This is not for me," she says. Dankin waves a kitchen worker over, speaking softly.

"You will get a new plate in a moment," he says, taking hers. "I will help myself."

She laughs. "Did we work up an appetite?"

"Using my magic like that can wear me out."

She turns serious. "I'm sorry. I forgot."

"It's okay. It's worth it, to spend a day like we had. You've needed one with everything I've put on you."

"It was a wonderful day." She smiles at him, taking his hand. He raises it up, kissing her palm.

"Maybe a wonderful night?" He chuckles as her cheeks grow red. "Sera, I'm teasing. Is it okay, though? If I tease like that?"

"It is. Mildly, not too much?"

"I promise."

They finish eating, returning to their quarters. She goes to the closet, finding a pink nightgown. "Oh, this is pretty." She looks over, her shoulders going down at the look on his face. She hangs it back up then sits on the bed.

"What's wrong?" Dankin asks.

"I feel bad for wearing your wife's clothing. Perhaps tomorrow I could have some made up?"

"You can, but you wear whatever of hers you want. I mean that."

"I see the pain on your face when I wear her clothes. I don't want to do that to you."

He sits beside her, taking her hand. "Sera, it's okay. It's something I'll get used to."

Watching her fingers trace over his hand, her jaw clenches. "It shouldn't be."

"Sera, I've grieved and moved on. Please, wear them. It's a good thing, because they aren't just sitting there."

She looks up at him. She brings her hand up and strums her fingers along his chin. "If you're sure?"

"I am. Can I dress you?"

She nods. "Okay."

He takes her to the closet and helps her remove her gown then gets out the pink nightgown she had picked out. Slipping it over her head, he lowers it down, smiling at her.

"Thank you," she says, her face flush.

"You're not going to pass out on me, are you?"

"No, I'll be okay. That was… different."

"How does your fluke feel?" he asks.

"I'm sorry, my what?"

He chuckles, shaking his head. "It's another word for tail."

"I see. It's okay. I can feel it, and it's not hurting. I guess I am getting used to it."

"That's good."

"Are you ready for bed?" she asks as she leaves the closet.

"In a moment." He changes out of his shirt and crown, then runs his fingers through her clothes as he thinks back. He sees his first wife, strawberry blonde and tan with a bright green tail. He smiles at the thought.

"Dankin?"

"Yes, Ko'era?" he asks, turning to Sera as he closes his eyes in shame.

"What does that mean?"

"It means wife," he answers, smiling at her.

She takes his hand and swims to bed with him. "Thank you for today," she says. "I hope tomorrow is just as good."

"It will be," he says, kissing the top of her head. He closes his eyes, praying that's true.

* * *

Sera wakes up as someone is knocking. Realizing she's alone, she swims to the door, opening it to a merman. He is dressed in a black dress robe with a red tail. His brown hair is just past his ears, his face youthful looking.

"Your Grace, I am Ric'aro." He bows. "His Majesty asked me to inquire about your family, and I have done as he asked."

She gestures him in, anxious to hear about her family. "Please, tell me what news you have."

He swallows hard. "Your brother is doing very well. He walks the market every day, and he is excelling in his studies."

"I'm glad to hear that. Any other news?"

He looks down, fidgeting with his robe. "One other bit. I apologize for being the bearer of bad news, but your father passed away."

She nearly sinks to the floor. He swims to her and reaches for her. "I'm okay," she says, gesturing him back. "When did he pass?"

"The night after your wedding."

"Oh," she manages as the grief is swelling in her chest.

"Shall I inform His Majesty?"

"No, I'll tell him. Thank you for your duty."

He bows. "Please, call upon me any time."

"Thank you." She watches him leave then sits on the edge of the bed. My father is dead. I can't tell Dankin. He will be happy! I can't say I blame him, losing a daughter to his blade. Still, I am heartbroken by this, and I cannot stand the thought of his reaction. I can't stomach it. She buries her face in her hands, grieving for her father.

She goes to the closet, looking through the various gowns, deciding on a black hanfu with a silver layer then picks out a silver crown with black diamonds. Leaning against the doorframe, looking in the mirror, she hangs her head as her grief overwhelms her. She sinks to the floor, her back against the wood of the frame. She brings her tail up, burying her face and weeping for her father.

He will come looking for me if I don't join him soon. She gets up, shutting the door and swimming out. She goes towards the great hall, passing a small parlor. She swims inside to look it over.

"Can I help you?"

She turns, seeing a young merman with black hair and a green tail. "I was just looking. I'm sorry—"

"Oh, no! Apologies, Your Grace." He bows. "I did not mean to offend."

"It's all right. What is this room used for?"

"It's a grieving room."

"Really?"

"It's so a family can have privacy upon receiving bad news. Otherwise, it's used as a standard parlor."

"Thank you."

"Of course. Anything else I can help you with?"

"That is all." She watches him bow and swim out. She looks around the room. *Appropriate, I guess.* She shakes her head, her heart heavy again. She pushes down her grief and anger, going to the great hall but stops in the doorway, seeing Dankin laughing with his brother. Her face is flush as her anger takes over. She turns away, swimming back to her smaller quarters. She goes inside, lying on the bed and crying herself to sleep.

* * *

"Sera?"

She opens her eyes, sitting up and looking at Dankin. "Yes?"

"You weren't at breakfast. Why are you in here?"

"I'm fine," she says, swimming past him. He grabs her arm. "Let go."

He releases her. "I'm sorry. Will you talk to me?"

"I'm fine," she says again, going to the great hall. He stays close to her, worried. They sit with Da'vae. A plate is brought over, and she eats. "See?"

"Did something happen?"

She closes her eyes, her head rolling back. She takes a breath before she resumes eating. "No."

He decides not to push. "Will you be with your handmaids today?"

"If I must."

"All right. What's wrong?"

"Nothing. I'm going to meet them in the library. I'll see you later." She swims off.

"What's going on with her?"

"Who knows?" Dankin asks, as he and Da'vae continue discussing the war. "So, you were telling me about the siren attack?"

"Right. They are moving in groups of four now, openly attacking us."

"They are brazen. They attacked us on our way back the other day." Dankin sighs. "This war has raged on long enough. What will it take to end it?"

"I wish I knew the answer. Now, onto happier tidings. How is your new bride doing?"

"As you see, she is still adjusting to everything."

"Was she really a land-dweller? And you turned her without asking her?"

"I did what I had to, in order to save us. If Maren had gotten her claws on this kingdom, she would've killed us all."

"Well, not you."

"Please. You know it's only a prophecy, probably not even true."

"What? I don't think you could kill her, either."

Dankin looks at him, skepticism on his face. "Tell me you don't believe the stories?"

"What? That Maren can't be killed by any merperson? Yes, I believe that. If it was just a mention or two, I wouldn't, but over twenty mentions in several books and scrolls cannot be ignored. You need to take it seriously."

They continue their discussion, stopping when Ava'lei approaches.

"Apologies, Your Majesty. We were wondering if Her Grace was joining us for her studies?"

Dankin looks at his brother, then back to Ava'lei. "She didn't meet you in the library?" Ava'lei shakes her head. Dankin rises from his seat. "Do not worry about her studies today, I will find her."

"Yes, Your Majesty," she says with a bow and swims off.

"I knew something was wrong with her."

He swims to their rooms but does not see her. From each guard he sees, he gets the same response. "I've not seen her, Your Majesty."

Groaning in frustration, his worry grows. Finally, he passes the chapel, and there she is, sitting alone in one of the pews. Dankin goes inside and sits behind her. "Sera, why are you here?"

She hangs her head. "I'm sorry. Could I have time to myself today?"

"If you'll tell me what's going on? You didn't finish your meal, then you didn't show up to the library. I'm worried about you." He swims around, sitting beside her. "Please, talk to me?"

"I can't."

"What do you mean?"

"We're doing so well together, and I'm afraid if I tell you…" she buries her face in her hands.

"Whatever it is, I'm right here."

"That's what worries me."

He takes her hand, gently lifting her face. "Please?"

"I need comfort right now, no matter what I'm about to tell you. Can you give me that?"

"I promise."

She squeezes his hand, swallowing her tears. "I heard back about my family."

"Your brother—"

"No, no. He's fine. My father passed away, the same day I said goodbye to them."

Dankin thinks a moment. "Sera, I mean this with utmost respect and sincerity. I am truly sorry for your loss. Why didn't you come to me and tell me this?"

She looks down at her hands. "Because I was afraid."

"That I would be happy to hear he had passed?"

"Or unable to comfort me. I wouldn't blame you. How could you comfort me grieving for the man who killed your daughter?"

"Because I'm comforting my wife." He gently grips her arm and takes her up to the altar. "Is this familiar? This is where we said our vows, and I meant every word of it. I want to help you, any way I can. I'm sorry you felt you couldn't talk to me about this. I never want you to feel that way again. Now, what do you need?"

She shakes her head. "I need hot tea, comfort food, and sunshine. All the things I can't have here."

"Come with me."

"Dankin—" They swim through the hall and out of the palace. He says nothing as he leads her through the ocean. They arrive at a small island. "Where are we?"

"This is Isle Toro'pikar. It's very similar to Isle Piscantur, but much closer. Less danger of running into sirens." They transform as they walk onto the shore. He takes her into the village where they find a small patisserie shop. "You can get tea and anything else you want, then we can go enjoy it on the beach, in private."

She leans up, kissing his cheek. "Thank you for this."

With their drinks and snacks in hand, they walk back to the shore and sit on a bench, watching the sun reflecting on the waves. She looks around, grateful it's just the two of them.

"I thought you might need to cry, too. Since you really can't do that underwater."

"It's kind of frustrating," she admits. She drinks her tea, savoring the mint flavor. "This was my father's favorite. I made it for him at breakfast." When her hand begins to shake, Dankin takes her cup. She cries into her hands, and he pulls her to him, holding her as she weeps. He strokes her hair, speaking softly as he reassures her.

"I'm sorry you weren't with him. That's my fault. I am so sorry."

"No, it's okay. At least he passed knowing I am queen, that I am married, and happy."

"Are you happy?"

"Well, not at the moment, but I am growing happy with you, with our life. You bringing me here to comfort me shows me how much you love me. You didn't need to prove your love, but thank you."

"I was worried, after what we talked about, with turning you human."

She shakes her head. "Honestly, I hadn't even thought about that."

"Really?"

"Yes. My heart aches too much right now."

"I wish I could kiss away your tears, carry away your grief, and only fill you with joy and happiness."

"My koy'lei." She buries her face into his shirt, crying again.

"Sera—"

"No," she says, quietly. "These are happy tears, for your words. Thank you for that."

"You're welcome. Um, your tea is getting cold."

She laughs, pulling back and wiping her tears. She takes her cup. "Thank you for the tea, for bringing me here, for being wonderful."

"Aren't I always?"

She giggles as she drinks her tea. "You think you are!"

"I'm hurt." He pouts at her, grabbing her cup when she nearly spills her tea laughing. "Sera!"

"It's your fault," she says, cleaning up. She looks at him. "I meant me spilling my tea—"

"Sera, it's okay. I know what you meant. I'm not upset."

"Not even with me for hiding?"

"No. You weren't hiding, you were grieving how you needed to. I am sorry you felt you couldn't come to me."

"You already apologized for that. It's okay."

"Sera, may I kiss you?"

"Please," she begs. His mouth joins hers, and she closes her eyes, letting her grief and heartache flow out as she takes his essence in. She holds him tight. "Could we stay here, on this bench, for the rest of our lives?"

He chuckles. "It's a nice thought, but our people need us."

"I know," she says. She picks up her tea again and finishes it, then eats the last few bites of her pastry. "Do we need to head back?"

"Only if you're ready."

"I am quite tired from crying."

"Come on," he says, helping her to her feet. They throw their trash away, before heading for the water. He scoops her up, kissing her again. "Ready?"

"Yes, my koy'lei."

He dives in, watching her sudden transformation. "Well?"

She laughs. "I don't know if I'll ever get used to that."

When they return to the palace, they are greeted by his brother. "What's wrong?" Dankin asks.

"Where have you been?" Da'vae demands.

"We had to take care of something," he answers.

Da'vae shakes his head. "Right. I need you in the briefing room. She's not allowed."

"She is the queen, and she comes where I say she can," he snaps.

"Fine."

Sera pulls back. "It's okay, really. I need to rest."

"I'll meet you in our quarters shortly."

She gives him a kiss on the cheek before going to their quarters. Inside their room, she lies down on the bed, exhausted from crying and swimming. She thinks of lying in the sun, falling asleep to its warmth.

* * *

"You were tired."

Sera's eyes open. She sits up, stretching and smiling at him. "I was. What did Da'vae want?"

"The sirens attacked one of our merchants, who was attempting to trade with another clan. They killed him and a few of the other merpeople. The clan wishes to form an alliance, to aid us in taking out the sirens."

"That's a good thing, right? Having help?"

"Yes. They haven't joined us before because the sirens didn't really mess with them. Maren's war isn't with all merpeople, just me and our kingdom. I'm sorry I brought you here to such danger."

"You brought me here to free you and your people." She takes his hand. "And because you love me. It's okay. I want to help, if I can."

"You are so incredible, how compassionate you are. You truly mean what you say, don't you?"

"I do."

"All right. For now, let's have supper. I'm meeting with their delegate in the morning, and we'll go from there."

"How many merpeople are left in this kingdom?"

"Only about twenty-five hundred. That may sound like a lot, but we had over six thousand before the war."

"So much loss."

"We've wiped out thousands of sirens in return, but they kept making more. However, since the mainland war ended, not as many ships pass around here. No sailors, no sirens. It's been a small blessing."

"I still don't really understand how that works. Why would the sailor willingly fight after becoming a siren?"

"No, no. This isn't like you becoming a mermaid. You are still you, just with a tail instead of legs. You saw the siren kiss the merchant and turn him. When a siren kisses you, you transform completely, inside and out. They take your body, your life, and your memories. All you know as a siren is to serve the queen and make more sirens."

Sera shakes her head. "That's awful."

"Now you see why we are fighting so hard against them."

"What would happen if they were all killed? Would Athe'nus make more of them?"

"She's not real, any more than the sea witch is real. It's just mythology, not religion."

"So, what do you believe in?"

"Like a higher power? Fate? Things like that?"

"Yes."

"I do believe there is something watching over us. What or who, I can't really say. I don't believe in fate or destiny, that our journey is pre-planned. I think each day is a fresh start, to learn from our mistakes and try to do better, to be better."

"I wish everyone felt that way. That's incredible."

"What do you believe?"

"Our spirit goes to heaven above. We are all reunited in death and have eternal life with our Maker."

"I see."

"You don't believe that?" Sera asks.

"I'm not sure. I want to believe that I will see my family again someday, but I really don't know."

"I'm sorry, I'm bringing up painful memories for you."

"You aren't. Now, we need to eat," he says, kissing her cheek.

* * *

At dinner, they are served fish again, much to Sera's dismay. Dankin laughs as she chokes it down. When they finish eating, he takes her by the hand and leads her around the palace. He shows her the briefing room, a small game parlor, even a theater. Eventually, they retire to their quarters and change for bed. He dims the lights and helps her lie down, then joins her in bed. He holds her in his arms, growing concerned when she yawns.

"What?"

"It's just, as merpeople, we don't yawn when we're tired. I didn't think of it before. Do you draw in air when you do that?"

"No, but I only do it when I'm tired. Force of habit, maybe?"

"Hmm. I don't know." He kisses the back of her neck as his fingers stroke through her hair. "I'm sorry about your father."

"Thank you. I've grieved today, so tomorrow I will resume my duties."

"You don't have to rush, Sera. Take as long as you need."

"I appreciate that, but I am ready for tomorrow. I think learning new things will help."

"Okay." He looks down at her, bringing his hand up and caressing along her neck and chin. He leans down and kisses her. "Good night, my sea nymph."

"Good night, my koy'lei. I love you."

"I love you, too."

Chapter 11

Gain…

"Queen Na'riti will be here any time to discuss an alliance. Are you excited to meet some of the other tribes?" Dankin asks.

"I am," she says, taking his hand. "What is her clan like?" Sera asks as they arrive at the grand foyer of the palace.

"The Tsun'ama are a beautiful people. Their skin is deep brown. They have curly hair and white tattoos on their arms. They are a tribal people, cunning and powerful. They will make a perfect ally."

"I'm glad to hear that, everything your—our people have suffered. Maybe with their help, we can end the war once and for all."

"That is my hope."

"Is it possible to turn the sirens back to sailors?"

"No, the curse is permanent, but they can lose their siren powers."

"How is that possible?"

"The siren queen would have to give her blessing."

Sera scoffs. "From what you've told me about her, I can't imagine that would ever happen." The large palace doors swing open then, and Na'riti swims in. Dankin and Sera return her bow with a half bow.

"How do you wish to be addressed?" Sera asks. Dankin smiles, grateful at her knowledge of customs for greeting fellow monarchs.

"Raa'ginna, which is our word for queen."

"Yes, raa'ginna. Please," Dankin gestures.

She gives him a look before turning back to Sera.

"Is something wrong?" Sera asks.

"No, Your Grace. You look… familiar. My apologies," Na'riti offers with a nod.

They go into the briefing room and sit at the large, round table. "Shall we get down to business?" Dankin asks.

"Please, Your Majesty. My people do not wish for war, but if we are unable to go around bartering and trading, we will not survive. We are willing to help."

"What do you ask in return?"

"If we defeat them, you will split her treasure with us."

Dankin thinks a moment. "You can have everything, but—"

"Oh, I know. That is yours. We would not dare ask for that."

Sera looks at them both, confused. Dankin squeezes her hand. "When would we strike back?" he asks.

"Tonight, if you're ready."

He laughs. "Raa'ginna, we have been ready. We will do whatever is necessary to stop this war, I assure you."

She rises up, bowing to them. "I will return at seven tonight, with my army."

"Until then."

Sera watches her leave, turning back to Dankin. "Why tonight?"

"Part of the siren's curse is their eyesight. They can practically see in the dark, so they usually sleep during the day and hunt in the evening or at night. When they first awake, around seven to eight o'clock, their eyes take a while to adjust. They are at their weakest."

"I see. Will you be going to battle with them?"

"I will."

"I don't want you to go," she admits.

"Sera, I have to. I have to protect my kingdom, protect you."

"I understand."

"Now, will you go and study with your handmaids? I have to prepare."

"See you at lunch?"

"Yes, my little sea nymph." He kisses her.

She leaves the room, finding Ava'lei and Fai'mi in the library.

"I would like to learn about the sirens today," she says as they greet her with a bow.

"Why the sirens?"

Sera shoots Ava'lei a look. "Because I need to know about our enemy."

"Of course, Your Grace. Apologies." She gathers a few books and brings them to the table. "We will answer any questions you have."

"Would you get us breakfast? I forgot."

"Of course." Ava'lei swims out.

Sera picks up the first book in the stack and flips through the pages. She comes upon a picture of a siren—the pale skin, black and red tail, and intense, vengeful eyes. Her chest hurts at the sight of her claws. She puts the book down.

"Your Grace? Are you all right?"

"Yes, Fai'mi. I'm fine. Thank you." She picks up the book and continues to look through it. She eats once Ava'lei returns with breakfast. "How many sirens are there?"

"We are unsure. We believe it is around five hundred, but we truly do not know. There are rumors of other siren nests, but I don't believe those. They seem to stay near their queen, under her influence and protection," Fai'mi says.

"That makes sense. What do you know about their eyesight?" Sera asks.

"Some believe it is worse when they first wake up. I think that sounds pretty ridiculous, but I would not venture a definitive answer on that. It is also said they have incredible strength. I have never encountered a siren, so I cannot say anything for sure."

"I have."

Fai'mi and Ava'lei swim closer. "Really?"

"Yes. She dugs her claws into my chest, but Dankin killed her."

"You survived a siren attack?" Ava'lei asks, looking at Fai'mi. "Do you think? Is she the one?"

"One what?" Sera asks.

"A prophecy—"

Sera laughs. "No, please. No magic, no prophecies. I do not wish to hear any nonsense right now. I need facts and answers, not myths."

"Of course," Ava'lei says, giving Fai'mi a wide-eyed look.

The three of them spend the morning reading and discussing what is known about the sirens before Sera returns to the great hall for lunch. When Dankin doesn't join her, she worries about him. When still he does not show, she reluctantly returns to the library. Her afternoon is filled with more reading and research, aided by Ava'lei and Fai'mi. She smiles when Dankin joins her in the great hall for supper.

"Sorry about lunch. We were heavy into discussing strategy for tonight. I believe this plan may work, but we are taking quite the chance."

"Can I ask?"

"I'll tell you about it tomorrow."

"I've decided to sleep in my quarters tonight. I can't stand the thought of sleeping alone in our bed."

He brings his hand up, gently gripping the back of her head as his lips crash on hers. He pulls back, smiling. "I apologize, I forgot where we are."

"It's okay," she says.

"Sleep there tonight, and hopefully, it will be the last time."

"I really hope that's true."

They finish eating, and he escorts her to her quarters. They stop outside her doorway, and she grips his hand. "This brings back memories," she says with a smile.

He chuckles softly, kissing her hand. "Good night, Miss Sera."

She looks up at him. "Please, kiss me before you go?"

He leans down, his mouth an inch from hers. "Sera, I promise you, I will return." He kisses her, hard and hungry. Reluctantly, he pulls back. "I love you."

"I love you, too." She watches him swim away, her heart heavy in her chest. "Please, keep your promise," she whispers.

* * *

Sera jerks awake, her heart pounding in her ears. She quickly dresses and leaves the room, unsure where she is going.

"Your Grace," a guard offers as he bows.

"Has the king returned?" she asks.

"No news, I'm afraid."

She sighs. "Thank you." She continues towards the front of the palace, hoping to wait for his return. The doors burst open and merpeople scurry about. She swims through the crowd and stops a young soldier. "What's wrong?"

"The king was gravely injured."

"What? Someone must heal him!" she commands.

The young guard shakes his head. "Only he has such magic."

"Take me to him."

"They are still—"

"I command you to take me to my husband!"

"This way."

He leads her to the infirmary. Tending to Dankin is a group of people who Sera can only assume is a doctor with her nurses. She swims over, trying to stay out of their way.

"How bad is it?" Sera asks.

"Get—" The doctor turns, stopping herself at the sight of the queen. "Your Grace, we are doing what we can. Please, wait in the hall?"

Sera swims closer, taking Dankin's hand. "No." She sees the gash across his chest. "Leave us!" she commands.

Once they swim out, she brings her hand to his chest, closing her eyes as she repeats the words he used on her brother. All of her energy is focused on saving him. She opens her eyes and watches as a blue streak of light emerges from her hand. It flows into his chest, and she watches the wound close.

Sera squeezes Dankin's hand as she nearly collapses onto him. "Please, come back to me, my koy'lei." She stays by his side all night, praying over him. She jerks up when he finally squeezes her hand in return.

"Sera?" He sits up. "Where am I?"

"You were wounded. They brought you here. I um, I said the same words you did when healing my brother, while I held my hand over your chest. I wasn't even sure what I was doing, but I had to try. There was the same blue light and… I healed you."

His eyes go wide for a moment. "I'm grateful you took the chance. Of course, since you are the queen, you share a little of my magic."

"Really?"

He laughs. "Not enough to turn human, I'm afraid."

"Dankin, I wasn't even thinking of that."

"I know. I had to tease. Thank you for saving my life."

"You almost broke your promise."

"I mean, technically I did return to you."

She gasps, rising up and turning away. "That's not funny!"

He leans over and pulls her against his chest, wrapping his arms around her. "I'm sorry."

She turns to hold him in her arm and looks up at him with hope in her eyes. "Is the war over?"

"I'm afraid not. We dealt a massive blow, but there are more of them than we realized. I'm afraid it's going to get worse before it gets better."

"What now?"

"Now, we take it a day at a time. You continue to learn your roles and duties while I oversee the war effort."

She sighs as she snuggles into him. "We will have peace. I know we will." She leans up and kisses him. "Now, are you well enough to go for breakfast?"

* * *

They go into the great hall. She smiles at the shrimp and clams on her plate. "This is different."

"They managed to get some on our way back," Dankin explains.

"How is your brother?"

"Not happy with me."

"What do you mean?"

"I fell into her trap. Maren was by herself, and I tried to sneak up behind her. I was confused when she laughed, and as I turned away, one of her sirens rushed at me, sword drawn. I never saw it coming. Da'vae thinks I was stupid."

"Why?"

"He is a great warrior, but stealth and strategy are not his strongest points."

"I see. So, you're saying he would have swam up, screaming, as he brought his sword down on her?"

Dankin laughs. "Exactly. As if that would work." He turns serious. "I'm sorry, today is going to be another like yesterday, as we go over strategy and regroup."

"I almost lost you. We need some time together," she says with a pout.

"I promise you, this evening we will."

"Until then," she says, planting a gentle kiss.

* * *

Sera sighs at the book in her hand, not really reading. She tries to concentrate but her mind is too distracted by thoughts of war.

"Are you all right, Your Grace?"

"I am, Ava'lei." She makes herself focus as she asks questions about the kingdom. "If Dankin had died in battle, what would happen to me?"

"You would become Queen Superior, our ruler. If you remarried, you would keep the higher title."

"Unless she married Da'vae, then he would, since he has royal blood," Fai'mi explains.

"If he is royal in blood, why would I take over?"

"You would inherit the throne from your husband."

"Really?"

"If you did not want it, then it would go to Da'vae."

"That's different from where I grew up. If our king or queen died, the throne went to next closest royal blood, whether a sibling or their adult offspring."

"Hmm, that is interesting," Ava'lei comments.

Sera has lunch brought into the library for them, and they continue working until supper. "When will I begin to fulfill these roles? Swimming about the palace and giving aid where I can?"

"Whenever you are ready. His Majesty wanted you to have plenty of time to learn everything, to be knowledgeable and ready," Fai'mi says.

"I see. I am getting there, I think."

"We will assist as well."

"Thank you for patience and discretion. I need supper."

"Until tomorrow?"

"Yes, Ava'lei. That is fine. Thank you." In the great hall, she eats alone, wishing her husband was there beside her. She returns to their quarters and finds herself looking through the gowns in the closet while she waits for him. She finds a short, ruffled dress, flirtier than she would usually wear. For fun, she slips it on. She blushes at her reflection in the mirror, smiling as she admires herself.

"You are truly beautiful."

She looks up, losing her smile. "Da'vae. Do you need something?"

He swims to her and looks her over. "I am surprised my brother chose someone like you."

"What do you mean?" she asks, trying to buy time.

"You look more like a siren than a mermaid," he says, gripping her by the neck. "You must make him very happy, to choose you."

"Please, let me go."

His grip tightens. He leans down, his lips caressing her cheek. "You and I should be on the throne. What do you think?" She claws his face, and he slams her against the door. "You'll pay for that!" he snarls, swimming off.

She looks at her hand in shock. *Maybe he's right, maybe I am more siren than mermaid. Why would Dankin choose me?* She quickly removes the dress and changes into a nightgown. She looks at the empty bed. *I can't sleep here alone. I just can't.*

* * *

"No!" she screams, sitting up and clutching the blanket.

"Sera, what's wrong?"

Dankin turns on the light. She realizes she's back in their quarters. She holds her face in her hand. "Nightmare," she murmurs.

"Why were you in the other room?"

"I told you."

"I'm sorry, I promised you some time tonight."

"It's okay," she assures him. "You have a lot going on."

"You are my wife, and you should be a priority. Get more sleep, and we'll do something special soon."

"Really?"

He kisses her forehead. "Really."

He turns the lights back off as she lies down, closing her eyes and losing herself in his arms.

* * *

She's surprised when she wakes up in bed with him.

"You're still here?"

He chuckles. "I am." He leans over her, kissing her as his hands explore down her neck. He opens her nightgown, continuing lower.

"Dankin—"

He pulls back. "What's wrong?"

She sits up, sighing. "I'm not ready."

"I am sorry if I rushed you."

"It's not that."

"Will you tell me?"

She looks at him, nodding. He sits beside her. "It's… it's a human experience I haven't had yet."

"I see. That's what you want?"

"When I'm ready, yes."

"Okay."

"Really?"

"Yes, really."

"Thank you."

He kisses her softly, smiling as her hand climbs under his shirt and onto his chest. "I am recovered from my wounds, thanks to you."

"I don't know what I would've done, had I lost you. I can't think of it. It's too painful for me." She starts to pull her hand away, when he takes it in his.

"Sera, why is there a bruise on your neck?" He leans over for a closer look.

"It's nothing—" she says as she pulls away.

"Is this why you had a nightmare? What happened?"

She thinks of Dankin and Da'vae laughing in the hall, fighting beside each other against the sirens, keeping watch over the kingdom together. "No, I—" She sighs, looking down at her clasped hands. "I must have done it to myself, in my sleep."

He takes her hands. "Really?"

She swallows hard, meeting his gaze. "Yes. Can we eat now?"

"Let's get dressed, first."

She changes in private, looking herself over to make sure there are no other signs of the previous night. Once she's dressed, Dankin takes her hand, and they swim to the great hall together. She looks up when Da'vae joins them.

"Morning, brother."

Dankin chuckles. "Back at you. How did you sleep?"

"Better, knowing we should have what we want, soon enough." He shoots Sera a smile. She immediately drops her head, staring at her plate. "How are you this morning, Your Grace?"

"I'm fine," she replies. She pushes her plate away and looks at Dankin. "I'm going to the library."

"Sera—" He watches her swim off.

"Our plan wasn't a total failure," Da'vae continues. "We have weakened them, significantly. I think we should be able to end this sooner rather than later."

"I hope so," Dankin replies, still looking in the direction Sera swam. "I'll be back."

"Brother, there are things more important than chasing tail."

Dankin turns to him. "Watch your tongue! That is my wife you are talking about."

"It was in jest, I apologize. We do have more important things to discuss this morning though. Shall we go to the briefing room?"

"Yes," he answers, his heart fighting his brain.

In the briefing room, they are greeted by Na'riti. "Morning, Your Majesty. I am glad to see you have recovered. May I ask?"

"It's part of my power," he explains as they take their seats.

"Of course. I have scouts telling me that Maren has a secondary location set up further west," she continues. "I think we should go there as soon as possible."

Dankin looks at Da'vae, who nods. "Yes, I agree. I'll join you. We'll take a small group with us, so we can attempt to sneak in. Da'vae, stay here and oversee things while I am gone."

"Of course, brother."

"Thank you." He nods to Na'riti, following her from the room. Da'vae smiles at the thought of having some time alone to become better acquainted with the new queen.

* * *

Sera closes the book. "I believe tomorrow I will be ready to take on my role as queen."

"You have done a fine job, taking in so much information in a short time. You are a quick study," Ava'lei says with pride.

"Thanks to you two. I couldn't do this without your help. Where should we meet tomorrow?"

"We'll meet you in the library at nine," Ava'lei replies.

"Perfect, thank you." On her way back to her room, Sera sees Da'vae approaching her. Fear grips her when she realizes they are alone in the corridor. She hurries inside, but he pushes his way in behind her and shuts the door.

"Hmm. You truly are a sight to behold."

"What do you want?" she demands.

He laughs. "You still haven't figured it out?"

Her eyes go wide. "Please, don't—" she looks around the room for a way to escape.

"Save it. I knew my brother was smart, but I had no idea he could be this… diabolical."

She freezes at his words. "What are you talking about?" she asks, raising her head to meet his gaze.

"He told me everything before leaving for his scouting trip." He smiles at the fear in her eyes. "Oh, yes. He will be gone a few days. Now, Sera Dahvaene, tell me, did you aid your father when he was hunting sirens? Or did he usually work alone?"

She propels backward, trying to create space. "I don't know what you're talking about."

"Save it. Dankin told me how lucky he was while trying to find a willing bride to save the kingdom, that you would appear right before him. Thank the goddess for small favors. As soon as they told him who you were, he set everything into motion. He took you from your father and forced you here. He made you believe he could actually love you."

"Everything you are saying is a lie. He does love me!"

Da'vae laughs, approaching her. "Wow, he really did a good job. You almost had me convinced. If he had not told me all about this himself, I wouldn't believe it, either. Now that he's away, I am excited to have this time with you."

Looking around again for a means to escape, her desperation creeps in. She raises her hands. "Please, don't hurt—" Her words die in her throat as he grabs her. She closes her eyes and prays for help.

Chapter 12

and Loss

"Your Grace?" Ava'lei knocks. "Are you okay? It's almost ten."

Fai'mi shakes her head. "No one has seen her this morning. What do we do?"

"Get a guard. Something is wrong."

Fai'mi swims down the hall, grateful to see a guard on patrol. "Do you have keys to the royal quarters?" she inquires.

"I do," he answers.

"Follow me," she commands.

He hesitates, then follows her, stopping outside the door. "This is above my grade!"

"Something is wrong with the queen. Open it!" Ava'lei demands.

Sighing, he pulls out his keys. "It's your head, not mine," he snaps as he unlocks the door. Once it's open, they all rush in then freeze at the sight of Sera on the floor.

"Your Grace!" Ava'lei cries, swimming to her. She kneels beside her, gently pulling her up. Her face is covered in bruises. There is blood on her arm and gown.

They rush her to the infirmary, where the doctor gestures them to an examination table. Ava'lei lays her down. The doctor removes her gown. Fai'mi gasps at the sight of the bruises covering her torso, arms, and tail, and one of her gills is nearly ripped open. She turns away in shock.

"What happened to her?" the doctor demands.

"We don't know. We found her like this, after she didn't show up for her lessons this morning," Fai'mi explains.

"I'll take care of her." The doctor takes her vitals. "That's strange."

"What?" Ava'lei asks.

"Her heart… it beats like a human, not like ours." She shakes her head in confusion then begins to clean her wounds. Stitching her gill and wrapping her in bandages, she checks her vitals from time to time. As she works, a guard swims in.

"Has she said what happened?" he asks.

"No, she is still—"

"Hmm," Sera moans, clenching the blanket in pain. "Where am I?"

"You're okay. You're in the infirmary. Who did this to you?" the doctor asks.

"Da'vae," she answers.

"Your Grace, are you sure?" Ava'lei asks.

"Yes."

The doctor looks at the guard, waiting for him to go. "You heard her, arrest him!"

"My apologies, but he is the Crown Prince and acting as ruler in Dankin's absence. I simply cannot—"

"She is our queen, and it is your job to protect her above all others. Arrest him."

"Yes, ma'am." He quickly leaves.

"How bad is it?" Sera asks.

"You'll be fine. A few contusions, and we'll watch your gill. I had to stitch it into place, so take it easy. No sudden movements. I'm Ish'a, by the way."

"Thank you."

"For now, you need to rest."

"Okay," she says as loses consciousness.

* * *

Sera opens her eyes, gasping in pain as she sits up and attempts to get comfortable. Ava'lei and Fai'mi swim to her side, and she does her best to give them a smile.

"You've been here this whole time?" she asks.

"Yes, Your Grace. We would not leave you so," Fai'mi assures her.

"Thank you for that, and thank you for saving me." She groans as she adjusts her tail. "What time is it?

Fai'mi and Ava'lei exchange glances, wanting to ask her more about what happened. "You slept most of the day," Ava'lei says, "but the doctor said that is normal while you are recovering. How do you feel?"

"Everything hurts. I think even my tail is bruised."

"Why did he—" Fai'mi backs up. "Apologies."

"No, it's okay. I don't really want to talk about it. At least it's not… at least he didn't—" She clutches the blanket in her hands. "At least it's not worse," she manages. She takes a breath. "I meant to ask, you two look alike. Are you sisters?" she asks, wanting to change the subject.

"We are cousins. I apologize for calling her cos in front of you the other day. It is not formal," Ava'lei explains.

"It's quite all right. I think it's wonderful that you get to work together."

"We enjoy it, Your Grace. Do you have any family?" Fai'mi asks.

"A mother and brother, back on the island. I don't know when or if I'll get to see them again."

"Wait, the rumors were true?" Ava'lei asks, glancing over at Fai'mi.

"What rumors?" Sera asks, confused.

"Apologies, but we had heard that you were a land-dweller turned mermaid," Fai'mi clarifies.

Sera laughs. "Yes, that's the truth." They talk over each other, asking questions about her life on land, where she's from. "One at a time!" She groans in pain when she laughs again. "I'm okay," she says in response to the concern on their faces. "Still tender, is all."

They look up when a nurse swims in with a plate in his hand. "Your Grace, can you eat?"

"Yes," she answers. "What happened to Da'vae?"

"He has been arrested and locked up. Once the king returns, he will decide his fate." The nurse explains, growing concerned when Sera nearly drops her plate. "Are you all right?"

"I'm a little weak."

Fai'mi takes the plate. "I'll help her."

The nurse bows and swims out. Fai'mi sits on the edge of the bed, holding the plate while Sera eats. "Thank you," Sera says.

When she is finished, Fai'mi puts the plate on the bedside table. "Rest now, Your Grace. We will send His Majesty to you as soon as he returns."

"Of course," she says, her smile unable to conceal the fear in her eyes. *That's what I'm afraid of. What if Da'vae was telling the truth, that Dankin never loved me? What will Dankin do with me? Oh, please help me heal so I can escape before he gets back!* She pictures him returning and choosing to free his brother from the dungeon instead of protecting her. Her body shudders at the thought.

"Your Grace, are you cold?" Ava'lei asks.

"Yes," she answers. Ava'lei brings over another blanket, covering Sera. "Thank you." She falls into a restless sleep.

* * *

Sera's eating breakfast when a nurse approaches her. "Your Grace, how are you feeling this morning?" he asks.

"I'm getting better, thank you."

"His Majesty has returned. He is down in the dungeon as we speak and should be up here shortly."

"I'm glad," she says, giving the nurse a smile. He bows and swims out. She turns to Fai'mi. "Would you go to my room and get me a gown?"

"Yes, Your Grace."

After she's been gone a few minutes, Sera looks at Ava'lei. "Oh, I forgot to ask for a crown, as well. Would you?"

"Of course, Your Grace."

She watches her leave then waits a few more minutes before sitting up, groaning in pain. Her hand trails gingerly over her ribs. She sees one of the nurse's tops on the table and slips it on, making it to the door before nearly collapsing in pain. She grips the doorway to keep herself up.

Leaving the infirmary, she looks out and sees the hall is clear on both sides. She makes her way to the parlor. *I'll hide in there and rest a little longer. Then I can—*

"Sera! Where do you think you're going?"

Her breath hitches in her throat as she looks back and sees Dankin swimming to her. She brings her hands up to protect herself. "Please, don't!" Sera begs.

He stops swimming, looking at her in concern. "Sera, what's wrong?" He sees her trembling as he reaches for her.

"Please," she begs again, "don't hurt me!"

"Why are you afraid of me? Sera, let me help you."

"He told me why you chose me. He said that you could finally have revenge!"

"Da'vae did? He lied to you, Sera. I swear on my very throne, I did not know who you were until your mother told me. Please, believe that, believe that I love you. I am not with you for revenge, nor do I want to hurt you."

She looks over as her handmaids approach. "Girls, please help me to my room. I need to lay down."

"Stop!" he commands them, turning back to Sera. "You will let me heal you, and we will talk."

"No."

"Sera—"

"I can't deal with you. I can't! I... I need to be alone right now."

"You need to heal!" He swims to her, holding her tightly as she struggles in his arms. He sinks to the floor, holding her in his lap as he uses his magic to heal her. "Sleep," he commands, caressing her face as her eyes roll back in her head.

Ava'lei swims forward. "Your Majesty, how can we help?"

"For now, I'll get her back to our room so she can sleep. Will one of you tell the doctor what has happened?"

"Yes, Your Majesty," Fai'mi answers, before swimming for the infirmary.

He carries Sera to their room, taking her inside and getting her into bed. He turns to Ava'lei. "She will sleep while her body is reacting to the magic. Please, stay in the hall in case we need you." He doesn't want to admit that he also needs to rest, after healing Sera.

"Of course, Your Majesty." She puts the dress and crown on the table, lingering a moment.

"Ava'lei?"

"I apologize if this is out of turn, but I feel you should know. She had a nightmare last night. She murmured mostly, but we could make out when she begged him not to hurt her, and she asked how could be so cruel, to exact revenge on her. She insisted she had done nothing to him. I don't know if that means anything, but I felt you should know."

"I see. Thank you for your care and for telling me."

"Yes, Your Majesty." She goes into the hall, closing the door behind her.

Dankin sits beside Sera on the bed and looks her over. Thinking of the bruises on her, his anger rises. He pushes it back, knowing she is healed now and will be all right. He lies beside her to rest, until he is summoned to the dungeon by his advisor.

He retrieves Ava'lei and Fai'mi from the hall. "Will you stay with her until I return?"

"We will, Your Majesty," Fai'mi assures him.

He hurries off, not wanting to be away from Sera for long. In the dungeon, he finds his advisor by his brother's cell. "Ma'like, what is going on?"

"Your brother is demanding to speak to you."

He swims closer, observing Da'vae through the bars. "What do you want?"

"Why am I still locked up?"

"Because you admitted to me you hurt the queen! How dare you—"

"I only did what you wanted."

"What are you talking about?"

"The day after your daughter's service, we sat in the parlor and talked. You said you would have your revenge, that you hoped he had a daughter so you could hurt him the same way he hurt you."

Dankin gasps. "That was ages ago. I was angry and bitter then, still in my grief from losing my wife and the loss of my other daughter. I was grieving for the three of them that day. Da'vae, I did not even know who Sera was when I met her." His hands clench in anger. "You will be banished—"

"Brother, don't. I misunderstood. I thought I was acting out your wishes. There must be something I can do to redeem myself?"

Dankin looks at Ma'like. "Our scouting mission was a failure. Do you have other news?"

"Unfortunately, yes. The sirens have moved into the abandoned kingdom to the west. They are better protected now."

Dankin looks at his brother. "Bring me Maren, alive, and you will be redeemed."

"Seriously? You ask me to do the impossible?"

"Or be banished. That is your choice. You brought this upon yourself."

"Fine! When will I leave?"

"Let me make the preparations."

"Then release me—"

"Oh, no. You are staying right here until your departure." Dankin leaves the dungeon and returns to his quarters. He opens the door to an argument.

"Your Grace, please. He will be back to speak to you any moment. I assure you, he healed you and is worried about you," Fai'mi tries.

"He doesn't care about me!" Sera cries out in exasperation.

"Yes, I most certainly do."

Sera stops. Looking at Dankin, she hangs her head at the sight of him. "Please, leave us," she commands her handmaids. Once they are gone, she swims towards him. "They told me you healed me and stayed by my side. Why would you do that?"

"Because I love you."

"Your brother knew so much—"

He sighs. "Because I'm an idiot who ran my mouth." He sees the confusion on her face. "Will you come sit with me?" he asks, swimming over and sitting on the bed.

She sits on the edge, leaving space between them. "What do you mean?"

He tells her of his grief, his anger, what he said to Da'vae in the parlor. "It was so long ago, and I was so consumed by grief, I didn't even remember saying such things. I am truly sorry, and I swear to you that I never meant for this to happen. I love you."

"I want to believe that," she replies softly. "I need to believe it, but I can't. I'm sorry."

"Will you tell me what he did?"

"He said it was your idea from the beginning, to use me to free you from the curse while exacting your revenge. He said you never loved me, that breaking my heart was part of your plan before you… before you killed me. He said he would do it himself, but he was saving that for you. He… he beat me all over, saying your daughter would be avenged. I passed out."

"I don't know what to do. How can I convince you he was lying?"

"You can't," she whispers, wrapping her arms around herself.

"Will you stay here?" he pleads.

"Where else would I go?"

"I mean here, in our quarters? Stay with me and let me prove myself?"

"I'm not sure. If you're telling the truth, you shouldn't have to. I'm sorry for that."

"I would rather spend every day proving my love to you than to lose you to your grief and heartache."

"What does that mean?"

"When you're hurting, you turn inward. Your body and mouth respond, but it's not really you. I don't want you to change like that because of me. Let me help you, please?"

"Because you've already changed me enough?" Sera asks.

He sighs. "That was low, but I deserve it." He brings his hand up to her face, growing concerned when she flinches. He caresses her jawline before bringing his hand back down. "Sera, please, I will never hurt you."

She turns away. "I need you to go."

"But—"

"Please? While I think things over."

"You promise you won't leave the palace?"

"I promise. I just… I need time."

"All right. Send for me if you need me. I want to help you."

"Wait," she says quietly when he swims past.

Hope in his eyes, he looks at her. "Yes?"

"What will happen to your brother?"

"He said he was sorry and asked to be redeemed. I told him he could if he brings me Maren, alive. Then he will be forgiven."

"That's impossible," she mutters.

"Now you see."

"But the risk—"

"It's either that or banish him, which would also be a death sentence with the sirens out there."

"Dankin, please, keep him imprisoned here. I don't want him hurt."

"Why do you care so much?"

"Because I don't want you to hate me if something happens to him."

"Sera, whatever happens to him from this day forward is his own fault, after what he did to you. Please, believe that."

"Thank you. You may go."

His mouth opens as he starts to argue, appalled that she would dare to command the king. Then he realizes she has every right, what she has suffered because of him. He leaves the room, angry over all that has happened.

"How is she?" Fai'mi asks.

"She's okay but continue to remain out here in case she needs you."

"Yes, Your Majesty."

"Thank you. Send for me if you need me."

Sera listens at the door, grateful that he is gone. She swims around the room, restless and anxious for something to distract her. *I feel like a prisoner in here.* Frustrated, she decides to dress and pin on a crown, then swims out the door. Her handmaids are surprised to see her.

"Can we see the galley now?" Sera asks.

"Of course, Your Grace," Fai'mi answers.

The three of them swim to the massive kitchen. "Obviously, being underwater we do not cook food like they do on land. I've never had cooked food. Is it good?"

Sera lets out a quiet laugh. "It can be. There is a lot of variety."

"Oh, I bet!" gushes Ava'lei. "This table is where the fish is prepared, over there are crustaceans and mollusks, then that table is where they do fruits or flowers, when we have them. We used to trade for them but haven't because of the war."

"What do you mean, flowers?" Sera asks.

"There are water flowers we eat. They are very sweet and are eaten at the end of the meal. I hope you can try one soon," Fai'mi says with a smile.

"It sounds… interesting."

"Part of your duty as queen is to oversee the kitchen, inspecting everything to make sure they are only using fresh ingredients and to address any issues," explains Ava'lei. "Would you like to see your office?"

"Wait, what? I have an office?"

Ava'lei laughs. "Yes, Your Grace."

They take her down the corridor and swim up to the next level. Ava'lei opens the door, gesturing Sera in. She swims around, surprised by the size of her office. "It's huge!"

"Do you like it?" Fai'mi asks.

"I do," she replies, admiring the marble columns and glass mosaic desk. "Oh, it's very beautiful," she says.

"This is where you will write orders for supplies, correspondences with other kingdoms, and meet with your people to resolve issues or anything else that is needed."

"Thank you, Fai'mi. Is it a busy post?"

"It can be."

"I'll start tomorrow, after breakfast. Will you make sure I have everything I need to begin?" She smiles when her handmaids nod. "Thank you. I'm going for supper. You are both dismissed."

"Um, Your Grace, I apologize, but His Majesty instructed us to stay with you," Fai'mi says timidly.

Sera waves her hand. "I'm just going into the great hall. I'll be fine, I insist."

Shaking her head, she swims into the hall. Sitting at their table, she looks over when Dankin approaches.

"May I sit with you?"

"Yes, that's fine."

He sits beside her, reaching for her hand when she pulls back. "Sera—"

"I still need time. Please?"

"Of course. Did you have a good afternoon?" he asks.

"I did. My handmaids showed me the galley and my office."

"Speaking of which, where are they?"

"I dismissed them. I know you commanded them to stay with me, but I was coming here and needed a break."

"All right. Will you let me escort you back after we eat?"

She studies the plate set before her. "About that—"

"What?"

"Just for tonight, I would like to sleep in my quarters."

"I see," he says, his voice rife with anger.

Shaking her head, she bites back her tears. "Please, don't get angry. I just need some space." She cries out when Dankin grips her arm. "Please, don't hurt me!" she begs.

"I told you I never will, Sera. Now, we cannot make a scene like this in here." A few merpeople sitting nearby glance over at them. Dankin's grip tightens as he leads her into the hall.

Once they are alone, Sera begins to cry. "All I asked for was one night, after what I just suffered, and it infuriated you. You couldn't even give me one night?"

"I was angry at myself for what happened to you. My brother did what he thought I wanted. I am not at all excusing Da'vae, but I want you to understand why I blame myself."

"It's not your fault," she whispers, looking away from him. "My father killed your daughter. It's what I deserve."

"Your father spent the rest of his life bedridden and in pain. He paid for his sins. You don't deserve what happened to you. I said those things in my anger, but I could never truly wish that on anyone. What can I do?"

"I don't know," she answers as she buries her face in his shirt. "I'm scared, and I can't get warm." She clings to him.

"Come," he says, swimming up. "I'll take care of that."

"It's too dangerous!"

"We'll be all right."

He carries her in his arms, swimming from the palace. Once at the grotto, he helps her in before joining her. She sighs and rests her head on his chest, soothed by the warm water.

"Thank you."

"I told you, Sera, whatever you need. I love you, my little sea nymph, and I want nothing more than to prove that to you."

"You risked yourself to bring me here?"

"I risked us both," he admits. "I thought it worth the risk, the way you are feeling." He wraps her tightly in his arms. "I love you."

"Thank you." She looks up at him, biting her lip as she caresses his face. He's surprised when she leans up and kisses him, her hand in his hair. His lips devour hers as she grips him tighter. "I love you, too."

"Sera, is this what you want?" he asks, turning human. She smiles at him as he turns her human, too.

"Yes," she responds, climbing up and kissing him fiercely. His hand trails down her back. She gasps softly when he pulls her to him. "I'm ready, koy'lei."

* * *

Lying on the beach, their tails resting on the warm sand, he smiles at her. "Why do you like laying on the beach in this form?"

Blushing, she returns the smile. "I like how it makes my tail feel."

"I do, too," he admits as he leans over her and kisses her. "Do you feel better now? About everything?"

Her cheeks flush redder as she bites her lip. "Any doubts I had about your love for me are gone."

"I'm happy to hear that. I never want you to doubt me or my love. I mean that."

She sighs. "We have to go back now, don't we?"

"Yes, but we will come here again soon, I promise."

"This is our special place? Just you and me?"

"Yes, my little sea nymph. It really is." He scoops her up, and she laughs as he dives into the water.

* * *

At the palace, Dankin carries her into their room and requests food be brought in for them. "We need to eat, since we worked up an appetite," he says, smiling at her.

She bites her lip as her fingers trail down his arm. "You were quite hungry…"

His face grows red in surprise. "How bold, Miss Sera."

"Because of you." She sighs as she thinks of resuming their duties. "I am ready for tomorrow, ready for whatever comes." A staff member knocks and brings their plates in. Dankin watches Sera devour her food and starts to laugh. Blushing, she joins his laughter. "What? I was hungry!"

He nuzzles his lips into her ear. "Hmm, I know what I'm hungry for."

"Dankin! I need to rest after all we did on our island."

"Me, too."

They finish their meal, then she changes into a white nightgown. "It's still so strange to me," she says, looking down at her tail and chuckling. "I catch myself sometimes, thinking I'm going to walk somewhere and then I remember. I guess it takes a while to get used to."

"I can imagine. I fell out of bed a time or two."

"What?"

"Well, I'm used to waking up and just rolling out of bed to start swimming. Can't do that on land, can I?"

She gasps, laughing. "Oh, I hadn't even thought of that! I'm sorry, I don't mean to laugh."

"It's all right," he says as he laughs with her. "It is pretty funny."

She floats in front of the mirror, running her hand over her tail. Dankin swims to her. "My hand running over it feels… weird. I can feel the soft pressure of my fingers, but not really feel the hand itself."

He kneels before her, bringing his hand up to softly stroke the length of her tail. "How does that feel?"

Her head rolls back. "Hmm," she moans, as her heart swells at his touch. He swims up and kisses her as he carries her to bed.

* * *

Sera wakes up, groaning when she realizes she's alone. Sitting up, she stretches and swims to the closet. Changing into a lavender and white gown, she goes to his side of the closet, looking through his shirts and crowns. She smiles at them before swimming to the great hall, seeing Dankin at their table.

"Are you all right?" he asks, taking her hand when she sits beside him.

"Why do I keep waking up alone?"

"Oh, I have a lot of things to tend to first thing…"

"Dankin, please, tell me the truth."

Looking down, he runs his fingers over her hand. "I don't want to be the one to wake up second."

"I don't understand?" she responds, as their plates are put in front of them.

"It would scare me to wake up alone, not knowing where you were. So, I make sure I'm up before you." He raises his head and looks at her. "I've woken up alone enough."

Her eyes go wide, pity on her face. "I am sorry. I didn't think of that. It's okay, I don't mind—"

"No, I shouldn't do that to you. You won't wake up alone again."

"Dankin, I know you are adjusting, too. It's okay." She finishes her meal. "I'll be in my office if you need me."

"I'll be in the briefing room. Can I kiss you in here?"

"Yes," she answers, leaning up to kiss him. "I love you."

"Sera, I love you, too."

She swims to her office with the biggest smile on her face. Her handmaids are waiting for her. "Everything okay?" she asks.

"Yes, Your Grace."

"Where do I begin?" she asks, sitting at her desk.

Her handmaids get out stacks of forms, going over necessities for the palace. The morning passes by as Sera responds to letters from other kingdoms, fills out requisition forms, and goes over supplies. At lunchtime, Ava'lei swims out to request food be brought in as Sera swims to one of the shelves that line the walls of her office.

She picks up a small portrait of three mermaids sitting on a rock with a fourth mermaid in the water beside them. Her eyes are drawn to the mermaid with strawberry blonde hair and a shiny green tail. She studies it closer, looking at the two blonde mermaids and one with silver-white hair. She looks up as Fai'mi approaches.

"Lunch is here, Your Grace."

"Thank you. I'll be just a moment."

"Of course."

"Wait, who is this?" Sera asks, handing her the painting.

Fai'mi looks it over. "This is His Majesty's first wife and three daughters."

Sera's heart skips a beat. "What were their names?"

"His daughters were Son'jia, the one with the blue tail, El'ena, who has the red tail, and Mei'ra, who also has a blue tail but platinum hair. "

"And his wife?"

She thinks a moment. "Oh, Ko'era."

"Ko'era?" she repeats, thinking back. *Ko'era? What does that mean? It means wife.* Angry, she shakes her head and places the portrait back on the shelf. "I'm sorry, I have to go I…" She swims to the door. "I left something in my room. I'll be back shortly."

In the hallway, she sees Dankin, who is escorting Da'vae in bindings. Da'vae tries lunging for her, but Dankin tightens his grip on the bindings.

"You! This is your fault!" Da'vae spits at her.

"What did I do?" she asks.

"Everything I did was for my brother, for my niece! Who are you to have claim to the throne? You're nobody!"

"Da'vae, if you want a chance at freedom, a chance to redeem yourself, you will stop this right now," Dankin warns him.

"No, let him speak. He thinks I married you to become a queen? That I long for treasure and acclaim?" She glares at Dankin, thinking of the portrait. "You're both liars. You deserve each other," she hisses, swimming away.

"What did you do to her?" Da'vae asks, laughing.

"Shut up."

"Oh, you don't even know?"

Dankin slams him against the wall. "I could leave you in a cell to rot or toss you out in these bindings. If you want a chance, you will stop this."

"Brother, you are too worked up. Now, where are you taking me?"

"The armory. We're going to get you ready. You leave tomorrow night."

"Why not tonight?"

"Bad storm on the horizon. I'm trying to at least give you a chance."

"You've always been too cautious. Get me ready, and I'll go tonight."

"If it was just you, I gladly would, but a few of my soldiers will be escorting you. It's an important task. I have to be sure you don't simply slip away."

"Let us go tonight. I'll use the storm to my advantage. I want to get this over with."

"Fine."

They go to the armory, getting everything he needs ready. Dankin returns him to the dungeon. "I'll come back for you at six."

"Can't wait," he jokes, flashing him a smile.

Dankin shakes his head as he goes to Sera's office. He looks concerned that it's empty. "We don't know where she went," Fai'mi admits, as she and Ava'lei swim to him. "She said she needed to get something from her room, but she never came back."

Dankin sighs. "All right, I will find her. What did she get done today?"

"She filled out the requisitions."

"Wait, all of them?"

"She's very efficient." Ava'lei smiles.

He swims to the desk and looks through the papers. "She did them all correctly. Very good." He looks up. "You are dismissed. We will call for you tomorrow."

"Yes, Your Majesty," they say with a bow before leaving the office.

Dankin goes to her quarters when he doesn't find her in their room. He lets himself in, seeing she is sitting on the bed. "Sera, why are you in here?" he asks as he's swimming to her. "What's wrong?"

"Oh, now you know my name."

"What are you—"

"Ko'era doesn't mean wife, does it?"

"No," he admits.

"That was your wife's name?" she asks, her jaw clenched.

"Yes. I'm sorry. We had just been talking about her clothes. I was looking through them and… it was a slip of the tongue. I still grieve for her, and I will not apologize for that."

"I'm not asking you to apologize for your grief. I'm upset because you lied to me. If you had admitted it that night and talked to me about it, I would understand. Instead, you lied and hid things from me. Sometimes I feel like you see me as her replacement."

"You could never replace her." Regret washes over him as she turns away, trembling on the bed as she buries her face in her pillow. "I didn't mean—"

"Go away!" she cries out. "I don't want to hear it. I have given you everything, only to find out what I truly am to you."

"Sera, what you are—"

"Is not your concern. Leave me alone."

He lays his hand on her back. "I'm not going anywhere. We are talking about this."

"There's nothing to talk about. I was right, wasn't I? You used me. You couldn't possibly love me when you had someone like her. I see now what I really am to you."

"You know how much you mean to me. I didn't use you—" she looks at him, anger flashing in her eyes. "I didn't intend to use you. I love you, and—"

"I hate you," she says softly, turning away.

"Give me a chance!" he demands.

She looks at him. "You mean another chance? How many have I already given you? You forced me from my home, turned me into this, your brother nearly killed me, then you wouldn't give me space as I was recovering. I have no chances left to give!" She slumps back onto the pillow. "I can't do this with you anymore. My heart can't take it. Please, leave me be."

"I promised you I would never leave you."

"And you're so great about keeping your promises, right? Just like you kept your promise to protect Ko'era from—" Seeing the hurt on his face, she instantly regrets her words. She sits up and reaches for his hand. "Dankin, please, I am so sorry. I shouldn't have said—"

He pulls away. "No, you're right. I failed my family and failed you. I can't set you free, but I won't bother you anymore."

"Dankin, wait—" She watches him swim from the room. She lies down, then buries her face in her hands and cries herself to sleep.

* * *

The next morning, Sera wakes up and knocks on Dankin's door, disappointed when there is no response. She goes to the great hall, hoping to find him there, and ends up eating by herself. Ignoring the looks from the other merpeople, she quickly eats. Ava'lei and Fai'mi meet her in her office after breakfast.

"Your Grace," Ava'lei says quietly.

"Is everything okay?" Sera asks.

They look at each other before Fai'mi turns to her. "I apologize that you haven't heard."

"What?"

"Da'vae and two soldiers were killed last night when they pursued Maren. His Majesty is in the parlor, and—"

Sera swims to the door. "Stay here!" she commands before swimming to the parlor. Slowly, she goes inside to find Dankin sitting on the sofa, his face in his hands. "Dankin?"

He raises his head, anger raging on his face. "You!"

She backs away as he rises up. "What—"

"Everything is your fault! He never would've been out there if I hadn't been trying to keep you safe. I lost my brother because of you!"

"Please," she tries, reaching for him.

"Guard!" He calls out.

Sera looks up in fear when a guard swims in. "Yes, Your Majesty?" she inquires.

"The queen is under house arrest, confined to her quarters until the command is lifted."

Sera looks at him as the guard grips her arm. "Dankin, please—"

"Now!"

The guard escorts her out and takes her to her quarters. "Your meals will be delivered to you. Two guards will be outside. Do not think of attempting to leave." She swims out, shutting the door behind her.

Sera sits on the bed. *He's just angry. I'll give him a day or two, then we'll talk. I can't blame him for this, as he's already lost so much.* Her heart sinks as she realizes it may be more serious than that. *Please, don't let me lose him. I've lost so much, too.*

Chapter 13

The Painful Truth

After four days locked in solitude, Sera decides she has had enough. She opens the door and darts past the guards, swimming as fast as she can. They chase after her, yelling for her to halt. She finds Dankin leaving the briefing room and is surprised to see his hair cut short.

She swims up to him. "Please, talk to me—"

"What are you doing out?" he demands.

"I escaped. I will not be a prisoner in my own home!"

He laughs. "This will never be your home." They look up as the two guards approach. He waves them away.

"Dankin, please—"

"Fine. Your house arrested is lifted, if you promise not to speak to me again!" He turns away from her.

She recoils at the anger on his face, in his voice. "I'm sorry. I'm so sorry for everything. I love you, you know. I thought you were the best thing that ever happened to me. Even coming here. I know I was angry in the beginning while I was trying to adjust. I love you, despite all we have been through, only for you to break my heart. I have done nothing to deserve your wrath!"

"My brother is dead."

"So is my father!"

He spins back to face her. "He murdered my daughter. I hope he rots!"

Sera stops, her heart racing as her hands clench. "Now I see the real you, see the truth. You never loved me, did you? I was a means to an end for you, nothing else. Well, you are free of your curse, so why am I still here?" she demands.

He laughs. "You know, I was tempted to return you to the mistress. I wondered what her reaction would be."

She gasps. "How can you be so cruel? Your brother wasn't lying to me, was he? You made me fall in love with you just so you could break my heart. He told me you would. I gave you my heart, gave you my love, gave you everything!"

Dankin leans down, his face inches from hers. "He was telling the truth. Now my daughter has been avenged."

"No!" Sera's hand flies to her mouth as her anger boils over. "I hate you!" she cries out. She rushes from the palace as fast and hard as she can, not caring where she is going. Glancing behind, she sees no one is pursuing her. Once she's certain, she floats down to rest on a rock.

"Hmm, what is Her Grace doing out here all by herself?"

She looks up as a siren approaches. "What do you want?"

"We want our revenge! I would kill you myself, but Maren would love to meet you."

Sera turns to swim away, only to run into another siren, who grabs her arms. "Let's take you to our queen!"

"Please, let me go. I beseech you."

They laugh. "Oh, so proper and polite. Maren is going to love you."

They are near the palace when Sera squirms and writhes, managing to break free of the siren's grip. She's swimming towards the palace when she's grabbed.

"I don't think so!" the siren calls out, pulling her to the ocean floor. She removes her gown, placing her claws over her chest. "Try that again, and I will end you. Do you understand?"

"Go eat a sea cucumber."

The siren's eyes go wide, before she and the other siren roll with laughter. "Oh, that is too funny!" She binds Sera's wrists behind her, then buries her face in the sand, the siren kneeling on her back and pressing her body down. Sera's gills fill with sand. Unable to breathe, she gasps and chokes. The siren's claws dig into her neck as she pushes harder, then she yelps in surprise when she's suddenly pulled off.

Sera tries to get up but is too buried to move. She cries out when Dankin lifts her out of the sand. She watches the sirens dissolve into sea foam while Dankin lowers her down.

"Are you all right?" he asks when he realizes she is trembling.

"What do you care?" she retorts, refusing to look at him.

"Good, you're fine. Let's go back."

"Would you at least remove my bindings?" Sera asks.

"Why? I like this look." He smirks at her when she shoots him an angry look. "Besides, I'm still waiting for my thank you."

She scoffs. "For what? It's your fault I was out here."

Shaking his head, he pulls out his knife. She backs away with fear in her eyes. "Sera, I am not going to hurt you," he assures her with a calm voice.

"You can't any worse than you already have."

He swims to her and cuts the bindings off. "We need to talk."

"Really? Because I have nothing else to say to you." She looks up at him. "Except, I am sorry about your brother. I mean that, too." She sees the surprise on his face.

"Such compassion and empathy."

"Don't you dare mock me!"

"I'm not—" Dankin starts.

"Take me back to your palace," she commands.

"Sera—"

"Now!" She picks up her gown and slips it on. She swims ahead of him. Once back at the palace, she heads for the library when he grabs her arm.

"I mean it, Sera. We need to talk."

"Your Majesty!" A guard calls out, rushing over. "A scout has just returned with news about the sirens."

He releases Sera's arm. "We'll talk later."

"Can't wait," she says, her words laced with sarcasm.

As soon as he is gone, she goes to the library and has food brought in. She tries to study their history, fighting back the tears and unable to focus.

* * *

Sera avoids him, spending twelve to fourteen hours a day in her office as he focuses on the war. One night, she's leaving her office when she sees him in the hall. She turns to go back inside when he notices her.

"Sera—"

Groaning softly, she faces him. "What?"

"How have you been?"

"Don't pretend you care," she scoffs. "What do you want?"

"We need to talk—"

"There is nothing to talk about. I am keeping my promise, fulfilling my oath to you as queen. After what you said," her voice hitches, "and after how you've treated me, it's more than you deserve. I have nothing else to say to you."

"Please—"

"Leave me alone!" she screams at him then rushes to her quarters. She sobs at what her life has become, full of bitter emptiness and heartache. She hopes the next day will be better.

* * *

Sera is eating breakfast at her desk and filling out reports when Ava'lei approaches her.

"Your Grace?"

"What do you need?"

"There is a situation that requires your attention."

"All right." She follows her out and looks up when Fai'mi joins them. She swims behind them and into the heart of the palace. "Where are we?"

"We are approaching the dungeon."

Sera stops swimming. "Why?"

"Please," Ava'lei gestures.

They continue down. The guard opens the door, locking it behind once they go through. Sera's heart is in her stomach as they go further in before arriving at a cell.

"This is a siren, one of Maren's. The king asked us to bring you down here and see if she will respond to you. She let herself be captured, but she will not speak to anyone. Perhaps you will have better luck."

"Why me?" Sera asks, nervous.

"You'll see," Ava'lei says, opening the door. They go inside. The siren is on a bench with chains around her wrists and tail. She looks up, hissing at them. Sera is taken back by her white skin and black hair.

She approaches, surprising everyone when she kneels before the siren. "I am Sera, and I want to help you. Will you let me?"

The siren stares at her. "If it's just the two of us, I will." Sera gestures for her handmaids to leave. They obey, reluctantly. "Very good. Now, what do you want to know?"

"Nothing."

"What?" the siren asks with a laugh.

"I mean that." Sera sits beside her, keeping her distance. "I just want to talk. I am new here, and I know very little of your war. Will you tell me about it, from your side?"

216

The siren gives pause as she considers it. "All right. Not that you'll believe me. We lived in peace with your kind for centuries. King Ak'emi, the previous king, descended upon us and declared war. He took our previous queen, Na'mika, and desecrated her. Why he didn't simply kill her, we don't know. Ever since, we have fought back to defend her honor and for our very lives. Once Ak'emi was killed in battle, King Dankin tried to implore Maren for peace, but our queen demands blood for blood, for the loss of her daughters."

"What do you mean, her daughters?"

"Besides Maren, sirens are not born as you are. Instead, we are made. We do not lure sailors to their deaths, but we bless them with our kiss and transform them into sirens. Maren considers every one of us to be her daughter."

"I'm sorry this has gone on for so long. Do you think there is any way to have peace?"

"Only with Maren's blessing."

Sera tilts her head in confusion. "What do you mean?"

"Her blessing is the only way to control us. Without it, we would have free will or be under the control of whoever she gives it to."

"I'm guessing that's not very likely," Sera sighs. "Any other ideas?"

"The sea witch."

"I beg your pardon?" Sera asks.

"Everyone says she's a myth, but she's not. She's very real. She hates mermaids and sirens alike. If anyone could broker a treaty, I think it would be her. She would require a great payment for such a service. Alas, she has no customers as the war rages on, so she would benefit from peace as well."

"Do you know where she lives?"

"Out east, there is an island with a grotto. She lives nearby, in a hut down below. That's only what I've heard, as I have never seen her myself."

"Thank you for all of this, I think it may help. What's going to happen to you?"

"I have been sentenced to death," the siren replies calmly.

"What? No!" Sera gets up. "There has been enough death already."

"You can't stop it. It's my fate to become one with the sea again. My life cycle will end, but that's okay."

Sera looks up as Dankin and a guard swim inside. "Did she tell you anything useful?" Dankin asks.

"We have to try for peace—"

He scoffs. "That ship has sailed. Now, it's time for her execution."

Sera swims up to him. "Please, don't kill her."

"You would plead her case?"

"Don't you think there has been enough death? If you want this war to stop, things have to change."

"Sera, I know your life wasn't easy, but you know nothing of what you speak. Her kind has taken everything from me. Now, let's go." He grabs Sera's arm. "I want you to see this."

The guard unchains the siren from the wall, lifting her by her tail. "Easy!" Sera cries out. "You don't have to hurt her!"

Dankin pulls Sera along as they follow behind the guard and siren. They swim out to the open water, where he lays the siren on the sea floor. The guard unsheathes his sword.

"Any last words?" Dankin asks.

The siren looks at Sera. "Please, bring peace. You're right, that there has been enough death. We are tired of it, too. I would give anything to see our kingdoms united."

"Go ahead," Dankin commands. Sera reaches for her, but Dankin grabs her arm and pulls her to him. The guard's blade runs the siren through. As her body begins to dissolve into foam, Sera buries her face in Dankin's shoulder. He grabs Sera's face and forces her to watch. "You need to see this. This is what happens, siren or merperson, when we are killed. This is what happened to my brother, to my wife, to my entire family."

"Please—" she gasps, crying out when he grips her tighter. She keeps her eyes open, watching in horror as the siren screams in agony, her body becoming one with the ocean. The silence after is deafening. Sera turns to Dankin, shoving him away and swimming to the palace as fast as she can. In her room, she locks the door and collapses on the bed, burying her face in her hands as she cries. She looks up when the door opens, and Dankin swims in.

"We need to talk."

"Please—" she implores. He swims to her and yanks her off the bed. "I need a moment!"

"No. Don't you dare embarrass me like that! Pleading for a siren? What is wrong with you? You aren't from here, you have no right—"

"Neither do you!" she screams at him, pulling away. "You killed an unarmed prisoner. You are no better than them," she declares.

His hands clench as his jaw tightens. Gripping her arms, he gets in her face. "You better watch it! Do you want to end up like her?"

"You—you would kill me?" she asks quietly, fear reflecting in her eyes.

"No! I meant—" He pulls away. "I meant that showing mercy like that would only get you killed. You really believe I would do that to you?"

"Yes," she admits. "I've seen what you are capable of. Not an ounce of mercy for her."

"Her kind have killed most of my people! They should all die!"

"You're a monster. I thought you wanted peace?"

"Can't have war if there are no enemies left."

"I can't believe what I'm hearing. I thought you wanted peace, but you are cruel. She could've stayed locked up, you could've worked with her, tried to convince her to join our side. She didn't need to die!"

"Well, you don't make that call. I do."

"I'm a prisoner here, too, like she was. At least now, she is free."

His shoulder's slump as his anger dissolves at her words. "Sera—"

"Just go. Your anger strikes me like a blade to my heart. It's too painful. I can't be around you anymore."

Without another word, he swims out. Her stomach churns as she thinks on his words. Deciding she has had enough, she swims to the door and looks out. She's grateful there are no guards. Quietly, she leaves the room, trying to remember her first tour with Ava'lei and Fai'mi. Without too much difficulty, she finds the vault and swims past the guards, who have no reason to question the queen.

She looks over the treasure, not sure what she's searching for, when she finds a box on a pedestal along the side of the room. Inside the box, she finds a massive, flawless, black pearl. A warning bell goes off in her mind, telling her to put it back. Ignoring it, she puts the pearl in her pocket and leaves the vault. She knows she has to wait, that she will need as much time as possible to slip away without being followed. Glancing at the clock in the hallway, she goes to the great hall for supper, surprised when Dankin gestures her over.

"Thank you for showing up."

Flinching at the anger in his voice, she looks at him. "Why are you so upset with me? What did I do?"

"You showed me how you really feel. Monsters? Cruel?"

"Dankin, please—"

"No, it's okay. I chose you as my queen for your kindness and compassion. I see now that was a mistake."

"If you don't love me, why am I still here?"

"Because of Maren's curse. We are bound to each other."

"Dankin—"

"We need to talk when we aren't so angry with each other. I have some things I need to tell you. Will you talk to me?"

"I have tried, but you always get so angry!"

He sighs. "Fine, whatever," he snaps.

Sera eats her meal, her resolve growing stronger with each second that passes. She tells him good night before retiring to her quarters for the evening. Knowing she has to wait, she swims in circles with the pearl weighing heavily in her pocket. At four in the morning, she goes to the window. A knock at the door startles her. She swims over and opens it, surprised to see Dankin.

"Can we talk?"

She gestures him inside, fearing he knows she stole the pearl. "What's wrong?" she asks with a lump in her throat.

"I want to apologize. I was angry at what you said about me, what you called us. I know you were upset and didn't mean it."

"I meant every word."

"What? How can you say that?"

"You said kindness and compassion are a mistake? You don't believe in showing mercy. Did you ever stop to think for a moment how different things would be if the siren who took your wife or daughter had shown compassion? If the siren who killed your brother had shown him mercy?"

"They can't even conceive of such a thing!"

"Dankin, they honestly believe they are fighting for their very lives, same as you. Is there no way to broker a truce so we can have peace with them?"

"You can't negotiate with animals."

She shakes her head. "They aren't animals any more than you are."

"Sera—"

"I spoke with her, had an intelligible conversation. They are afraid, too. They want peace! You heard her, they are sick of death and killing. She could've thrown a curse at you or said something awful. Instead, her last words were begging for peace. How can you be so deaf, so blind to what is right in front of you?"

"You haven't been here. You haven't fought in our war, haven't risked your life for our people. You haven't lost everything you love to them! You have no right to even speak of it."

"Then why did you come in here?" she demands.

"I thought we could talk, maybe see eye to eye. I wanted to try and understand how you see them the way you do, but I can't."

"Then we have nothing else to discuss."

"Sera—"

"No! I have given up everything for you, only asking for your love in return. You swore to me you loved me, swore to protect me." Her voice hitches in her throat. "Then you treat me this way? I won't have that. I may not be free, but I will not live like this." She takes a breath. "Not again," she whispers.

His eyes close at her words. "I never meant for you to feel like that."

"I feel like I'm going to be sick, dealing with all of this. I need time to myself. Please, go."

"All right," he agrees, unable to meet her gaze. "Perhaps we will speak more at breakfast."

She watches him leave, shaking her head. "That's what you think," she says before going to the window and pushing it open.

* * *

Grateful it's a clear morning, Sera goes to the surface of the water and looks at the stars to find east. She swims to the grotto as fast as she can. The first rays of morning light start to come through the water as she swims around, looking for any signs of life. She continues further east, frustrated and about to give up when she sees movement to her left. A beautiful siren swims through the water, near a small hut.

Sera approaches her. "I am sorry to trouble you. Are you the sea witch?"

The siren turns to her. "Your Grace!" She bows. "Yes, I am called Tori'uki. How may I serve you?"

Sera is taken back by her beautiful silk robe, silver-blue with white accents. Her red hair is wavy and runs the length of her back. "I wish for peace between the sirens and merpeople. Is it possible to achieve this?"

She thinks for a moment. "Not that I have seen. Maren and Dankin seem intent to destroy each other. I long for peace as well."

"Can I ask why?"

"The merpeople hide in the safety of the palace, while the sirens travel in groups. Hard for me to get good business that way," Tori'uki explains.

"I see." Sera keeps her distance as the sea witch approaches her.

"It's all right, my child. I won't hurt you." She lifts her hands to gesture peace. "I wouldn't want to invoke the wrath of your mighty king."

"I have another question to ask."

"Please, go ahead."

"Can you turn me human?"

Her curiosity piqued, she swims closer. "Human? Yes, I have the power to turn merpeople human. Is that what you want?"

"It is," Sera answers.

"And how would you pay for this magic?"

Sera removes the pearl from her pocket. "Would this be enough?"

Tori'uki's eyes widen, her hand reaching out when she stops herself. "That would suffice, I suppose. It's not much more than a bauble, but I would accept it."

Don't do this. Something is wrong, the voice in her head tells her. Thank her for her time, then leave quickly. This isn't right.

"Perhaps another time—" Sera starts, when the witch snaps her fingers and has her ensnared in seaweed. Tori'uki takes the pearl from her hand, rolling it between her fingers.

"Oh, no, my dear. This is the perfect time. That is the deal you wish to make? Legs for a pearl? Because I will grant that."

"I won't drown? You won't make me a monster?"

"Oh, don't be silly. You'll be fine, I promise," she assures her with a grin.

Unable to free herself from the seaweed binding her, Sera realizes she has no choice. "Fine, yes. The pearl for legs."

"Very well." Tori'uki speaks in a strange language when a bright blue light emits from her hand and forms a ball. She looks at Sera, laughing as she turns from her and sends the blue light streaking away from them.

"What was that?" Sera asks.

"My magic that will turn the tail into legs."

"I don't understand? I'm right here—"

"Oh, no, my dear. Not your tail, but your king. He will turn human. Will he make it to the surface in time, I wonder?"

"What? You lied to me!"

"The deal was a pair of legs for the pearl. You didn't specify who would get the legs, did you, Your Grace?" She cackles.

"You tricked me! Release me now," Sera demands.

The sea witch laughs and snaps her fingers.

As soon as she is free of the seaweed, Sera swims as fast as she can towards the palace. She sees Dankin, who is out looking for her. He is struggling to get to the surface. When she reaches him, she grabs his arm and starts to pull him up when he kisses her. Confused at first, she realizes he can get air from her and keeps her lips on his as they make their way to the surface. She takes him to their grotto.

"What happened?" he asks.

"I—I made a mistake."

"What do you mean? What did you do?"

"I found the sea witch, and I bartered with her to make me human."

"Sera!" He looks down. "Wait, but I'm the human?"

"She tricked me. She took the pearl, then she—"

"What pearl?"

"I took a black pearl from the vault as payment for her services."

"Oh, you stupid woman! That wasn't just a pearl!"

"What is it?"

"It's the source of my power! Now she will team up with the other sirens and destroy all of my people. You have doomed us. I know you hate being a mermaid, but did you hate us so much you would kill us all?"

"This wasn't supposed to happen! She was supposed to make me human so I could return to my family." She rests her head in her hands. "I know you never loved me."

"No, Sera. That's what I've been trying to talk to you about. I—"

"I don't have time! I have to make this right," she interrupts.

"What are you going to do now? Leave me here and take over my kingdom?"

"What part of this are you not getting? I want nothing to do with you, your people, or your kingdom. You can rot in hell, as far as I'm concerned!"

"Sera!" he cries out, surprised at her words. "So, you're going to face the sea witch on your own? It's too dangerous."

"Even so, I am going back to her. I have to fix this. I'm sorry. I never meant for this to happen."

"Take me with you."

"I can't. She's too far down. Even with me helping you, you would drown. I will make this up to you. I'm so sorry."

"Sera, please!" he cries out as she dives under the water. "Don't," he says quietly, sitting on the shore.

* * *

She swims back to where the hut was, looking everywhere for any sign of the sea witch but finds nothing. Even the hut has disappeared. *This can't be! She has to be here. I have to fix this, to save him and his people. His people!* Realizing they are in danger of a siren attack, she swims to the palace as fast as she can, alerting the guards to gather and watch for sirens coming. She leaves the palace, and heads west, where Maren and her sirens live, knowing she also has magic. Sera thinks she can barter with her to save Dankin. As she approaches their small city, Sera is shocked at how efficient and organized they are. Two guards are at their post with their swords crossed, blocking the entrance.

"Tell Maren that Queen Sereia requests an audience with her."

The guards give each other a knowing look. "She's expecting you," the siren with red hair says.

"What?" Sera asks, confused. The sirens part, gesturing her to follow them. They swim inside the city walls and take her into their palace. Sera stares in amazement at the sheer size of the room. Maren sits on her throne, looking up as the guards leave them. Sera's eyes go wide in shock. "You're the sea witch!"

"Of course," she laughs. "I knew when I sent that siren to get caught by your king's soldiers that you would fall right into my trap." She moves the black pearl around in her hand. "Thank you for giving me Dankin's power. With it, I can finally destroy the rest of you."

"I beg you, let us have peace."

She laughs again. "Peace? After so much death? I don't think so."

"I know you can't kill Dankin, I've heard the prophecies. How will you kill them all if you can't kill him? He will never stop fighting for his people."

She scoffs. "He's a human now, harmless. No matter how powerful his lust for revenge, he cannot come here now."

"I wouldn't underestimate him if I were you."

"Then what would you suggest?" Maren asks, curiosity playing on her face.

"I'll serve you. Take my life, and in return, Dankin gets his pearl and all of his powers back."

Maren looks down, skeptical. "What sort of trick is this?"

"I mean it. I'll serve you. Think of it, the mermaid queen herself serving you personally."

"You aren't a mermaid, though, are you? Where are you from? What are you?"

"I'm a human from Isle Piscantur. Dankin turned me into a mermaid so we could marry and stop the curse."

"How creative of him!" She laughs. "Hmm, you may look like a mermaid, but I assure you that you are not."

"What do you mean?"

"My child, you may have the body of a mermaid, but you will always be human at heart. No amount of magic can change that."

"Regardless, I am the queen. I offer my life for theirs. Let me serve you."

"I do like how that sounds. Besides, we have killed off most of the merpeople, and with or without the pearl, their end is nearly here."

"You'll accept my terms? I offer my life for theirs, Dankin gets his pearl and all of his powers, and there are no tricks," Sera says, clarifying the bargain to avoid being tricked again.

"Let me think about it," Maren says, snapping her fingers. Sera cries out as she is bound to the floor in cold, metal chains. Maren swims around for a moment, unable to refuse Sera's offer. "Yes, I will accept your life as payment." Maren casts her spell, her magic flowing into the ocean. She smiles at Sera.

"You would give it back so easily?"

Chuckling, Maren grips her chin. "Oh, sweet child, you truly are naïve."

"What do you mean?"

"You'll understand soon enough," she says. "In the meantime, I am famished. I will return shortly."

Sera watches her swim out, joined by her guards. She shakes her head. I'm sorry. I never wanted any of this! I only wanted my brother to be well, and I wanted a better life. At least part of that came true. Resigning herself to her new position, she slumps to the floor. While she's waiting, she thinks of Dankin, praying the spell found him and turned him back.

* * *

Maren returns and takes her seat on her throne. They look up as Dankin charges in, back in his merman form.

"Release my wife!" he commands, unsheathing his sword.

Maren chuckles as she swims to Sera. "Oh, she isn't your wife anymore. No, she belongs to me now. Don't you, child?"

Nodding in agreement, Sera looks at Dankin. "She's right. I gave my life for you and your people. I'm sorry, for everything." She cries out as pain radiates through her body.

"You do not apologize to him!" Maren roars. "Speak out of turn again, and I will increase the pain. Do you understand?"

"Yes." Another bolt of pain shoots through her. "Yes, Your Grace!" she cries out as the pain intensifies.

Maren reluctantly hands Dankin the black pearl. "This is yours."

He takes it, placing it into the hilt of his sword. "What do you want?" Dankin asks. "What will it take to free her?"

Maren brings her finger up under her chin, pretending to think for a moment. "Oh, I don't know. How about… your kingdom?"

"What?!"

"She thought with the pearl I could go in and eradicate you all! She doesn't understand how things work here. She doesn't understand the law of the sea. However, if you agree to give me your kingdom, you and she could become human. Go live your life on a sunny beach, unharmed by me. I will take over, making your people my slaves. I promise you they will be safe."

"No!" Sera calls out. "She'll kill them!" Her body writhes as the pain shoots through her. "Dankin!"

"Please, stop this. Don't hurt her!" he begs.

"You know what I want."

He looks at Sera with regret in his eyes. "I'm sorry. I won't give you that. I will not give up my people. It is my duty to protect them."

"That's your final answer?"

He hangs his head. "It is." He looks up when she laughs.

"Watch!" She points to Sera, and a blue light bursts from her hand and flows into Sera. Sera's tail splits, growing into two legs.

"Stop, please!" she begs. She grips her neck as she struggles for air once her gills disappear. As Sera is trying to free herself of her chains, her ring falls off.

Dankin rushes towards her. Maren grabs him, but not before he sends a spark of blue light in Sera's direction. Maren looks over as an air bubble forms around Sera's head, and Maren laughs at the sight. "How long will that last?"

"One hour," he admits.

"Perfect! You have one hour to decide the fate of your kingdom. Give it to me and take your wife, or you watch her drown. It's up to you."

"I need to think."

"Then go."

Looking at Sera once more, he reluctantly swims out. She struggles against the chains, unable to free herself. She cries out as the chains burn her flesh.

"Struggle against them, and you will feel the fire of them!"

Sera nods, going back to the floor and sitting in silence, praying for a solution. *This is completely my fault. There is no way for him to save us both. I'm sorry, Dankin. I am so sorry for this. I know you never loved me, that you used me for revenge. Even so, I am sorry that I nearly cost you the lives of your people. You are right, I'm selfish. If I had simply continued with my duties, we wouldn't be in this mess. I pray some day after I am gone, you can forgive me for this.* Waiting for him to return, she longs to look upon him one last time.

Chapter 14

Freedom

Maren laughs when Sera's air bubble shrinks again. "Not much longer, child."

"You would let me die rather than serve you?"

"Dankin gave me a gift. See, I personally cannot kill any merpeople. Why he can kill sirens, I do not know. However, I will gladly take credit for killing the beautiful, new queen who was supposed to bring peace to her people." She laughs again. "It will be enough to watch the look of horror and helplessness on Dankin's face as you gasp for your last breath."

She looks up when she hears a scuffle in the hall. Dankin charges in, Na'riti and several soldiers with him. Maren grabs her sword, surprised at the sight.

"What are you doing?" she asks.

"Freeing my wife!" Dankin cries, rushing to her, only stopping when Maren smiles, opening her mouth to unleash the most beautiful song Sera has ever heard.

"Come with me, where you'll have peace.
Come into the sea and be with me.
Come with me, into my arms,
come with me, into my heart.
Come and be free, come be with me."

Dankin's laugh cuts through the enchanting melody. "I am immune to your pathetic song! We all are, thanks to my magic."

She smiles at him as she charges toward Sera, her sword popping the delicate air bubble. Dankin reaches for Sera when Maren strikes at him with her blade. He swallows hard as he turns his attention back to Maren, dueling as Sera struggles for air. Her ring glimmers on the floor, catching her eye. She swims down as fast as she can, pulling on the chain. She picks up the ring and slips it onto her hand. Once in place, the chains fall away from her as her legs merge together, and her silver scales ripple down her body. With a swish of her tail, she picks up a sword from one of the fallen sirens.

"Maren!" Sera calls out.

Laughing at the sight, Maren shakes her head. "Don't you know my fate? No merperson can kill me!" Her eyes reflect her certainty.

Sera charges forward. "What did you say? I may look like a mermaid, but I will always be a human at heart," she says as her sword penetrates Maren's chest.

"No! This wasn't supposed to happen!" An ear-piercing shriek echoes through the room and ripples out across the open ocean. The ground beneath them shakes as Maren begs for help before she dissolves into a bubbling mass of sea foam, her body slowly disappearing and blending in with the water. A hush falls over the chamber. Sera swims down and picks up Maren's white pearl off the floor as dozens of sirens rush in. She faces them.

"I offer you peace," she says, holding it up. "Any siren who will come to our kingdom and willingly serve will be spared. If not, you will meet the same fate as your queen. What do you choose?"

Unsure of how to proceed, the sirens look at each other, waiting for one to speak up. An older siren swims forward, ready for peace. "We will bind ourselves to you. We will serve King Dankin and Queen Sereia, we swear." She bows, looking behind to see her fellow sirens bowing with her.

Sera turns to Dankin. He nods, holding out his hand. Reluctantly, she hands him the pearl. He combines it with his in his hilt and slams the sword down, sending out a wave of blue light that fills the room.

"Your curse is broken. You can no longer create sirens using your kiss. Now, my soldiers will escort you to the palace. Any sudden move, any hint of treason, and you will be struck down." He looks at his captain. "Take them away," he says, swimming to Sera. He takes her hand. "Are you all right?"

"I am. I—" She looks down. "I am so truly sorry for what I did. You were right, that I am not meant for this position. I'm sorry I failed you, failed your people."

"Sera, you killed the siren queen and brought us peace. How is that failure?"

"Because I nearly cost you everything with my selfishness. Regardless of how you feel about me, I never meant for that to happen. I swear, I—"

He pulls her to him, kissing her softly. "Let's go."

"Where are we going?" she asks as she follows him through the water.

"I have a surprise for you."

As they get closer, she recognizes that they are heading for Isle Piscantur. When they arrive, they go to the shore and lie on the sand in their cove, sunning their tails in the warmth of the afternoon sun. After a few minutes of silence, he looks at her.

"Sera, I said and did things in anger, things that I truly regret. If I could go back, undo the horrible things I did, I would. Even if it cost me my life to do so. Instead, I offer this." He removes her ring. She watches as her tail grows back into legs, then looks at him in confusion. "You're free, Sera. You saved my people, in more ways than I had imagined possible. Go home, go be with your family. I am so sorry for everything I did to you. You've earned your freedom." He stands up and runs to the water.

"Dankin, wait!" she calls out as he dives into the ocean, disappearing beneath the surface. "Please come back!" she cries as she runs up and down the shore. Collapsing to her knees, she weeps into her hands. She waits on the beach as the sun sinks lower in the sky, hoping he'll realize his mistake and return for her. Heartbroken when she realizes he is truly gone, she collects herself and walks the familiar path to the estate. Rae'lin is returning to the house when Sera arrives.

"Sera? I thought you wouldn't be back. Is everything okay?"

"The war in our kingdom is over, and travel is safe again. I wanted to come and apologize for how I left." She hesitates, debating what to say next. "Dankin wanted to join me, but he had to stay and oversee the transition. He sends his regards."

"I understand. I imagine the life of a monarch isn't easy."

She laughs. "You have no idea."

"Please, come in. We'll have tea and talk," Rae'lin offers.

Surprised by the kindness in her voice, Sera follows her into the parlor. Rae'lin calls for Chi'yo and requests tea. "What does the kingdom look like?" Rae'lin asks.

"The palace is beautiful. Everyone has been very kind. I have two handmaids."

"Really?"

"Yes."

"And married life?" Rae'lin asks.

She sighs. "We haven't really got to experience that yet. He has been too focused on the war."

"Can I ask, why did he come here in the first place?"

Sera thinks for a moment. "He was looking for a wife. He needed help to carry the kingdom."

"That must be difficult for you." Chi'yo walks in and sets a tray on the small table beside them, with two cups of peppermint tea and a platter of honey scones.

"I was angry, at first. Then, learning my roles and helping where I can, I see now why he did it. He had to put his people first. I can't blame him for that," Sera says then blows gently over her tea.

"Sera, I want to apologize. A lot has changed around here recently, with your father's passing and your brother healing so suddenly." Her gaze is focused on her cup, too ashamed to meet Sera's eye. "I watch your brother, so happy and healthy, making friends and living his life. I see now what I deprived you of, what I did to you." Rae'lin looks up, a single tear falling from her cheek. She quickly wipes it away before continuing. "I am so truly sorry for everything. I will understand if you can never forgive me, but I had to say it."

Sera takes a sip of her tea, thinking on Rae'lin's words. "I won't lie and say it makes everything okay. Still, I appreciate your apology. I will think on it."

Rae'lin sighs in relief. "Thank you," she says, taking a bite of her scone. "I know you're a queen now, but do you have any interest in helping Chi'yo with supper tonight?"

"Do you need a break from her spices?"

Rae'lin laughs, nearly spilling her tea. "I do."

"Yes, I'll help her, of course. I do miss cooking. Where is Na'ito?"

"He's at the market. He and a boy named Kye work the stall in the morning then study together in the afternoon."

Sera smiles. "I'm happy to hear that."

"Kye said you helped him when you could, that he wouldn't still be here if not for your kindness. I know you did not get that from me, but it made me so proud to hear him say that. I don't know how you became so kind, so compassionate."

Sera smiles, unsure how to respond. She finishes her tea and scone before joining Chi'yo in the kitchen. "I am helping tonight."

Chi'yo argues with her. "But, Your Majesty—"

Sera laughs. "I am still me, still Sera. I want to cook, really. It was always something that relaxed me, and I never get to cook at the palace."

She relents. "Yes, Miss Sera."

Sera shakes her head at the sight of fish in the icebox, getting out the beef instead. They fix it with rice and potatoes.

"Sera!" Na'ito runs into the kitchen, nearly knocking her down as he hugs her.

"How are you?" she asks, looking him over. He is taller than her, his skin back to its healthy bronze, his dark brown hair, flowing just past his ears, is no longer matted to his head from sweat. His blue eyes match hers, full of joy at seeing each other.

"Very well. I didn't know you were back!"

"For a few days. Go clean up, supper will be ready soon." She looks over as Rae'lin walks in, gesturing Na'ito to go do as Sera said. He leaves the room. Sera is surprised when Rae'lin takes a plate and helps set up in the dining room.

"The family eating together at the table? I don't remember the last time we did that. I only wish your father were here for this."

"I wish I could have been with him in the end. I'm sorry for your loss," Sera offers with sincerity.

"Thank you. He is at peace now, and that is what matters."

"Of course."

Na'ito walks into the dining room as Chi'yo carries in platters of food. They sit and eat together.

"Mother said you are friends with Kye?"

"I am. We work the stall together. He's teaching me how to read and write. We study our history, math, and science together."

"I'm glad to hear that. I am so grateful you are better."

"Will you ever tell me how Dankin did it?" Rae'lin asks. Shaking her head, Sera opens her mouth to argue. Rae'lin laughs. "Don't bother. I know it was him."

"I… I can't discuss it."

"I understand. As long as he knows how grateful we are, too."

"I promise you, he does."

When they've finished with their meal, Na'ito begins to gather their dishes and clear the table. Sera excuses herself to go for a walk. Strolling along the beach, she looks over the water, hoping to catch a glimpse of Dankin. *I will find him, I will earn his forgiveness. I love him so much. I don't know if he really loves me, but I have to tell him how I feel. Please, give me a chance.* She sighs when there isn't a hint of him to be seen.

Returning to the estate, she steps into the shower, relishing the hot water raining down on her. *Oh, I missed this! Nothing like a hot shower.* Thinking of the grotto, she blushes as she imagines being in his arms with the warm water splashing around them. *I would give anything to be there right now*, her heart heavy at the thought it may not happen.

She dries off and changes into pajamas before climbing into bed. Lying on her back, she stares at the ceiling. *I know I will see you again. I will find you, and I will prove myself to you, show you how much you mean to me. Please, goddess, return my love to me!*

Chapter 15

A Chance

She wakes up early the next morning, going to the beach and searching for him. Wiping her tears, she has never felt so alone. Every morning and every evening, she returns to the shore. Sometimes she swims, but she always sits and watches for him. Her grief at the thought of never seeing him again is more than she can bear. She pushes it down, thinking of her love for him. She will find him, and she will beg his forgiveness, she swears upon the tides.

He is an ocean, dangerous, deep, and an adventure waiting to be explored. An adventure I may not even survive, but I'm willing to take the risk. Does he know he has my heart trapped in the water with him? That as I walk the shore, I cannot breathe, only feeling my longing for him…

* * *

One morning, as the sun is slowly rising, she sees movement on the water. Without thinking, she rushes in, fully dressed. She gets caught in the current, swimming hard and struggling as she nearly gets swept out with it. Dankin grabs her in his arms, pulling her to the surface.

"Are you crazy? You could've been killed!"

She gasps for air, her arms wrapped tightly around his neck. "It was worth it to find you."

"What do you mean?" Dankin asks.

"I've been looking for you all week!"

"Why?" he asks, as they reach the shore. He stops once their feet are on the sand, keeping her in the water as they talk.

"I don't know how you feel about me. I don't know if you only married me to break your curse or if you love me. Either way, I have to tell you. I love you, Dankin. I love you so much, and I want to be with you. Even as a mermaid, away from my family and under the sea. I will give up everything to be with you, because I love you so."

"Do you mean that?"

"With everything I am."

"Sera, I love you, too. I released you because I thought it was what you wanted, after how I treated you. I never meant to hurt you, to scare you away. I am sorry for everything."

Her lips attack his as his hand grips the back of her head. Her legs wrap around his waist, and he covers her neck and face with kisses, whispering his love over and over. "Will you take me back?" he asks, clinging to her.

"Yes, of course. Will you take me back?"

His answer is another passionate kiss. "You don't have to give up everything, though."

"What do you mean?"

"The war is over. The ocean will never be completely safe, but it's much safer than it was. We can come and visit your family from time to time. If that is what you want."

"Really?"

"Really."

"Oh, thank you!" she says, hugging him. He starts to pull her down into the water. "Wait! I can't just leave. I told my family that I was visiting. I didn't tell them any of what happened, obviously. Even about our fight, because I held out hope I could earn your forgiveness. I have to say goodbye to them."

"I'll wait for you."

She kisses him again. "I'll be back shortly." She walks to the shore, quickly drying in the sun. Running to the estate, she finds her mother and brother in a parlor, reading.

"I am heading back."

"So suddenly?"

"My duties call."

"Of course. Will we see you again?"

"Yes. I believe Dankin will join me on the next visit."

"That's good." They hug and say goodbye.

Sera returns to Dankin, smiling when he runs to her and lifts her into his arms, kissing her as she holds him tight. "I'm here to stay?"

"As long as you want," he assures her. "Now, we need to talk about what happened and discuss these pearls."

"Could we go to our grotto?" Sera suggests.

"Of course."

He carries her into the water, transforming them both. They say nothing as they swim, Sera admiring the sharks and jellyfish swimming nearby. Her smile grows at the familiar sight ahead. Dankin starts to take her to the pool.

"For right now, could we lay on the beach and rest our tails while we talk?" Sera asks. She laughs in delight once he lowers her onto the sand. "How are the sirens doing?"

"They are doing well. Some have already begun courting merman, while a few are helping with tasks around the palace. They seem sincere in wanting to work with us and keep the peace. Only time will tell."

"I really hope so," Sera says with a sigh.

"What's wrong?"

"Maren said I look like a mermaid, but I will never truly be one. She said I will always be a human at heart. Is that true?"

"What do you think you are?"

Looking down, she runs her fingers over her scales. "I don't know."

"Give it time, and you'll see exactly who and what you are."

"You really believe that, don't you?"

"Yes, I do."

"All right."

"Sera, I have to say something. Please, let me get through this?" He continues when she nods. "I said horrible things to you, things I never meant. I was angry and overwhelmed with grief. Even so, you are the best thing that has ever happened to me. I meant it, when I told you I never thought I would love again. You were right, you have given me everything while I lied to you, hurt you, said and did horrible things! I don't deserve your love, certainly don't deserve your forgiveness. Even so, I am begging you for both."

"Begging won't help."

"Sera—"

"Because you already have them."

"How can you possibly?"

She laughs. "Compassion and empathy, remember?"

"Still, what can I do?"

"We both have hurt each other. I really want to move forward, to move past this so we can be husband and wife. Is that what you want as well?"

"More than anything," he admits.

"It will take both of us to do it. We have to work together."

"I want to make this up to you, to prove myself to you. Please, let me."

"The only true test is time. Show me you will never treat me that way again. You can say you love me, but I need to see and feel it for myself. I need action, not words."

"I'm not that patient," he admits, grinning at her.

"I know."

"Sera, even so, I am truly sorry for what I said about your father. For making you think my brother was telling the truth about using you for revenge. I don't know how I could say such horrible things."

Wiping his tears, she kisses him softly. "You did, and you've been forgiven. Now, do you forgive me? I said I hated you—" her words die in her throat as his mouth crashes on hers again.

"You only did what you had to in order to protect yourself." He pulls back, stroking her hair and looking down at her. "Sera, any time you need a break, whether to walk here on our little island or see your family, say the word. I will gladly take you."

"Will we do much walking on our island?" She giggles when he blushes.

"Where did you learn to be so improper?"

She laughs. "I think you're a bad influence on me!" He kisses her, his hands on her back. She pulls away. "I love you, but—"

"I know. Let's ease back into our role as husband and wife. I am sorry I've gotten upset when you needed space. I swear to you now, that will not happen again. I will always give you whatever you need."

"I'm sorry that I sometimes need space, but I am still adjusting to all of this, from becoming a mermaid to fulling the duties of a queen."

"I meant to tell you what a great job you did."

"With what?" she asks.

"Everything. The requisitions, the reports. I am very impressed."

"Oh, I'm glad. I was terrified I was going to screw something up."

"Not the case!" He laughs.

"I guess tomorrow we'll get right back into work."

"Sera, you killed the siren queen and brought peace. I think you've earned a day or two, really."

"I just had the week with my family—"

"And now you have to adapt to everything all over again. I mean it, no rush."

"I won't argue," she says, resting her head on his chest. Listening to his heartbeat, she lets his heart calm hers. "I love you, koy'lei."

"I love you, sea nymph."

Giggling, she buries her face in his shirt. "Dankin!"

"Is that not what you are?"

"Of course I am," she answers, studying his face as he leans down and kisses her. "I missed you, missed this. I walked the shore every morning and every night, praying for the chance to see you again."

"Then you nearly died."

"It was worth it, if it means I get to be here now."

"What were you thinking? Running out like that?"

"Um, I wasn't. I was just so happy to see you again!"

"If it hadn't been me—"

"I know. It was reckless and stupid. I'm sorry."

"But you would do it again?"

"What? No, of course not..." She blushes, pulling his shirt to her face. "Yes," she admits, the word muffled by the fabric.

He smiles as he takes his shirt, gently pushing her back. "Sera, you cannot be so reckless."

"You know I am not usually like that. I had been waiting so long, was so desperate to see you!"

"I'm surprised you hadn't seen me sooner."

Sitting straight up, she faces him. "What?"

"I did come there, every morning. I figured you would be out swimming, and I had to see you."

Her eyes narrow. "I don't believe you," she teases.

"Which dress did I like best? The blue and silver, or the pink with turquoise? Oh, I know, the red and black was nice."

"You really were there!"

"I was. I would watch my sea nymph swimming, wishing I could swim with her. It was bittersweet."

"Why didn't you talk to me? How could you leave me like that?"

"I was ashamed of how I acted, and I thought you truly hated me for the things I said and did. You told me you made a deal with the sea witch to become human so you could return to the island. I thought I was giving you what you wanted. I saw you out swimming, but I didn't know you were searching for me. I didn't mean to add to your pain."

"I would swim, then sit on the beach to dry. Sitting in the sun as its warmth washed over me, I would picture us in our grotto. Your arms would be around me," she smiles as he tightens his grip on her, "and you would kiss me." Leaning down, he kisses her softly. "I thought of that every morning and every night."

"I don't see how you can forgive me, me or Da'vae after what we've done, after we—" He clears his throat.

"Dankin, everyone makes mistakes."

"Sera, we did not make mistakes. He nearly killed you, then I broke your heart! We both hurt you so badly…"

Looking up at him, she trails her fingers over his jawline and down his neck. "You were lost in your grief, saying and doing things you didn't mean."

He buries his face in the nape of her neck. "But I hurt you!"

"Dankin, I told you I hated you, remember? I started this. We were already angry at each other."

"Yeah, what was that all about?"

"Between finding out what Ko'era meant, everything with your brother, then your anger at me, I was overwhelmed. We both said things we didn't mean, trying to protect ourselves."

"I was outright cruel to you!"

"In your grief. You had already lost your family, then to lose the only one you had left—"

"No, Sera, you are my family, too."

"You know what I mean."

His eyes close as shame washes over him. "Even so, how could I be so cruel to the woman who possesses my heart? Threatening to return you to the mistress, what I said about your father—"

"Again, grief and anger. Not excusing it, but I understand."

"You truly are my opposite."

Worried, she glances at him. "What do you mean?"

"I have been angry, bitter, and hateful because of the war, because of my loss. You have been kind, loving, and compassionate despite yours. You have made me a better man, made me into the man I was before the war. That truly is a miracle."

"I'm sorry for everything you've been through."

He pulls away, hanging his head. "How can you say that to me after what I've done, what I've said?"

Kissing his hands, she brings his palm to cup her face and smiles. "Because I love you so." He buries his face in her hair. "Oh, koy'lei, why are you crying?"

"Because I am overrun with guilt and shame for what I've done to you."

She brings her hand up, gripping the back of his head. "No, Dankin. Let this go, be with me now. You don't need to feel like this anymore."

"Can I take you over to our pool? I want to hold you in the warm water, to let all of this out."

"Please, koy'lei."

He carries her over then sits in the water, holding her on his lap. "Is this okay?"

"Yes." She gasps softly as they both transform to human. "Dankin?"

"I want us to hold each other as tightly as we can."

She wraps her legs around his waist, adjusting her gown in the water. "Not the easiest thing," she admits with a laugh. Holding her to his chest, he runs his fingers through her hair as she nuzzles in. "Hmm, I have missed this."

"Sera, are you okay for me to kiss you?"

"Please," she answers, leaning up to him. She pulls back, smiling at the love reflecting in his eyes. "This really is ours, isn't it?"

He returns the smile. "It is." He kisses her again, reaching for her sash. His smile grows when she bites her lip, nodding. "Sera, is this okay?"

"Yes, koy'lei," she answers as the gown slips off.

* * *

Sera and Dankin rest on the beach, watching the afternoon sun on its slow descent.

"You love this warm sand."

She giggles, hiding her face in his shirt. "Yes, I do."

"Do you still feel cold underwater?" he asks in concern.

"A little," she admits.

"I'll see what I can do to help with that. You should feel normal."

Smiling at him, she pulls back as she rolls onto her stomach, bringing her tail up with the fins resting above her head. "Normal?"

He falls to his back as he laughs. "That's normal to me." He climbs to her, caressing her face. "I like this pose. It's different."

"I'm trying to be more comfortable with my tail."

"You are absolutely gorgeous." He leans up, kissing her.

"Hmm," she moans softly as her tail lowers down. She climbs to him, kissing him as his hands are on her back. She looks down at him. "I love you."

"I love you, Sera. I love you as a human and as a mermaid, as my wife and as a queen, I love every single thing about you."

She gasps, kissing him again. "I love you so much."

"We need to get back before dark. You get cold enough as it is."

"Yes, koy'lei." He picks her up, carrying her into the ocean. "How quickly you transform! It always amazes me."

"You will, soon enough. I'll show you how. You will not be my prisoner anymore."

She laughs as he kisses her. "That's good to know!"

* * *

Arriving at the great hall, Sera is surprised to see it so full with sirens and merpeople.

"Wow," Sera whispers.

"This is because of you."

"Because of us," she corrects, smiling when he gives her a confused look. "If you hadn't come looking for a wife, you would still be at war. You may have been looking for a wife to break the curse, but in doing so, you found the woman who would free not just your kingdom, but your ocean."

"Our ocean," he clarifies as food is set before them.

"What do you mean?" Sera inquires as she looks over the platter with clams, shrimp, and oysters. Smiling, she fixes a plate and eats as he continues explaining their positions.

"We aren't just king and queen. I am Ruler Supreme, reigning over all water and the life within. Now, as my wife, so are you."

"I—What?"

"The pearls we have were gifts from Calyp'seidon, according to the legends. Two pearls, one for each ruler, to keep the peace and be fair. How Maren ever got ahold of one, I will never understand. It was missing for as long as I can remember."

"It was payment."

Sera and Dankin look over at a young siren eating nearby. "Beg your pardon?" he asks.

"Apologies, Your Majesty, for listening in. The pearl was payment from your father to Maren's mother, the previous queen."

"Payment for what?"

The young siren looks down. "Um, for what he did to her. Athe'nus demanded compensation from him. At least, that's what Maren told us."

Sera's eyes go wide as she looks at Dankin. "Wait, you don't think… Dankin is it possible that…" she shifts uncomfortably. "Well, I don't really know a delicate way to ask this but, is it possible that Maren was your sister?"

"Half-sister, and no, that's ridiculous! Maren lied and accused my father of many things, but he was a good man. Besides, sirens are made, not born. He couldn't have gotten Maren's mother pregnant even if he did—"

"Just because we are typically made, doesn't mean it's not possible for us to be born as well," the siren interrupts again. She gestures around the room. "As you will see soon enough."

Sera takes Dankin's hand. "There must have been a reason why Athe'nus made your father compensate Maren's mother with the pearl. Dankin, I hate to say it—"

"No, you're right. It would make sense, why she hated us so much." He sighs and looks at Sera. "I wish I had listened to you sooner. I regret the lives that I took, the prisoners I had killed." Looking back at the siren, he continues. "I am filled with regret for what I have done."

"It was war," the siren answers. "We all did things we didn't want to. We were growing weary of the war, tired of all the killing. Maren commanded us, made us, but we didn't want to."

"For being so young, you are aged in spirit, aren't you?"

"I was a cabin boy, I think. Around twelve or thirteen when I was turned. After the things I've seen, I am grateful Maren is dead."

Sera looks at Dankin, gesturing to the platter in an attempt to change the tone of their conversation. "This is a nice variety."

"Now that the sirens are no longer a threat, our gatherers can venture out to check traps and explore."

"I see."

"Sera, was that a pun?" he asks.

Giggling, she winks at him. "I would never."

He feeds her a shrimp. "Seeing you happy like this is so important to me. Never again do I want you crying because of me. I want you to always be this happy."

"Then laugh at my puns."

"Well, tell one that is funny, and I will."

She feigns hurt. "How mean!" Dankin kisses her suddenly. "We are in public," she whispers, looking down.

He gently lifts her face. "I'm sorry."

"No, it's okay. Of course, a kiss is fine. I'm still thinking of my customs from the island, having to be proper at all times. I know it's a little more relaxed here."

"Especially since we are married."

Sera and Dankin resume eating when Dankin looks at her, seeing utter shock on her face.

"Sera?"

Gripping his chin, she turns his head. He immediately rises up at the sight before him. Swimming over, he hugs his brother tight.

"How is this possible? We were told you were killed!" Dankin says, pulling him in and hugging him again.

Da'vae pulls back, placing his hand on Dankin's shoulder. "Maren killed two of the soldiers with me, then had her sword at my throat. That's when I commanded the other soldiers to leave, to use my death as a distraction to escape. Once she realized who I was, she threw me in her dungeon and left me to starve as punishment. She came to me and said Sera was dead, and I was next. I didn't understand. Then she never came back. A soldier found me when they were searching her palace. He told me it was Maren who was killed, not Sera."

Dankin grips him again as Sera swims over. "You still have to answer for her!"

Da'vae kneels before her. "I offer my life as restitution. I am sorry for hurting you. I was very close with my niece and took out her loss on you. You are an innocent woman who did nothing to deserve such pain."

"You have fulfilled your end of the bargain, going after the siren queen. I will not forgive you right away, but I will give you a chance."

He straightens up. "That is more than I deserve. Thank you." He looks at Dankin.

"I'm with her. What she says, goes."

"Yes, brother. For now, can I eat? I'm starving!" He sits with them, telling of what he overheard.

"I am grateful you are still with us," Dankin says. "I grieved your loss."

"Yes, I see you cut your hair."

Sera looks up. "I was going to ask about that, but things were so busy I didn't get the chance."

"It's our custom for men. We cut our hair in our grief."

Da'vae looks from Dankin to Sera. "What happened while I was gone?"

Sera averts her gaze while Dankin shifts in his seat. "We… we had a fight. We're okay now, as you see."

"Because of me?"

"I blamed her for your death."

"What? Really?"

"Yes," she answers. "Then I killed the siren queen."

He nearly chokes on his food. "You are the one? I knew she had been killed, but I didn't know any details."

"Yes, Dankin and I went after her together," Sera explains as she grips Dankin's hand. "I'm grateful to be here."

"Excuse me." Da'vae swims over to speak with one of the soldiers who had left him behind, to dissuade any guilt that may linger.

Lifting her hand, Dankin kisses her palm. "I'm sorry I drove you away."

"Um, you laid me on the beach and swam off!" She laughs. "Don't ever do that to me again."

"I swear to you, here and now, I will never leave you."

"Please, don't. My heart couldn't take it." She looks down, thinking about the pearls and his power to transform them both.

He cocks his head at the look on her face. "Sera, do you have something you want to ask?"

"Well, yes and no…"

"Sera?"

"Is one of those pearls mine?"

He gasps, feigning shock. "I knew you only wanted the throne! How dare you?" He rolls back laughing at the look on her face.

"Why are you so mean today?"

"Because you are making it easy for me to do so."

"Hmph! See if I let you accompany me to the grotto again," she teases.

"Your Grace, a thousand apologies."

She laughs, squeezing his hand. "Of course. Today really has been a special day, one that I haven't had in a long time."

Da'vae joins them again. Dankin gives him a smile before he turns to Sera, serious. "About the pearl, yes, it is yours. I'll have to teach you how to use it, to possess its power."

"If I don't want it?"

"You don't have to. It is preferred though, for the power to be split, to keep an equilibrium. If you don't, I will give it to Da'vae, as he is next in line after you."

"I see. Can I think on it?"

"Take as long as you need. I know it will be something else for you to adjust to, and I don't want you overwhelmed."

"Thank you." She looks at Da'vae, seeing anger in his eyes.

"How are things in the kingdom?" Da'vae asks, stuffing shrimp into his mouth.

"Since we are no longer under threat of attack, things are running well," Dankin replies.

"I am glad to hear that," Sera says.

"Do you want us to throw you a parade?" Da'vae asks, his voice thick with sarcasm.

Sera gasps softly, looking down when Dankin turns to Da'vae. "Get out."

"It was a joke—"

"Now!" he snarls.

"Fine." Da'vae swims off.

Dankin looks at Sera. "Are you okay?"

"Yes. I should not get so upset by a joke—"

"It wasn't just what he said, but how he said it. He is jealous of the fact that you killed Maren. He wanted the glory for that." He grows concerned when she doesn't look at him. "Sera?"

"Does… does he want the throne?" she asks.

"What makes you think that?"

Eating a few bites, she keeps her head down. "Nothing."

"Please talk to me. Is it from the night he nearly killed you?" Dankin asks.

"No. A few nights before."

"What? What do you mean?"

"You're getting angry—" she says with worry.

"At him, not you. What did he do?"

"You found me in my room and took me to our quarters, then I had a nightmare. Do you remember?"

"How could I forget?" Anger burns through him as he realizes what she is saying. "The bruises on your neck? He did that?"

"Yes. He held me by the throat, kissing my cheek and telling me he wanted to be on the throne, with me by his side. I don't know if he meant it or if he was testing my loyalty."

"What else did he say?"

"He didn't understand how you could be with someone like me."

"I don't know what that means."

She looks at him. "Because I look more like a siren than a mermaid. After I clawed his face, I felt like one, too."

"You did that? He said he did it shaving. I'm sorry I didn't piece this together myself."

"It's okay. I protected myself, then he slammed me against the door and left. I couldn't bear to sleep alone in our bed, so I went next door."

"He should be punished for what he did to you."

"Twenty days in the stocks?" she suggests quietly.

She's surprised when he laughs. "Don't tempt me! I might not let him out. I'll think of something. Still, I'm sorry for what he did to you," Dankin says.

"But what he said, that I look like a siren?"

"Sera, you are beautiful. What does it matter if you look like a siren? They are a part of the kingdom now, because of you."

"You think I look like one?" she asks timidly.

He sighs. "I only meant—"

"No wonder it was easy for you to be cruel."

"Sera, you are getting upset when you have no reason to be. Please, believe me that I did not think that. I see it now, only because you mentioned it."

"I'm sorry. I worry that you are going to get upset and hurt me again, and I… I make a pre-emptive strike that is hurtful and unnecessary."

"Then we talk it out. See? No anger, no tears. We talk about what we're feeling."

"Yes, you're right. Thank you."

"Will you come to me if he does anything like that again? You will not come between us, and I am truly sorry for blaming you when I thought he was dead. I don't want that to happen again."

"I will come to you."

"Please, do. I don't want us to hide anything anymore. I want us to be able to come to each other, open about everything. No secrets, no hiding."

"I want that, too."

* * *

They retire to their quarters. "We'll just sleep tonight, since I know it's your first day back after everything."

"Thank you," she says with a yawn. "Hmm, I guess I still do that."

He laughs. "I think it's cute."

"It doesn't worry you that I yawn?"

"No. I think it's just a habit for you, when you're tired. I know you are still part human, though I don't know why."

"Is that a bad thing?"

"It doesn't seem to be." He sighs.

"I don't feel weird, I have no pain or anything like that. I will tell you if anything changes."

"Please, do. Now, can we sleep?"

"Yes." She laughs when he picks her up, carries her to bed, and snuggles with her. "I've missed this. What a perfect day with you."

"I um, I slept in your room the night I left you on the beach," he admits.

"Really?" she asks, looking at him. "Oh, koy'lei—"

"Please, don't. I deserved the pain I felt. You did nothing wrong."

"Still, that you slept there…"

"My heart ached for yours."

"My heart was with you the whole time. Every day without you, I felt as though I were drowning in my grief."

He brings his hand up, caressing her face when she buries herself in his chest. "Sea nymph, don't cry."

"I'm so happy to be in your arms. This is the best present I could ever ask for," she says, looking up. "I… I ached for you. I sat on the beach every day, closing my eyes as I felt your lips brushing mine, your hand in my hair. To open them and be alone…"

"Never again. I mean that."

"I know you do." She moans softly when he kisses her. "I need sleep." She giggles.

"All right." He holds her tight, kissing her on top of her head. "Sleep now, my little sea nymph. I'm here now, and I promise you, never again will you wake up alone."

"I better not!" She snuggles in, closing her eyes with a smile on her face as she drifts off to sleep, happy to be home.

Chapter 16

Redeemed

Dankin wakes up and reaches over. His eyes fly open as he sits up, seeing he's alone in bed.

"Sera?"

She swims from the closet, tying her sash. "I'm here. What's—" She gasps when he grabs her, pulling her to him and wrapping her tight in his arms.

"I thought you left, or that yesterday was a dream!"

"I'm right here." She looks at him. "Do I have to ask for a kiss?" she teases.

He leans down and kisses her softly. "No, Sera, you never have to ask for that. Although, I may make you earn it from time to time…" he adds playfully.

"Well, I may have to make you beg, just for being mean." She swims away from him and laughs when he reaches for her.

"I'll catch you!" he threatens, joining her laughter as she swims to the ceiling. "That is not proper, Your Grace."

She pauses when she hears this and begins to drift back down towards him, concerned that she has done something wrong. When she is within reach, he grabs her hand and pulls her to him, kissing her again. "You trickster!" she cries out. "How dare you?"

He bows. "My apologies, Your Grace. How shall I make this up to you?"

"Hmm, promise me we won't have fish for breakfast?"

He rolls with laughter. "I wish I could. I really don't know what we're having this morning. That is your responsibility, by the way."

"Well, if my husband would let me do my job," she huffs.

They laugh, and then she kisses him again.

* * *

In the great hall, they take their seats as she watches the merpeople and sirens. "I'm still trying to get used to how busy it is in here."

"You and me, both. The tension is gone, too."

She looks over when Fai'mi and Ava'lei approach. "Your Grace! We thought we had lost you," Fai'mi says as they bow.

Flashing a wink at Dankin, she turns her attention to her handmaids. "No, girls. You won't get rid of me that easily."

They laugh. "Are we working in your office today?" Ava'lei asks.

"Yes, I will meet you there after breakfast." She watches them bow and swim from the hall.

"Sera, are you sure?"

"I am. Any other tasks I can help with, let me know. I want to help, especially now that we are rebuilding." Smiling at the plate set before her, she lets out a quiet laugh. "No fish," Sera observes.

He laughs with her. "I try."

"Thank you." She leans up and kisses him, blushing when she pulls back.

"Forget where we are?"

"Yes," she admits, eating. His sudden laughter causes her to raise her head. "Not funny!" she says, laughing with him.

"Now be a good girl and finish your meal," he commands playfully.

"Do I get dessert?" she teases.

"Actually, you do."

"What?"

"Eat, and you'll see."

Giving him a look, she finishes her meal. She looks up in surprise when a plate is set before her, holding a pink flower she doesn't recognize. Leaning in, she looks up at him. "I eat this?"

He laughs. "Yes."

"How?"

He picks up his flower, pulling a petal off and eating. "Like so."

She watches others do the same, shaking her head. "Okay, this is too weird!" She places the petal on her tongue, before gently chewing. The sweet flavor fills her mouth, making her think back to eating some of the candies at the festival.

"Weirder than turning into a mermaid?"

"Ha ha, no."

He smirks at her when she shoots him another look. She finishes her flower, leaving the middle on her plate like everyone else.

"Did you like it?"

"Yes, it's very good. Where do these grow?" Sera asks.

"Only in one place, where a trench and volcano meet. They create just the right conditions for them. We trade with the Sol'lun'a clan for them."

"Mermaids?"

He nods. "Hmm, merpeople, yes."

"What do we give them?"

"Medical supplies, as they do not live in a protected palace like us. They prefer to be out in the open, dangerous as it is."

"I still have a lot to learn."

"You're doing just fine, I assure you."

"All right." She kisses him. "I'll see you at lunch?"

"Yes, my little sea nymph."

* * *

She swims to her office, seeing her handmaids have organized her paperwork. "Thank you."

"Yes, Your Grace."

"You said you are cousins? What does your family do?"

Ava'lei swims closer. "My mother works in the infirmary while my father is a bard."

"I see. Fai'mi?"

"I lost my parents in the war."

"I'm sorry."

"Thank you, Your Grace."

"I lost my father not too long ago."

"My condolences," Fai'mi offers.

"Now, let's get this paperwork done, shall we?" Sera asks. They work through the morning, pausing for her to ask questions from time to time. They finish the stack when Dankin swims in.

"Your Majesty," they offer with a bow.

He gives them a nod. "Afternoon, girls. Is one of you to blame for my wife missing lunch?"

Sera's face flushes in surprise. "We got lost in the work. I am so sorry. I didn't even realize."

He chuckles. "No worries. Lunch will be delivered here." He turns to her handmaids. "Could we have a moment?"

They bow and swim out, closing the door behind them. He swims up to her, looking her over.

"What?" she asks.

"Sitting here, working in your crown, you really look like a queen."

"Do I? I hope I know what I'm doing." She bites her lip, looking down. "This was Ko'era's office, wasn't it?"

"Yes."

"Do you want her portrait?" she asks, looking at him.

"What portrait?"

"Her portrait with your daughters."

"I've never seen it," he admits.

She swims to the shelf, picking it up and handing him. "I would've given it to you sooner. I'm sorry."

Taking the portrait from her, he looks it over as grief is written on his face. "They were so beautiful."

"They truly were. I wish I could've met them."

"The grotto…" he says, running his hand over it as he turns away.

Sera looks over his shoulder, trying to see the portrait. "Our grotto?"

"Yes. It was—" He clutches the portrait to his chest. "It's unimportant. I'll put this in my office and be back shortly."

"Dankin—" she tries, but he swims from the office. Her handmaids come in to set up lunch. "Let's go ahead and eat. He should be back any time." She eats her meal, worrying over him. They resume their duties until three, when she decides to stop for the day. "I need to rest. I'll meet you here tomorrow after breakfast."

"If you could meet us in the galley for the weekly inspection?" Ava'lei reminds her.

"Oh, of course!" She smiles at her. "Thank you." They bow and leave. Wondering where Dankin is, she goes to their quarters, where he is sitting on the bed with the portrait still in his hand. "You never ate, did you?" Sera asks with concern.

He jumps at her voice. "No," he admits, looking at her. "I think I need to be alone right now."

"Okay," she says, hiding her hurt. "I'll be next door if you need me." Swimming into the smaller quarters, she sits on the bed. "Let's be open and talk about everything, instead of hiding." She shakes her head. "Right, I'm not staying in here. Not after everything I just went through!"

Leaving the palace, she swims to the grotto where she lies on the beach, letting the warmth of the sun and sand lull her to sleep.

* * *

Dankin takes the portrait, placing it on the shelf in the closet before going next door. "Sera?" He knocks, opening the door when he gets no response. He swims around the palace, growing more concerned when he cannot find her.

"Your Majesty, can I be of assistance?" a guard inquires.

"Have you seen the queen?"

"She left a few hours ago, Your—"

"You let her leave?" Dankin snarls.

"I— She—" He sighs in relief when Dankin swims away.

Dankin looks around, trying to think. *Would she go home? No, she can't transform yet. Where could— the grotto.* Thinking of every possible worst-case scenario, he rushes to the island. He runs up the shore, calling her name. "Sera?"

"Dankin? I'm over here," she responds weakly.

He rushes to the other side, finding her on the beach. Her tail is covered with slashes, and there is blood on her gown. "Sera!" He runs to her, kneeling beside her. He carefully lifts her up and carries her into the water, murmuring softly and healing her. He takes her to the beach, sits down, and holds her on his lap. "What happened?"

"I came here and fell asleep on the beach. I woke up to a fisherman standing over me. He raised his knife, told me to come quietly, then tried to throw a net on me. He said he would get me to his boat on the other side. I ducked away, avoiding the net then kicked my tail over, knocking him down. He slashed wildly at me in anger, but I was able to get the blade from him. He jumped on me, when I brought it up. There was so much blood..." she cries into his chest.

"Why did you come here without me?"

She wipes her tears as she attempts to collect herself. "You were grieving and asked to be alone."

"So, this is my fault?"

"Please—" she tries. "Please, don't. I… I'm so scared right now," she cries as she clings to him.

"Good! Maybe that will make you think twice about leaving the safety of the palace. What were you thinking? You could've been killed!" He looks down as she sobs into his chest. Taking a breath, he strokes his hand through her hair. "I'm sorry. You left because of me. I shut you out, closing you off in my grief. I never should've done that." He grows concerned as she trembles, her tears falling fast. "Please, Sera. I'm sorry."

She grips his shirt, holding him as tightly as she can while taking small breaths to calm herself down. "You're right. I never should've left. I was upset that you were shutting me out, and I wasn't thinking." She looks up at him. "Please, don't be mad at me."

"Sera, I'm not. I was angry that you left, angry for how I treated you. I just got you back! Then I—" He looks away.

"You are grieving for your family."

He looks at her. "I will never understand how you do that."

"What?"

"Have so much compassion."

"Growing up in the house, I had to. I would see servants in tears, or worse, and—" She shakes her head. "We helped each other when we could. That's all I'll say about it."

"Okay."

"Hmm, I need to wash my hair. I think there's still some blood in there." He picks her up, carries her to the waterfall, and places her on the ground. She rinses her hair.

"Is his boat around here?"

"I don't know," she answers, running her hands through her hair. "I rolled his body away and watched it sink. I think I fell unconscious. Then I heard you calling out for me." Dankin steps away to look for the boat. Closing her eyes, she thinks of better times in the grotto. Her body goes tense when she's suddenly on her feet. "Oh!" she cries out. Her eyes fly open as Dankin runs over, surprised at the sight.

"How did you do that?"

She looks down at her legs, shaking her head. "I don't know. I wasn't even thinking about transforming. Oh, if that had happened underwater!"

"The pearl. I need to teach you how to use it, so something like this doesn't happen. What were you thinking about?"

"Happier times here, enjoying being with you," she admits sheepishly.

"When we transform together then stroll along the beach?"

"Yes."

"It wasn't on purpose, but you were thinking of transforming."

"What do I do for now?"

"Stay close to me until you learn how to control it."

Sera looks down, sighing at the sight of cuts and blood on her dress. "This gown is ruined. I'm sorry."

"Not your fault. It's just a dress. Let's get back to the palace and into clean clothes." He picks her up, carrying her into the water and growing concerned when she doesn't transform with him. "What is going on?"

"I don't know."

"Okay. Close your eyes. Picture yourself as a mermaid, swimming the ocean with me, laying on the sand as it warms your tail."

Doing as he says, she concentrates. She groans in frustration when nothing happens. "What now?"

"I don't want to leave you here, but we need the pearls. I left in such a hurry I forgot to equip my sword."

"I'll be okay. I'll hide in the grotto, and I have his knife."

He sighs. "I really don't want to leave you alone."

"What else can we do? Are you going to kiss me all the way to the palace?"

"No, you're right." He carries her over, getting her to her feet, and kissing her fiercely. "I will return for you."

"I know you will." Her heart sinks as she watches him swim away, thinking back to when he left her on the beach. "Please, come back," she whispers, wiping her tears. She goes further into the grotto, sitting on the edge of the pool and soaking her legs. Closing her eyes, she waits for him, stepping out from time to time to keep watch.

Crying out suddenly, she falls to her back as her legs give out, burning, and her feet go numb. She looks down, pulling the gown up as her legs are covered in silver scales and fusing together. Desperate, she attempts to stop it, to maintain control over her own transformations. She falls to her back, her knees coming to her chest as the transformation continues.

"Ow!" she cries out as her body is overcome with sharp pain. "Help!" she tries, clawing at the gown when she cannot catch her breath. She rolls onto her stomach then reaches out, attempting to grip anything she can. Sand runs through her fingers as she looks up, seeing Dankin approaching with fear and confusion on his face. "Help!" she begs, as he races to her and kneels beside her. Taking the black and white pearls from his sword, he holds them against her palm, murmuring softly and watching with concern as she loses consciousness.

* * *

Sera opens her eyes, groaning in pain when she moves.

"What's wrong?"

She looks up as Dankin is by her side. "Everything hurts." Examining herself with her hands, she runs her fingers over her tail. "What happened?"

"Best guess? I screwed up."

"What do you mean?" She sits up but instantly regrets it as vomit threatens to rise into her throat. "Oh." She realizes they are still in the grotto as Dankin eases her onto her back.

"When I transformed you the first time, I put some of my magic into your ring. Those pearls are from the same oyster as ours," he says, opening his hand to show her their two pearls. "I thought the magic would be enough for your transformation. I don't know what I did wrong, but instead of making you into a mermaid, I made you a half human, half mermaid."

"Isn't that basically what you are? The top half human and the bottom half fish?"

He chuckles softly. "No. That may be what we look like, but our anatomy is more complex than that. I think I'm glad I made the mistake, because you were able to kill Maren, but it's what caused this. You should be okay now. How do you feel, besides sore, I mean? Do you feel different?"

"I don't know. I can't really tell while I'm hurting like this. Will you help me into the pool? I think the warm water will help."

"Of course." He picks her up and carries her over.

"Why do I still hurt? If you used your magic?"

"I'm not sure. I basically undid everything I had previously done, redoing the magic. Your body may still be undergoing change, and I can't do anything to ease that until the transformation is finished."

"I understand." She sighs as she is lowered into the water. "Oh, that feels so much better!"

"Can I join you?"

She laughs. "You don't have to ask."

"Still," he says, transforming as he hops in.

"I can't wait to transform like that on my own. It's incredible to see." She's confused by the fear on his face. "What?"

"I'm afraid if you transform too many times, you may not change back. And I can't say for certain if you would remain a human or a mermaid," Dankin admits.

"You don't think I should change anymore, once this takes?"

He looks down a moment before meeting her gaze. "No, I don't."

Her breath sucks in. Sera looks at the pearl in her hand. "Does this share magic with yours, or does it have its own power?"

"I believe it has its own power, but I'm not really sure."

"My pain has eased."

"That's good."

Closing her eyes, she focuses on her body, moving her tail slightly while the water flows in and out of her gills, moving the air through her. She runs her fingers over her tail as she looks at him. "I think it worked this time, that I truly am a mermaid."

Surprise flashes across his face when she hands him her pearl. "Sera?"

"Take it for a moment. I want to see something."

"All right." Doing as she asked, he eyes her cautiously.

She lies back, closes her eyes, and pictures her tail splitting, growing into legs as the scales recede. She imagines herself standing up, walking along the beach, and feeling the sand warm on her feet. She looks down, seeing her legs before looking at him. "I think the magic is in me now. I should be okay to transform."

"If I can't change you back—" He watches as she is transformed back in an instant. "Sera, how did you know you could do that?"

"I feel it now, feel the magic. The magic in my ring is much more powerful, and that magic is connected to me, its power flowing within me. I feel… complete."

He swims to her. "Still, we should be careful."

"We will."

"I will keep this pearl in the hilt of my sword when I'm away from the palace and in a pouch in my pocket when I am there. What will you do with yours?"

She takes it from him, looking it over. "I will do that, as well."

"I want you to have this with you at all times," he says with utter seriousness.

"Why? In case I transform without warning? Dankin, it's not going to happen. I know how I feel, what my body has been though. I control it now."

"You can't know that for sure."

"All right. For now, since I am staying with you, will you keep it safe?" Sera asks.

"Yes. Now, we need to do something about your gown." He takes off his shirt, revealing a short sleeve shirt underneath. He looks at her when she sighs. "What?"

"It's… it's not proper for me to be in your shirt. I saw the looks I got last time we did that."

He thinks for a moment. "I can't believe I'm saying this. Uncover and turn human."

Confused, she says nothing as she transforms and pulls the gown off. He helps her get his shirt on, buttoning it up and looking at her. He takes her hand, holding it between his as she transforms back, the shirt growing into a gown. "Much better! How do you do that?"

He laughs. "I'll show you someday. For now, let's return to the place. We both need to rest after this."

"Did you find his boat?"

"Yes. It was docked on the other side. I released it, so as not to draw attention here."

"Good thinking." She looks at him. "I am exhausted. Are you sure you're okay to get us back?"

"I will."

"I don't want you to overdo it. We could rest here."

"It's too dangerous. What if he had fisherman friends who knew he was coming here? We will come back, but after some time has passed. I'll be okay. We'll rest and have supper in our quarters."

"That sounds good," she answers as he scoops her into his arms. He carries her to the ocean, diving in and carrying her to the palace. On the way to their quarters, he stops a guard and requests food be brought in.

"At once, Your Majesty," he says, trying not to stare at the queen in his arms. He hurries away.

Dankin takes her inside and carries her to the bed. "I know you need to sleep, but food will be here shortly."

"I know." She smiles at him, taking his hand. "I like this gown. You may have started a new fashion trend."

"What? A mermaid dress?" He laughs. "I don't know about that."

"It's not quite proper to wear around the palace, is it?"

"No, but it's perfect for being in here." He grins at her, laughing when she blushes. "Sera!"

"What? You're the one teasing!"

He goes over to get their plates as she sits up. He sits beside her, happy to see her eat. "How do you feel?"

"I can barely keep my eyes open!"

"Hmm, yet you haven't yawned. Maybe you are correct, that you truly are a mermaid now."

"We'll see," she says. He takes their plates and hands them off. She goes to the closet and opens the door, looking herself over. "Oh, this is different!" She smiles at him. "Thank you for sacrificing your shirt."

Laughing, he swims to her. "Seeing you in it is payment enough." As she turns to him, he pulls her forward, his mouth on hers.

Giggling, she pulls back. "We are supposed to rest now!"

"Yes, Your Grace."

She laughs as she swims onto the bed. He follows behind, holding her to him.

"This is what we both needed. It's what you should've done in the first place, instead of pushing me away," she says softly.

"I know, but I'm grateful now that I did."

"Why?"

"What if you had transformed down here? And I couldn't turn you back? I still worry over that, but I feel a little better after the work we did in the grotto."

"I'll be okay now."

"Still, if anything happens, wake me."

"I will, I promise." She leans up, kissing him before snuggling against him.

He kisses the top of her head. "Stay with me, Sera. I can't lose you again."

"I'm right here, koy'lei."

* * *

Sera wakes up, smiling at his arms wrapped around her. He squeezes her gently. "How do you feel?" Dankin asks.

"Better than I have in a long time."

"That's what I want to hear. What time is it?"

"It's still early. We can sleep a little more before breakfast."

"Just sleep?" Dankin teases.

A giggle escapes her. "Dankin!"

"All right," he relents. "We'll get more sleep."

Realizing she's no longer tired, she listens to his soft snoring, and she lets her body be calmed by his warmth, his heartbeat, his breathing. She looks up when the lights slowly come on.

"Koy'lei, are you ready for breakfast?"

"I am," he says, pulling back to stretch.

Sera swims to the closet and slips out of the nightgown. Looking herself over in the mirror, she studies the scales leading from her tail up her stomach and covering her chest. She runs her fingers over the scales, sucking in air at the feeling. Blushing furiously, she hangs her head.

Dankin swims over. "What's wrong? Do you hurt?"

She giggles, looking at him. "I didn't realize how… sensitive my scales are…"

Sighing in relief, he shakes his head. "Don't scare me like that."

"I didn't mean to. I was examining myself, after my changes yesterday." Her breath catches in her throat when he brings his hand to her side, gingerly running his fingers over her scales. He pulls back. She looks over when he removes his shirt. "How come you don't have scales on your stomach?"

"Merpeople don't…" he admits.

"What?" she asks, swimming to him. "I don't understand?"

"Sirens are covered like that."

"What?"

"I'm sorry. I could try and fix it—"

"Oh, no. I like it. You know how shy I am, and with my attacks, I'm grateful to be covered like this. I was curious, was all."

"They don't bother you?"

"No," she says as she looks through the gowns, deciding on a blue and white hanfu with gold accents and pinning in a gold crown to match. He smiles at the sight. "What?" she asks when she catches him staring at her.

"Just admiring my beautiful wife."

She takes his hand. "Are you staying with me today?"

"I am. I know I won't be every day, but I want to for the next few to be sure nothing else happens like yesterday."

"Thank you."

* * *

They go for breakfast, then to her office. Ava'lei and Fai'mi approach, bowing. "Your Grace, we were supposed to meet in the galley," Ava'lei says.

"Oh, my apologies! I forgot. Yesterday was… well, eventful. Please, let's go." She sees them eyeing Dankin. "He will be with us today, as he is making sure I am all right with everything that happened. This is nothing against you."

"Yes, Your Grace," Fai'mi says.

They go into the galley to begin their inspection. They find a few spoiled fish and promptly throw them away. Sera looks at Dankin as he helps her inspect. She holds up a fish, making a face when he chuckles.

"Ah, yes. That is sardina del mar. It's a… smelly fish," Dankin says.

"That's how it's supposed to smell? And people here eat it?" Sera asks with a crinkled nose.

He laughs. "Yes, they do."

"Ugh," she says, laughing with him. She looks at her handmaids. "Do you eat this fish?"

"No, Your Grace. It's gross," Fai'mi responds.

They all laugh as Dankin takes her to the next table. "I don't really know much about these, the clams, oysters, and such, so I'm glad you're here," she admits as she looks at him.

"They will help you."

"I know, but—"

"You're trying to show them you can figure his out? Sera, there is nothing wrong with asking them to help. It's literally their job."

They inspect the last table when Sera turns to Fai'mi. "What's next?"

"Now we go to your office, where paperwork awaits."

Sera laughs. "Does the paperwork ever end?"

"You could assign someone, but then we might end up with another pillow mishap," Dankin answers.

"What's that mean?" Sera asks.

"When Ko'era was bedridden with pregnancy, we assigned a handmaid to fill out the paperwork. She put in for 4,000 pillows instead of 40.00 pillows."

Sera chuckles. "What happened to all of them?"

"Well, everyone was happy to get new pillows."

She laughs when Ava'lei shakes her head, smiling. "Right, I see what you mean. No, I will take care of this. It's my duty, right?"

"It is, but you can take a break any time. Have a snack and read, if you get overwhelmed."

"I'll keep that in mind."

They work through the morning, filling out paperwork and exchanging glances. He reaches over, squeezing her hand. In return, she smiles at him before continuing her work. They go for lunch, Sera happy to see the flower with her meal.

"You like those, don't you?" Dankin asks.

"I do. Um, could we visit the island this weekend?"

"Our grotto?"

She shakes her head. "Isle Piscantur, so I can see my family." She tilts her head when he makes a face. "I know you're worried about me transforming, but that's why I want to. If this did become permanent, I at least want some good memories with them before that happens."

Sighing, he thinks for a moment. "All right. We'll leave here Friday morning and return Sunday evening."

"Thank you!" she perks up, smiling at him before suddenly turning serious. "I'm sorry."

"Whatever for?"

"That I…" She looks away. "That I can go and see my family. I wasn't thinking and—"

"Sera, look at me. It's okay. You are fortunate to have them. There is nothing wrong with being happy to see them."

"I know, but I can't imagine what you've been through."

"That was in the past, and now I want to focus on the present, on being here with you. Can we do that?"

"Yes, Dankin. Sorry."

He sighs as he finishes his meal, looking over at her handmaids. "You are dismissed for the rest of the day. Her Grace will see you in her office in the morning."

"Yes, Your Majesty," they say with a bow and leave.

Sera looks at him, confused. "What's going on?"

"Come with me."

He takes her hand, leading her from the palace. "Where are we going?"

"You'll see."

* * *

They swim for nearly an hour before arriving at an underground grotto. He swims inside with her and together they break the surface.

"Oh, this is incredible! I've heard stories of these, but never thought I would see one!" She transforms and starts to walk around when she hears him groan. "What?"

"I thought we were taking it easy with that?"

She walks over, kneeling before him. "You really thought you could bring me somewhere like this so I could, what, lean up and try to see?"

He walks out of the water, approaching her and taking her hand, kissing her palm. "I know you're right, but I worry."

"We both do. We have our pearls, we're fine."

They explore the cavern, where she is impressed by its size and beauty. She shivers as the cold and damp penetrate her skin. Smiling at Dankin, they walk back to the pool where they had entered.

"Do you have more secret places like this to show me?"

"Yes. We'll visit them soon enough, I promise."

"Can we go to our grotto? It's beautiful here, but so cold! I'd like to warm up in the sun."

His smile grows. "Of course."

They dive in, transforming and swimming to their island. He takes her up on the shore, carrying her as she stays in her mermaid form. Dankin lies with her on the sand as they both soak in the sun's rays.

"Thank you."

"You really don't like the cold, do you?" he asks.

Sera shakes her head. "No. Ugh, I hate being cold."

He laughs as he leans over her and kisses her. "Well, get warm now. Let's relax for the afternoon, then we'll head back for supper."

"I feel like I'm neglecting my duties."

"We both are. It's okay. The palace won't fall apart because we leave for a few hours."

She laughs. "Are you sure?"

Shaking his head, he chuckles softly. "I assure you, it's fine." His eyes go wide when she climbs over him, kissing him as he caresses her face. She gasps in surprise when he transforms and wraps his legs around her tail.

"No fair," she calls out, laughing. "Free me," she begs playfully.

"Do you submit?"

"Never!" He kisses her again, transforming back. She eases into his arms while his kiss comforts her body, heart, and soul. He rolls over her when she looks at him, biting her lip. "Will you help me get warm?"

He smiles as he lowers down. She grips the back of his head as her lips devour his. He pulls back. "Are you sure?"

She smiles and nods. "Yes," she begs, losing herself in his kiss as her tail wraps around his.

* * *

"Hmm," she moans as she shifts on the warm sand. "Why does my tail like this so much?" She laughs.

He leans over her, smiling at her. "I like how it makes you feel."

"Dankin!" Her eyes close as her face turns red.

He chuckles, then kisses her. "What? You are my wife, am I not allowed to say things like that?"

"Of course, you are. I didn't expect that, is all." She looks over the horizon as the sun is slowly lowering down. "We need to head back, don't we?"

"We will soon enough. For now, enjoy this warmth. I see how much good it does you, you and your tail."

Blushing, she smiles at him, content to lie in the sun. "It really does."

"Do you wish we could live in the grotto?"

"Hmm, no. I like that it's our special place." She looks at him. "It was special for you and Ko'era, wasn't it?" She grips his arm when he transforms and starts to stand. "Please, don't shut me out again. I was just asking. If you don't want to talk about it, that's all you have to say. Please?"

He looks at her with sorrow in his eyes as he brings his knees up to his chest. "Yes, it was special for me and her, too. I was afraid you would get upset."

"Why? You have a lifetime of memories with her. We'll make our own, I know. We already have, right?"

He smiles at her. "Right."

She sits up, pulling herself onto his lap. "I want you to talk about her, when you can. I swear to you, I will never be jealous or angry. I see how much you love her still, and I want to know about her."

"Really?" he asks in surprise.

"Yes. She was an important part of your life, she and your daughters. I'm not saying you have to tell me everything, but don't feel like you can't bring them up, either. 'Ko'era really liked that dress' or 'that was one of my daughter's favorite places' or anything like that. I want to hear about them."

"You are such an amazing woman. I love you so much."

She smiles at him. "I love you, too." She looks over as the sun is nearly on the horizon. "We need to get back."

"I tell you what, once a week, we will come here or the underground grotto or similar places. How does that sound?"

"Hmm, just once a week?" she asks, grinning.

He laughs. "Okay, at least once a week."

"Much better!" She gasps softly when he picks her up. "Wait," she says.

He stops walking. "What's wrong?"

"Nothing. I just love being like this, a mermaid in your human arms." She looks down, embarrassed at her own admission. "Is that weird?"

Laughing, he brings a hand up to cup her face and raise it up before kissing her softly. "No, it's not. I love holding you like this."

"Really? Why?"

"Because you can't escape," he says with a grin.

She laughs as he kisses her again, before attacking her neck and face with smaller kisses. "All right, you win!"

"Hmm, for now, let's eat."

He dives into the water, swimming with her to the palace. They go into the great hall, curious that it is quiet. Sera sees Ava'lei and gestures her over. "Did something happen while we were gone?"

She sighs, looking at Dankin then back at Sera. "Yes, Your Grace. Some of the mermen were out to get food, when a pirate ship attacked. Most of the mermen made it back," Ava'lei explains.

"Most?" Sera asks.

"Two were killed by the pirate divers."

"Who?" Dankin demands.

"Oga'wa and Ma'lao."

"When did this happen?"

"About half an hour ago," she backs up as he raises over her. "Your Majesty—"

"Sera, stay here with your handmaid!" he commands, swimming off before she can protest.

She looks at Ava'lei. "Is he going after the pirates alone?"

"I believe so, Your Grace. It wouldn't be the first time."

She thinks of the merchant throwing her into the cold tank and speaking of selling her on the mainland. "No, he can't go alone!" She swims from the hall, trying to follow him but not seeing him. She ends up in the armory, picking out a sword and fitting the sheathe into her sash. Going to the entrance of the palace, she sees him in the distance and follows behind.

They swim for a while before coming upon a ship. She surfaces long enough to see how massive it is, diving down when she's suddenly caught in a net. A pirate in a small boat pulls her up, laughing.

"Well, well, what do we have here? What is a woman doing, swimming all the way out here by herself?" the pirate asks as he examines her.

Sera sighs in relief, grateful he hadn't seen her before she transformed. "I was knocked off my ship with these high winds. Thank you for rescuing me. I assure you, you will be rewarded greatly."

"I'm sure—" He stops when he sees the crown on her head. "And who are you, Your Majesty?"

She laughs nervously, glancing up. "Oh, no. We…We were putting on a play to pass time on the ship, when the storm blew in and knocked me overboard."

"Right. Let's get you back. The captain will find out exactly who you are," the pirate says.

She struggles to unsheathe her sword, but her arm is twisted in the net. He climbs up the rope ladder, Sera draped over his shoulder, when she sees Dankin swimming rapidly to the ship.

"No, stay back!" she pleads with him, grateful when he suddenly dives under the surface.

"Who are you talking to?" the pirate asks, looking behind.

"You!" She spits at him. "Get your hands off me!"

"Right," he says with a chuckle. They climb onto the deck. Lowering her down, he unravels her from the net then grips her arms behind her back, walking her to the captain. "I found her struggling out in the ocean." He throws her down. Sera groans in pain as she lands.

"And who are you?" the captain asks, kneeling beside her.

"No one of importance. Just—" He reaches up, ripping the crown off her head. She cries out as the pins pull her hair. "Please—" Sera tries again.

Standing up, he examines the crown. "This is real. No one of importance, eh? Then why do you have this?" he demands, his sword at her throat.

She jumps backward with her hand reaching for her sword. Her head jerks up at the sound of laughter, and she sees the pirate who had brought her up flashing her sword at her.

"Looking for this?" He grins. "Did you think I would let you keep it?"

"Now, tell us who you are, and it may work to your advantage. If we know you are from a rich kingdom who is willing to pay a fine ransom for you, I will take good care of you myself." The captain stares at her lips. "Otherwise, my boys will insist you dance for them, entertaining them all. So, answer me, who are you?"

"I am no one of importance," she tries when his boot meets her ribs. She cries out. "Really, I am a servant, and my queen insisted I wear her crown and perform a play to pass the time. Please, let me go!"

"I don't believe you. As much as I want to, because I know my men would enjoy your company, I see the look in your eyes. You are a princess or a queen yourself, aren't you?" the captain demands.

Lowering her head, she refuses to answer any more questions. When he turns away, she sweeps her leg around and brings him crashing down. She dives onto him, grabs the dagger from his belt, and aims for his throat. "Now, you will release me back into the water. Do so, and you will return to your life. Otherwise," she says as the blade digs in, blood drops trailing down his neck. "What do you choose?"

Before his men can do anything, the captain jumps to his feet, pulling her up with him. He throws her over his shoulder. The air is knocked from her lungs when she lands hard on her back. Laughing, he looks down at her as he rests his boot on her stomach.

"Nice try, princess." He kneels down, binding her with rope, then looks at his second mate. "Take her to the brig." Smiling, he looks her over again. "No, better yet. My quarters. Make sure she is nice and… comfortable."

"Yes, captain!" The pirate picks her up and carries her over his shoulder. He takes her down to the captain's quarters, loosening the rope so he can tie her to the bed. As he leans over her, she brings her knees up and kicks him away. She grabs a dagger off the captain's nightstand then quickly turns back to him. She keeps it at his throat.

"Did you kill the mermen earlier?"

His eyes go wide. "Who are you?" he asks quietly.

She scoffs. "You do not ask the questions! Tell me, did you kill them?"

"No, it was Vex. He was diving for treasure when he came upon them. He told me what he did, and I told him it was dangerous, messin' with the merfolk like that." He looks at her in surprise. "You're their queen, aren't you? You've come to avenge them!" His eyes go wide in fear.

"I have," she says, looking him over. She jabs the dagger toward his throat. "You will be first!"

"Please, Your Majesty, I've never killed a mermaid, I swear. Please, show mercy," he begs.

Compassion can get you killed. She pushes Dankin's words away, swallowing hard. "Fine!" Picking up the rope, she tosses it to him. "Tie yourself up." She watches him obey, then reaches over, quickly retying them even tighter before tying him to the bedpost. Gagging him with his bandana, she flashes him a smile. "Stay here." She sneaks up to the deck, grateful to see most of the men are back in their beds. Coming up behind the captain and first mate, she listens in.

"She is a fine catch," the first mate says with envy.

The captain laughs. "Yes, one I will enjoy tonight. I may share with the men tomorrow, we'll see."

She rushes behind him, her blade going into his back. She turns to the first mate.

"Please, don't kill me!"

She grabs her sword from the captain's body, bringing it up as the first mate charges at her, impaling himself on it. Lowering him down, she looks over as Dankin climbs onboard. He rushes to her and looks her over, relieved she is not hurt.

"What were you thinking?"

"I was following you, keeping back in case you needed me. They caught me and brought me up here. I've tied up one and dispatched two, but there are at least six more."

"I would've been here sooner, but it was near impossible to climb up once they pulled up the ladder. Thank the goddess you're alive. Now, I will take care of them. Return to the water," he commands.

"Dankin, I can help—"

"Now!" he yells with his hands clenching. "I will deal with you later!"

Running from the ship, she dives off and transforms on her way down. She swims away as fast as she can, stopping and rising to the surface when she realizes she is hopelessly lost. Groaning in frustration, a pale green light catches her eye.

She swims closer, relieved to find their grotto. Trailing her fingers over the luminescent flower, she thanks the goddess for leading her somewhere she knows. She swims inside, resting along the pool and soaking her tail to keep warm. She knows it's too dangerous to venture back to the palace, so she opts for staying in the safety of the grotto, ready to head back at first light.

Chapter 17

A Misunderstanding

Sera wakes up, stretching and looking over. She gasps when she sees Dankin sitting beside her, looking at her with anger on his face. "What's wrong?" she asks, slowly sitting up.

"What were you thinking?" he asks through clenched teeth.

"I don't—"

"You went after pirates? You could've been killed! Then you come here instead of—"

"As you can see, I wasn't killed," she retorts with defiance in her eyes. "I am a capable fighter."

"You were taken straight from the water! Doesn't seem capable to me." He snorts. "Sounds pathetic."

She turns away to hide her tears. "Go away." She crawls towards the water when she turns human. "Dankin?"

"You aren't leaving. We are going to talk about this. You are the queen, and you will take my throne if something happens to me. I am entrusting you with my kingdom. You cannot be so reckless! Do you not understand?"

"If it's so important, why did you go instead of sending your soldiers? Why risk the life of the king over two gatherers?"

"Because it was my duty to avenge them. Now, about the pirates, you were lucky you survived—"

"It wasn't luck," she says, getting to her feet. "It was years of practice and skill. You would know this, if you tried to learn anything about me instead of keeping me locked away in an office all day."

"Sera—"

"No! How dare you be angry at me for fulfilling the same duty as you?"

"Because, as if that wasn't bad enough, you came here instead of returning home. You could've been hurt or killed here! Did you forget about the fisherman? Coming here was reckless," he says, walking towards her.

"I didn't come here by choice," she snaps.

He stops walking, looking at her skeptically. "What does that mean?"

She sighs. "You were so angry last night, and I swam away as fast as I could, then realized I was lost. I didn't know which way the palace was. I saw the flowers glowing and swam over here, relieved to find the grotto. I knew staying here was the safest place for me until I could find my way back."

"You didn't come here to escape my anger?"

"No. I just told you, I was lost! It was too cloudy last night, and I couldn't make out the stars."

"Then I was wrong," he admits.

She looks at him. "About what?"

"I was angry, thinking you swam here to get away from me. I… it was wrong to take that out on you."

"I should be used to it by now."

His eyes close when he realizes there is no emotion in her voice. He takes a breath before looking her over. "Don't shut yourself off to me. I know I deserve it, that you're protecting yourself after how I've behaved. Please, don't."

"What do you care?" she scoffs.

"You know I do. I wouldn't be so angry that you could've gotten yourself killed, if I didn't care."

"Oh, so this was my fault? Right."

"That's not what I said!"

"You scared me, you were so angry. And I'm pathetic? I deserve better than that, especially from my own husband."

"How can I make this up to you?"

"I need food," she admits, her stomach grumbling.

"I'll get it."

She looks at him before turning away again. "Fine." As soon as he's gone, she walks around, trying to think of some way off the island. She looks at her ring, closing her eyes as she focuses. Falling to the ground with her tail back, she crawls to the shore, and dives into the water.

* * *

On Isle Piscantur, she lies on the beach as she dries off, grateful when she turns human.

"Did you think I would fall for that?" Dankin asks as he kneels beside her.

"What?"

"You are predictable."

"I wanted to come home," Sera says, seeing the hurt in his eyes.

"I thought the palace—"

"It was." She leans up on her elbow, looking at him. "What do you want from me? Do you want me to be a quiet, submissive queen who hides in her office? Do you want me to be a warrior, able to defend myself and my people? Because it seems like no matter what I do, it's the wrong thing."

"I think of my wife and daughters—"

"Don't you dare use your guilt against me. That is low, even for you," she snarls, getting to her feet. "I wasn't lying. I need food, and I have no money."

"Hmm, maybe I can help? Let me buy you breakfast, and we can talk?" he offers, standing up.

"What can you possibly say that will make this better?"

"Give me a chance, please? I know you have given me so many already, but once more? I love you, and I'm truly sorry for hurting you. I never should've said that."

"So why did you?"

"I was angry," he says, hanging his head. "It was wrong."

She scoffs. "I'm going to the estate. I can't stand to look at you!" She turns to walk towards the estate.

"Sera, please. I'm sorry." He grips her hand, pulls her to him, and kisses her passionately. She backs away, slapping him across the face as she turns to run away.

"Sera—"

"No!" she cries out when his grip on her hand tightens. "How dare you?" She cries out in shock when her legs are turning silver and fusing together. "What are you doing? Stop this!"

He picks her up, carrying her into the water as she struggles and cries all the way to the palace before giving into her exhaustion and passing out. He takes her to their quarters, goes inside, and gets her tucked into bed. "You need to eat and rest, then we will have a serious discussion," he says, his hand caressing her face. "I really do love you, and I would give anything for you to believe that."

* * *

An hour later, she opens her eyes, immediately turning away from him. "Please, don't."

"Will you talk to me?"

"Why? What else is there to say?"

Letting out a sigh, he tries again. "Sera, whatever happens after today, I at least want to talk it out. Will you work with me for that? All I'm asking is for us to talk."

She sits up. "Go ahead."

"I escorted Ko'era and her two handmaids to our grotto. The handmaids would keep watch so we could have some time to ourselves. If they spotted a ship, a siren, or any other dangers, we could move quickly. It was stupid and reckless, but I knew how happy it made Ko'era to go there. The last time we went…" he turns away, collecting himself.

"The last time we went, her handmaids were grabbed by the sirens, with no chance to warn us. We had fallen asleep on the beach. When I woke up, Ko'era was in the water, desperately battling a siren. I swam to her as fast as I could, but I was too late. I watched her turn to foam, then I killed the siren. I lost the woman I loved that day."

"I'm sorry for your loss," Sera says, her words ringing with sincerity. "I truly am. I'm sorry that I am not Ko'era, that I am not the wife you want. I have been trying to be who you want me to be, but apparently, I failed you. Please, stop punishing me for that!"

"I'm not. Did you hear a word of what I just said? I was reckless and stupid, and it cost me my wife. It's why I get angry when you do the same thing! Especially when I found you in our grotto. I know this does not justify my actions in any way, but I wanted you to understand. So when you do leave, you will know why I behaved the way I did."

"You're letting me go?"

"If it's what you want. I brought you here so we could talk, so that if or when you do leave, you know why I did what did."

"You say I'm reckless and stupid? After spending my whole life in servitude to the estate, then to finally be free. Here I am, twenty years old and now a queen! Then you tell me what to do, where to go, what duties to fulfill, but I do it because I love you. I was happy here, finally happy. I had forgiven you for leaving me on the shore, forgiven your words about your brother. How do I forgive your cruel words?"

"With time. I know that's asking—wait, what do you mean, twenty years old? You're nineteen, right?"

"I was, up until my birthday."

"When was that?" Dankin asks.

"It doesn't matter."

"Sera, please. Why didn't you say anything?"

"It's just a birthday. It's no big deal. I haven't celebrated it in years, so why bother now?"

His heart aches at her words. "I want to celebrate with you. Please, just tell me, when was it?"

She sighs. "Now you're changing the subject."

"Sera?"

"It was the day we went to the grotto and made up, after I found you in the ocean. It doesn't matter," she says, swimming to the closet and leaning against the doorframe. "I'm going to change into one of my gowns. I don't want to take any of your wife's clothing."

"Please," he begs, swimming to her and taking her hand. He kneels before her. "Please, stay and talk with me? That's all I'm asking is for us to talk."

"Why? We talk, we make up, we love each other as husband and wife." She turns away. "Then you break my heart again with your cruelty! I won't survive another... I won't."

"I would give anything to prove to you how truly sorry I am. Right now, my stomach is in knots, my heart aches, and I can't bear the thought of watching you leave. Please, forgive me?"

She sighs. "How can we make this work?"

He looks at her, hope in his eyes. "Whatever it will take, I will do it. Tell me what you need."

"Some space and time." She turns away. "I was called pathetic by Rae'lin when she was training me to clean. Hearing you call me that..." Her hands clench as she bites back the tears. "I don't deserve that."

"I know. Not from either of us," he says, taking her hand and kissing it. He brings up the palm of her hand to his face, closing his eyes. "I love you."

"I want to believe that. I really do." Her hand caresses his cheek. "I'm sorry I hit you."

"I grabbed you and kissed you when you were angry. It's no less than I deserve."

"No, regardless of the situation, I should never hit you. I am truly sorry and ashamed for it."

"I forgive you because I love you and want to prove how much. I don't expect the same right now. One thing at a time, right?" he asks as his fingers intertwine with hers.

"Yes, Dankin. Thank you." She looks up at him. "I still need to eat. I feel as though I could pass out."

"Here or in the great hall?"

"In here, please."

He swims over, requesting food as she changes gowns. She looks up, gasping. Dankin rushes to her side. "What's wrong?"

"My crown! The captain took it. I am so sorry. Please, don't be—"

He reaches in the closet, getting it out. "This one?"

She sighs in relief. "How?"

"I got it back, that's what matters. I came here first, thinking you had returned. When I couldn't find you, I went to the grotto." He sees the pain on her face. "Sera, please—"

"No, it's okay. It's what we're working through."

He swims to the door to get their plates. He sits on the bed, watching her as she swims to him. "I love watching you swim. You are magnificent in the water."

She smiles at him as she takes her plate. "Thank you. Even as a human?"

"Especially as a human! I've never seen anyone swim as beautifully as you do."

She looks at her plate, smiling at her salad with crab. "This looks good."

"I told them to give you a little break from fish."

Laughing, she takes a bite. "Thank you for that." She eats her meal, looking at him. "What do we do now?"

"We can resume our duties or have the afternoon to ourselves, if you still want to talk over things. Please, tell me what you want, and I will see to it."

"I know it's not the weekend, but could we visit my family? I miss my brother dearly."

"I'll pack a few things, and we'll go."

"Really?"

"Yes."

"Thank you. Um, while we're there—"

"Pretend we are happy, normal couple?" Dankin asks.

She laughs softly. "We will be, soon enough. I'm sure."

"Yes, that's fine."

She takes out the plates while he gathers some clothes and packs up. He reaches for her hand then pulls back. "Is that okay?"

She takes his hand, swimming from the palace with him. "What about while we're gone?"

"Da'vae and my advisors will oversee everything. Same with your handmaids and your duties."

"I feel bad, leaving that on them."

"It's okay, it's just paperwork. I was kidding about the pillows. Not the mistake, she really did request four thousand pillows, but we caught it before the order was filled. Your handmaids will be fine."

"All right."

* * *

They arrive at the island, where he carries her out as she transforms in his arms. They sit on a bench, his clothes laying around them to dry. "Don't want them to think we were shipwrecked, do we?"

She laughs. "Of course not. Oh, I didn't even think of that."

"What?"

"You lied to me the first time we met."

"Well, I mean, I kind of had to. What would you have said, had I walked up, taken your hand, and said 'Excuse me. I am a merman king, looking for a bride. Will you help me?' What would've been your reaction?"

"I would've had you arrested for being intoxicated."

He laughs. "I wouldn't blame you."

"My shipwrecked worker…"

"That I was."

"How did you ever go from being king to taking orders from someone like me?"

"I knew what was at stake."

"You told me you had to find a bride. What would've happened if you had not found one in time?"

"We would've been cursed to serve Maren, meaning we would belong to her, and she would've had the power to take us out."

"She said she couldn't kill you?" Sera asks, curious.

"There was a prophecy that one could not kill the other."

"She said she would leave you as a human, so you wouldn't be a threat to her. I told her not to underestimate you."

"Really?"

She nods. "Yes. I offered her my life for you to get your powers and your pearl back, to protect your kingdom. I nearly ruined everything, so I had to offer everything to make it right."

"Because I drove you away. Why did you go to Maren?" he asks, his fingers stroking along her neck.

"I didn't. I went looking for the sea witch out by our grotto. I didn't know she was the siren queen, and she tricked me." She shakes her head. "How did you find me at Maren's palace?"

"I used my magic," is all he will say.

She sighs. "Maybe you were right, that I am too reckless to lead. I nearly cost you everything you have fought so hard for."

"You were scared and hurting, and you made a mistake. It was meant to happen, to finally free us of her."

"Do you really see it that way?"

"I do now. I also think everything is dry." He packs his bag up. "Are you ready to see your family?"

"I am," she replies quietly.

"Sera, it's okay. You can be excited to see them."

"Thank you." She takes his hand, walking with him to the estate. They approach the front door. "I guess I knock?"

He laughs, shrugging his shoulders when the door opens.

"Sis!" Na'ito runs out, nearly tackling her.

Gripping Dankin's arm, she keeps herself up right. "Na'ito, watch it!" She laughs as he pulls back.

"I missed you!"

"I see that. I missed you, too. Now, can we get inside the house?" Sera asks.

He laughs, grabbing her hand and running inside with her. "Mother, look who's here!"

Rae'lin walks in and smiles at them. "Your Majesties, welcome." Dankin is surprised when she hugs them both. "Here to visit?" Rae'lin asks.

"Yes. I'm sorry we didn't message you first."

"Sera, please, you are both welcome any time. Now, are you staying in your old room?"

"If that's all right?" Sera asks.

"Of course. Why don't you freshen up? We'll have tea in the parlor."

"Thank you." Dankin takes her upstairs, unpacking as she goes into the washtoire to freshen up. He walks over when she steps out and takes his hand.

"Ready for tea?" he asks.

"Always."

* * *

They meet Rae'lin in the parlor.

"So, what brings you to the estate?"

"I missed you and Na'ito."

"We miss you, too. How is the kingdom?" Rae'lin asks.

"Running smoothly," Dankin responds.

"That's good. Oh!" She stands up. "I'll be right back. I have something for you."

Sera looks at Dankin to see he is as confused as she is. Sera stands up when her mother returns, handing her an envelope.

"What is this?" Sera asks as she looks over the cream envelope, her name written in plain script across the front.

"Your father left you a letter. I'm sorry I didn't give it to you last time. You showed up, then left just as suddenly."

"I understand. I'll open it later." She gently folds it and puts it in her pocket. "Thank you."

"Is there anything I can do while we're here?" Dankin offers.

Rae'lin looks at him. "Um, Your Majesty—"

"Please, when we are here, we are Dankin and Sera. I mean that."

She looks at Sera, who nods in agreement. "I… Thank you, Dankin. I believe we are okay at the moment, but I appreciate the offer." She looks at Sera again. "Queen Kery'oto has requested an audience with you."

"What? Why?"

"I received the message last week. What do you want to do?"

"We'll message her to let her know we are in town through the weekend." She looks at Dankin, who nods.

"I'll see to it," Rae'lin says, getting to her feet.

"Mother—"

"It's no trouble." She walks out.

Dankin looks at Sera. "What am I missing?"

She gasps softly. "Oh, right. After you left me here, I told her I was staying for a few days. She brought me in here, had tea with me, and told me she was so sorry for everything she put me through. She asked for my forgiveness. I told her I would think on it."

"We've both wronged you so much. Goddess knows you didn't deserve any of this. I'm sorry that I've put more on you right now."

"I won't say it's okay, but thank you for saying that. Will you take me to the clothing merchant so I can get a new gown?"

"For meeting the queen?" He smiles when she nods. "Yes, I will go with you."

"Thank you."

Rae'lin walks in. "The message has been sent. Now, what are we doing?"

"Dankin is taking me to the market to pick out a gown for the occasion."

"I see. You'll be back for supper?"

"We will," Sera assures her.

"Okay." Rae'lin squeezes her in a hug. "I know it's only for a few days, but I'm glad to have you here."

"I missed you."

"Oh, Sera, I missed you."

She takes Dankin's hand. "Shall we?"

He brings her hand up and kisses it. "Yes, my little sea nymph."

Sera giggles as they leave the estate. "Hmm, walking to the market with you. This brings back memories…"

"I did miss this."

"Selling fruit all day? It wasn't boring?"

"It was a break from the war."

She stops walking, looking at him. "I didn't think of that. I'm sorry."

He gently tugs her along. "It's all right."

* * *

As they walk through the market, people stop and stare when they notice a king and queen are walking among them. Some bow and wish them a good day while others walk past, minding their own business. They go into the clothing shop, Sera unsure of what she is looking for.

"One of the times I could use a handmaid."

He chuckles. "I'm sure Kea'nda can help you."

Kea'nda steps out. "Sera, wel—" She stops at the sight of their crowns, instantly bowing. "A thousand apologies, Your Majesties."

Sera walks over, putting her hand on Kea'nda's arm. "No, it's all right. When we are here, we are simply Dankin and Sera. I insist."

"All right, Miss Sera. How can I help you today?"

"Queen Kery'oto has asked to meet me. I need an appropriate gown."

"I see. The ladies of the court are wearing komo'waii gowns. They are similar to the kom'ono, but with lace and ruffles."

Sera thinks a moment, unsure. "Could I see one?

"Of course!" She walks over, getting a garment bag off the rack. "This is actually for a duchess, so it will give you a pretty good idea." She raises up the gown. Sera walks up, admiring it. It's pale pink with white layers and ruffles, a slight V-neck opening, with a pink and lavender obi wrapped around.

"Something like this will be fine. I've never worn anything like it! It's very different."

"Hmm, I think I have the perfect one." Kea'nda hangs the gown up, walking to another section. A moment later, she brings Sera a seafoam green and pale blue gown, with a matching blue obi wrapped around, layers of gossamer fabric hanging off the sleeves with a ruffle skirt.

Sera's eyes light up. "It's beautiful!"

"Well, let's see how it fits so I can make adjustments."

Sera gives Dankin a small smile as they go into the fitting area. She opens her hanfu, sliding it off. Kea'nda helps her into the gown then Sera looks in the mirror. "It fits perfectly!" She smiles at Kea'nda. "I'll take it."

"Do you need shoes or accessories?"

"Let me change back, then we can look?"

"Of course, Miss Sera." Kea'nda takes the gown. "I'll wait for you."

Sera dresses and steps out, seeing Dankin with Kea'nda looking at shoes. "What are those?" she asks, pointing at a pair of silver shoes.

"Another new trend. They're called a low-heeled hanbok."

"I like them, but are they difficult to walk in?"

"Try them on and see for yourself," Kea'nda suggests.

She does so and finds she loves them. She picks out jewelry to match and goes to the counter. Dankin follows her. "I've got this," he says, pulling out his coin pouch.

He pays and takes the bag, offering Sera his arm. She laces hers through and turns to Kea'nda. "Thank you for everything."

"Yes, miss Sera. You are always welcome here."

* * *

Once in her room, she hangs the bag in her closet then looks at Dankin. "Excuse me," she says, going into the washtoire. Sitting on the edge of the tub, she pulls out the letter from her father. She debates reading it, but the pain is still too great. She wipes her eyes and returns the letter to her pocket, unread.

"What else are we doing at the estate?" Dankin asks when she joins him.

"Could we see the orchard? The next crop should almost be ready. I'm curious to see how it looks."

"Of course," he says with a smile.

She takes his hand, and they go downstairs. Rae'lin walks up to them. "The queen has requested you for tea at two o'clock tomorrow."

"I will be ready. Just me?" Sera asks, glancing at Dankin.

"Yes," Rae'lin replies.

"Thank you. We are going to inspect the orchard."

"Habit?"

Sera laughs. "A little."

They walk around back. Dankin smiles at the sight of fruit on the trees. "It looks like it will be a good harvest." He takes her to the blueberry bush, plucking one off and popping it into his mouth. Sera looks at him, feigning shock.

"How will you pay for that, Mister Dankin?"

He pulls her to him and kisses her with fire in his lips. "Is that payment enough?"

Sera laughs as they walk back into the house. "I'm going to help Chi'yo with supper."

Dankin starts to answer when Rae'lin walks in. "I'll spend time with my son-in-law. Join me in the parlor?"

He kisses Sera on the cheek, following Rae'lin in. "Looks like a good crop," he says to break the silence.

"Hmm-hmm. So, are you going to tell me why Sera is upset with you?"

"What are—"

"Oh, no. She's a sweet girl, but she thinks we don't see the emotion in her eyes, the look on her face. I can see she is angry. What did you do?" Rae'lin asks.

"Why do you assume it's with me?"

"A mother knows these things."

Dankin sighs. "It was a… misunderstanding. She did something reckless, and I got angry. We'll be all right."

"And last time she came?" She laughs at the look on his face. "She said you were busy with the kingdom, but I could hear it in her voice and see the pain on her face. Another fight?"

"It was… What matters is, we're okay from that one."

"Is that all you do? Fight with each other?"

"Of course not! Look, the war had just ended, we had a few other skirmishes. She's still learning her place, as queen."

"And you gave her a firm reminder?"

He scoffs. "Nothing like what you did to her."

"I know. I have asked her forgiveness."

"I guess we're both waiting for that."

"Is it wrong—" Rae'lin looks up when Sera walks in.

"Dinner is ready."

"We'll be right there." Rae'lin smiles at her. As soon as Sera is gone, she turns back to Dankin. "My daughter deserves everything for what I put her through. She deserves love, comfort, and happiness." Her breath hitches in her throat. "Everything I denied her. I know it's not fair to ask of you, but can you do that for her?"

"I'm trying," he answers honestly. "We both are adapting."

They go into the formal dining room. Dankin admires the dark walnut oval table. He sits with Sera, taking her hand and kissing her palm. "I missed you."

She blushes, giggling softly as Chi'yo serves. "You, too."

"Nervous about tomorrow?" Rae'lin asks.

"I am. I can't imagine why she is hosting me."

"I've racked my brain trying to think, but I have no idea, either. Will you wear your crown tomorrow?"

She looks at Dankin, who nods. "Yes. I have a new outfit, too."

"That's good."

They finish supper and retire for the evening. Dankin takes her into her room. "Want me across the hall?"

She laughs softly, looking up at him. "No, you can stay here."

He sees the sorrow in her eyes. "You read your father's letter, didn't you?"

"No, I can't," she answers, turning away. She takes the letter out, her fingers stroking over the paper. She traces the lines of the envelope. "I miss him too dearly." Knowing it will not survive at the palace, she places it carefully in her nightstand.

"Regardless of how you feel about me right now, will you let me comfort you?" he asks. She nods as her tears stream down. He pulls her into his arms, holding her as she cries. He sits with her on the bed and strokes her hair, wiping her tears. "I'm sorry for your loss." Unable to speak, she sobs into his chest.

He holds her until she falls asleep. Getting out a nightgown, he removes her dress, and changes her before tucking her in under the blanket. Turning off the overhead light, he changes into pajamas and holds her to him as she sleeps.

* * *

Sera wakes up, looking up and smiling at Dankin.

"I must've been really tired last night."

"You've been through a lot," he agrees. "I'm sorry that I'm part of that. Hurting you is… is the last thing I should ever do." He turns away and buries his face in his hands.

She gets to her feet, walking around the bed and pulling him into her arms. He cries into her gown when his shame is overbearing.

"I won't say it's okay, but please, you don't need to feel such guilt. You have asked for forgiveness."

"Even so, I don't know what I was thinking."

She sighs, running her fingers through his hair. "Dankin, you have lost more than I could even think of. You were angry and scared, and you said something stupid. If anyone can relate to that, it's me."

He looks up at her. "What do you mean?"

She wipes his tears. "I went to the sea witch, imploring her to help with peace between merpeople and sirens. She said it was impossible." Sera closes her eyes, turning her head away. "Then I asked her to turn me human. After what you had said, thinking you never loved me, I almost cost you everything in my heartache."

"It was still my fault! All of this. If it's too much, if… if you can't forgive me, I'll understand."

"I'm working towards it. I love you, and I want us to be together. I need to know that you are my partner, that you will hold my hand and support me through anything, instead of growing angry and pushing me away."

"I know. I want that, too." He looks up at her.

She gives him a small smile before pulling away. "Can we go to the beach after breakfast?"

"You're not tired of the water yet?"

She shakes her head. "I told you, it's always felt like home to me."

"It's part of why I thought you would be okay, becoming a mermaid. I could tell how much the ocean means to you, how much you love it. Still, I should've talked to you instead of just changing you."

"It's okay. You did what you had to in order to save your kingdom. Now, we need to get dressed."

"We… need to?"

She blushes when she looks at him. "Behave!" She laughs as she goes to the closet and slips into the pale blue hanfu she knows he likes. "Well?"

"I love that gown," he says, buttoning up his silver shirt. He walks over to caress her face. "You know what else I love?"

"What?" she asks, eyeing him suspiciously.

He leans down, his mouth by her ear. "Not having fish for breakfast."

Her head rolls back as she erupts with laughter. "Really?"

Smiling, he nods. "Yes, really."

"What to do with you? Hmm?" She takes his hand. Once downstairs, he sits at the table as Sera and Chi'yo cook breakfast. She looks at Chi'yo. "I think we should add fish to his pancakes. Don't you agree?"

Chi'yo chuckles. "Okay, why are you punishing him?" They both laugh.

She shoots Dankin a teasing look, blushing when he winks at her. She walks over to him. "Are you going to do anything besides sit today?"

"Would you like me to set the table?" he offers.

"Please."

"Yes, Your Grace." He smiles when she sticks her tongue out at him as she returns to the stove. She and Chi'yo talk and giggle as they cook. "What are you two over there planning?" Dankin asks with a raised eyebrow.

"I have no idea what you mean," Sera says, batting her eyelashes at him. Dankin laughs as he finishes setting up and takes his seat. Sera fixes his plate and sets it before him.

Nearly falling out of his chair with laughter, he grins at the plate. "Really?" he asks, looking down at the fish-shaped pancakes.

She sits beside him and starts taking his plate. "Well, if you don't want it—"

He reaches up and gently grips her wrist before taking the plate with his other hand. Then he brings her hand up to plant kisses along her wrist and palm. "You made it. Of course I want it."

She sighs, looking at the clock. "I wish the tea with the queen was over already. I am so nervous."

"You'll be fine," Rae'lin say as she walks in. "I can help you get ready after lunch, if you'd like."

"That would be nice, thank you." Sera replies.

Dankin gives Sera a reassuring smile. "Like your mother said, you'll be fine."

Sera looks at Rae'lin. "We are going to the beach after we eat. Would you like to join us?"

"I am helping Na'ito at the stall this morning. Kye's mother is ill."

"Not again," Sera sighs. "Please tell Kye I hope she feels better soon."

They finish eating and go upstairs. She packs a small bag with towels. He walks over, takes the bag off her shoulder, and sets it on the dresser. His hand gently caresses along her neck and chin. "Sera, may I kiss you?"

She looks at him, tears in her eyes. "I don't know," she answers, looking for any anger on his face. Seeing none, she nods. "Please?" His face lowers down, his mouth on hers, as she grips him by the back of his head. Reluctantly, she pulls back. "Can we go to the beach?"

He smiles at her. "Of course."

* * *

Once at the beach, she unrolls her towel and sits on it. He laughs as he joins her. "What's funny?" she asks.

"Not laying on your tail?"

She gasps. "We could be seen!"

He looks around. "It's a private spot you've picked, and no one seems to be out. Live dangerously?"

She hangs her head. "That hasn't worked out for me in the past."

Turning serious, he squeezes her hand. "I'm sorry for all of that. You rest here how you are comfortable. What you do, I'll do."

She smiles at him as her legs transform into her tail. "Like this?" Her smile grows when he does the same, his fingers trailing along her stomach as she caresses his face.

"Enjoying the sand?" he asks.

"I am. I didn't care for it as a human. Now, I love how it makes me feel."

Dankin leans over her, studying her face. He lowers further so his mouth is mere inches from hers. "Sera, may I kiss you?"

"Yes," she responds. He kisses her fiercely until she pulls away, and she surprises him when she strips the gown away, taking his hand and tracing it over her scales. "Is it still just us?"

He glances around before smiling at her. "It is." She leans up, kissing him as he surprises her by wrapping his tail over hers. "Is this okay?" Dankin asks.

She blushes. "Yes, koy'lei."

"Now, what to do until lunch?"

She laughs, looking out over the water. "What are we to do?"

Chapter 18

The Unexpected Queen

Sera sighs as her legs return, the gown growing down to her ankles. "It's time to go back to the estate. Light lunch, then getting ready to meet the queen. I know I'll be okay, but I'm still worried."

"I'm accompanying you."

"What?" she asks, sitting up.

"Not to the tea itself, but to the mainland at least."

"Thank you." She leans up and kisses his cheek. "I didn't want to ask—"

"Why not?"

"I don't want you to think you have to stay with me and hold my hand," Sera explains.

"What if I want to? And no, I don't think I have to. I know better, as strong and tenacious as you are!"

"Thank you."

They gather their towels, rolling them up and putting them into her bag. Once at the estate, they go into the washtoire to clean up. She changes into a simple pink and blue hanfu, going downstairs as he finishes in the shower.

"Did you have a nice time at the beach?" Rae'lin asks.

"We did. How is the market?" Sera asks.

"Busy, but that's good. We have people now coming from other islands to try your fruit. Word is spreading. I'm sorry, I feel like I should pay you for your work, your creation—"

"I don't need it, I assure you. Use the money for Na'ito, give him a future. Will you do that?"

"Of course." When Dankin joins them, they eat lunch, with Sera laughing at the fish and rice. Rae'lin takes her hand. "Let's get you ready to meet another queen."

They go to her room, where Sera gets out her purchases. Rae'lin helps her dress. "Do you like it?" Sera asks.

Rae'lin turns away. "I'm sorry."

"You don't like it?"

Rae'lin spins on her heel. "No, it's not that. I'm sorry, I've always been so jealous of how unique looking you are, how beautiful. Your father would rave about your beauty when you were born. I never had offers from noblemen like you did. You see, I was forced to marry your father because I am not as beautiful as some. We fell in love and were very happy together, but I was jealous that you had a duke and a lord interested in you. You had prospects I could only dream of. Now, married to a king? I never saw that coming, but I am so happy for you and so proud of you."

"Thank you," Sera says, surprised when Rae'lin hugs her. "I wish you and I could've had more time together, had a real relationship."

"I hope it is not too late for us now," Rae'lin says.

"It isn't," Sera assures her with a smile. She pulls out a silver crown studded with emeralds and smiles as she pins it into her hair. Her mother watches intently. "What? The crown?" Sera asks.

"You attach it so efficiently, as if it's something you've done your whole life. You really were meant to be a queen, weren't you?"

Sera looks down. "I've made mistakes—"

"Life is full of twists and turns, full of unexpected events. All we can do is roll with it and let it lead us where we need to go."

"Is that what happened to me? Unexpected events?"

Rae'lin laughs. "My daughter, the unexpected queen. This is more than I could ever want for you. As long as you are happy, that is everything in the world to me."

"Do you mean that?"

"I do," Rae'lin says with a smile.

"I am happy."

"Have you forgiven him?" Rae'lin asks.

Sera nearly drops the necklace in her hands, looking up. "What?"

She laughs. "He didn't tell me, but I could see and hear it, the way you are with him. Until this morning."

"I haven't told him I've forgiven him," Sera admits.

"Oh, you little minx! That's right, make him earn it." They laugh again as Sera finishes getting ready. She turns to Rae'lin. "So beautiful. The queen will be most jealous," Rae'lin exclaims.

"Dankin is accompanying me to the mainland."

"I'm glad to hear that. I was going to offer, but I have a lot to do here."

"It's okay."

Sera walks downstairs to find Dankin waiting for her. He shakes his head and smiles when he sees her, as if he can't believe she is his. "Oh, my beautiful queen!"

She walks up and takes his hand as she kisses him softly on the cheek. "My escort?"

He holds out his arm, and she laces hers through his. "Don't wait up," he jokes to Rae'lin.

She laughs. "Sera, what are we going to do about him?"

"Don't worry about that. I'll take care of it." They all laugh as he walks her to the door. She gives her mother another smile before she and Dankin walk out. "I don't know why, but I feel a little better."

"Is your heart pounding?" Dankin asks.

"It was when I was getting ready, but it's not now. I think you have a calming effect on me."

* * *

They walk to the harbor and board the next ferry going across. People part ways and stare in shock at the sight of them. Dankin hands over the tickets, and the man is so nervous, he nearly misses the punch before handing them back. Dankin places the tickets in his pocket, winking at Sera.

"Did you enjoy the beach this morning?" he asks.

"We both did."

"I love you," he says, his breath warm on her ear.

She smiles at him. "I love you, too," she replies, kissing him softly. "Oh, I have to be careful. I forgot about my make-up."

"It looks perfect, I promise."

She sighs. "I wish this was the return trip."

"Sera, you get to partake in something few women do. Enjoy the time with her, then you can tell me all about it as we walk around the market."

"Really?"

"Yes, really."

"Thank you," she says as she rests her head on his shoulder, enjoying the view of the water.

* * *

Two young women, with hair carefully put up with flowers and fans, dressed in silk kom'onos, and adorned in white face paint, approach them as they disembark.

"Sera Dahvaene?"

"Yes," she answers.

"Her Majesty welcomes you, and—" she stops, seeing their crowns. She looks at the other girl, and they quickly bow, "She is most excited to meet you. Please, follow us," the young woman says as she extends her arm out in a welcome gesture.

Sera turns to Dankin. "Where will we meet up?"

"I'll be outside the palace, I promise."

"I'll hold you to that." Sera pulls away and follows the young women to the palace. She smiles at the contrast of white marble with the dark wood exterior. Guards dressed in black pants with royal blue jackets patrol around the gate and entrance. She walks with them inside, through a large corridor with bright colored banners, until they arrive at the tea parlor. They gesture for her to enter first, per custom.

Inside, Queen Kery'oto sits at the low table with an intricate silk rug underneath. The rug is deep purple with embroidered silver lotus blossoms. Upon Sera's entrance, the queen stands up. Her gown is lavender and pink silk, with a pale blue obi and silver ruffles. Her hair is up in a katsura style.

"Please, Sera, welcome." She gestures her over, a warm smile on her face. Sera can't help but notice her beauty.

Following custom, Sera drops to one knee. "Your Majesty."

"Well, this is unexpected."

Sera looks up. "Did I do something wrong? A thousand—"

"Oh, no. I did not expect to be meeting another queen." Kery'oto gives a half-bow. "The pleasure is mine."

"Yes, Your—"

"Please, let us try not to be so formal, since it is just the two of us? Saying that over and over would be cumbersome."

"How shall I address you?"

"By my first name, since you are also royalty."

"Yes, Kery'oto," she says, her face growing even more red.

"Sera, please. Don't be nervous. Just two women sitting to tea, right?" Kery'oto gestures Sera to sit. The young women walk over and set the cups before the two queens. Music plays, and they do a special tea dance with fans and ribbons.

"Are you enjoying the ceremony?"

"I am. I've never attended one before." Sera turns to her. "If it's not too bold—"

"Why are you here?" Kery'oto laughs when Sera nods. "Well, originally I was going to ask you to be a Ga'ishi, like them. To serve tea and dance for me. I see now, you were meant for something more."

"I don't understand?"

"They are not my servants. They are noblewomen, and this is part of their coming-of-age ceremony. I knew you were not a noble, but we have heard your family name, know of your contributions to the island. When I saw you at the ball, I wanted to ask. I was waiting for a better time, when it would be just us."

Sera sips her tea, following Kery'oto's movements. "It would be a great honor. I apologize—"

"For what? Running off and marrying a king?" She laughs. "You owe no apology, I assure you."

Sera sets her cup down. "May I ask a favor?"

"Please."

"Could I dance for you?"

Kery'oto's eyes go wide. "You know how?"

"Not exactly like them, but a traditional dance from the isle. It would be an honor to dance for you. I just, um, I'm a little shy, is all."

Kery'oto turns to the Ga'ishi, gesturing them out. "The honor would be mine. What sort of song shall I have them play?"

Sera tells her the name. Kery'oto smiles. "They know that one." She instructs the small band, which is behind a curtain for privacy.

Sera picks up a gold fan from the table as she walks to the open part of the room. Opening the fan as the music begins, she is grateful that each step is flawless. Nervous as she is, she takes a breath and enjoys the movement. Once the song ends, she closes her fan and bows. Kery'oto gets to her feet and claps fervently.

"What a beautiful Ga'ishi you would've made," she exclaims as she approaches Sera.

Sera lays the fan down, turning back to her. "I am glad you liked it."

"Well, Sera, I enjoyed this time together. I won't say it was a waste, because while I may not have you as one of my Ga'ishis, I truly enjoyed watching you dance. It has been a pleasure getting to know you."

"The feeling is mutual."

"I don't have many friends," Kery'oto admits. "After losing Kae'li in the war, I haven't left the palace much. I want you to know, you are welcome any time. I wish to see you again."

"You will, I promise."

"Until then, may the tide always wash up in your favor."

"Thank you, Kery'oto."

"They will escort you out," Kery'oto explains as she returns to the table.

Sera says her goodbyes and sighs in relief when she sees Dankin leaning against the wall, waiting for her. She rushes to him, breathing easier as he wraps her in his arms.

"Well?"

"It was wonderful," she admits.

"Will you see her again?"

"I promised her I would."

"Then we will."

She tells him everything as they walk about the market. She purchases a gold lotus pendant for Rae'lin, a book of legends for Na'ito, and a new apron for Chi'yo. Dankin acquires their tickets for the ferry then takes her onboard. They drink tea and take in the sea air for their trip back.

* * *

Rae'lin meets them in the hall when they return to the estate. "How was it?"

"It was better than I expected," Sera replies, unable to stop grinning. "Let us freshen up, and I'll tell you about it over supper." Upstairs, Sera admires her gown in the mirror and notices Dankin watching her. She turns to him. "You want to see, don't you?"

He looks at her, confused. "See what?" She laughs as she lies down on the bed. He walks towards her but stops suddenly as he watches her transform. He admires the sight of her silver tail in her gown. "You are so beautiful." He continues walking to her and kisses her as he leans over her, trailing his fingers over her tail. "No pain? Nothing bothering you with this?"

"No, thank goodness." She leans up and kisses him, gasping when he transforms, too. "We are expected at supper soon," she laughs.

"I know. They can wait for us."

Kissing him again, she blushes as her tail wraps around his.

* * *

Rae'lin helps Chi'yo set the table, looking up. "To be young and in love."

Chi'yo chuckles while she plates the food. "Should I put their plates in the warmer?"

She nods, laughing. "Yes, please." She looks up as Na'ito walks in. She's concerned at the look on his face. "What's wrong?"

"Kye's mother is going to the mainland for treatment. He says he can't afford to stay in their ab'odo. I don't know what to do."

"He could stay here," Rae'lin offers.

"Really?"

"Of course. He means a lot to Sera, too. I see how hard he works, and he has done so well teaching you. Please, let him know."

"Thank you!" He hugs her, then runs off.

Rae'lin eats her meal at the small table before retiring to the main quarters. She walks over to her bed and runs her fingers over Tsuji's pillow. "I miss you, my love. Our daughter is a queen. Can you believe it? It's what she deserves, after everything she suffered here. I wish I could see you one more time." She lies on the bed, closing her eyes as she weeps for her lost husband.

* * *

Sera and Dankin go downstairs. She checks the warmer, laughing. "Yes, they kept it for us." She carefully gets out the plates, laying them on the counter. They stand together and eat, talking and laughing quietly when Na'ito and Kye come in.

"Kye! How are you?"

"Very well, Miss Sera. Miss Rae'lin and Na'ito are taking me in while my mother is at the mainland for treatment."

"I am glad to hear that."

"How will you afford the treatment?" Dankin asks, taking a bite of his bread.

Kye looks down. "We used the gold you gave us as a down payment, but we also had to sell everything we have. The clothes that I am wearing are all I have left."

Sera reaches out and rests her hand on Kye's arm. "Why didn't you come to us?"

"Miss Sera, it's not your problem—"

"Tell them to send the bill here, and Sera and I will take care of it. I mean that," Dankin says as he digs out a small coin pouch and hands to Kye. "Get yourself some clothes and shoes tomorrow, as well."

"Thank you, both of you! Please, how can I ever repay this?"

"Just do anything Rae'lin asks and help where you can. Deal?"

"Yes, Miss Sera!"

They boys each fix a plate and go upstairs. Sera sighs.

"What's wrong?"

She looks at Dankin. "I am grateful for what we have, but—" she looks down. She runs her fingers over her gown and traces them on her legs.

"Sera, do you want to stay here?"

"With you?" she asks.

"I'm afraid that's not possible. You know the duty I have."

"I do. I could dream for a moment." She turns away, wrapping her arms around herself. "I can't have both worlds, I know."

He walks up behind her, pulling her back to his chest as his arms wrap around her. "Tell me what you want, and I'll do my best to see that you have it."

She spins around and faces him. "I want to be with you, no matter where that is."

"Will you forgive me?"

"I already have. Then seeing you now, with Kye and his mother, I know you are a good man."

He smiles at her words, holding her tight in the quiet kitchen. "I am sorry. Regardless of why I did it, or how I felt, what I was thinking. There is no excuse for what I put you through."

"I know. You'll make it up to me."

"How?"

She laughs. "Hmm, you'll see." She yawns. "For now, I need sleep."

"I see you're yawning again."

She laughs. Dankin scoops her up and carries her upstairs, where she changes for bed. Dankin walks up behind her as she is slipping on a short, red satin nightgown.

"What is this little thing called?" he asks as he takes her all in.

"A cheng'pao. It's a traditional sleep gown."

"Really?"

She laughs. "For a married woman."

"Right. I wondered why I hadn't seen you in this before."

Sera shakes her head. "Rae'lin left it in here for me."

"I'm glad the two of you have made up."

"I pity her. I see the grief she carries for my father. She loved him so much." She looks at him. "If I'm a mermaid, will I be immortal, too?"

He sighs, thinking for a moment. "I believe so, but I can't say for sure. I didn't mean—"

She laughs. "I know, I was curious, is all. I don't look forward to the day that my mother and brother are both—" She stops, catching herself. "I need to use the washtoire," she says, stepping towards it. Dankin stops her and takes her hand. She hangs her head. "I'm sorry."

"Sera, you have family. Everything you are thinking and feeling is completely understandable. Why do you worry so much over me?"

"I don't want to upset you. I know you still feel guilty over changing me without my permission. And you are still in the midst of your grief over your wife and daughters."

"You won't upset me, I promise." He strokes her cheek, wiping a tear away. "I want to be the man you deserve."

"That's all I can ask. I don't deserve to be treated like that. I know I've had moments, too. In my defense, you took me from my home and forced me to marry you. Even so, we both can do better."

"Sera, we will do better. Now, I have to ask. Are you still mad at me for taking you from here, for using my magic to make you marry me?"

"Not anymore. I was, oh, I was. You healed my brother, kept your word about our wedding night, and have helped me through it all. You already are the man I deserve."

"So, I can kiss you?" he asks, his eyes meeting hers.

She smiles. "Any time you want." He pulls her up, kissing her fiercely. "I do need to use the washtoire, though," she says.

"Of course." He lets her go. While she's inside, he turns the overhead lights off and gets ready for bed then waits for her. As soon as she steps out, he scoops her up with a laugh. He carries her to bed. "Didn't get to do this the night I proposed."

"I mean, you technically did. I was just unconscious through it," she teases.

"I'll be right back," he says before going to the washtoire.

Sera relaxes and closes her eyes, picturing their morning on the beach. She bites her lip when Dankin takes her into his arms, his hand tracing the lace of her nightgown. He rolls on top of her, pinning her underneath his weight. She laughs and closes her eyes, letting herself get lost in his kisses.

* * *

"Will you wear this for breakfast?" Sera asks as she gets a pao out of the closet.

"Your traditional attire for men?"

"Yes."

Dankin looks it over. "I will, if you'll help me with it."

"Of course," she answers with a smile. Removing it from the hanger, she sets it on the bed then she unbuttons his shirt and lets it fall to the floor as she admires his muscular build. Biting her lip, she lowers down to help him out of his sleep pants. He watches her wrap the satin silver robe around him. A gasp escapes his lips when she suddenly tightens it before tying the sash to the side. Stepping up behind him and wrapping the navy-blue outer layer over him, he runs his hand along the fine silk. A chill runs down his spine as she trails her fingers over his shoulder blade when she walks behind him. She smiles at him, as she smooths it over and ties the outer sash. "So handsome."

"It's different."

"If you aren't comfortable—"

"Oh, no. It's fine," he assures her. She takes his hand and leads him to her mirror. She stands back as he looks himself over. "I like it."

"Then I do, too," she says as she steps up and kisses him.

They go downstairs, where Rae'lin joins them for breakfast. "I missed you at supper last night."

Sera blushes, smiling at Dankin. "Sorry."

"Oh, no, it's okay. However, I am dying to hear how yesterday went."

Sera tells Rae'lin all about the tea with the queen. "I had a very nice time. She is friendly and kind."

"And she wants to see you again?"

"Yes."

"That's wonderful."

"Oh, we told Kye to send his mother's bills here. Dankin and I are taking care of them."

Rae'lin shakes her head in wonder. "You both have been such a blessing to this island."

"We do what we can," Sera answers.

"What are you doing this morning?" Rae'lin asks.

Dankin looks at Sera. "I have some business to take care of on the mainland."

Sera looks at Rae'lin. "Would you like to do something while he's gone?"

"Yes. I have to take care of a few things here, first."

"I'll get a bath while you do."

Sera walks Dankin to the door. "I'll be a few hours, just because of travel time alone," he says.

"I know." She leans up and kisses him. "I love you."

"I love you."

Sera watches him walk out before running upstairs to fix her bath. She climbs into the tub, sighing as the warm water eases her body. Relaxing deeper as the steam soothes her, she imagines being in the grotto and lying with her tail on the warm sand. She smiles at the thought, until her tail flicks in the tub.

Her eyes fly open in surprise. Closing her eyes, she concentrates then lets out a groan of frustration when she doesn't change back. "Please, not now."

"Sera, are you all right?" Rae'lin asks, right outside the door.

"Oh, yeah. Um, I'll be out—" Panic rises in her chest when the door opens. "Mother, no—"

Rae'lin walks in and takes in the sight before her. "Sera, if you needed to go to the ocean, why didn't you just ask me?"

"You knew about this?" Sera asks in shock.

"Not exactly. Your father left me a letter, telling me of his days hunting sirens. He was friends with a few mermaids."

"He killed Dankin's daughter."

"Actually, he did not. Sera, didn't you read your letter?" Rae'lin asks.

"No, I wasn't ready. What are you talking about?"

Rae'lin walks over, sitting on the edge of the tub as she tells Sera snippets from the letter. "Are you going to tell Dankin?"

"Yes. He deserves the truth. Whether he believes it or not, I can't say."

"Honestly, when I read the letter, I was worried Dankin only took you away from us for revenge."

"Well…" Sera tells her everything about the ball, the proposal, the wedding, even the siren war, and her deal with the sea witch. "I didn't mean to change in here. I'm still adapting to having this ability, and sometimes it just happens."

"What do you mean? Can you not change back?"

Sera hangs her head, forgetting about her pearl as she tries to turn herself back. "Not at the moment."

"Should we drain the water? Maybe drying off… wait, will you suffocate?"

Sera lets out a small chuckle. "No, that's not how it works." She reaches over but can't grasp the stopper with her tail in the way.

Rae'lin leans down and her fingers accidentally brush along Sera's tail as she pulls on the chain. "I'm sorry."

"No, it's okay." Sera sees her staring. "You want to touch it, don't you?"

Rae'lin laughs, embarrassed. "I do, yes."

"It's okay."

Rae'lin brings her hand down to where Sera's knees would be, trailing her hand down to her fins. "It's so beautiful!"

"Thanks."

She gets a towel and helps Sera dry. With her eyes shut tight, Sera thinks of walking the beach with Dankin, strolling through the market, and running through the orchard. She cries out in relief when her legs return.

"Does it hurt?" Rae'lin inquires, her curiosity piqued over the process.

"It was horrible the first time, but I fell unconscious right after. It doesn't hurt now."

Rae'lin fetches a gown and helps her dress. "Are you still up for going into town?"

"I should be okay." Sera's face flushes when she goes to the dresser and gets out the pouch with her pearl in it. She says nothing about it to Rae'lin as she slips it into her pocket, too embarrassed to admit she had forgotten it.

They go downstairs to find Kye and Na'ito loading the cart with produce to take into the market. "Look familiar?" Rae'lin asks.

Sera laughs. "Yes. I actually kind of miss that. I know, that's probably weird, right?"

"Says the girl who is half human, half mermaid."

She laughs harder. "Not exactly, but close enough."

They walk towards the market when Rae'lin takes her arm, leading Sera to the beach and sitting with her on a bench.

"I thought we could talk a moment."

"Of course. Are you all right?" Sera asks.

"I'm worried about you. So much change in such a short time. Please, tell me, are you really okay?"

"I'm fine," she tries.

"Please?" Rae'lin asks.

Taking in a deep breath, Sera trails her fingers over her arm. "I am happy with him, swimming together and seeing things in the ocean I never would see as a human."

"But?"

"He's worried if I change too many times—"

"You may get stuck?"

She nods, looking at her mother. "I'm not worried. It might take me a bit to learn how to control it, but I think I will be fine with my transformations. Still, he doesn't want me to."

"What will you do?"

She sighs. "It's one of the reasons we came."

"To say goodbye?"

"I hope not. I want to still come from time to time, but it won't be as often as I would like."

"Honestly, I didn't expect to see you that much anyway. You have a kingdom to run, after all. I'm grateful for whatever time we can have."

Sera looks out over the water. "I don't belong to either world."

"Why do you say that?"

"When I lived here, I dreamed of exploring the ocean. When I'm there, I miss being here."

"Sera, that's normal. You grew up here, it's your home. Sitting here, seeing you watch the tide flowing in and out, I see how much you miss it, too. Maybe it means you belong to both of them."

"Really?"

"Like your father. He loved being here, spending time with us. I could see it, though, that he missed being on his boat. Then when he would come home after being at sea for months on end, he would take me in his arms and hold me for an hour, happy to be back. You're like him, a child of land and sea."

"That's wonderful," Sera says, wistfully. "I wish I could've known him better. After the war, he wasn't the same man."

"His body was damaged, with his spirit, but he still loved you, loved us. He was a good man."

"Were you with him?"

A sad smile crosses Rae'lin's lips. "It was… bittersweet. In his final moments, he talked about you. He was so happy that you are married and living the life he wanted you to have. Hearing him speak of a future he wouldn't see…" she turns away a moment, wiping her tears. She looks back at Sera. "He loved us all, but he always loved you best."

Sera understands but says nothing. This was not the time or place for that discussion. "I remember him teaching me to fight with a sword, telling me no daughter of his would be unable to defend herself. It certainly came in handy, when I faced the siren queen and fought off pirates."

Rae'lin laughs, until she realizes Sera is serious. "I beg your pardon?"

"That's a story for another day. For now, come with me."

"Where?"

"I know you want to see." She smiles, taking Rae'lin's hand and leading her to the water. Once she's sure it's just the two of them, she dives into the water, transforming in mid-air.

"Well?" Sera asks as she swims towards Rae'lin.

"I was right about you." Rae'lin watches Sera swim about, her tail coming in and out of the water. She watches in awe as Sera approaches the shore, her tail transforming then she walks out of the water. "It's incredible to see!" She takes her back to the bench, letting the sun warm and dry her. "What's your favorite part of being a mermaid?"

Sera laughs. "Um, you wouldn't believe me."

"Sera?"

"Laying on the beach."

"I don't understand?"

"My tail on the sand is so comforting, warm, and relaxing in ways I can't explain. It's my favorite thing to do."

"Your favorite thing?" Rae'lin asks.

Sera laughs again, telling her about their private grotto and beach, describing their trips there. "Then we lay on the shore. It's perfect."

"It sounds wonderful." She looks her up and down. "I think you're about dry. Do you still want to go into the market?"

"It's almost time for lunch. Let's get it there."

"That sounds nice."

They walk into the village with their arms laced together, feeling closer than they ever have. They order their meal and sit together outside, the scent of the sea wafting and blending with the breads and meats. Sera watches the people coming to and fro. "I miss this dearly. The bustle of the market, my regular customers, people milling about, and walking together."

"It's what you've known your whole life. I can understand that."

Out of nowhere, Dankin appears at their table. "I didn't expect you to still be here," he admits. Sera and Rae'lin exchange a glance. "Everything all right?" he asks.

Sera takes his hand. "I'll tell you about it back at the estate, but yes, everything is okay. Do you need to eat?"

"No, I bought something there and ate on the ferry."

They finish eating and return to the estate. Sera looks at her mother, who gives her a small nod of understanding. She leads Dankin up to the bedroom and sits him on the bed.

"Hmm, what are we doing in here this time of day?" he teases.

Trying to compose herself, she lets loose a nervous giggle. "We need to talk."

He steps up and kisses her softly. "How was your morning with your mother?"

"It was wonderful. We had a nice time. Now—"

He holds her to him, his mouth on hers as his hand strokes gently through her hair. "Do we have to talk? For now, I need to have you in my arms."

She nods, as he walks to the bed, and sits down with her on his lap. He kisses her again. He lies down and pulls her on top of him. Caressing his face, she looks into his eyes. "Dankin—"

"Shh. Just be with me right now. I missed you."

She lays her head on his chest, gently bobbing with each breath. His heartbeat pounds in her ear, soothing her. "Yes, koy'lei." He holds her tightly, smiling when she falls asleep.

* * *

Sera wakes up from their nap and snuggles back into his chest, letting his breathing roll her up and down softly. She laughs when he wraps her tightly in his arms.

"You're mine now!" he calls out.

"As long as you'll have me," she answers.

He sits up, pulling her with him. He gently brushes her hair out of her face. "How long? Hmm?" He looks away, pretending to think. "I know. How about forever?" He smiles as his fingers caress along her ear.

She giggles softly. "That sounds like a good start." She takes a breath. "We need to talk—"

"Sera, Dankin, supper is almost ready," Rae'lin calls from the bottom of the stairs.

"Thank you," Dankin calls back. "We'll be down momentarily."

"Are you sure? I can put it in the warmer?" she offers with a laugh.

"Rae'lin!" He chuckles. "Yes, we're coming down."

Studying his face, Sera traces her fingers along his neck and jawline. "Having fun here?"

"I am, actually."

"Good."

"Now, let's freshen up."

She goes to the closet, getting out a lavender and pale blue hanfu. She undresses, when he walks up and kisses her.

"You told her—"

He laughs. "I know. I wanted a kiss. Now, how am I dressing for supper?"

"Strip down, and you'll find out."

"With pleasure."

"Dankin," she says with a laugh.

They dress for dinner, with Sera selecting another traditional outfit for Dankin, then they meet Rae'lin in the dining room. Chi'yo and Kye come in to serve the meal. "I helped cook, Miss Sera!" he beams with pride.

"Yes, Kye is a natural. I think you will be impressed," Chi'yo adds.

Sera looks up in surprise when Hi'tob'a joins them. "Miss Sera, Mistress Rae'lin said I could join you this evening. Is that all right?"

His eyes widen in surprise when she runs up and hugs him. "Of course! How are you?"

He tells Sera about his work in the orchard as he helps her sit back down. The table is set, and everyone is looking at Sera. She takes the first bite then smiles at Kye in approval.

"Kye, I would've had you cook sooner. This is fantastic." Dankin and Rae'lin try theirs, agreeing with her. "Did your mother teach you?" Sera asks.

"We never had much food in the house, so I would have to make do."

Kye and Chi'yo bow before returning to the kitchen. Dankin and Sera tell Hi'tob'a all about their life at court, running a kingdom, and keeping the peace. Hi'tob'a leans in and listens intently to Dankin's tales of pirates and other adventures on the high sea.

"Thank you for regaling me with your stories," Hi'tob'a says as he stands. Dankin shakes his hand, and Sera gives him another hug before he returns to his quarters.

Dankin looks from Sera to Rae'lin. "We will be leaving in the morning."

"That's what I thought. We will all miss you here."

"I'll miss you," Sera admits, looking down. Dankin looks over when he hears her sniffle.

"Sera?"

"I'm okay," she says. She leaves the table and runs upstairs.

Dankin sighs. "She wishes she could stay here."

"I do, too. However, I know how important your duties are. I hope you appreciate what she is sacrificing, for you and your kingdom."

"Believe me, I do," Dankin says before going after Sera. She's on the bed with her face buried in her pillow. Sitting on the edge of the bed, he places a comforting hand on her back. "I'm sorry. I forced you into a decision, without thinking you might not want to leave. The way you were treated here, the way you spoke of the ocean, I thought I was doing the right thing."

"I know being with you, being your wife and queen, is what I'm meant to do. Still, it hurts to leave here, not knowing when or if I'll be able to return."

He sighs. "We could stay another day," he offers.

She shakes her head. "That will only make it harder." Looking at him as she sits up, she takes his hand. "I'm not angry about what you did, because I understand your reasons. Please, don't take this against you."

"I don't." He brings his hand up, wiping her tears. "Now, let's visit some more with your mother."

She climbs over to him and into his lap, clinging to him. "Hold me a moment?"

"You never have to ask for that," he says as he takes her into his arms. "I love you, Sera. I love you more than I ever thought possible. I was looking for a wife, looking to break a curse. I had no idea I would find the love of my life in the process."

"Why did she curse you?"

"She wanted the kingdom—"

"No. I mean, to find a wife? Of all things?"

"She knew I had lost mine to her sirens. She thought it funny and cruel, making me search for someone to love me. She was a trickster, you know. I think part of her curse was that I had to fall in love, which she didn't think was possible for me. Then I met you."

"Your smile was the first thing I noticed."

"Really?"

Her face grows warm as she thinks of the first time she saw him, when he was walking around the market. "The stranger with the perfect smile."

He laughs, kissing her. "I would say the same about you. Now, let's get back downstairs. I'm sure your mother is worried."

They go back downstairs. Rae'lin stands as they walk in. "Are you all right?"

"I am. I'm sorry."

"It's okay, Sera. I'll see you again soon, I'm sure," Rae'lin says.

"We'll leave after breakfast in the morning."

"I understand."

"Could you and I have a moment in private?" Sera asks her mother.

"Of course," Rae'lin answers.

Rae'lin and Sera go into parlor while Dankin helps in the kitchen. Sera sits with Rae'lin. "I don't know what my future has in store for me, but I will do what I can to get here. Any chance I get."

"I know you will."

She takes a breath. "Um, merpeople are immortal."

"What?"

"They live forever. We don't know if I will, since he turned me into one. Truly, only time will tell. I had to tell you though, because whether I am or not, you would understand why he doesn't come as I get older, or why we stop altogether if neither of us age."

"I didn't know that."

"Even if we are, we can still come around for the next few years, maybe even a decade or so before anyone would notice."

"Does this scare you? The prospect of living forever?"

"Not really. I was a little overwhelmed when he told me, but knowing how happy he and I are together, knowing we have a future ahead of us with peace, I'm okay with it."

"Do you think you will have children?"

"Maybe one day. I don't want to rush into that, not while I'm still adapting to everything myself."

"Smart choice."

Sera leans up, hugging her tightly. "I love you, mother."

"I love you, too."

"I forgive you," she says, pulling back.

"Really?" Rae'lin asks, tears in her eyes.

"You've proven yourself to be my friend and my mother."

"Thank you." She pulls her in, squeezing her. "My beautiful daughter." She holds her tight, not wanting to let go. "I can't bear the thought of you leaving tomorrow, but I know you must."

"Growing up, I dreamed of leaving here, to have a better life."

"Now you have that."

"You allowed it to happen."

"It never should've been for financial gain. I am sorry—"

"It's custom here. I know. Like you, when you married father. Then you fell in love with him. That's what happened with us, except we fell in love first."

"I'm grateful you have him. I was only thinking of myself, of what I could gain with the transaction. Seeing you happy with him, seeing how much he loves you and cares for you, is worth every gold coin on the island."

"Thank you."

"I know you need to retire now. I'll see you in the morning." She pulls back, kissing Sera's forehead.

"Until then," Sera says, standing up. She gives her a small smile then finds Dankin having wine with Chi'yo in the kitchen. "Hmm, are we having the good stuff?"

Chi'yo laughs. "I tried, since he is the king. He insisted on the 1378, not even fifty years old yet! I told him we have older, better vintages."

"I like this one," he says. "Nothing wrong with that."

Sera laughs, walking over. He brings his glass to her mouth. She cups it in her hands as he helps her try a sip. "Hmm. It is good."

"What's your preference?"

She laughs. "Oh, no. I don't really drink."

"You don't?" Dankin asks.

"I will take a sip with company to keep up appearances, but I don't have much tolerance for it."

He finishes his glass, walking for the sink when Chi'yo takes it. "Thank you," he says, flashing her a smile.

"The king himself cooking and washing dishes. I never!"

Sera and Dankin laugh as he takes her hand and leads her upstairs. Once in their room, she walks to the mirror and removes her gown.

"What's wrong?"

Sighing, she looks at him. "Nothing," she says as she turns to the mirror. "I just don't know when… or if I'll see myself like this again."

He rushes to her and pulls her to him. "You will. I swear you will. We'll figure it out, make it so you can still be human from time to time. I've taken enough from you, I will not deprive you of your humanity."

"Dankin, you have taken nothing and given me everything."

He pulls back, surprise on his face. "Do you mean that?"

"I do. I love you, whether we are like this or in the water. As long as I am with you, that is what I long for."

"Longing for me?"

Blushing, she leans up and kisses him, fire in her eyes. Her hand reaches for his sash when he gently grips her wrist. He picks her up and carries her to bed.

"I love you."

He kisses her. "I love you, my little sea nymph."

Chapter 19

Unspoken Loss

Waking up to Dankin kissing her forehead, she snuggles into his arms. "Hmm," she moans. "I love waking up with you."

"Me, too. Now, we have a little time before breakfast. What would you like to do?"

"Can we try something?" she asks shyly.

"Okay," he answers, confused by her question.

She stands up and faces him, then climbs into his arms. Wrapping her legs around his waist, she kisses him. "I wanted to enjoy our legs while we still have them," she says.

He chuckles softly. "All right." His hand strokes through her hair as his lips are on hers, kissing her and fueled with passion. His other hand trails along her nightgown, running down her leg. "I see what you mean."

Blushing furiously, she gets to her feet. "Dankin!"

"What?"

"If you're going to make a joke—"

"No, no. I wasn't, really. I misunderstood what you wanted. I'm sorry." He steps up to her.

She looks up and kisses him again. He grows concerned when he tastes the salt of her tears. She pulls back, looking at him. "I'm okay—" she tries.

"Sera, what's wrong?" He sighs when she looks down. "This isn't your last day as a human. I mean it. We'll use the pearls and figure this out."

"That's what I was trying to talk to you about yesterday. I transformed in the bath and couldn't change back. I had to dry off and focus completely before I would. Then I tried again and changed with no problem!" She doesn't admit she did it at the beach in front of Rae'lin, worried he it might anger him, especially since she had forgotten about her pearl.

"I know you're scared. It's going to be okay," he assures her as she clings to him, trembling as she cries. "Let's see about breakfast and spend some time with your family. We'll talk more once we're back at the palace," he offers.

She nods, pulling away from him.

* * *

Sera helps Chi'yo cook while Dankin gets out plates and silverware. She laughs at the look on Chi'yo's face. "I will never get used to that," Chi'yo admits.

"We are still us. Why is this surprising to you?"

"He is a king, and you a queen. You should be sitting, letting us serve you—" she argues, until Sera raises her hand.

"Chi'yo, as I've said, when we are here, we are simply Sera and Dankin. We need a break from the palace, from duty, from titles. Please, indulge us?"

She sighs. "Yes, Miss Sera."

Rae'lin walks in, and they sit together. "You're leaving right after breakfast?"

"We are. I'm sorry," Dankin says.

"I understand. I've enjoyed your visit," Rae'lin responds.

"So have we," Sera agrees, looking up when Dankin takes her hand and kisses it. She gives him a small smile before turning her attention back to her food.

Na'ito walks in. "Thanks for waiting."

Dankin laughs. "How is everything?"

"Going really good," he says.

"Really well," Rae'lin corrects him.

Na'ito shoots Sera a smile while eating. "Right."

"We hope to come back soon," she says.

"Wait, you're leaving already?" Na'ito asks.

"Yes, after breakfast. We have to return to our duties."

He sighs. "I know. I wish we could've had more time together."

"We will on our next visit," she says, reassuring him.

They go upstairs and pack. Sera looks around the room, certain it's the last time she will see it. Dankin takes her hand, giving it a squeeze to reassure her. They go downstairs to find Rae'lin, Na'ito, Hi'tob'a, and Chi'yo waiting for them.

"Quite the going away party," Dankin says.

Sera walks up and hugs each of them, and Rae'lin holds her tight. "Be safe, my daughter."

"I will."

Dankin and Sera say their goodbyes then start on the path to the beach. She holds back her tears, not wanting him to see her cry. Arriving at the beach, they go to the small cove for privacy. He picks her up and carries her in, then dives as they transform. Neither of them notices the man, watching from a distance with his spy glass, taking notes.

* * *

Sera pulls away, holding his hand as they swim back to the palace. He gets her into their quarters.

"How do you feel?"

"I'm okay," she answers, looking down at her silver tail as they sit beside each other on the bed.

"Will you look at me?" he asks. She meets his gaze. "I need to check on things. Do you want to stay here or come with me?"

"I'll stay in here."

"What if you transform?"

"I have my pearl, and I'll be fine."

Looking unsure, he gives a small nod. "I'll be back shortly."

"I know. I should check on things, too." She sighs.

Dankin grows concerned when she lies down. "Sera?"

"I'm tired."

"You shouldn't be." He looks her over. "You don't hurt? Don't feel sick?"

"No, just tired."

"Hmm. Okay, lay here and rest. I'll be back shortly."

"You have a kingdom to run—"

"And a wife to worry about." He leans down, kissing her forehead. "I'll have your handmaids wait outside, in case you need anything."

"Thank you." She watches him swim out of the room, then closes her eyes and falls asleep.

* * *

Dankin returns, swimming to the bed and sitting on the edge, watching her. He chuckles softly at her quiet snores. Holding her hand, he worries over her sleeping so much. She wakes up shortly after.

"How long was I out?"

"I was gone about an hour."

"Then an hour. I feel a little better. I think it was just my worries over everything. I'll be okay now." She gives him a reassuring smile.

"You better be," he says as he helps her sit up. "Do you feel up to studying with Ava'lei and Fai'mi?"

"Yes, that's fine. I'll go with them to the library."

"Can I join you?"

"Of course."

They swim out to the hall, where Dankin instructs Ava'lei and Fai'mi where to go. They arrive at the library. Sera swims over to the culture section to pick out a few books. She sits with her handmaids, excited to learn about the different merpeople clans, their customs, and their religions. They break for lunch.

"What are you reading about?" Dankin asks when he joins them to eat.

"Right now, the Sol'lun'a clan," Sera answers.

"Oh, they are interesting. Their skin is as white as yours, and they use magic to create glowing blue tattoos on their body. Their magic isn't near as powerful as ours, but it's beautiful to see," Dankin says with envy.

"Will we meet them?" Sera asks.

"Yes. We tour some of the other merdoms and, sometimes, we host them here. Their ruler is called a'poto, which works for king or queen. It basically translates to 'one who is reigning.' They are a friendly clan." He gives her a smile as they finish eating. She resumes studying with her handmaids as he reads off to the side. He comes over at four.

"Would you like to freshen up before supper?" Dankin asks.

"Please," Sera replies.

"Handmaids, you are dismissed."

"Yes, Your Majesty." They bow and swim out.

He turns to Sera, who gives him a look. "What?"

"If they are my handmaids, why do you dismiss them?"

"Apologies. It's a habit, being the…" he clears his throat, "the only ruler for so long."

"It's okay."

"No, they are your handmaids. I will do better."

They go back to their quarters, getting changed for supper. He watches as she looks herself over. He swims closer.

She turns her attention to him as he approaches her. "Just admiring the gown."

He changes into a black shirt with his sword on his hip. She looks at it, remembers the grotto, and quickly turns away. "What's wrong?" he asks.

"Nothing," she answers. He takes her hand, surprised when she pulls away. "Let's go to supper, shall we?" Sera says.

He decides to let it go for the time being.

* * *

They're getting ready for bed one night, when he notices she is cold to the touch. "Are you ill?"

She looks at him, as he runs his hand up her arm. He brings it to her forehead. "I don't feel sick," she says. "I've just been tired lately."

"Hmm."

"Do merpeople get sick?"

"Not generally."

"If I'm not better tomorrow, we'll go to the infirmary. I promise."

"I'll hold you to that." He takes her to bed, wrapping her in his arms and prays she really is okay.

* * *

Sera wakes up and smiles at him. "Morning, koy'lei."

"Morning. How do you feel?"

"Better."

He runs his fingers over her arm and hand. "You aren't cold, so that's good. Still, I worry."

"I know you do." She kisses him. "I love you for that."

"Let's get ready for breakfast."

"Do you think we could go to our grotto today? We haven't been in a while."

"Yes. After breakfast, I'll check on a few things, then we'll go."

"Great!" Taking a moment, she builds up her courage. "Since I have been doing so well down here, do you think we could go and see my family?"

Dankin rubs his chin as he thinks it over. "I say we wait just a little longer."

"Dankin—"

"It's too dangerous for you. We will go again, I promise. Now, let's eat then we'll go to our grotto."

* * *

Sera enjoys meeting some of the merpeople while she is waiting for Dankin, who had to check on a few things before leaving. Once he returns, he takes her into the grand foyer. "Oh, one thing I forgot. I'll be right back."

"Of course, koy'lei. I'll wait here." She smiles at him while watching him swim away. She looks up when Da'vae approaches her. "Good morning."

"Morning, Your Grace. How are you and my brother doing?"

She looks him over, not liking his tone of voice. "We're fine," she says, trying to appear calm. She looks behind him to see if there's a guard or anyone else in the entryway. She becomes worried when she realizes she is alone with him. "Are you courting anyone?"

"I met a siren."

"You?"

He laughs. "Yes, it's surprising. Now that they're free of their curse, they are actually sweet once you get to know them."

"I'm glad to hear that. Dankin will be back any moment, and we are going for a little swim."

"Hmm, why wait?"

She laughs. "You're funny."

He swims up to her. "I wasn't joking," he whispers in her ear. His hand is on her side as he pulls back. "It's just the two of us."

"I thought you were trying to make amends?" She gasps when he whispers inappropriate things in her ear. She pulls back, bringing her hand up to slap him when he grabs her wrist.

"I don't think so!" He jerks her over, folding her into him. "Hmm. This feels nice and cozy, doesn't it?"

She struggles to get away when he tightens his grip. Easing her body, she smiles at him. "You're right, it does." As soon as he eases, she flips back, her tail slapping him in the face. He swims to her when she pulls out her dagger. "Stay back!" she cries.

"What is going on?" Dankin asks, swimming up.

"I asked if I could go with you two on your swim, and she flipped out! Literally!"

Dankin looks at him, then at her. "Sera?"

She puts the blade away, raising her hands and looking at Dankin. "That is not what happened." She swims up to him and takes his hand. "I was polite, wishing him a good morning. Then it went downhill from there." She tells him everything Da'vae said and did.

Dankin sighs, looking at him. "Da'vae—"

"She's lying! She just wants to drive a wedge between us. She hasn't forgiven me for hurting her, and she took a little harmless flirting the wrong way. That's all."

Sera looks at Dankin, clasping his hand with both of hers. "Please, Dankin. I told you the truth."

Dankin looks from Da'vae to Sera, remembering the morning he was told Da'vae had been killed. He shakes his head, pushing down the pain. "I believe you saw it that way," he says to Sera.

Her eyes go wide as she pulls her hand back. "What?"

"Look, the two of you need to get along. Why doesn't he accompany us—where are you going?" he asks as she swims to her quarters as fast as she can, going inside and locking the door. She rushes to the closet. Dankin comes in, keys in hand, and is confused when he doesn't see her. "Sera?"

"Go away!" she calls out.

"Sera, please. Let's discuss this." He places his hand on the closet door, wanting desperately to see her and reassure her everything is okay.

"I told you exactly what happened. Not what I think or what I feel, but literally what happened!"

"You are upset—"

She opens the door, shock on her face. "Really? Do you think? Your brother just attacked me! Of course I'm upset!"

He sighs. "You just don't understand his sense of humor—"

"You're defending him?" Her mouth opens at the realization. "Because he's the only family you have left. Please, I don't want to do this, but I am telling you the truth. Please, please, believe me."

"I want to give him the benefit of the doubt, and I want you to give him another chance. Will you do that for me?"

She shuts the door, slumping against it, and sinking to the floor. She brings her tail up as she buries her face in her hands.

"Sera—"

"Go!" she cries out. "I don't want to see you or your brother!"

"Fine. I'll talk to him. Maybe I can find a way to make you two work together."

"Give me some time to think about it?" she asks, a plan formulating in her mind.

"I'll be back shortly. Please, stay here," he begs before leaving.

She changes gowns, feeling disgusted after what Da'vae did. She lets the gown she was wearing sink down as she slips on a pale blue hanfu. Opening the door and looking out, she sighs in relief when she realizes she's alone. She goes to the window, forcing it open and swims towards Isle Piscantur, ready to see her family. Arriving at the beach, she climbs up onto their private cove and groans in frustration when she doesn't transform. "Not now, please. I need this."

She pulls herself to the sand, relishing in the warmth on her tail. Her eyes close as she thinks of walking the market with her mother, walking along the beach, picking up shells and tracing her fingers in the sand. Relief floods her body when she her legs return. Walking to the bench and sitting down, she enjoys the sun as she finds comfort in its warmth.

"Why are you here?" Dankin asks.

She looks up as he sits next to her. "Because right now, I need to be around people who care for me, who will believe me if I tell them something."

"I'm sorry."

"Right," she scoffs.

"No. He told me everything you said was true."

"How did you manage that?"

"You won't like my answer." He looks down before meeting her gaze. "I gave him another chance. I told him to tell me the truth, or he would be banished."

"I'm glad he did, but I'm still angry that you didn't believe me. You had to see how scared I was, how upset."

"I was blinded by the fact that he is family," Dankin explains in earnest.

"Please, return to the palace. Let me have tonight with my family, then I will return tomorrow."

He takes her hand, kissing it. "Whatever you need. Do you forgive me?"

"I want to. I need some time away, after what happened."

"All right." He kisses her forehead. "I love you, Sera."

"I love you," she says, fighting back tears. "I'll return tomorrow."

"Until then," he says, getting to his feet. "I'll miss you."

She watches him swim into the ocean. Her thoughts wander back to Dankin and Da'vae, and she cries silently, unsure again of what her future will hold. When at last she calms down, she strolls along the familiar path from the beach to the estate. She smiles when she sees Rae'lin walking up from the orchard. They hug and go inside.

Rae'lin gestures her into the parlor. "So, why are you really here?" she asks.

"What do you mean?"

"Middle of the week, no husband. What happened?" She gestures for her to sit, surprised when Sera folds into her arms, crying. Sera tells her everything his brother did. "And he didn't believe you?" Rae'lin asks in disbelief.

"No, he defended Da'vae."

"I'm sorry, Sera. That must have been terrible."

"I don't know what to do now."

"I believe Dankin is a good man. He'll come around and realize what he needs to do." Rae'lin strokes Sera's hair. "For now, you can stay here as long as you need."

"Thank you. Will you help me cook lunch?" Sera asks.

"Of course."

They discuss the upcoming festival while they eat. "I wish I could come back for this one. The Amphit'ran festival was so much fun." Looking at her ring, she thinks of Dankin asking her to marry him, and how happy she was. She wipes a tear. "Um, are you going?"

"I'm planning on it. The harvest festival isn't usually as exciting, but it is a nice gathering."

"I'll return to the palace tomorrow. I have work to catch up on."

"You stay as long as you need," Rae'lin insists.

"Thank you. I'm going to lay down."

"Are you all right?"

"Yes, just tired." Sera hugs Rae'lin before starting up the stairs. When she gets to the third step, she collapses against the rail. Rae'lin runs to her, takes her back to the parlor, and is frightened when Sera passes out on the couch.

"Fetch the doctor!" Rae'lin cries out. Chi'yo runs in, shocked at the sight before she runs from the room as fast as he can. "Sera, can you hear me?" Rae'lin asks, her voice full of concern.

* * *

"What happened?" Rae'lin asks.

"…wasn't far along… No pain now…"

Sera doesn't recognize the man's voice as she tries to listen. Her eyes flutter as she fights to stay conscious.

"What now?" Rae'lin asks.

"She'll be fine. Maybe sleep a day or two, but…"

Sera passes out again.

* * *

Slowly coming to, Sera listens to her mother and brother speak softly, only catching pieces of their conversation.

"Whatever she needs…do not speak of this… Please see to supper…"

"Hmm," Sera moans, moving slightly.

Rae'lin walks over to take her hand. "Sera, how do you feel?"

"Exhausted. What happened?"

Rae'lin clears her throat. "You overdid it, was all. You need your rest now."

"Will you help me to bed?"

"You are in bed, Sera. We moved you up here after the doctor left."

Sera's eyes flutter open. "Oh, I thought I was still in the parlor. I must've been out."

"You were. The doctor said for you to rest a day or two. Will you do that for me?"

"I will."

"Do you think you could eat something?"

"Yes. I'm sorry, I didn't come here to inconvenience—"

"Stop. You are my daughter, and we want to take care of you."

"Thank you."

Na'ito walks in and hands Rae'lin the plate. "How are you, sis?" he asks, looking at her with worry drawn on his face.

"I'm okay. Apparently, I was overdoing it."

Na'ito shifts uncomfortably and clears his throat. "From what I've heard, you have a habit of that." He smiles at her, sorrow in his eyes.

"I'll take it easy for now," she assures him.

Rae'lin helps her eat, then hands her empty plate to Na'ito. He runs it downstairs. "Can I get you anything else?" Rae'lin offers.

"A cup of mint tea would be great."

"Of course. I'll be back with that."

Sera watches her go before weeping into her hands. When she hears Rae'lin's footsteps on the stairs, she wipes her tears. Rae'lin walks to her side and set the tray of tea on the nightstand.

"Here you are," Rae'lin says as she hands Sera the cup and saucer. "Careful, it's hot."

"Thank you for making this." She sips it slowly, enjoying the flavor and warmth. Rae'lin sits in a chair beside her bed, and they spend the next hour talking about Sera's father, her life at the estate overseeing the orchard, her kingdom in the ocean, the people she has met. Na'ito brings in tea and fresh lemon scones.

"How are you feeling?" Rae'lin asks.

"Better, but still tired," she says, looking down at her hands. "Thank you, for taking care of me."

"Of course."

Sera finishes her tea. Na'ito takes the plates as Rae'lin helps her to the washtoire, then into a nightgown. She gets her back in bed, covering her up. She kisses her forehead.

"I love you, Rae'lin."

"I love you, my daughter. Now rest."

"I will," she says, pulling the blanket to her chin. She falls asleep, dreaming of her grotto and the warm sand.

* * *

Yawning and stretching, Sera groans when she feels how heavy her legs are. Confused, she pulls the blanket off and looks in surprise at her tail. She falls back against the pillow.

"Sera, how are—" Rae'lin walks in and freezes at the sight. "Again?"

"I dreamed of swimming and being in the grotto, laying on the sand. I swear I thought I had better control than this by now."

"It's okay."

"I have break—" Na'ito walks in, freezing in place and dropping the plate at the sight of her. "Sera? What—what happened to you?"

Rae'lin grabs his arm and pulls him inside before shutting the door. "Dankin is a merman king. He turned her into a mermaid so they could marry."

Na'ito looks at his mother in shock, before turning back to Sera. She gives him a small nod. "Okay…"

"Rae'lin, that's one way to put it. Na'ito, I promise you, there is much more to it than that. I can turn myself now. Sometimes it happens on accident."

"What do you need?" Rae'lin asks while Na'ito cleans up the mess he made.

"For now, I need water. Once I'm dry, I think I can turn myself back."

Rae'lin goes in and starts the tub filling up. Na'ito approaches. "How can I help?"

"Getting her into the tub," Rae'lin answers.

He walks over to pick Sera up, when she holds up her hand. "Brother—"

"I am strong enough," Na'ito assures her. "I have been working in the orchard, and my strength is fully returned."

She sighs. "All right."

He scoops her up, carries her into the washtoire, and gently lowers her into the tub. "I'll give you privacy," he says as he leaves the room.

"Is the water okay?" Rae'lin asks.

"It's perfect, thank you. I am supposed to carry a magic pearl with me, but after the things Da'vae said to me, I changed gowns and left in a hurry. I forgot to grab the pearl. There should be enough magic in my ring, at least I hope so."

"For the time being, lay back and enjoy the water. Don't try to force anything, just relax. Can you do that?"

"I will."

"I'm going to see to a few things, then I'll be back."

She steps out, closing the door behind her. Sera pushes down thoughts of how she left things with Dankin and thinks of her grief at what she just experienced while wondering how she could possibly tell him. She decides to focus instead on trying to transform back. She imagines herself walking on the beach with the heat of the sun flushing her skin, the warmth of the sand on her feet. She opens her eyes, sighing at the sight of her tail.

*Don't force it, like she said. Relax. How can I relax? After everything—no. She's right. I overdo things, and I need to take it easy. I've already—*She stifles the sob, calming herself down. *It's going to be okay. Dankin and I will make up, and we will live a long, happy life together. That's what I want, more than anything.*

She bends her tail up so she can reach the chain. The water drains out slowly, leaving her sitting in an empty tub. With a long stretch, she manages to reach the edge of a towel and pull it from the rack. Rae'lin walks in as she's drying her tail.

"Do you think you can help me to the bed? I'm pretty heavy with a tail."

"I used to lift your father, so I think I can," Rae'lin replies. Sera brings her arm around Rae'lin's shoulder. She picks Sera up before carrying her slowly to the bed. She gets her on and watches as Sera rolls over.

"Thank you."

"Is there a way I can send for Dankin?" Rae'lin asks.

"There is, but I don't want to see him yet. Give me a little time, and if I still can't change back by supper, we'll send for him."

"All right. I'm only agreeing because I know it means you have to lay here and take it easy until you can."

Sera smiles at her. "Thanks."

They both laugh. "Seriously, though. Rest today, then we'll see what happens."

"How is Na'ito? Is he in shock?"

Rae'lin chuckles softly. "A little, but he understands now why you can't visit as often as he would like."

They look up when there's a knock at the door. "Come in," Sera answers.

Na'ito walks in. "I wanted to see how you're... um, doing."

She laughs. "I'm okay. Still trying, though."

"I see," he says, trying not to stare.

"It's okay. You can look. It's just a mermaid tail."

"You say that like it's not a big deal."

"It's not, at least, not to me."

"Did you marry him for me?" Na'ito asks, meeting her gaze.

"What do you mean?" Sera asks.

"So he would heal me?"

"He asked me to marry him at the lantern festival, and I said yes. I didn't even know who or what he was until after. This is not your fault, do you understand?"

Na'ito nods. "We're going to the market, unless you need me here," he offers.

"No, go ahead. We'll be fine," Sera answers.

He walks over and hugs her. "I'll see you later."

"You will. I won't leave without saying goodbye, I promise."

He gives her one last look before leaving. Rae'lin stands by the door. "Rest now."

"Honestly, I think I'm going to sleep some more. I am quite tired."

"It's weird."

"What?"

"You usually yawn… a lot," Rae'lin says with a laugh.

"Apparently, we don't. As mermaids, I mean."

"I didn't think of that. Get some sleep, and I'll check on you shortly."

As soon as she's gone, Sera sits up. She looks at her tail, determined to change back. She groans when nothing happens. "Please?" she begs. "Please, just change back for me. I can't—" she buries her face in her hands, crying in defeat.

* * *

Sera jerks awake as her legs return. She looks up to see Rae'lin and Dankin standing at the foot of the bed. She pulls away. "What—"

"He showed up, worried about you. I'll give you two some privacy." Rae'lin explains as she walks out.

Sera looks at Dankin before turning on her side. "Thank you for that," she says as she pulls the blanket up.

"So, your mother knows?"

"She does."

"How are you?" Dankin asks, his voice quavering with worry.

"I'm fine," she responds quietly. "I need more sleep. Thank you for coming to check on me."

"Sera—" She raises her hand and gestures him out. His hands clench, and he takes a breath. "Of course. I'll see you tomorrow?"

"The doctor said I should be fine by then."

"Wait, what doctor?" Dankin asks, his concern growing.

Sera's eyes squeeze shut. "Rae'lin didn't tell you?"

"No, only about your tail. What happened?"

"Please, go," she begs as tears are streaming down her cheeks. "I can't—"

He sits on the edge of the bed and takes her hand. "Talk to me?"

"I'm okay. I overdid it, is all," she says as she looks at him, giving him a reassuring smile.

His heart aches at the sorrow in her eyes and pain in her voice. "All right. Rest for now, and I'll be in the parlor until you need me."

"Dankin, I know you have a kingdom to run. I'm still trying to—" she rolls on her stomach and buries her face in her pillow. He caresses her back, trying to bring her some comfort.

"I know, and I'm sorry. All right, I'll return to the kingdom if you'll promise to be back tomorrow by supper."

"I promise," Sera says, muffled by the pillow.

He stands up and kisses the back of her head as his hand strokes through her hair. "Until then," he says, putting the pearl in her hand. Once she hears the door shut, she sits up and studies the pearl. Gripping it tightly, she transforms from human to mermaid, then back to human. She opens the drawer in her nightstand, removing a small pouch and placing the pearl inside.

* * *

"Dankin, I won't tell you anything that she won't."

"Why did she need a doctor?"

"Please, stop asking. She will tell you when she is ready. She is okay now and just needs rest."

"Rae'lin—"

"No. After what you and your brother have put her through, you need to give her some time."

"She told you that? She told you our business?" he asks, getting angry.

"She didn't have to! I could hear and see it. She was devastated when she got here, then she nearly fainted on the stairs—"

"What do you mean? She fainted?"

"Yes, as soon as I got her into the parlor."

"Tell me what happened!" he demands, his anger dissolving into worry over Sera.

She laughs. "You will not give me orders, king or not. Especially not when it's my daughter involved."

"She's been my wife longer than she was your daughter. For most of her life, she was only treated as your servant!"

"Well, she is my daughter now, and I will do whatever I have to in order to keep her safe. It's sad I even have to say that to her very husband!"

"My brother will be punished for all he has done to her. I have him locked up now while I debate how best to proceed. You have to realize, I lost my wife and daughters, and he was all I had—"

"You have my daughter!" Rae'lin yells.

"He was all I had for so long," Dankin finishes, "and I didn't want to believe he could be capable of such things. I pray she will forgive me, though I know I do not deserve it."

Rae'lin scoffs. "At least you can admit you don't deserve it."

"I'm not a bad guy. I have been cruel to her, mistreated her in ways I regret, but I truly do love her. I don't ever want her crying because of me. I will show her what a husband is supposed to be. That's what she deserves. Not because of what she has already suffered through, not because she saved my people, saved me, but because she is worthy simply by being her."

"Do you really mean that?" Sera asks.

He looks over to see Sera leaning in the doorframe, then rushes to her. "With every fiber of my being," he says as he takes her hand and kisses it.

She meets his gaze. "Then I forgive you."

He pulls her to him, crushing her to his chest. He grips her tightly as his tears flow down. "Thank you." Rae'lin walks out, giving them privacy.

Sera pulls back and looks at him. "Why were the two of you fighting in the first place?"

"I was worried about you, especially after you mentioned the doctor had been by. I was trying to get her to tell me. I'm sorry. I wasn't trying to go behind your back, but—" His words die in his throat as she leans up and kisses him.

"Thank you for loving me and caring for me so."

"I mean it, I will do better. I promise you."

"I know you will. I believe in you, if nothing else."

"I'm not worthy of it."

"Yes, you are. You protected me here when I was most vulnerable. You saved my brother, helped my family. Believe me, you are."

"Are you ready to return or do you want more time with your family?"

"Both," she admits. "Let's stay for lunch, and then we'll return home."

"All right." They walk into the kitchen where she helps Chi'yo prepare lunch as Dankin sets the table. Rae'lin walks in.

"I'm leaving after lunch. Thank you for everything."

Rae'lin walks over and holds her tight. "Sera, any time. I mean that."

"I know. Thank you."

Kye and Na'ito walk in just as they are sitting at the table. Na'ito smiles at Sera. She gives him a slight nod. "Busy today!" Kye remarks, washing his hands. He looks at Dankin. "Welcome, Your Majesty." He bows.

Dankin smiles. "How are you? How is your mother?"

"I'm well, and she is doing much better. The treatment is helping, and they think she should be released in the next few weeks. I am trying to find us somewhere to live—"

"Kye, you may both stay here while she is still recovering," Rae'lin says. "Once she is healthy enough, we will help you find a place."

"I don't know what to say."

"Then say yes," Sera replies, smiling at him.

"Yes, Miss Sera. Yes, Miss Rae'lin. Thank you so much."

Dankin helps Chi'yo clean up after lunch while Sera and Rae'lin go upstairs. She gets out her pearl, showing her mother.

"It's beautiful," Rae'lin comments, staring at the large pearl in awe.

"I thought it was just a pearl. I had no idea it was so powerful."

"Will you show me? If it's not too much for you, I mean."

Sera gets on the bed and transforms to a mermaid then back to human. "See?"

"Wow. It's incredible." She helps Sera to her feet. "You'll still be careful though? About turning back and forth?"

"I'll only do it as long as I have the pearl."

"We'll see you again soon? And not just because you've had a fight?" Rae'lin asks, giving her a small grin.

Sera laughs. "Yes, we'll come visit when we can."

They go downstairs and say their goodbyes. Dankin walks with her, holding her hand in his as they begin their walk to the beach.

"You look better."

"I feel a lot better," Sera says.

"Will you tell me?" he asks.

She squeezes his hand. "I will, in time."

"When you're ready. I won't push you. I see now that I can be too harsh, and that is something else I am working on."

"Thank you." They arrive at the beach and go to their private cove. She looks up at him. "Can I ask a favor?"

He laughs, picking her up as he sits on the sand, while they both transform. "Didn't even have to, did you?"

She joins his laughter. "No. I love laying like this. It's soothing."

"I'm glad to hear that."

Lying together on the sand, she lets the sun comfort her sorrow and warm her cold heart. Hearing voices, she looks over and sees people are walking towards the beach.

"It'll be getting busy soon. We need to get back." She gasps softly when he rolls on top of her, kissing her. "Dankin!" she laughs.

"What? I don't get to kiss you on the beach like this as often as I would like."

"Well, we have a private beach…"

"Tomorrow, my little sea nymph. For now, let's return to the palace." His eyes go wide in surprise when she grips him by the back of his head and kisses him with all the love inside her. He melts into her arms, getting lost with her. Reluctantly, he pulls away. "We should go before we're seen."

"Yes, my koy'lei."

* * *

"I need to go to the library," Sera says when they arrive at the palace.

"Let's have supper—"

"I'll eat in there."

"Okay," he says, taking her to the library, where she gives him a soft kiss.

"I need to look something up, and… I need privacy. Please?"

He looks at her, confused and worried, but he doesn't argue. "I'll see about having supper brought here while you look. You know you can ask me about anything, right?"

"I know," she answers, giving him a small smile.

Once he's gone, she goes over to the health and anatomy books, getting a few off the shelf and sitting at a table. She reads about mermaid design. Dankin is watching her in concern when she looks at him, forcing him to look away a moment. She considers asking him, but her skin grows flush, and she realizes she cannot, so she returns to her book. After a while he brings over a plate and sets it on the table beside her.

"Thank you," she says.

"Sera—" He tries looking at the book in her hands, but her arm covers the title.

"Just a few more minutes, please? Then I'll go wherever you want. You can sit there," she gestures to the table beside her. "I'm almost finished."

"All right." He leans down and kisses her, trying once more to catch a glimpse.

Taking the plate, she eats as she continues to look through the book. When she's done, she puts the books back. "Where to?" she asks.

He takes her hand, swimming into a corridor she doesn't recognize. He takes her inside a luxurious suite. "This is my office."

"It's beautiful," she says. She runs her fingers over the shells and statues on his shelves, then swims over to the clamshell chaise and sits. "This is really comfortable. I love it."

He laughs. "Jealous?" he asks.

"A little," she admits. "Now, what are we doing in your office?"

"Our duty," he answers as he goes to the desk and picks up a stack of papers. "The Sol'lun'a clan have asked us to broker a treaty with the Tsun'ama clan. I agreed. Will you help?"

She swims over. "I don't know how much help I'll be, but I'll try."

"Only way you'll learn, right?"

"Of course."

He goes over their history, why they fought in the past. He shows her other treaties still in effect. They write a new treaty based on information from both sides. "I'll send this over, and their leaders will meet with us to negotiate."

She looks up at him. "Are we about to turn in?"

"We are." He locks the papers in his desk. She looks at the keys in his hand. "What?" he asks.

"I want the keys to my room."

"I don't understand, we both have keys—"

"To our quarters, yes, but when I need space, I like to use the smaller room next door. I've taken to calling it my room, I suppose. I want your key, so I can have privacy when I need it." She holds out her hand.

"I have keys to every room in this palace. What if something were to happen, an emergency or—"

"Please?"

He sighs, removing the key and handing her. "Hopefully, you won't need it anymore."

She laughs. "That's true." She adds it to her key ring then they swim back to their quarters. She changes into a nightgown. He comes up behind her, wrapping his arms around and placing his hands on her stomach. "Dankin, please—"

He pulls back. "I just wanted to hold you. What's wrong?"

She shakes her head, looking down. "I thought… I—"

"You thought I wanted more?"

"Yes, I'm sorry. I'm really tired."

"We both need sleep," he admits.

She gets into bed and covers up with the blanket. Snuggling into his chest, she smiles as he holds her. "I love you."

"Oh, my little sea nymph, I hope you know how much I love you."

"I do," she says.

He kisses the top of her head. "Good. Now sleep."

She closes her eyes, pushing away her sorrow, as she falls asleep in his arms. Concern drawn on his face, Dankin watches her sleep. *Please, Sera, I wish you would let me in.*

Chapter 20

Making Promises

Dankin is still sleeping soundly when Sera wakes up. She gets dressed and goes to the great hall, not wanting to disturb him.

"Morning, Your Grace," Ava'lei says as she and Fai'mi both bow to Sera.

"Morning. Weekly inspection today, right?"

"Yes," Fai'mi confirms.

"I'll meet you in the galley after breakfast." She watches them swim off as Dankin comes in. "Morning," she says as he approaches her.

"Morning to you," he replies, looking her up and down. "Why didn't you wake me?" he asks, concern in his voice.

She laughs. "You were sleeping really hard." Seeing the serious look on his face, she gasps. "I'm sorry. I forgot. It wasn't on purpose."

"I know. You aren't cruel like me," he says, winking at her.

"You better not be cruel!"

"I won't be. Well, not to you, at least."

Their breakfast arrives. "I'm meeting my handmaids in the galley after we eat for the inspection."

"Right. I'll be in my office."

"I don't want to be away from you," she blurts out.

He stops eating and looks at her. "What's wrong?"

"Nothing," she says, hanging her head. "I'm sorry. I should be stronger—"

"Sera, it's okay. I can join you for the inspection, then we can work together in my office. Just admit it, it's because you like my chaise."

She laughs, looking up at him. "I do like it." She squeezes his hand. "I mean it, though. I want to be with you today."

"We will do the inspection, get a few things done, then we'll go to our grotto. Is that all right?"

"Yes," she answers, not much above a whisper.

"I wish I knew what was going on with you," he stops when she gives him a look. "Only so I would know how to give you comfort."

"Just be with me? That's what I need right now."

* * *

In the galley, she watches him swim to the head chef while she inspects the tables with her handmaids. Arriving at the flower table, she looks at Fai'mi.

"They are starting to wilt," she points out.

"We know," Ava'lei says, picking one up. She and Fai'mi smile at each other before turning back to Sera. "We thought you would like to learn how to make hair pua'au."

"What is that?" she asks, interested.

Ava'lei opens her bag, getting out pins, ribbons, and clips. She helps Sera pick her flowers, wraps the stems together, and runs a pin through to secure it. She brings it up to Sera's hair, clipping it in. She takes her to a mirror on the wall. "Well?"

"It's beautiful! Thank you."

"We do this as tribute, so the flowers are not wasted," Fai'mi explains.

"That is really nice. I like that." She looks over, blushing when Dankin gives her playful wave and smiles at her. She shakes her head, turning to back Ava'lei. "Are you and Fai'mi making one, too?"

"We are. As queen, you received first pick."

"Tradition?" Sera asks.

"Yes."

They each make up their hair pua'au then pin them in.

"We are going with Dankin to his office for some work, then he and I have plans," Sera says.

"Yes, Your Grace."

She swims to Dankin. He brings his hand up to gently touch around her flowers. "So beautiful, like you." He kisses her, watching her blush and look down. "Apologies, my sea nymph."

"It's okay," she says as she takes his hand and swims with him to his office. Her handmaids sit with her to help her learn about the clans they are trying to broker peace for while Dankin catches up on the reports he missed. Near lunchtime, a kitchen worker knocks on the door. Ava'lei answers and brings a basket to Dankin's desk.

"Your Majesty, this was delivered for you."

"Yes, thank you." He looks at Sera.

"Handmaids, you are dismissed until I call upon you," Sera says.

They bow and swim out.

"Are we ready to go?" Dankin asks.

"Yes," she answers, eyeing the basket. He smiles as he takes it with one hand, taking hers in his other.

* * *

When they arrive at the grotto, he pulls them up onto the beach and opens the basket. He lays out a small blanket to dry and sets out a delicious spread of food, with crab, oysters, mussels, and shrimp. They sit and eat together, when she catches him staring at her.

"What?" she asks.

"You, sitting here. You have your tail resting on the sand, flowers in your hair, you look as if you were made to be here."

"I'm starting to feel that way, too." She finishes her shrimp, looking up at him. "I want to tell you, but I'm afraid of your reaction."

"I don't understand."

"I worry that you will blame me or… blame yourself… and I can't bear that right now. I need comfort and support, not blame or anger."

"I swear to you, I will never blame you again. I blamed you for my brother's death, and that was one of the worst mistakes I've ever made, next to not being able to save my wife or daughters." He looks up when she gasps. "What?"

"That was the other thing we need to talk about."

"Sera?"

"You don't have to believe me or him, but I will tell you. My father left Rae'lin a letter once he knew his life was drawing near the end. He told her about the merpeople and sirens, the war between them. He told her how he saw a mermaid and siren fighting, when he rushed over to help. He killed the siren quickly, but when he tried to assist the mermaid, her wounds were too great. She dissolved before him. He blamed himself for your daughter's death, but he was not responsible."

Dankin sits in silence for a moment, taking in everything she's said. "I can believe that," he replies. "I came to the surface as I saw him pulling his blade back. From where I was, it looked like it came out of my daughter. I see now what you're saying."

"Do you still blame him?"

"How can I? Had the situation been reversed, I would've done the same thing he did. I am sorry he carried guilt for so long, as that was not his fault."

"Thank you," she says, reaching her arms around his neck and holding him tightly. "I was so hoping you would feel that way."

He holds her to him, squeezing tighter when she begins to cry. "Are these tears because of your father or the other thing you want to tell me?"

"A little of both."

He looks at her as he wipes away her tears. "Whatever you tell me, I will listen with love and compassion, with no anger or blame. I promise."

She takes a breath, picking up another shrimp. She eats it, smiling at him. "I will hold you to that." She sits in his arms, telling him what happened at the estate. She traces her fingers over his hand. "Do you… do you blame me?" she asks quietly.

"How could I?" he asks, cradling her face in his hands. "I'm sorry you had to deal with that without me and after everything that happened with Da'vae."

"Rae'lin comforted me. She took good care of me."

"I know, but that's my job. I never want you to feel so isolated from me again. I will do better, I promise."

"Thank you. Can we soak in our pool?" She gasps when he picks her up and carries her into the soothing water. "I love when you do that!" She laughs. He joins her in the pool, holding her in his arms as he transforms back. She relaxes in his arms. "I love coming here, especially with you." She looks up, kissing him. He grips her tighter, his kiss hungry. She pulls back, looking down. "I—I'm not—"

"I'm sorry. I know what you're going through. I didn't mean to make you feel that way. I just needed to kiss you."

She kisses him again, returning his hunger. He pulls back, looking into her eyes. "We don't have to do anything right now, except relax in the pool and let the afternoon run away. Is that what you want?"

"Please?" she asks, lowering her head to his chest.

"Whatever my sea nymph needs."

She laughs. "Why do you call me that?"

"It's what you are, aren't you?"

"You called me that before I turned into a mermaid!"

He smiles, looking down at her. "To us, a sea nymph isn't just a mermaid or other sea creature. She represents the magic of the sea, it's wonder and beauty. That's why I call you that."

"Really?" she asks.

"Really," he answers, kissing her. "How are you feeling?"

"Better. I'm not as tired as I had been, and I know we will deal with your brother once we get back to the palace. What will you do with him?"

"Imprison him."

"How long?"

"A year."

"Really?"

"Yes, then we'll talk again and see how he feels. If it makes him angry or bitter, I will banish him. If he seems truly remorseful, we will go from there. How does that sound?"

"It sounds okay. It's just—I hate the thought of you doing that to your own brother."

"It's no less than he deserves."

"Thank you. When you believed him over me, I was so scared. I knew if he had free reign, thinking you would take his side—" she trembles in his arms.

He strokes her hair. "Never again. I will never doubt you. For now, let me hold you."

After some time has passed, she looks up at him. "Could I swim here for a bit? I love being in this warm pool."

He smiles, "Of course, my little sea nymph. I will sit up there and watch. All right?"

She leans up and kisses him. "Yes."

He climbs onto the rocks off to the side from the small waterfall as she watches him. He gets settled, smiling at her. "So, which feels better on your tail, the hot sand or warm water?"

She bites her lip. "Your tail wrapped around mine," she admits. She smiles as he blushes in response and enjoys being in the water. He seems okay with what I've told him. I know we haven't talked much about the future, and I pray he truly is all right. She looks back, seeing him watching her. "I love you, koy'lei."

"Sera, I love you so much. I am sorry for how things have been, but please, never doubt me, never doubt my love? I promise I will do better with my anger."

She gives a small nod, then continues swimming. As the sun lowers on the horizon, he scales back down the rocks and into the pool, smiling when she swims to him. He stands up, picking her up and carrying her to the beach, lying together on the sand.

He leans over her, staring at her lips. He looks into her eyes, lowering down when she nods and kisses her as he is overwhelmed with love, his hand trailing down along her tail. Reluctantly, he pulls away, packing everything up from their lunch. She holds the basket as he picks her up, carrying her into the water.

They swim back to the palace. He drops the basket off at the galley, thanking them for making it before they return to their quarters.

"Dinner in the great hall?" she asks.

"Yes, then we'll go to the dungeon."

She smiles as she runs her hand over the pink ruffled dress she wore when Da'vae first attacked her, knowing the effect it has on him. Slipping it on, she pins on a diamond crown. Dankin swims to her.

"You look lovely in that," he says as he looks her up and down.

"Thank you."

They go to supper, sitting at their table. She smiles at the fish on her plate then looks at Dankin when he chuckles.

"We can get you something else—"

"No, I get enough variety now. I'm okay to eat it."

They eat and go to the dungeon. Da'vae is in a cell, chains around his neck and tail. He has his back to them, turning when he hears them.

"Da'vae, how are you?" Dankin asks.

He laughs. "I was starting to think you had forgotten about me."

"Don't be so dramatic. You've only been down here a few days while I have debated how to proceed. Now, Sera and I—"

"Hmm, yes. Your piece of… sushi. How are you doing?" Da'vae asks as he turns and looks at them. His eyes go wide at her dress. She grins at his reaction, which only angers him further.

"We're fine. So, we have discussed it," Dankin continues. "You will be imprisoned for one year, then we will see how you feel."

"About what?" Da'vae asks.

"Sera, the throne. All of it."

"I never wanted either of those things. I was only testing her loyalty to you, I can assure you."

Dankin swims closer to the cell. "I want to believe that, but after everything you've done to her… I can't."

"You believe that tail over me?" Da'vae asks with a laugh.

"I do. And she's my wife and your queen, so you will show her respect, or I'll add gagging to your punishment."

"Of course, Your Majesty," he bows as best he can, despite the chains. "And these?"

"Oh, no. Those stay on. I know how fast you are. They are under strict orders not to remove those for any reason. I have the only key. I may open them, in one year," Dankin says.

"Until then, thank you for your… hospitality."

"Brother?"

"I have no interest to see either of you until then."

"That doesn't show remorse or interest in trying again," Dankin points out.

"Is that what you're looking for? Oh, well. I am so very sorry I hurt her little feelings," he says, laughing.

"Why are you doing this?" Dankin asks.

"You chose her over me! For the throne, to help you with the kingdom. You shoved me aside for her!"

"Da'vae, I did no such thing."

"You gave her my pearl. That was my inheritance. She is not meant to have that."

"She earned this pearl by saving us from Maren. Look, I did not plan to fall in love when trying to break the curse, it just happened. Even so, you know how much you mean to me. I would never cast you aside."

Da'vae grips his chains, shaking them. "Then what do you call this?"

"Fair punishment!" Sera snaps back.

He snarls at her. "Oh, if I weren't in here…" he says, gripping the bars.

"Fine," Dankin says. "You get your wish. We'll leave, and we won't see you for one year. Enjoy your stay," he says, taking Sera's hand and leaving the dungeon.

"Please, don't leave me alone! I was joking!" Da'vae tries. He lowers back down, once he realizes they left him.

Sera looks up at Dankin as they return to the main corridor. "I know that wasn't easy for you. I am so sorry."

"Thank you, but you owe no apology. He hurt you, so he deserves his punishment. For the time being, I'd rather not talk about him."

"I understand."

* * *

Sera is grateful the last few months have been without incident, with Da'vae locked up. The two clans tried to keep the peace but are still disputing their land rights. They requested she and Dankin aid after all. She is in her closet with Ava'lei and Fai'mi as they help her pick out a dress and crown for hosting the two clans. Fai'mi decides on a silver and gold hanfu with matching crown, adorned with diamonds. Ava'lei agrees with her choice.

"I'm nervous about meeting them," Sera admits.

"You'll be fine, Your Grace. We'll be nearby for anything you need. You've studied their history and are more than prepared," Ava'lei assures her.

"Thank you."

Dankin comes in as she adjusts the crown into place. "Very regal, Your Grace." He smiles at her.

She laughs as she swims to him. "Hmm, what are you wearing?"

He looks her up and down. "Something to match you."

She and her handmaids leave the closet so he can get dressed. He comes out in a silver shirt with gold embroidery and matching crown. "So handsome," Sera says, laughing when he blushes. He swims to Sera and takes her hand. "Are we ready?" she asks.

"We are." They go to the palace entrance to await the two tribes. Sera had suggested they come a half an hour apart, hoping to avoid any unnecessary interaction before the meeting. "That was smart thinking. I'm glad you thought of that," Dankin says with pride.

Sera smiles at him. "I try, Your Majesty." He chuckles, kissing her forehead.

The Tsun'ama clan arrives first. Introductions are made, and Dankin has his royal guards escort them to the meeting room. When the Sol'lun'a clan arrives, Dankin and Sera escort them. Once everyone is settled, Sera studies the people on both sides. The Tsun'ama are beautiful with dark skin and brown curly hair, white tribal tattoos on their arms and neck, dressed in dark blue and black tribal attire. The Sol'lun'a are pale with red or pink hair, contrasting the bright blue tattoos that cover their bodies, and wearing green and black tartan robes.

Dankin starts the meeting by welcoming both parties and addressing their grievances. "So, you both believe you are entitled to the undersea volcano that is between your lands? And the flowers and plants that grow around it?"

"We do," Nar'iti answers.

"Why not share?"

The a'poto of Sol'lun'a, Ri'kia, rises up. "We have tried, but only had fights when we were there at the same time."

"Okay. I will send an ambassador to reside with each of you. When you go to the volcano, they will accompany you. You both are entitled to the volcano and surrounding fauna. We will make a schedule, so that you will not have parties there at the same time, to avoid any further confrontation. You will evenly divide up the fruits and flowers."

Nar'iti rises as well. "That is agreeable to us."

"Us, as well," Ri'kia agrees.

"Then let it stand," Dankin says. He writes it out and watches them sign the treaty. As they discuss the ambassadors, Sera tries to focus and learn the process, but she is distracted by a sudden pain in her stomach, followed with a wave of nausea. She looks at Ava'lei, who swims over low, trying not to attract attention.

"Is something wrong, Your Grace?"

"I'm not feeling very well. Will you take me to my quarters?"

"Of course."

Sera writes a quick message, folding it up, and passing it in front of Dankin. He takes it, looking at her then placing it in his pocket. He turns back to the matter at hand while her handmaids help her from the room.

"Do you need the infirmary?" Fai'mi offers, concerned when Sera's face bunches in pain.

"No, I just need to lay down."

They get her to her quarters and help her into bed. "We will be in the hall," Ava'lei says as she covers Sera with the blanket.

"Thank you." She watches them leave, lying in the bed as her hands clutch her stomach. She moans in pain, turning to her side. She looks up when the door opens a short while later. Fai'mi swims into the room.

"Apologies, Your Grace. Can we get you anything? Something to eat, perhaps?"

"No, thank you."

"I hope I'm not being too forward, but are you sure you don't want the infirmary? It's just… we don't really get sick. I am concerned for you, Your Grace," Fai'mi admits.

"I appreciate that. For now, I'll stay in here and rest. If I require food or the doctor, I will let you know. I promise."

"Yes, Your Grace." She leaves the room.

Sera stares up at the ceiling. She thinks of swimming in the ocean, trying to push her nausea back. She looks over when Dankin comes in. He rushes to her. "Why didn't you tell me you were ill?"

"You were negotiating for peace. I couldn't interrupt."

He takes her hand as he lowers onto the bed. "What's wrong?"

"My stomach hurts, and I feel like I'm going to throw up."

"I'll send for doctor."

"No, I'll be okay. Is it not possible for you to heal me from something like this?"

"I believe I can, but I need to see if this is a one-time occurrence or if something is wrong with you. Do you need me to heal you?"

"No, just to rest for a bit."

"If you aren't better by supper—"

"We'll request the doctor, or you can heal me then."

He sighs. "All right. Have you eaten anything?"

"I can't."

"Should I take you to a doctor on the mainland? They can run tests there. Our doctor basically treats wounds and such. As I've said, we don't really deal with illness."

"No, I'm starting to feel better, really. The pain is easing. I think I could try to eat a salad."

"I'm sorry, a what?"

"I don't know what you call it here. The plate with various leafy greens and underwater plants?"

"Oh, right. Sar'ada."

"That's one of my favorite things to eat here."

He swims to the door and sends Fai'mi to the kitchen to fetch one, then returns to Sera's side. "Do you want to change? Get more comfortable?"

She laughs, sitting up. "I do, but if either party requests an audience with us, I want to be ready."

"They are staying for supper, then they will all leave after."

"I'm grateful they can have peace."

"Me, too. After the war with the sirens, I don't want to think of another."

"What would've happened if you couldn't get them to agree?"

"More skirmishes and attacks, then I would sanction them both. They depend on us for medical supplies, modern weapons, and other necessities to survive in the ocean. The Tsun'ama have advanced well, whereas the Sol'lun'a tribe prefer to stay in the past."

"I see. Their tattoos are beautiful."

"They offered to do us each one, if you want."

She laughs. "Oh, I can't think of that! Maybe later."

Fai'mi swims in with food for them both. "Thank you," Dankin says, taking the plates. He sees the concern on her face. "She is feeling a little better." She looks relieved as she bows and swims out to the hall. He takes the plates over, helping Sera eat.

"I'm not as nauseated now. Maybe it was just my worry over the treaty and everything."

"That would make sense. You're sure you are feeling better?"

"I am, really." She smiles at him as she finishes her plate. "Thank you. That was what I needed."

"We'll be eating supper where we had our reception, since we are hosting guests tonight."

She sighs. "I'm feeling better, but not really up for being around so many new faces."

"It's just for tonight. You don't have to, if you need to stay in."

"I won't be rude. It's my duty, and I will fulfill it."

"Thank you."

"Can we go to the grotto tomorrow?"

"We'll have to wait and see."

"More business to attend to?"

"I'm afraid so. I know we haven't been in almost a month, I'm sorry."

"It's okay. I would like to see my family again, too."

"We will. This is a busy week, but things will calm back down. Then you and I can have some time, and we'll go to Isle Piscantur."

"Thank you. How long until we leave for supper?"

"We still have over an hour. Why don't you get more rest?"

"Will you lay with me? Or do you have things you need to do?" Sera asks as she pulls up the blanket.

"I can lay with you," he offers, getting into bed. He pulls her back against him, wrapping his arm over her. "Sleep, my sea nymph."

She closes her eyes, letting his heartbeat soothe her to sleep. Dankin plays with her hair as she sleeps in his arms and thinks of what she has been through. He thinks of taking her into the grotto, knowing how much she loves relaxing in the pool. When it's time to get up he nudges her gently and sprinkles her neck with kisses.

"Hmm, what?"

"Time to get ready. How do you feel?"

"Much better. Do I need to change for supper?"

"Yes, I believe so. Although I'm not sure what is best for the occasion."

He swims to the door and hands off their plates, then brings Fai'mi and Ava'lei back into the room with him to help her change. They select a beautiful lavender and silver gown, with a crown lined with amethysts and pearls. Dankin swims into the closet to see her, and his jaw drops at the sight.

"You look beautiful in that."

"Thank you," Sera says with a smile.

She and her handmaids swim from the closet so he can have privacy to change. She sits on the edge of the bed. "Do you know any of the visiting merpeople?"

"Not really. We stay in the palace and only serve you, so we haven't met the other clans. They are… interesting," Ava'lei says.

"Yes, they are," Sera agrees. Dankin swims out, wearing a black dress shirt with a silver and purple cravat. Sera swims to him and runs her fingers over the cravat. "We match!"

He smiles as he takes her hand and leads her to the ballroom, surprised to see merpeople already inside. "I guess they are excited for dinner."

She laughs. "Or ready to go home."

Before dinner is served, they go to each table to greet their guests. Sera is surprised at the looks she gets from some of them. Once back at the table, she looks at Dankin.

"Why do they stare at me like that?"

He sighs. "You do look a little like the sirens. I think it surprised them, is all."

"You really think I look like them?"

"We've talked about this. You are similar, but you don't look exactly like them."

"I've never really fit in anywhere," she says quietly.

"Sera?"

She smiles up at him. "I'm okay." She looks around the room. "I miss dancing."

"I know you do. We can, in our quarters. I know it's not the same—"

"Still, it will be nice. Thank you."

"You look absolutely stunning tonight."

"Thank you, my koy'lei."

The night winds down, and both clans depart, much to Sera's relief. She and Dankin return to their quarters. She swims to Dankin and removes his crown. He helps her remove hers, and she puts them both in their spots on the closet shelves. Swimming back to him, he reaches for her hand when she backs up. He gives her a confused look when she swims up to him and unbuttons his shirt. He says nothing as she takes it off, then removes her gown, both pieces of clothing floating down to the floor. They swim around the room, swirling and moving together as she hums her favorite song.

She stops humming when he leans down and kisses her, leading her to the bed. He sits on the edge as she swims backwards and hums a different tune, curving her body and dancing for him. He smiles, thinking of the first time she danced for him. When she finishes, he holds up his hand. She takes it in hers, laughing when he suddenly pulls her to him and kisses him.

"Ready for bed?"

"Oh, yes," she answers.

* * *

Sera wakes up and smiles at a sleeping Dankin. She climbs on top him, planting soft kisses on his mouth and chin. Gently, he wraps his hand around the back of her neck, as his kiss grows in hunger.

"This is how I want to wake up, every morning."

She smiles at him. "I'll see what I can do."

"Did you have a good time last night?"

"Everything was wonderful. Could we have breakfast in bed this morning?"

He sighs. "That sounds nice, but we have too much to do today. No time to be idle."

"Oh, okay." She swims to the closet to get dressed then swims out as he goes in. "I'll see you later," she says, going for the door.

"Sera—" He comes out of the closet, buttoning his shirt. "Stop." She freezes in place, unable to move. He swims in front of her. "Tell me what is wrong this morning."

Unable to control herself, she does as he commands. "I wanted us to have a little time together before our busy day." She strains with all her might, trying to move her tail forward, but it doesn't budge. "What did you do to me?"

He lifts up her hand, running his finger over the ring. "I imbued my command into the ring. I'm tired of you running away and—"

"Right now, I wish I could run away."

He sighs, dropping her hand. "Okay. I'm tired of you *swimming* away when we are trying to have a conversation. I don't have to worry about that now."

Sera seethes with anger. "So, you've made me your prisoner once again?"

"You are not my prisoner. I thought this would help us, allow us to face our issues when they arise instead of avoiding them."

"Release me!" she demands.

"Fine, you are free, for now."

She laughs, taking off the ring and letting it fall to the floor. "I may still be your wife, but I will not be your slave!" She swims to her office as fast as she can and loses herself in paperwork. Ava'lei and Fai'mi come in to help. They stop at lunchtime when Dankin comes in.

"Your Majesty," her handmaids say with a bow.

Sera swims to Dankin. "Your Majesty," she offers with an exaggerated bow. The girls give each other a look before swimming out to give them privacy. "How may I serve you today, my liege?"

"For one, you can grow up."

"You're one to talk, keeping your wife prisoner!" she yells.

"Now you're stretching things." He holds up her ring.

She scoffs. "If you think I'm putting—"

He grabs her hand and slips it on. "The only magic that's left in it, is to help you stay in mermaid form. I swear to you."

"Prove it."

"Sera, stop now!" he commands.

She backs up. "I see. All right, then I will wear it. Anything else you require of me? I still have quite a bit of work to do."

"Why are you so angry with me?"

She looks down. "All I wanted was breakfast in bed with my husband, and you dismissed the idea without a thought. It's as if you thought I was lazy for wanting that, for wanting a few minutes with you."

"Because I was afraid if we had breakfast in bed, we might spend the whole day there. Especially since we haven't been able to see each other as much lately."

"You get mad at me for keeping to myself, but you're no better! I at least asked for what I wanted. Why didn't you talk to me? Instead, you hid behind our duty."

"Sera—"

"Do you realize that in the time you have been here, explaining all of this, is the time we could have this morning together? Just go. I don't want to be around you right now." Her heart aches as her throat swells.

"I will give you space, then. I am sorry that this morning was screwed up. I would give anything to fix it."

"You can't," she says, turning away. "Your anger—" she wraps her arms around herself. "I'm afraid you would blame me or yourself for… for what happened at the estate. Is that why you are controlling me now?"

"What are you talking about?"

"When you get angry, I'm afraid it's going to grow, and I've seen how you get. I'm waiting for the day you get so angry at me, that you blame me."

His eyes go wide. "That day will never happen! I am so sorry, for this morning, for what you're dealing with. You are still reeling from that while I am putting so much work on you."

"It's okay," she tries.

"No, it's not. Look, let's finish our work today. Tomorrow is Friday. What if we left after supper tonight and stayed in the grotto until morning?"

She shakes her head. "I can't."

"Sera?"

"Last time I slept there, you… you said horrible things."

"I'd like to think I've done better since then. I'm far from perfect, I know. However, I think I am a better man now. I've learned from my mistakes."

"Let me think about it? I'll give you my answer at supper?"

"All right. I'll be in my office, if you need me."

"I always need you," she softly replies, looking at him. "I just wish you felt the same way."

"I do."

She shakes her head. "No, after this morning—" she swims over to her desk. "I'll see you later."

He sighs, debating. "All right." He leaves the room and sends her handmaids back in. They finish the paperwork then Sera looks at Fai'mi.

"I need a change of scenery, and I need to do some research." Her handmaids escort her to the library to teach her more of their history. "You didn't know Dankin's family, did you?"

"No, Your Grace. That was before our time," Ava'lei answers.

"Of course."

* * *

She looks at the clock. "It's almost time for supper. You are dismissed until Monday, unless I call for you before then."

They bow before swimming from the library. Sera gathers a few more books, takes some notes, then puts them back before going to Dankin's office.

He smiles when she comes in. "I'm almost done."

She goes to his chaise and sits. "No rush."

He signs a few more papers before swimming to her. "Are we going for supper?"

"Yes. Then we can go to the grotto, if you still want to."

"Okay." He looks at her hand. "What's that?" he asks, nodding to the folded piece of paper.

"Oh, just some notes I made," she says, tucking it into her pocket. They go to the great hall for supper.

"We'll stop by the galley on the way out."

They eat and return to their quarters to pack a few things for their overnight trip. She slings the bag on her shoulder and takes his hand. They stop in the galley, and Dankin is handed a basket. He smiles at her.

* * *

They say nothing as they swim together, Sera enjoying the movement through the open water. Aware of Dankin glancing at her from time to time, she keeps her head forward and focuses on swimming. At the grotto, Sera climbs onto the beach and lies on the sand. Dankin puts the basket in a cool, shaded corner of the water and tethers it down before joining her.

"I'm sorry," he says as he settles in beside her.

"For which thing?" she asks, turning to her side and looking at him. She sees the anger flash across his face, as he takes a breath and calms himself down.

"For everything. I've put too much on you. You have done a great job, and instead of seeing how hard you were working to do so, I gave you more work. Why didn't you tell me?"

"I'm fine. I just thought—" She shakes her head. "It doesn't matter what I think. Like you said, it's our duty to the kingdom that is most important."

"When it comes to their health and safety, yes. Not to a few trade requests. You're right, that we should've had that time this morning. I want to make it up to you."

"You already are, by bringing me here."

"This really is your favorite place, isn't it?"

"Out of the entire ocean, it is. It's peaceful, relaxing, beautiful. I feel safe and happy here." She looks down. "Usually."

"I know."

She climbs over to him and rests in his arms.

"This is wonderful. It's what we've needed, for a while now," she whispers.

"I should've listened to you."

"Yes, you should have," she agrees. "Your anger scares me," she confesses.

His eyes close at her words, his heart aching for her. "Sera, that is the last thing I ever want you to feel. I am sorry, and I am trying. That's all I can say."

"No, it's not."

"What do you mean?"

"Out of all the women on the island, why did you choose me?"

"I wanted a woman with a big heart, kind, compassionate, smart, cunning, and beautiful. I knew I probably wouldn't find someone with all of that, but I had an idea of what I wanted. I asked for help, and every single person sent me your way. I saw you helping Kye, heard about the fruit you created, saw how kind you were to every customer who came to your booth. I couldn't believe I found a woman who was everything I wanted."

"I look so different—"

"Different, but beautiful. Your smile lights up the room, your eyes reflect the heart of the galaxy, and your soul is as heavenly as the stars. Believe me, it wasn't a hard decision. So, let me ask, why did you say yes?"

She looks at her ring, then back up to him. "You were a good friend, understanding of my family's situation. You defended me and protected me at your own risk. I fell in love with you from the start, but I fought it because I never thought Rae'lin would allow me to court a simple commoner. You came in and saved me, from a life of servitude, a life without love, no life at all. You gave me a future, when I never thought one would be possible."

He kisses her as it grows dark and begins to rain. He's pulling away when she kisses him, her mouth devouring his.

"Please," she begs, "stay with me."

"I will never leave you, I promise." He kisses her again as the storm moves past. She looks up at the stars, thanking every one of them for the loving husband in her arms.

Chapter 21

Breaking Promises

Sera wakes up as Dankin lowers her into the pool. "What's going on?" she asks.

"You were shivering. It got colder than I expected."

"Hmm," she moans, relaxing in the warm water. "I love our pool."

"I do, too," he says, joining her. "How did you sleep?"

"In my husband's arms under the stars? Wonderfully. You?"

"It was the perfect night." He retrieves the basket, and they eat breakfast as they soak.

"When are we heading back?"

"We could go see your family for the weekend, if you want."

"Really?"

"Yes."

She thinks a moment. "I would like that. Let's enjoy this a little longer, though. Is that okay?"

"Of course."

Once they finish eating, he sets the basket against the wall of the grotto, then he carries her to the beach so they can rest on the sand. She closes her eyes, basking in the sun's warmth. A moan escapes her lips when she moves her tail, causing her to blush.

"I'm sorry," she says as she lowers her gaze.

"For what?" he asks.

"I—it's nothing." She looks down, biting her lip.

He chuckles. "Sera, it's okay. I know how the sand makes you feel. It does the same for me, too. You would think something gritty and hot would be uncomfortable. Instead, it's relaxing."

"It really is!" She laughs, sitting up. "I am ready to see my family, though. I miss them."

He carries her to the water. Once in the ocean, they swim side by side, holding hands. She's surprised when he leads her to the surface.

"This is different," Sera says as they glide along the water.

"It's safer to stay lower, obviously. Since I don't see any traffic out, I think it's okay."

They arrive at Isle Piscantur and dry off in their private cove. "I'm grateful we can come here now, the way I've been feeling." She looks at him as she squeezes his hand. "I have to admit, I've kept my distance with you. I'm worried that your anger will boil over because I say or do something to set you off. I've been careful—"

"Sera! You should never have to walk on eggshells for me. Why do you feel this way?"

"You've gotten so angry in the past, when I asked for space, or I told you I needed some time alone…" she looks away. "I didn't want to add to your burdens, because you give so much of yourself for your people."

"So, you're worried something will set me off, then my anger will erupt?"

"I'm trying not to think that way, but yes. I tell myself we haven't fought because you've been working on it, since you promised you would. Still, I fear that one day I'll set you off."

"I have worked on it, because I never want you afraid of me." He caresses her face. "Please, continue to be open with me like this. Let me in?"

She nods. "I will. Can we see our family now?"

"Yes."

When they arrive at the manor, Rae'lin gestures them in, excited to see them. A short woman with dark brown hair, green eyes, and a narrow waist, walks into the foyer and greets them with a bow.

"Sera, this is Kye's mother, A'lina," Rae'lin says.

"Nice to meet you! How are you?" Sera asks, admiring her pink and white hanfu.

"I am much better. Thank you, Your Majesties, for my son and for me. Please, how can I ever repay your kindness?"

"The Maker blesses us so we can bless others," Sera answers. "We ask for nothing in return."

She bows again. "You are both too kind."

Rae'lin smiles, looking at Sera. "She plays the flyte. Would you like to hear her play?"

"After supper, if you are up for it," Sera suggests.

"Of course, Your Majesty," A'lina replies with a bow.

"A'lina, please. Call us Sera and Dankin. We insist."

She nods and returns to her room.

Sera and Dankin go upstairs to freshen up. She sits on the bed, running her hand back and forth across the blanket.

"Are you okay?"

She laughs. "I miss how soft this is."

"Of course. Will you see the queen on this visit?"

"I'll let her know we are here, then she can summon me if she wishes."

"I think I'll take a shower before supper," he says, walking towards the washtoire.

"You miss those?"

He laughs. "A little."

Looking through her gowns, Sera picks a silver-blue hanfu with white and silver layers. Humming softly as she changes, she returns to the closet and picks out a matching pao for Dankin. She's pinning her diamond and pearl tiara in her hair when Dankin steps out. He smiles at the robes on the bed. His smile grows as she helps him dress.

"Do I need to have some of these made up for when we're in the palace?"

She laughs. "What would our people think, seeing you dressed like this?"

* * *

They bump into Rae'lin on their way to the kitchen, and she informs them that the queen has sent several messages to see when Sera would be on the island again. Sera requests for a note be sent to the queen about her arrival, and Rae'lin hurries off to find a messenger.

In the kitchen, Sera helps Chi'yo prepare supper as Dankin and Na'ito play a game at the small kitchen table. Sera watches a moment, as she thinks fondly of the meals she and Dankin had shared there before turning her attention to the pan of vegetables before her.

Dankin laughs. "Cheater!"

Na'ito chuckles, collecting the pieces. "Hmm, sore loser?"

"Another round!"

"If you want to lose that badly…"

Sera smiles when they both laugh. She turns back to Chi'yo. "What's it like, having a full house now?"

"It's very nice. Although, we miss you terribly."

"I miss you, too."

"Where is he from? His kingdom?"

Sera takes a worried breath. "Um, Dankin?" He walks over. "What's the name of our kingdom? Chi'yo would like to know."

Dankin shakes his head. "Sera, one of these days you will remember. It's the Mar Reinado Kingdom." He gives Sera a confused look but quickly hides it with a smile.

"I am unfamiliar with that one," Chi'yo admits.

"It's pretty far," Dankin explains.

"That's one reason we don't get to visit as often as we would like," Sera adds. "I wish we could."

"You're here now," Rae'lin says, walking in and giving her a squeeze on the arm.

Dankin and Na'ito carry the food into the dining room while Sera and Rae'lin set the table. Kye and A'lina join them, and they all sit for supper

"Sera, you look well," Rae'lin comments.

"Thank you."

"What's it like, living in a castle?" Kye asks, practically attacking the cooked beef on his plate.

"Hello to you, too."

He laughs. "Apologies, Miss Sera."

"It's okay. Um, living in the palace is incredible. It's several thousand years old, and it's so beautiful." Dankin smiles as she recites a little of the history behind it.

"I would like to see that sometime," Kye says.

Sera and Dankin exchange a glance. "Of course," she says. "How is the orchard doing?" Sera asks, changing the subject.

Kye begins talking excitedly about the work he and Na'ito have put in. "Last month, we added three more rows of trees, and we opened up a half-acre for tilling."

"That's wonderful," Sera says with a smile.

"More and more people are coming here just to try your fruit!" Na'ito says.

"Really?"

"Yes. Even from Isle Ky'oto," Kye adds.

"Wow! That's incredible," Sera says. "How was the harvest festival?"

"It was so much fun. Na'ito and I went almost every day. The fireworks were spectacular. We were disappointed there weren't lanterns like the last one," Kye answers.

"What was the lantern release like at your last festival?" Na'ito asks Sera.

She looks down at her ring, smiling at Dankin. "It was one of the best nights of my life. The lanterns were beautiful. That's when Dankin asked me to marry him. He whisked me off to his kingdom, where we married immediately."

"Why the rush?" A'lina asks. "Apologies—"

Sera laughs. "It's okay. Um…" She looks at Dankin, smiling at the affection in his eyes. "His people have suffered war. We wanted them to have a happy occasion to celebrate. As much as we love each other, we saw no reason to wait, either."

Dankin smiles at her answer, taking her hand and kissing her palm. "I love you, my little sea nymph."

She blushes. "I love you, too."

Kye and Na'ito give each other a grossed-out look, giggling quietly, until Rae'lin shoots them both a look. They turn serious before looking down at their plates.

"You can see the love between you. That's rare, since most marriages are arranged for financial gain, for land and business, or to keep peace between kingdoms."

"Rae'lin's right," A'lina chimes in. "I was married off to my husband so his father and mine could combine their business on the mainland. Instead of building it up, they drove it into the ground. I lost my husband, and I worked as a servant for a duchess for fifteen years, until I became ill. Then she fired me and kicked us out."

Sera shakes her head. "I'm so sorry. Years of loyal service, and that's how you were treated? It's not right."

"It's how things are. You and Dankin have been the talk of the mainland, once people learned how you were helping me and my son. Some see it as quite controversial, while others see it as a blessing."

Dankin looks at Sera. "Controversial? How?"

"Because we are helping someone below our station. If other servants had helped her, no one would think anything of it. If the duchess had fallen on hard times and other noblewomen helped her out, it wouldn't be controversial."

"The queen herself is most impressed with your compassion," A'lina continues. "She is trying to create a better system, with access to healthcare and education to help all of her people. Not just for the islands, but around the world."

"What do you mean?" Dankin asks. "The world?"

Sera clears her throat. "Kery'oto is the queen over this realm."

"I… I did not know that," Dankin admits.

"I'm glad to hear it." Sera says as she looks at her brother. "We were blessed to be able to buy your medicine. I can't bear to think of the people out there who need something like that but are unable to afford it. They aren't looking for a handout. They are literally just trying to live," she says with a shake of her head.

"Sera, I know how hard you worked, day after day without rest, to get me my medicine. Mother and a few workers have told me about it. I can never repay you for all you did, you and Dankin both."

"We're family," Dankin answers. "That's how it should be."

Sera smiles at him, squeezing his hand. Once they finish supper, everyone retires to the parlor, where A'lina plays a few songs for them on her flyte. Sera admires the instrument as A'lina places her mouth on the lip-plate and strums the strings. Sera and Dankin applaud once she finishes playing the last song.

"Thank you," she says, bowing. She steps out to clean and store it. Sera looks at Rae'lin.

"How long is she staying with you?"

"She may stay on as a servant." She sees the concern on Sera's face. "She offered, and I promise you, things here are much better now. She and Kye will live in the servants' quarters."

"Is that the small cottage beside the orchard?" Dankin asks.

"It is. For now, they are staying in guest quarters, to make it easier for me and the doctor when she needed him. She has recovered really well here."

Sera looks at Dankin. "The cottage is rather nice inside."

"I never did see the workers' quarters."

Sera giggles. "I almost put the king in those! Oh, my!"

Rae'lin laughs. "What are you talking about?"

"When I first met Dankin, I put him in the room across from me because the workers' quarters were full. I told him once the seasonal pickers returned to the mainland, if he was still here, that's where he would go." She looks down, clasping her hands.

"It's all right," he says, taking her hands between his. "You have no reason to be embarrassed about this now. You obviously didn't know who I was, and I was not about to break character for anything. I did what I had to do for my people."

"Our people?"

Dankin chuckles. "Of course, Your Grace. How could I forget?"

She laughs, squeezing his hand. "Well, at the time, they weren't my people, yet. I'll allow it this time." She laughs harder when he sticks his tongue out. "Your Majesty! That is grossly inappropriate for present company."

He looks over when Rae'lin chuckles, shaking her head. "You two."

Na'ito tries to tempt Dankin with another game, but Dankin has learned his lesson and turns him down. The evening continues with more laughter and storytelling, until everyone is ready to retire.

"Sera, could I have a moment alone with you before you go up to bed?" Rae'lin asks.

"Of course," Sera replies. Dankin kisses her forehead and steps out.

"Sera, have you read your letter from your father?"

"No, I left it here so it wouldn't get ruined in the salt water."

Rae'lin gestures her to sit beside her. "There was something else your father told me in his letter. I don't know if it's mentioned in yours, and I wasn't sure if I should tell you, but seeing you two tonight, how well you're doing, I think it will be okay. Just know, it is your decision how to proceed."

"You have me worried, mother. What is it?"

Rae'lin sighs. "Tsuji's grandmother, your great-grandmother… she was a siren."

"What?"

"Her name was Auri'elle. I'm not sure how, but she wasn't under the siren spell like the others. Instead, she maintained her free will. She met your great-grandfather when he was out fishing. He recognized what she was and immediately returned to his ship. Then she found him again, clinging to his boat and begging to speak to him. She swore it wasn't a trick, that she just wanted to talk to a land-dweller, to hear stories of where he was from. She didn't remember her own time on land, but she missed it. He took a chance, returning to her night after night to tell her of people walking the markets, dancing in the great halls."

"How were they able to be together?"

"She prayed to the goddess Calyp'seidon, begging for her help. She would trade her siren voice and her ability to turn people into sirens, if she could become human. Calyp'seidon, curious as to the outcome, agreed. Auri'elle walked onto the land, dressed in a shimmering gown, the color of the sea, and found your great-grandfather. It's why you look the way you do. I'm sorry he didn't tell you sooner."

"I—I'm part siren?" Standing up, she wraps her arms around herself. "Oh. What will Dankin think?"

"You don't have to tell him. Honestly, he may already suspect, with your white skin and pointed ears."

Sera takes a breath. "Thank you for telling me the truth. I'll ask Dankin if he wants to get some air, then I'll see where the evening takes us."

"Of course."

"Wait… doesn't this mean Na'ito is, too?"

Rae'lin thinks it over a moment. "If so, he doesn't show any of the characteristics. Not the way you do, at least."

Sera goes into the kitchen, where Dankin and Chi'yo are each enjoying a glass of wine. "More of the 1378?"

Chi'yo laughs. "I actually got him to try the 1214 vintage."

"Oh, that is a good vintage, so I've been told." Sera sets his empty glass behind him before taking his hand. "Let's go for a walk."

* * *

Dankin leads Sera from the estate and takes her to the beach. They walk over to the small dock. "I haven't been to this spot since the night you gave me this," she says, holding up her left hand. "Everything changed that night."

"Your legs included?"

She laughs. "If I said that—"

"It's okay, since I'm the one who did it to you."

"Dankin!"

He laughs, pulling her to him. "I have to tease," he says, his lips brushing her cheek. "Sera, did you forget the name of our kingdom?"

She laughs softly. "No, but I couldn't remember if we use that name in front of humans."

"It's fine."

She looks down as her legs grow into a silver tail. "Dankin, what are you doing?"

He sits down with her on the dock, holding her on his lap. "This is what I wanted to happen the night I proposed. I thought you would transform, then we would sit here and discuss our future. I had no idea it would be too much for you."

"You didn't pass out the first time you turned human?" she asks as he turns her back.

"No. It was painful, but I was okay after. Of course, it wasn't a surprise for me like it was for you. I knew what was happening. You were in shock."

"I remember you saying you were sorry."

"What else?"

"I was watching the scales climb up and couldn't keep my legs apart. The next thing I remember, I was waking up in bed, thinking I had too much to drink the night before because my head and body hurt, and I didn't feel… right."

"I never wanted you to hurt. I did everything I could, but it's how the first transformation has to be. I am sorry for the pain I put you through."

"You did what was necessary to save your kingdom. I understand, now. I was so angry at you that day, I—" she looks down as her fingers strum along his arm. "Even after I agreed to marry you, I was still upset and hurting. I hid it so I could make sure you kept your promise to heal my brother."

"Did you only marry me because of that?"

"When you proposed, I said yes because I love you and wanted to marry you. Our wedding night, however, was about my brother. I was so angry about everything, and I was afraid if I told you, you would punish me."

"Sera, why would you ever think something like that? You saw everything I did to protect you from Rae'lin."

"I'm sorry! I was scared and overwhelmed, and I felt so alone." She clings to him. "I wish we could've had more time before getting married, more time for me to adapt. I know why we couldn't, I get there was a tight timetable because of the curse."

"You asked me to take it slow, and it nearly killed me every time I agreed, knowing what I was going to do. I prayed that by the time I proposed, that you would truly love me and want to marry me."

"What did you think would happen, when I saw my tail for the first time?"

"I knew it wouldn't be good, but I hoped you would give me a chance."

"Still, making me swear on the ring?" Sera asks.

"I know, that was low of me to do. I didn't want to, but I had to ensure we would marry that night. I tried using magic, doing everything I could think of to break the curse. Nothing worked, and I was running out of time, running out of options."

"The stocks!" Sera suddenly remembers. "You agreed to go into those for me. How could you, knowing you had to break the curse?"

"Well, I wasn't going to."

"What?" she asks, pulling away and looking up at him. "What do you mean?"

"Don't misunderstand. I tried to think of a way I could send a thousand gold to the lord without you figuring out it was me. Then you would've been free of him while I could break the curse in time." He looks away. "It broke my heart, not helping you with him. I couldn't let you know who I was or what kind of wealth I had. So much was at stake—"

"I know. It's okay." She brings his hand to her face, holding it against her cheek. "I love you, so much. I couldn't imagine being anywhere but here, with you."

He leans in, kissing her softly under the moonlight. "This is where you belong. I love you, too."

She gasps in surprise when he transforms her, then wraps his tail around hers. "Dankin!" She looks around, making sure no one is around. "We could be seen."

"Hmm, you're right," he says, rolling them off and into the water.

"How dare you," she teases as she hits his shoulder.

Splashing her, he lets out a laugh. "I'll get you for that!"

She dives under, laughing as he tries to catch her. She hides behind one of the dock's wood supports. As Dankin swims by, Sera playfully grabs his tail. He spins to her as he laughs and grabs her arm, pulling her to him before they melt into a passionate kiss.

"Most inappropriate," he says as Sera joins in the laughter.

"We need to dry off before going back," she says as they swim for the shore.

He sighs. "I know. I'm sorry."

"For what? Making me laugh? I needed this, so thank you."

Once on the shore, Dankin lights a fire in the pit and holds Sera. "I didn't realize it would get this cold."

They warm by the fire as she lays in his arms. "What would my mother think, knowing you rolled me off the dock with you? I still can't believe she knows what we are."

He laughs. "Could you imagine her as a mermaid?"

"Oh, goodness! No, I don't think I can imagine that." Her laugh stops suddenly when she remembers why she brought Dankin to the beach. "Oh," she sighs.

"What's wrong?"

She takes a breath before smiling at him. "Just a chill. You're right, it did get cold fast." Letting the fire warm and dry her, she snuggles into his arms. She sighs again. "I need to tell you something."

"Hmm, all right."

She sits beside him, holding his arm in her hands. "I'm part siren."

"What?"

"My great-grandmother was a siren who fell in love with a fisherman." She tells him about the conversation she'd had with Rae'lin, observing his face for any sign of anger. When she's done, she waits for him to respond.

"How do you feel, knowing this?" he asks, looking down at his hands.

"I'm okay. It explains a lot, but I worried how you would feel."

"Sera, I don't hate sirens for being sirens. I hated them for killing my family, especially now that I know they killed my whole family." He looks back up at her. "This doesn't change how I feel about you," he assures her.

"Do you mean that?"

He takes her hands, kissing them all over. "I swear it to you."

"Thank you."

"No, Sera. Thank you for being honest about this."

They put out the fire and return to the estate. The rest of the house is asleep, so they go upstairs as quietly as they can. In bed, she snuggles into his chest.

"Are you warm now?" he asks.

"Finally," she answers with a laugh. She looks up at him. "Are you sure you're okay, after everything I told you? I'm sure thinking about me being a siren brought up memories of your family…"

"I am. I promise you, Sera. I've had a wonderful day with you."

"Please, don't hide again."

"What do you mean?"

She looks down. "The day I gave you the portrait—"

"It was a surprise, that's all."

"Dankin, we had just agreed not to hide anymore, to have no more secrets, and that we would talk about anything. Instead, you pushed me away."

He sighs. "And nearly lost you."

"I don't blame you for what happened to me. It was my fault, leaving the safety of the palace. No matter how angry I was, I never should've left."

"You were angry? Because I was grieving for my family?" he asks, his voice thick with anger.

She looks at him. "How could you possibly think that's what I mean? I'm sorry," she says, looking down. "Just please, don't be angry!"

"Why do you think that I am?"

"It was in your voice… I would never be angry with you for grieving. I told you once, and I meant it, that I want to be here for you. Will you let me in? Will you open up to me?"

He shakes his head. "I've grieved so long on my own. It's not that I don't want to, but I don't know how. You can't understand what I'm feeling, so I don't see the point—"

"I know I can't understand what you're coping with. I didn't realize I had to, in order to comfort you. I am trying to be your wife, your partner. It's what you've asked for, since I woke up in bed that first morning as a mermaid. Why are you rejecting me now?"

"I'm not, and I never meant for you to feel that way." He strokes his fingers through her hair. "I'm sorry. I see now, that you're right about me, my grief and anger. I carry it too close, and it makes me angry to think of or to talk about."

"I won't bring it up again. I'm sorry I did."

"Sera, no. You're right, that we are partners in this. I should be able to talk to you about anything." He hesitates before continuing. "There's something I haven't told you. When I would think of my family, my grief would be so intense, it clouded my judgement. One day, I went out hunting for sirens after a scout had spotted them. I was sneaking up on them when Maren ensnared me. I fell into her trap, sure it was the end. Honestly, I was okay with that. Then she laughed and said she had bigger plans for me. That was when she cursed me that I had to marry for love before the next full moon, or my kingdom would become enslaved to her. She released me. I tried going after her, but she disappeared."

"Why haven't you told me this?"

"I was embarrassed by how easily she tricked me."

"She tricked both of us," she reminds him.

"I know. You're right, that I need to talk with you, let you in."

"You will always carry this grief, and I understand that. We don't have to talk about it, if you don't want to. I know we talk about being open, but I don't want you to feel as though you have to, either."

"Even so, I shouldn't get so angry. I blame myself, that I couldn't protect my family. I couldn't protect you."

"You did. You saved me from the mistress, the fisherman—"

"I couldn't save you from me." The pain on his face pulls at her heart.

"You have. Like you said, you have been doing better," she assures him. She sighs, yawning. "I need sleep. I'm sorry, I know we are talking about something important—"

"No, you're right. We were going to sleep when I caused this." He slips from the bed and covers her up with the blanket. He kisses her forehead. "Maybe it's best I don't sleep in here tonight." He starts for the door.

"Please," she begs softly. "Please, don't leave me."

His hand is on the handle as he hangs his head. "Sera—"

She jumps from the bed, running to him then she slips her arms around his torso and pulls him to her, nuzzling her head against his back. "Please, you promised me."

He turns around, drawing her in. "How can you want to be around me, after I made you so upset? Aren't you afraid of me?"

"Because I love you, and I need you. I know you are dealing with tremendous pain and loss. Why won't you believe me, that I want to help you carry this?"

"Because I never want to burden you. I've done that enough. I've forced so much on you."

"Sleep in bed with me? Hold me and be my husband, please? Will you do that for me?" she asks, looking up at him with love reflecting in her eyes.

He leans down, kissing her fiercely as he picks her up and carries her to bed. "Yes, I will be your husband, I will be the husband you deserve," he answers, climbing into bed with her and wrapping her tightly in his arms. "Now sleep, my little sea nymph. You need it, putting up with me."

She laughs softly. "I love you, my friend, my husband, my king."

"I love you, too."

* * *

He slips the ring on her finger. "I'm sorry," he says, as the ring tightens. Her entire body goes tense as she collapses against him. He sits down, holding her to him. "You'll be all right, Sera."

She watches as her legs fuse into a silver tail, gasping as the koi markings appear, red, black, and orange blotches. She looks at Dankin with red eyes, her skin shining white under the moon. "Kiss me," she hisses.

He pulls out his dagger…

* * *

Sera's eyes shoot open as the scream flies from her lips. Dankin jerks awake, then turns on the lamp. "Sera?"

She crawls onto his lap and clings to him as she sobs hysterically. "I—" she tries, burying her face into his chest.

"Shh. It's all right. Are you hurting? Is something wrong?"

"Nightmare," is all she can manage.

Rae'lin rushes in. "What's wrong?"

"Nightmare," Dankin answers.

Rae'lin nods her head. "I'll make tea," she offers, then she leaves the room.

Dankin looks down at Sera, stroking her hair as she cries. "It's okay. You're safe now. Nothing can hurt you." He grows concerned as she clings to him tighter. "Sera, please. Will you tell me about it?" He sighs when she says nothing. Rae'lin returns, setting a tray with two cups on the nightstand. She gets out a kerchief and hands it to Dankin. He helps Sera wipe her face. "Can you talk now?" Shaking her head, she buries her face deeper into his chest. He looks at Rae'lin.

"I'll go back to bed. Call for me if you need."

"Thank you," Dankin responds. He holds Sera until she calms down. "Are you all right?"

"Yes," she answers quietly, taking the cup of tea from him.

"Drink and relax. You don't have to talk about anything right now."

"Thank you." She sips her tea, avoiding his gaze. She finishes her cup and holds it in her lap as she mindlessly traces her finger over the rim. "If I had turned into a siren instead of a mermaid the night you proposed, what would you have done?"

He thinks carefully before answering. "I don't really know. Why?"

"Would you have killed me?"

His cup nearly falls from his hand. "Sera! Why would you think—" he takes a breath as the realization sinks in. "That's what your nightmare was?"

"Yes."

"Will you tell me about it?"

She swallows hard. "It was the night you proposed. You slipped the ring on, and I started to transform. Only, as my tail grew silver, it also formed the orange, red, and black koi markings of the sirens. My eyes were red, and I reached for you to kiss you. You pulled out a dagger, and—" She clutches her gown above her heart. "I dissolved into foam, right there on the dock!"

He takes her cup with his, setting them on the tray. He pulls her back into his arms. "It was just a nightmare. If that had happened, I would've brought you back to the palace, and we would've figured it out. I swear to you, I would not have killed you."

"You can say that now, because you know me and love me so, but back then? Still so angry in your grief, to look down and see a siren?"

"Sera, it doesn't matter. You turned into a beautiful mermaid, we are happy and in love. Right?"

"I know, but—"

"Then just forget about it!" he snaps.

She jerks away from him, running into the washtoire, and slamming the door before falling to her knees as she weeps in fear.

His voice is muffled through the door. "Sera, I'm sorry. Please, let me in?"

"You are too angry! Why?"

"You think so little of me, that I would kill the woman I love?"

"You scare me when you're angry. Right now, you're doing a fantastic job of it!" She goes to leave the room when her legs give out from under her. She looks up at him from the floor, her tail stretched out behind her. "Dankin?"

"I told you, you aren't running away."

She sighs, crossing her arms over her chest. "What do you want?"

He picks her up and carries her to the bed as she struggles in his arms. "I want us to talk. I'm sorry you had an awful nightmare. I am trying to help you through it."

"You were helping, until you got angry. Back then, do you really think that the thought wouldn't at least cross your mind, as much as you hated sirens?"

"Fine, you're right. I would've at least thought about it. I would not have done it, though."

"Turn me back!" she demands.

"Not until we finish this discussion."

She wriggles free, falling to the floor and letting out a cry of pain when she hits. He rushes to her, concerned when she pushes him away. "Stop!"

He backs away, raising his hands. "Sera, please—"

She brings her tail up, folded under, and buries her face in her hands. "Why do you keep doing this to me?"

"What?"

"Transforming me as a means of keeping me prisoner? It's not right."

The door opens and Na'ito runs in, shocked at the sight before him. "What's wrong?" he asks.

Sera looks away, ashamed. "I'm sorry we woke you. We were—"

"Are you having trouble turning back?" Na'ito asks.

"I— A little."

He looks at Dankin. "Why aren't you helping her?"

Before he can answer, Sera retorts. "He did this to me so I can't leave the room!" Na'ito starts for Dankin when Sera lifts up with her arms and flings herself between them. "No! You two are not fighting. There has been too much violence in this house already. Na'ito, go back to bed. Now!"

Na'ito wants to argue, but huffs instead. "Yes, Sera."

Looking at Dankin, she's not surprised by the anger flaring in his eyes. "There you are. I knew it would only be a matter of time. I had a nightmare, needed comfort, and have to suffer your anger instead." She weeps into her arm.

Dankin crawls over to her, putting his hand on her shoulder. "I'm sorry. What can I do?"

"I need water."

"I'll turn you back—"

"No. You can after, but right now, I need water. I need to soak."

He quickly draws her a warm bath, carries her into the washtoire, and lays her in the tub. "Were you hurting?"

"Yes," she admits.

"I'm sorry. It's one thing to change you, but to keep you from water, too. I didn't do it on purpose." He sits on the edge of the tub. "Please, Sera. Forgive me?"

"I need to be alone," she says.

"All right. I'll be in the bedroom, if you need me."

"Thank you."

As soon as he's gone, she hangs her head as she concentrates, trying to make her legs reappear. Defeated when she can't, she lays her head back. Her hands clench as she thinks of how he treated her, and she looks at her tail in anger. "Ahhh!" she cries out, turning human again. Dankin rushes in.

"Sera—"

"I'm okay," she answers, exhaling loudly. "I just needed to let it out." He helps her from the tub, then she dries off and gets back into her nightgown when she looks up at him. "What did I do to deserve such anger from you? No, I don't think so little of you, but I know how you were back then, when it came to sirens. Can you really blame me for thinking something like that?"

"No, but—"

"I didn't just randomly think you would kill me. Between Rae'lin telling me the truth and then walking along the dock, I had a nightmare."

"Yes, one that you believed would be true, had it happened that way."

She walks over to the bed, sitting down. She shakes her head. "Maybe you should sleep across the hall."

"Sera—"

"I need my husband, not anger!" she cries out. "I was scared, and lost, and—" she buries her face into her hands. Dankin sits next to her and lifts her onto his lap.

"That's who I am, your husband."

"Then act like it."

He sighs. "Okay, I deserve that. Now, please, look at me?"

She wipes her tears and meets his gaze. "What?"

"Can we go back to sleep? I can see how much you need it, and I think we can discuss this better once we've had some rest."

"Okay," she agrees, lying beside him. He turns away, giving her space. She cries softly as she thinks of his anger until she falls asleep.

* * *

Sera wakes up first, remembering what he had said. Regretting how she reacted the night before, she leans up and plants soft kisses on his mouth. She smiles as he opens his eyes. He sits up, gently pushing her back.

"No."

"No?" she asks.

"I'm still upset with you, for last night."

Her eyes go wide in surprise "I thought we would be—"

"I told you we would discuss it this morning."

Her head hangs, as she fights back the tears. "If you're waiting on apology from me, you won't get one. I did nothing wrong!"

"Neither did I."

"Then why did you apologize?"

"Because I was trying to keep you calm. Truth is, I laid awake last night and thought over what you said. How can you love someone you're afraid of? You caused this, Sera, because you couldn't just let things go and let me comfort you. So, no more apologies from me."

She scoffs, getting to her feet. "Then I guess we're at a standstill." She goes into the closet, quickly dressing and shooting him a look of anger as she leaves the room. Downstairs, she helps Chi'yo prepare breakfast.

Rae'lin walks in. "Sera, are you better this morning?"

"I'm trying to be."

Rae'lin walks over, taking her hand and leading her to the parlor. "What happened last night?"

She tells her about the nightmare, about Dankin's reaction. "I don't understand why he got so upset. And he thinks this is my fault?"

"I see both sides, and I think you owe each other an apology."

"What? What did I do?"

"Sera, you know how much he loves you. He was a different man back then, so why bring up the past? Why ask about something that will never happen? You should've let it go and let him comfort you."

Sera sighs, clasping her hands. "I know you're right, but I am too stubborn to break first."

Rae'lin laughs. "You have always been willful. I couldn't break you, no matter how hard I tried." She looks away a moment in shame before returning her gaze to Sera. "So, what will you two do?"

"I don't know. I tried to make it up to him this morning, but he pushed me away."

"He put his hands on you?"

"Oh, no, nothing like that. I was kissing him, but he said he was still upset with me and nudged me back."

"Wait, you were showing him you love him, and he did that? Okay, now I see why you're angry. He is a stupid man!" They both laugh.

Chi'yo steps in. "Breakfast is ready."

They go into the dining room. Sera is surprised when Dankin comes in and sits beside her. She says nothing as she eats, thinking of her nightmare. As she looks down at her ring, she grows angry for the power he has over her. They finish eating in silence, and Chi'yo gathers dishes. Rae'lin helps, giving Sera and Dankin privacy. Sera removes her ring and sets it on the table before him.

"Sera—"

"I want you to remove your magic from it. All of it!"

"It's only enough to help—"

"I don't care. I won't wear it again, until you do."

He sighs. "What is going on?"

"It's how you can transform me, right? You can override my power?" She looks at him, seeing the surprise on his face. "I'm not as stupid as you treat me." She scoffs.

He picks up the ring, clenching it in his fist. "Why should I bother to give this back at all?" He regrets it, seeing the hurt in her eyes. "Sera—"

She runs from the room as Rae'lin walks in. "Why do you hurt her so?"

He looks down, ashamed. "I don't know. I give in to my anger."

"I see how much my daughter loves you. I've seen how much she has sacrificed, changed, and even lost being with you. Still, you treat her this way? For what?"

"I was angry— wait. What do you mean, lost?"

"Oh, no. That's between you and her, I'm not getting into that. If she hasn't told you what happened when she came here after your fight about Da'vae, I am not telling you, either."

"How can I make this right?"

"Show her you forgive her, show her you love her. Don't say it, don't tell her, but show her."

He nods his head. "All right. Let me step outside a moment to gather myself. I know she fears my anger, and that is the last thing I want her to see or feel right now. I'll come back in shortly."

"In the meantime, I will speak with her. Maybe the two of you can work this out. You know how stubborn she is."

"That I do," he says, leaving the room.

Rae'lin goes upstairs and knocks softly on the door. "Sera? Are you in here?"

"Come in."

She enters the room and walks to Sera, who is sitting in a chair in the corner of the room. "Dankin went to get some air. He seems sincere in his regret."

She shakes her head. "You're right, all we do is fight."

"Really?"

"No, but it feels that way, sometimes."

"You've had to adapt to so much, change in ways I can't even comprehend. He should be grateful to have a wife like you, who loves him so much. A wife willing to change for him."

"He is. He takes me on picnics to our grotto, he holds me when we sleep, he—I know he loves me. I wish he would do better with his anger."

Thinking back to when Dankin defended Sera from her, Rae'lin realizes it could've been worse last night. "He seems to have calmed down some. Otherwise, the whole house would've heard your argument."

"I guess that's true." She looks up at her. "What do I do?"

"When he gets back, give him a chance and talk to him. Will you do that?"

"I will because I don't want a humiliated husband trying to return me."

Rae'lin turns away. "I still can't believe I said such things to you. I guess Dankin isn't the only one who lets his anger get the best of him. I'm so sorry, Sera."

"I know. You've proven yourself to me since then. I wish I could do the same for him."

"Don't you mean he should prove himself to you?"

She shakes her head. "No. He knows I'm afraid of him, especially his anger. He doesn't see though, that I'm afraid of my own reaction. I feed off of him, and I hurt him as I try to protect myself. I need to prove to him how much I love him, that it's not just him causing this rift."

"How will you do that?"

"I don't know. It backfired this morning…"

"Wait here," Rae'lin says. She returns a moment later with a garment bag draped over her arm. "I am ashamed to admit this, but I was so heartbroken after losing your father, I used some of the gold Dankin paid for the agreement, and I bought more gowns. Right now, I think you need this more than I do." She pulls out a pink hanfu, gold and white layers underneath, with a sheer, rose-pink outer layer, embroidered with pink and white flowering vines.

"It's exquisite," Sera says, reaching out to touch it.

"Come, let's get you ready." Rae'lin helps Sera get into the gown, then watches as Sera pins in a pearl and diamond tiara. She turns Sera to the mirror.

Sera holds her hands together at her waist, gasping at the sight. "Oh, mother. It's beautiful!"

She laughs. "Because you make it that way," Rae'lin says, kissing her on the cheek before they go downstairs to the parlor. "Wait here, please?"

"Of course." Sera fidgets nervously with the gown, worrying over her relationship.

I want to fix this, to fix us. Does he still want me? After what I said last night, I wouldn't blame him if he didn't. She swallows hard, fighting down the tears. When Dankin walks in, she stands up and faces him.

Unable to hide his joy at the sight of her, he clears his throat before attempting to speak. "You look lovely," he manages to get out.

"Thank you. Can we talk now? Or do you still need space? I'll understand—"

He pulls her to him, clinging to her tightly. "Will you come with me?"

"Yes."

They walk around the orchard until they reach the pond, where he has set up a small picnic for her. "Now, we can talk."

She shakes her head, looking over the setup before her. "Thank you for this. I don't deserve it," she says as he helps her sit.

"Sera?"

"I've told you before, how sometimes I worry over your anger and make a pre-emptive move, trying to protect myself. Last night was one of those.

And in trying to protect myself, I only made you angrier and drove you away. I never meant for that to happen."

"We both acted out to protect ourselves. The question is, how do we move forward?" He holds up her ring. "Do you want this back?"

Her eyes go down. "I don't know."

"Sera?"

"I thought I did, but now—" She gets to her feet, looking over the glassy surface of the water. "I love you, and I don't doubt you love me. Two people who love each other should not behave the way we did last night."

"You're right. I should've comforted you."

"And I never should've asked you that."

"So, why did you?"

Her hands clench. "Because I was terrified!" She takes a breath, turning away. "Maybe coming with you was a mistake."

"Why?"

"If all you're going to do is question me—" She looks up as he pulls her to him, kissing her softly.

"No more questions. Except one. I am truly sorry for everything I said and did last night. Please, will you forgive me?"

"I tried to this morning—"

He turns away. "Sera, why didn't you just say yes? We could be sitting on that blanket, talking and laughing, being happy together. Why do you ruin this?"

"As I was going to say, I tried this morning, but you needed time. I see now we both did, and I was going to say it was for the better, having that time to think. I was going to forgive you, forgive us, but I ruined this?" She shakes her head. "Why do I bother?" She walks past him when he grabs her arm. "Dankin—"

He picks her up and cradles her in his arms, planting soft kisses along her neck. "You're right. I was giving in to my anger, because I am terrified of losing you. You give me light, and hope, and beauty, when my life has been loss and war. Losing you—" his breath hitches in his throat, "would destroy me." He puts her on her feet, kneeling before her. "Please, stay?" He holds up her ring.

"Did you remove all magic from it?"

"Sera—"

"No. It's not right for you to control me."

"It's for your own protection."

She scoffs and tries to walk away when he grabs her arm. "Let me go!"

"I'm sorry. I am a stupid man, I am too full of anger and grief. You're right, that I should not have so much control over you."

"Good for you, now let me go," she demands.

"Sera, please," he says, pulling her closer. She shoves him back, his hand coming up to protect himself when she flinches. "I would never hurt you!"

"What would you call last night? I needed love and comfort, only to receive anger instead. You control me, you hurt me with your venom! I deserve better." She tenses against him, holding back tears. "All I wanted was to wake my husband up with loving kisses, to show you that I forgive you and that I wanted to move past what happened last night."

"Wait, really?"

"Yes." She sighs. "I wanted us to be together this morning, to be husband and wife. Not enemies, not fighters, just us."

He takes her over to the pond, walking in with her. He holds her to him as they transform. "Will you be with me now?" he asks, slipping the ring on.

"Dankin, please—"

"Let me hold you in here, that's all I'm asking."

She looks at him. "I'm angry..."

"I know, and I deserve it. Here," he lays her back, sitting across from her. "I swear to you, I will never make you transform against your will, and I will never let you hurt like that again."

"That's assuming I forgive you." She looks down, running her fingers over her silver tail. "I thought being turned into a mermaid was bad enough, then watching as I became a siren? I know it was just a nightmare, but it scared me horribly." She shakes her head. "It was too much for me. I don't hate sirens, you know how hard I fought for them, fought for peace. Even so, I didn't want to become one. In the dream, I wanted to kiss you and it terrified me. I didn't feel like I was in control of myself, which is how I feel when wearing this ring."

"I'm sorry. I had no idea it was so powerful for you. I am doing everything I can to make this right. What can I do?"

"I just need some time to deal with this."

"Sera, please—"

"I'm angry, and I don't want to say or do something I will regret. Please, give me a little time?"

"All right," he says, getting out of the pond.

"Wait!" she calls out, when she realizes she's stuck.

He walks over to her. "What's wrong?"

"I—I can't turn back."

"Call for me when you're ready."

"Dankin?"

"I'm not having you run away from me. It kills me when you do!" he admits.

She looks at him. "I didn't know that."

He turns away, wiping a tear before facing her. "Please, don't run from me? Not anymore?"

She scoffs, looking at her tail as she crosses her arms. "I literally can't!"

"Then call for me when you're ready to talk. I'll change you back."

"You would leave me here like this?"

"I'm not going anywhere. I'm stepping away to give you the time you asked for."

"Dankin—"

He waves his hand, walking off. Her shoulders slump. She tries to pull the ring off, groaning in exasperation when it won't budge. *I am his prisoner again. He is holding me here, and for what?* She sighs. *I may as well relax and think, while I'm stuck here.*

* * *

A sudden movement in the water draws her attention. "What was that?" she asks aloud. She gasps as she watches a water snake slither over her tail. She's about to climb out when another is right behind her. Her breath catches in her throat as she watches them. They swim past, then suddenly one turns and swims straight for her. "Dankin!" she screams. "Help!" She gets out her dagger, grateful she remembered it this morning, as the first snake reaches her. She strikes quickly, stabbing it in the mouth and tossing it aside as the other snake swims back and forth, watching her intently. "Dankin!" she tries again.

"Sera?" He walks over in time to see her slash with her blade, cutting its head off as it lunges for her. She looks at Dankin, trembling.

"Please?"

He jumps into the water and tosses out the snake carcasses. "Are you all right?"

"Yes. Why did you leave me?"

"We both needed time to ourselves. I got lost in thought and didn't realize how far away I had wandered."

"Still!"

"Are you ready to talk?"

"I was just nearly killed!"

"How could I have known something like that would happen?"

"You want to prove to me you love me? Turn me human and remove my ring."

"Really?"

"Really!"

"All right." He kneels down and takes her ring off, watching as she transforms back into a human. "Better?"

"Yes," she says, as he helps her to her feet. She looks down, grateful her mother's gown isn't ruined. They step up onto the grass, hoping there are no more snakes nearby. "You want to talk, so talk."

"Not if you're going to give me attitude," Dankin replies.

She turns away. "I wasn't trying to. I was giving you the floor. Apparently, nothing I ever give you is enough, is it?"

"Why do you say that?"

"First, I was a servant, then the daughter of Tsuji Dahvaene. I was a prisoner, then I fought and killed pirates. No matter what I do, it's never enough for you! Whether I'm shy and meek, demanding and headstrong, timid or brave, I can never seem to make you happy. What do you want from me?"

"You do make me happy, Sera. I want you to stop being afraid of me. That's all I want."

"I don't know how," she confesses.

"Are you still afraid of Rae'lin?"

"No, but she asked for my forgiveness, and she has not hurt me since. With you, it's when I need your love and comfort the most, but I get your anger instead. It... it scares me so."

He looks down at the ring in his hand. "Maybe you were right."

"About what?"

"That you aren't right for me, not if I scare you so much."

Sera steps forward. "Dankin, no—"

"I can't live with someone who is afraid of me. That's not love, and that's certainly not a life you deserve. You deserve as much love as you give, deserve to feel safe, to never be afraid of the person you are with. I don't deserve you, Sera."

"Please—" she tries, taking his hand. "Don't—"

"I'm sorry," he says, pulling away. "I'll leave you in peace." He heads for the beach. She's in shock, unable to move as she watches him walk away from her, away from their marriage, away from their life.

"No!" she cries out, running after him. She jumps on him, knocking him to the ground. He rolls onto his back as she pummels him on his chest. "How dare you!" she screams. "You promised you would never leave me! I love you, and I won't lose you, not again!" Seeing the smile on his face, she freezes, her fists in the air. "What? Why are you smiling?"

"This is what I wanted to see. Would you let me walk away or would you fight? You had to see for yourself, what you feel, what you want. Do you see it now?"

She lowers her hands. "I don't understand."

"I wasn't really leaving you. You said words weren't enough, so now that you've been forced into action, do you see what you want for yourself?"

"You made me think you were leaving? You were testing me?"

"No, Sera, not testing you. I was showing you what you want, seeing what you would fight for, if you would fight." He brings his hand up, gingerly rubbing his chest. "I didn't expect you to literally fight."

"I'm sorry!" She collapses on him, her face in his chest. "I didn't mean to hurt you. I was just so angry and scared at the thought of losing you."

"Sound familiar?"

"That's why you react that way?" she asks.

"It is. I become terrified I am going to lose the best thing I have, become overwhelmed with grief, then I give into it. Which you do not deserve, at all."

"Oh!" She buries her face in his shirt, sobbing. "I'm so sorry."

He sits up, holding her to him. "Sera, I'll be fine."

"No, I should never hurt you like that, not when I know what it's like. I am truly sorry."

He laughs. "Only difference, you did it out of love. I know that probably doesn't make sense—"

"No, it does. Still, I am sorry. Please, forgive me, koy'lei?"

He holds up her ring. She watches as he speaks quietly, the blue light leaving the ring and flowing back into him. He hands it to her when she lifts up her hand, smiling when he slides it onto her finger. He kisses her, softly at first then growing in intensity as she clings to him. He pulls back. "Sera—"

"Take me to the house, please?"

He stands up, helping her to her feet. They go inside and are greeted by Rae'lin. "Everything okay with you two?" she asks as they go up the stairs. Rae'lin remains at the foot of the stairs with her hand on the rail.

"Yes, mother," Sera answers, as they go into her room.

Rae'lin shakes her head. "Kids, I swear," she says with a laugh. She goes into the kitchen, helping Chi'yo prepare their meals. "Kye and Na'ito should be back any time. We'll have a full house for supper," Rae'lin observes.

"Yes, mistress."

Hearing something in her tone, Rae'lin looks at her. "Chi'yo, are you all right?"

"Yes, I am sorry."

"For what?"

"That Mister Tsuji could not see such joy in here."

"Believe me, I wish for that as well. To see his son healthy, working hard and studying. His daughter happily married and a queen. I would give anything to have him here for this."

"I'm sorry. I hope that wasn't out of line."

"No, Chi'yo. It's okay. We all miss him."

"I can see it on Miss Sera's face. She really grieves for him, doesn't she?"

"She does. He loved her so much, and I know losing him—" she wipes a tear. "Well, let's discuss more pleasant things, shall we? How is your son?"

"His practice is doing very well, and he's courting a noblewoman. I believe he is very happy."

"Can I ask, why doesn't he visit here?"

"I asked once, and you said it wasn't allowed. I'm sorry—"

"No, Chi'yo. Please, things have changed. They are both more than welcome, any time. I mean that."

"Thank you."

Once supper is prepared, they set the table then Rae'lin goes upstairs and knocks softly on Sera's door. "Supper is ready."

"We'll be down in a moment," Sera calls out.

She turns away and comes back downstairs, giggling.

"Mistress?" Chi'yo asks out of curiosity.

"Young love."

Chi'yo returns the laughter. "Of course."

Rae'lin sits, waiting for them. Dankin and Sera walk in, holding hands and dressed to match in shades of blue and grey. They join Rae'lin at the table.

"So, I guess you two are okay now?"

"We are. We had a long talk, about everything," Sera answers, taking Dankin's hand. She smiles up at him.

"I'm glad to hear that. Oh, the queen responded. She would like you there tomorrow at noon for tea and lunch. I messaged back that would be fine. I hope you don't mind?"

"Oh, no. It's okay. I told her I would see her again," Sera says. "What will you do while I'm with her?" she asks Dankin, squeezing his hand.

"I'll attend to some business on the mainland."

"Of course." Sera wants to ask but thinks it better to wait when it's just the two of them. She looks at Rae'lin. "I'm sorry. We came here to visit you and Na'ito, but—"

"Sera, it's okay. You have so much responsibility now. It's understandable." She looks up as Kye and Na'ito walk in. "Hello, boys. How was the market?"

"Packed!" Na'ito answers, sitting down. "We are selling out every day so far."

"That's good."

"We're actually turning a good profit from the orchard," Kye says.

"Really?" Sera asks. "That's great!"

Na'ito looks at Sera. "We want to ask, but—" he looks down.

"What?"

"Would you go with us to the stall in the morning?"

"I will, but can I ask why you want me there?" Sera asks.

Kye and Na'ito smile at each other. "You'll see," Kye answers.

"All right. We'll stop by on the way to the ferry."

"Going to the mainland, Miss Sera?" Kye asks.

"Yes, to have lunch with the queen."

Kye lets out a whistle. "Wow!"

They all laugh as they continue eating. Telling them about her last encounter, Sera explains that she was surprised by the queen's kindness and interest in Sera. "I did not expect her to like me so."

Dankin laughs. "What's not to like?"

Once they finish eating, the boys gather the dishes and take them into the kitchen. Dankin looks at Rae'lin. "Thank you for having us."

"You and my daughter are always welcome, you know that." She looks at Sera. "Are you better now? From your nightmare?"

"I think so."

"I'm going to retire for the evening. See you for breakfast?"

"Yes, mother." She watches her leave, trailing her fingers over the table.

"Are you still upset from your nightmare? And please, I don't mean what happened after. The nightmare itself?" Dankin asks.

"No, I'm okay," she responds as she stands up. "I think I'm about ready to turn in, as well. It's been a long day."

"Sera, don't hide from me."

"Yes, I'm still upset from my nightmare. I'm getting over it, I'll be fine." She gives him a reassuring smile. "Please, don't take it personally."

"How else would I take it?"

She closes her eyes, pulling away. "Dankin, please—"

"I'm sorry. You're right, I am getting angry and have no reason to be. You can't help what your nightmare was about. Can I hold you?"

"Let's go upstairs so we can have privacy."

Upstairs, as they get ready for bed, Sera's thoughts return to her nightmare. She looks in the mirror, dreading the thought of the dream recurring, when she suddenly falls to the floor. "Dankin!" she cries out.

He runs in, shocked to see the markings on her tail, her eyes glowing red. He kneels beside her, holding her as he speaks softly. Rae'lin comes in to see what's wrong.

"What is happening to her?" she demands.

Dankin ignores her and continues to speak softly until Sera transforms back into a human. "Are you all right?" he asks, panic in his voice.

She nods her head. "I'm okay. It didn't hurt this time, it just scared me." He helps her to her feet. She looks at her mother. "What you just saw was me, as a siren."

"What?"

"It's a long story, and I need to rest now. We'll talk later?"

"Of course." She shoots Dankin an angry look. "Call on me if you need anything," she offers as she leaves.

Dankin looks at Sera. "I know you said you don't want any magic in—" Before he can finish, she removes her ring and hands it to him.

"Please, fix this! I don't know how I changed myself into that, but I never want it to happen again!"

"I will." He sits on the bed and speaks quietly into the pearls as she finishes getting ready. She sits beside him, and he slips the ring back on. "This will help you stay in whatever form you are in, mermaid or human, and should prevent siren transformation."

She sighs in relief. "I don't want to think about if that had happened at lunch with the queen."

"Let's be grateful it didn't."

She goes into washtoire, turning on the shower and stepping in. Shock washing over her, she sits in the tub, holding her knees to her chest as she cries. Dankin pulls the curtain back, concerned at the sight of her.

"You're in your nightgown!" Turning the water off, he gets her out of the tub. "What happened?" He helps her out of the wet clothes and wraps a towel around her. He gets her dried and dressed, then carries her to bed. "Sera?"

"I think I went into shock from it all."

"Honestly, I'm surprised it took this long. You've had so much thrust upon you." He covers her with the blanket, his hand stroking her arm. "Can I get you some tea?"

"Please?"

He smiles, leaning down and kissing her forehead. "I'll be right back." As soon as he's gone, she goes to the mirror. Thinking of herself as a mermaid, she pictures herself swimming in the ocean and lying on the sand. She shakes her head when nothing happens.

He gave me this ring to help, but he also took away my own power! She gets the pearl out of her bedside drawer and tries again, to no avail. Listening for footfalls on the stairs, she gets his pearl out, holding one in each hand. Recalling the words she heard him use a few moments ago, she whispers into the pearls, feeling the flow of magic between them. She returns the pearls and slides the ring on her finger before climbing back into bed. She looks down, smiling as her tail appears, then her legs. She sighs in relief, happy to have some control back. Dankin walks in with tea.

"Thank you," she says as she takes her cup.

"Of course. How are you feeling?"

"Much better. I am quite tired, though."

"Drink this, and we'll turn in."

"Okay." She smiles at him, sipping her chamomile and honey tea. When they're finished, he takes their cups downstairs and returns to find her asleep. He climbs into bed, pulling her to him and holding her tightly as she sleeps.

"I love you, sea nymph," he whispers, kissing her on her forehead. "Please, no bad dreams tonight."

Chapter 22

Spill the Tea

Dankin opens his eyes, stretching when he looks over to find he's alone. He bolts upright. "Sera?" he calls out, getting to his feet.

"I'll be out in a moment," she calls from the washtoire.

He walks to the door and turns the knob. "Sera? Let me in!" he says when he finds the door locked.

She rinses her mouth then opens the door. "What's—" before she can finish, he crushes her to his chest, holding her tightly.

"Please, I'm sorry. I woke up alone…"

She eases in his arms, holding him and caressing his back. "I had a taste in my mouth, I guess from the tea." She laughs. "I woke up and had to brush. I wanted to kiss you, but not with gross breath."

"Sera, I don't care about bad breath. Please, don't let me wake up like that again?"

She looks up at him, nodding. "I promise."

He leans down and kisses her, chuckling. "Minty fresh!"

They go downstairs, surprised no one is awake yet. "Hmm," Sera murmurs as she goes to the ice box, getting out the ingredients to cook breakfast. Chi'yo walks in.

"Oh, a thousand apologies!" she says as she blows her nose.

"Chi'yo, you sound awful! Are you ill?"

"Yes, Miss Sera."

"Go back to your bed. We will take care of this."

"But—"

"The queen commands it," she says, smiling at her.

Chi'yo nods and bows. "Yes, Your Majesty." She leaves the kitchen.

"She does not get sick very often. Must be something going around, I wonder?" Sera asks.

"Let's hope we don't get it."

"Oh, right! Have you ever been sick before?" Sera asks as she stirs up the eggs, adding a splash of milk.

"No, but I hadn't been on land this much, either."

"You're lucky. It can be awful."

"I remember when you were sick. I took care of things around here. I hated seeing you like that."

"Why didn't you heal me?"

He looks down. "I did a little, but I couldn't just make you suddenly better. I was still trying to just be peasant Dankin, remember?"

"Oh, right."

"I don't think I could, now. I would probably take the chance."

She smiles up at him, as he brings over the chopped veggies and adds them to her pan. She seasons as she cooks, smiling at the smell and taste. "I miss cooking."

"Hot foods? Hot drink? Hot shower?"

"Yes," she admits. "All of it."

"Any regrets?"

"No! Not at all. It's worth it, being married to you. Oh, I just realized I don't know your middle name."

"I don't have one. As merpeople, we don't." He begins to plate the food. "What's yours?"

She laughs. "Oh, no. You have to earn that."

Rae'lin walks in then. "It smells incredible in here! And what are we talking about this morning?"

"I'm sure your beautiful, kind mother will tell me?" Dankin grins.

"Oh, he is buttering me up!"

The three of them laugh. "What is Sera's middle name?"

Rae'lin takes her plate, following them to the small table. "If she's not saying, neither will I."

"That bad, huh?"

Sera laughs. "No."

"I am begging you. Please, tell me?"

"All right," Sera relents. "My full name, before getting married, was Sereia Ba'ra Dahvaene."

"Ba'ra? What does that mean?"

She blushes, looking down. "Rose."

He laughs, kissing her hand. "I think it's beautiful."

"Thank you. Now, can we eat in peace?"

"Yes, my little water rose."

She smiles at him as she eats. After breakfast, Dankin takes her upstairs. "Do you have a gown to wear for your visit with the queen today?" he asks.

"No, I meant to go yesterday," Sera answers. She watches him open her closet door and smile at her. "What are we—"

"Get out the nicest gown you have," he instructs.

"Okay." She pulls out the dress she wore last time. "But she's already seen this one. I can't wear it again."

He laughs. "Trust me?" She nods, slipping into the gown. He looks through her closet and gets out a pale pink gown. "Are you partial to this one?"

She gives him a confused look, shaking her head. "No."

He instructs her to lie down on the bed and drapes the pink gown over her. Then he puts his hands on her arms, speaking softly as she transforms into a mermaid and back again. He helps her up and guides her to the mirror. "Well?"

She stands in awe, admiring the pink ruffle gown. "It's gorgeous!" She runs her fingers over the dark pink ribbons, contrasting the white and pale pink layers. She looks at him. "How do you do that?"

He kisses her forehead. "That's for me to know…"

She laughs, turning back to the mirror. "Thank you." When Dankin steps into the washtoire, Sera goes to the dresser and removes her pearl. She puts it in the pocket of her gown, along with her dagger.

Rae'lin stands as they enter the parlor, jealous of the breathtaking gown. "Sera, that is beautiful! Where did it come from?"

She blushes, looking at Dankin. "He… surprised me with it."

"You have good taste," Rae'lin admits.

They visit until it's time to leave. Rae'lin helps Sera with her hair and makeup, smiling at the sight. Sera hugs her tightly. "I'll tell you everything when we get back."

"Unlike last time?"

Sera laughs, blushing. "I—"

"It's okay. Have a good time."

At the market, Sera's mouth drops at the sight of her stall. The cover now provides shade for the entire stall, and they added shelving space to hold more produce. She looks over when Kye steps up.

"Well?" he asks.

"Very impressive!" she beams with pride.

"Thank you. You look… nice."

She laughs. "Thanks. We'll be back in a few hours."

"Have fun!" Kye calls out as Sera and Dankin walk away.

* * *

On the ferry, they find their seats and enjoy the cool morning breeze. Once at the mainland, they go to the market, where Sera buys Na'ito a few books and her mother a bottle of perfume.

"I never got you a birthday present," he realizes.

"It's okay. I haven't—" She looks away, clearing her throat. "I haven't gotten one in a long time."

"Sera?"

"My father always gave me something special before he was wounded in the war."

"What was the last thing he gave you?"

"A sword. It's too small for me now, as I was just a child."

"Really? A sword?"

"He trained me in fencing and self-defense. As you've seen, I'm perfectly capable of protecting myself."

"Taking on pirates, sirens, and snakes. I wouldn't want to cross you." He winks at her.

They walk up to the palace to see the Ga'ishi are waiting for her. They bow to her. "Your Majesty, the queen is ready for you."

"Thank you," she says, stepping forward. She turns back to Dankin.

"I'll be here. I promise," he assures her.

She smiles at him before following the Ga'ishi inside. They take her into a tea parlor, nicer than any she's ever been in. The trim is bamboo with dark wood floors. Sera admires the ornate round table. She smiles as the queen gets to her feet. Sera bows to her, watching as Kery'oto returns with a half-bow.

"Sera, how are you?"

"Doing well. Thank you for having me today."

They sit at the table as the Ga'ishi perform the tea ceremony. Lunch is brought in. Sera stifles a laugh, when she sees the platters of fish, lobster, clams, and oysters. Kery'oto gestures the Ga'ishi out.

"Is something wrong?"

"Oh, no. Apologies. I was trying to decide what to eat first."

"I didn't think when planning this menu. I'm sure you are quite tired of food like this."

"Whatever do you mean?"

"Sera, please? Between us, I know who you are, you and Dankin."

Sera swallows hard, keeping the smile on her face as her ears are ringing. "I'm sure I don't know what you're—"

"Please, don't insult me?"

Sera looks down. "Yes, Kery'oto."

"You are still my friend. I am curious about you, though."

Sera looks up to see Kery'oto studying her. "How so?" she asks.

"My scout told me how quickly you transform. I was wondering if I could see it for myself? You will not offend me if you refuse. I'm asking as your friend, not commanding as the queen."

"I see. Can I ask, who all knows?"

"Just my scout and myself. I assure you, he is loyal and trustworthy. I would not have sent him on such an important mission if I did not believe so."

"Why send him in the first place?"

"I've heard mentions of the Mar Reinado Kingdom, but I could not find anyone who was from there. We couldn't find it on any map. I was worried that Dankin was a con artist or something worse. I couldn't imagine who else he could be, so you can understand how surprised I was to find out the truth."

Sera sighs. "Where would you like me to do it?"

"Oh, we can eat lunch first. Unless you'd prefer to get it out of the way?"

She looks around the room, seeing the chaise by the wall. "Over there?"

"Yes, that would be fine."

They walk to the chaise, and Sera lies down, looking up at Kery'oto. "You realize I am trusting you with something no one outside of my family knows about?"

"I do, and I thank you." Sera nods, closing her eyes. She looks down as her tail grows. Kery'oto gasps. "Oh, it's so beautiful," she murmurs in disbelief.

"Thank you." Sera closes her eyes to turn herself back.

"No, wait. Just another moment, please?"

Sera nods again, retaining her mermaid form. "What would you like to know?"

"Does it hurt to change like that?"

"Only the first time."

"What's it like, going so deep into the ocean?"

"Beautiful. You get to see things you never would've thought possible." She notices Kery'oto staring at her fins. "Do you want to touch it?"

She backs up, blushing. "It's inappropriate."

"It's just the two of us. If you want to, go ahead."

Kery'oto leans down, gently brushing two fingers along her tail. "It's so soft! Not at all what I expected."

"May I change back now?"

"Of course. Thank you for indulging me."

They return to the table, where Sera pushes her food around with her fork. "Thank you for having me."

"What's wrong? Are you upset with me?"

"No. I'm upset that we weren't more careful. I told him—"

"Sera, it's not your fault. My scout had to follow you many times before he finally saw you transform, and he only saw it from a distance, for fear of being discovered."

"That makes me feel a little better, thank you."

"Please, eat with me?"

She nods, picking her fork up and taking a bite. "Of course." Looking at the food, Sera shakes her head as she loses her appetite. "I apologize, it's not you." Her nose crinkles.

"Is something wrong with the food?"

"I hope I don't offend you, I just don't have an appetite at the moment."

"Let me help." Kery'oto gestures one of the Ga'ishi back inside. She leaves, returning a moment later with a bowl of warm soup that she sets in front of Sera before pulling out a message for Kery'oto.

"Your Grace, this is from the Maristellar Kingdom."

Kery'oto takes it from her, admiring the satin paper and silver engraving. "Thank you."

The Ga'ishi bows and leaves the room.

Sera inhales the aroma. "Hmm. Beef, truffles, and," she inhales again, "a hint of saffron?"

"Very good! Do you cook as well?"

"I do."

"Cook, dance, turn into a mermaid. Is there anything you can't do?"

They laugh as they finish their meal. "Thank you, Kery'oto. This has been a nice lunch."

"I truly hope I did not put you on the spot. I have loved hearing and reading stories of mermaids for as long as I can remember. To actually see one has made me very happy. I haven't felt like that since… Well, in a long time. Thank you so much."

Sera gives her a smile, seeing the sorrow in her eyes. "Of course."

"I assure you, your secret is safe with me."

"I appreciate that."

The Ga'ishi escort her out, but Dankin is not waiting for her when she leaves the palace. She looks at the clock. *Lunch didn't last as long as we thought. He's probably still dealing with some business.* She goes to a bench and sits down, waiting for him.

After an hour goes by, she can't wait any longer. She gets to her feet and wanders around the market, trying desperately to find him. Finally, she goes to the ferry, where a messenger flags her down.

"Sera Dahvaene?"

"Yes."

Upon seeing her crown, he bows as he hands her the message. She gives him a gold coin in return. Once he disappears into the crowd, she rips the message open.

I had to return to the palace. Please,
go back to the estate and wait for me.
I am truly sorry I had to leave.
I will tell you everything once I get back.
Love, Dankin

She crumples the note, worry flooding her veins. The ferry horn blasts, but she turns and runs the other direction. When she gets to a private spot on the beach, she dives in and rushes for the palace. Inside, she inquires after Dankin and is immediately escorted to the infirmary. He is on one bed, his brother next to him on the other.

"What happened?" she demands.

A guard swims forward. "The dungeon wall started to crumble. Da'vae was hurt, so we sent word to the king. His Majesty was removing Da'vae from the cell when the whole thing collapsed. Da'vae dove on His Majesty, taking the brunt of the hit."

Sera swims up to Dankin, looking over his bruised face. She gets out her pearl and holds it in her hand as her other holds his arm. She speaks quietly when the magic sparks out, healing Dankin. She goes over to his brother, doing the same for him. Then she waits, biting back her worry as she sits on the edge of Dankin's bed, fighting to stay conscious and holding his hand.

"What happened?" Dankin asks when he comes to.

"The dungeon wall collapsed."

"Da'vae!" He looks over, grateful to see his brother.

"I healed him as well."

"You... healed my brother? Even after what he put you through?"

"Of course. He's family, isn't he? From what I heard, he landed on top of you to protect you."

Da'vae sits up, groaning. "What was that?" he asks.

He looks at Sera and Dankin in surprise. "How do you feel?" Dankin asks.

"Surprisingly, okay. Your doing?"

"No. Sera healed you."

"I need to get back," Sera says as she pulls away. "I'm sure my mother is worried sick, wondering why we haven't returned."

"I'll escort you."

"Dankin, you need to rest—"

"So do you, using magic like that!"

"All right." She looks at Da'vae. "What about him?"

Dankin looks at him. "Well?"

"I'm sorry for everything I did to you, Sera. Down there alone, all I've done is think on how I acted. No matter my reasons, I was wrong. I'm not just saying this. I know I will serve out my sentence. But I am truly sorry."

Dankin looks at Sera, who nods, then gives his attention to the guard. "Put him in his quarters, under full house arrest until I return."

"Yes, Majesty."

Dankin swims up to her, taking her hand. "You continue to impress me, Sera Rose."

She laughs. "Anything for you, koy'lei."

They swim back to Isle Piscantur as it's starting to get dark. They dry by the fire on the beach before returning to the estate. Sera suggested it, to avoid any questions about why their clothes are soaked.

"Are you all right?" Rae'lin asks, rushing out to meet them.

"Yes," Sera answers. "Everything went fine with the queen. We had an issue back at the palace that needed our immediate attention. I'm sorry. I didn't mean to worry you."

"As long as you're all right?" she asks again, looking them over.

"We are, just exhausted now."

"Have you had supper?" Rae'lin asks.

"No."

"Well, come in and freshen up. I'll bring you each a plate."

Sera smiles at her. "Thank you."

Once they've both showered and changed into pajamas, Sera flops down on the bed. "How are you still awake?" Dankin asks when she yawns twice.

She laughs, looking up at him. "Because I do need food."

"I have it," Rae'lin says, walking in. Dankin steps over to help her with the tray. She pulls up a chair as they eat. "How did things go with the queen?"

Sera looks down before looking at Dankin. "She knows about us."

"Knows what?" Dankin asks.

"What we are."

Dankin gets to his feet. "What? How?"

"She was suspicious, having heard of King Dankin and our kingdom, but never meeting anyone from there. She had a scout follow us. He—he saw us at the beach."

"Should I be worried?"

"No. She wants to be friends, and she swore to me that she would keep our secret. She only brought it up because she was fascinated to learn of us. She said she has heard and read stories since she was a child, and she was excited to meet a real mermaid."

"I could see that," Rae'lin agrees. "I mean, walking in and seeing you like that in the tub surprised me, but I thought it was one of the most unique experiences of my life."

"Wait, did you transform in front of her?"

"Yes, because she asked me to. She told me I did not have to, but—"

"How did you?" Dankin asks.

Sera looks down. "After you went to get tea last night, I used our pearls and put magic back into my ring." She looks at him. "You should not be the only one to control my transformations."

"That wasn't my intention. I was trying to keep you from turning into a siren again." Dankin leans over and kisses her forehead. "But you're right, and I'm not upset you did that."

"What was that all about, Sera?"

While Dankin takes their dishes downstairs, Sera tells Rae'lin about the nightmare and the pond. "I had no idea I would change so much being with him."

"Do you regret it?"

Dankin stops, standing in the hallway and listening in. "No. I love him, and it's worth everything we've been through. I've had moments where I did, because I've been hurting or because of him, but I am grateful to have him. I love him so much."

"I can see that."

Dankin walks in and takes Sera's hand in his. "You need to sleep now, after everything you did today."

"So do you."

Rae'lin leans forward to kiss Sera on top of her head. "Sleep, my child. I'll see you both in the morning."

"We're leaving after breakfast, aren't we?" Sera asks Dankin.

"No, I know you and your mother did not get to spend much time together. Have some time tomorrow, then we'll leave after."

"Thank you."

Rae'lin leaves, shutting the door behind her. Dankin adjusts the lights before climbing into bed with her. He holds her to him, stroking her hair.

"Thank you."

"For what?" she asks, yawning.

"Saving me and my brother."

"I healed a few bruises—"

"Sera, we had internal injuries."

Her eyes fly open as she sits up, looking at him. "Are you serious?"

"I am. Sera, you need to rest. Lay back down."

She lets him hold her wrapped in the comfort of his arms.

* * *

Dankin is still asleep when Sera wakes up. Knowing how much it upsets him to wake up alone, she leans over and kisses his cheek. His eyes open.

"Is—is that okay?" she asks softly, thinking about when she woke him up with kisses the day before.

He looks at her. "No."

"Dankin—" Before she can finish, his lips are on hers.

"That's better."

"Don't do that to me." She laughs, rolling onto her back. Her eyes go wide as he climbs onto her, kissing her again. She holds him tightly, as his kiss grows in hunger. "Dankin, we need breakfast."

She gets dressed and goes into the washtoire. He goes to the closet and starts to pull out a pair of black pants when he hears her retching. He rushes to the door, surprised to find it locked.

"Sera? Are you all right?"

She opens the door, brushing her teeth. "I'm fine," she says, confused.

"I thought I heard you getting sick?"

She laughs. "I had a hair in my throat."

"Not something we deal with underwater."

She spits, rinses her mouth, and laughs again. "No. I didn't mean to have you worried."

"It's okay."

Downstairs, they are surprised to see Chi'yo cooking breakfast. "How are you feeling?" Sera asks.

"Much better."

"I am glad to hear that."

"Your mother sent for the doctor, and the medicine he gave me helped a lot." She looks at Sera, speaking quietly. "I don't know what happened to make her change for the better, but the mistress is such a different person now. I like to think you had something to do with that."

"I only showed her who she was. She made the decision to change. Like you, I am grateful she did."

They finish cooking and set up at the small table. Rae'lin walks in. "Can I ask why you prefer this table?"

Sera looks at her as she's setting down her plate. "I have eaten at this table for as long as I can remember. This is where I always had breakfast." She smiles up at Dankin. "And not alone for the last few weeks I was here."

He smiles, taking her hand and kissing her palm. "Never again, either."

Rae'lin sits with them. "I didn't think of that. You would bring us our tray, but I never thought about you eating out here alone." She looks away a moment, before facing Sera. "You never should've felt so alone in your own house."

"It's okay—"

"No, it's not. You needed a mother, not a master."

"You are now."

She sighs. "I know."

"Rae'lin, what's wrong?" Sera asks.

"I guess if you have children, I'll never get to see them?"

Sera looks over, seeing Chi'yo at the sink and washing dishes. "We could meet in the cove to have privacy," she answers quietly. "I can't make promises that we can come here. But I will try everything to make sure you get to meet them."

"Thank you."

She looks at Dankin, who nods. "If that time comes, we will figure it out," Dankin assures them both.

They finish eating and go into the parlor. Sera visits with her mother while Na'ito and Dankin play a game. Sera looks at the clock. "I'm sorry, we need to get back."

Rae'lin stands, taking Sera's hand and pulling her in for a hug. "I know. I'm thankful I got to see you, both of you." She smiles at Dankin. "Please, come back soon?"

"We'll try," Dankin answers, surprising Rae'lin when he gives her a hug.

* * *

Back in their quarters at the palace, Sera lies down on the bed while Dankin requests lunch. He swims to her, worried. "Are you all right?"

"Just tired. I think it's from yesterday."

"I see. Eat lunch and rest, while I check on things."

"Okay."

As he leans down to kiss her, his hand slips under her pillow. She tries to grab his arm as he pulls out a few pages of handwritten notes. "I found these the other morning. Why didn't you ask me about this?"

She takes the papers from him, sitting up. "It's how I learn. The mistress taught me manners and customs, but I had to learn history, science, and literature myself."

"Sera, this isn't history of the palace—"

"I know that. Still, it's how I learn."

He gets their food and brings it to her, sitting while they eat. "Do you have any questions?" He nods to her papers.

"No," she answers, keeping her head down.

"Sera? Why are you embarrassed? You literally transformed into something else. It's only natural for you to want to know what you are, inside and out. I just don't understand why you hid it?"

She hands him her plate and lies back down, pulling the blanket up over her head. Dankin sighs.

"I love you," she says quietly.

"I love you. I'm going to check on things and see how the dungeon repairs are coming. I'll be back before supper. I hope by then you can talk to me about this."

"I wouldn't hold my breath," she answers.

He chuckles, shaking his head as he swims from the room. As soon as he's gone, Sera gets up. She gathers her notes and sits at the small vanity in the corner. Laying them out to look them over, her eyes begin to droop with exhaustion. She rests her arm on the vanity and lays her head on it, falling asleep.

* * *

Dankin returns, holding a tray with their supper. He grows concerned when he doesn't see Sera in bed, then sighs in relief when he sees her at the vanity. Setting the tray on the table, he swims to her and gently wakes her.

"How are you feeling?" he asks.

"Better. Do you have supper?"

"I do. Let's eat and talk."

She swims with him to the small table. "I'm sorry."

"Whatever for?"

"That I didn't tell you what I was studying."

"I'm not upset. I just don't understand?"

She sighs, looking down. "I'm still adjusting to so much, and having these pictures and charts help."

"And the drawing of the mermaid's purse?"

She blushes, setting her fork down. "I—It's—"

"Sera?" He takes her hand. "Please?"

"I wasn't sure if... as mermaids, if it's a live birth or... um..."

"Or if you lay eggs?" She hides her face in her hands. "It's a live birth. Think about it, if each mermaid laid thirty to forty eggs, the ocean would be overrun!" He laughs, turning serious when she doesn't respond. "Sera, why is this so embarrassing?"

"We shouldn't discuss these things. It isn't proper!"

"Sera, you're not on the island anymore. Things are different here—"

"Like I don't know that?"

"Sera, take a breath. You're getting upset when you have no reason to be. I am simply explaining to you that we can talk about things like this without me worrying you are going to pass out."

"I know. I'm sorry."

He pulls her from the chair, holding her in his arms. "I love you, and I want you to be comfortable talking to me, about anything."

"I love you, too. I'm working on it…"

"I know you are. Please, I mean it. Ask me anything, any time. I will answer whatever questions you have."

"Can I finish eating?"

He laughs as she returns to her seat. "Of course." He brings his hand under her chin. "First, will you look at me?"

She raises her head, meeting his gaze. "Yes?"

"I love you. I wanted to see your beautiful face."

She smiles, taking his hand and squeezing it. "Thank you for your patience with me."

"I did this to you, so helping you with it is the least I can do."

She finishes eating. "I'm still tired. I'm going to turn in."

"Are you sure you're okay?"

"Dankin, I used so much magic yesterday, more in one day than I have in all the time I've had it."

"You're right, of course. Hmm, about that?"

"What?"

"Your ring?"

She sighs. "Do you want to undo what I did?"

"Oh, no. As long as it works for you, I'm not upset, but I still don't understand why you didn't talk to me about it."

"You seem to view using magic as a... a personal thing. I didn't want to upset you, but I wanted to have some control myself."

"You have every right to. It was wrong enough that I forced you the night we got engaged. I never should transform you without your permission."

"Unless we're on our island on the sand?"

He laughs, kissing her. "Okay, maybe a surprise like that from time to time, but I swear, never in anger or to keep you prisoner. Never again."

"I don't believe you."

"What?" His eyes go wide, when she grabs his hand, pulling him to her and kissing him back.

"Hmm, okay. I guess I will now."

He laughs. "Get ready to turn in. I'll tuck you in."

"You're not coming to bed yet?"

"They need me for some of the repairs."

"Oh, please be safe."

"I will."

He gets her settled into bed. She takes his hand. "I have a confession to make," she says.

"Okay?" he asks with worry.

"Um, I almost rolled off the bed at the estate."

He laughs in relief. "Really?"

"You're right, that it becomes such a habit to roll off here. It's your fault, you know." She laughs, pulling him to her.

"Hmm, do you forgive me?" he asks.

"Kiss me, and I will."

He leans down, kissing her gently as he pulls the blanket up. "Now, Your Grace, get some sleep."

She giggles as he attacks her face and neck with kisses. "Thank you, my koy'lei." She closes her eyes, and he watches her a moment before leaving the room.

Chapter 23

Unexpected News

At five in the morning, Sera wakes up, stifling a scream. She sits up when she realizes Dankin isn't with her. Deciding to check on him, she slips on a dress and crown. She goes into the hall, seeing it empty as she heads towards the dungeon. Rounding a corner, she nearly bumps into a siren.

"Your Grace," she bows.

"Hello. What is your name?"

"I am Ka'lael'a."

"That's a beautiful name."

"Thank you."

"What are you doing out this time of night?"

"We are creatures of the night. Well, we were…"

"Oh, right. I apologize, I had forgotten."

"I just came from the dungeon, and the repairs are almost complete."

"The dungeon?"

"I thought he told you? I am courting Da'vae."

"I see. He mentioned a siren, but I apologize that I did not know your name." Her skin grows cold as she realizes it's just the two of them in the corridor. "Dankin is expecting me—"

"Of course." She gives her a small smile before swimming away.

Sera sighs in relief. She flags down a guard. "Where is the king?"

"He is in his office. I'll escort you, Your Grace."

"Thank you." When they arrive at Dankin's office, the guard returns to his post. She opens the door. Dankin is at his desk. "I missed you," she says.

"I apologize. Trying to catch up on work."

"Did you wake up early?"

He sighs. "I never came to bed."

"I need to catch up, too. I'm sorry—"

"You have nothing to be sorry for. I enjoy the time we get to spend with family. If it means a little paperwork piles up, then so be it. It's worth it."

"Thank you. Will you come to bed soon?"

"I will."

She swims to him and kisses him. "Promise?"

"I promise."

"Hmm, all right." She looks at him again.

"Sera?"

She turns away. "I'm okay."

"Nightmare?"

Her head goes down. "Yes. The snakes in the pool…"

He swims over, holding her tight. "I'll come to bed with you. You'll be safe and warm."

She looks down. "Warm?"

"Do you want your grotto?"

She looks up at him, biting back tears. "Please?"

He pulls her up, swimming with her. They leave the palace, getting to the surface as the sun is rising. He takes her to their grotto and helps her into the pool. He holds her tightly and looks down when her stomach grumbles. "We didn't think to bring food. I was more concerned with getting you warm!"

"It's okay. I don't have much of an appetite at the moment, despite the noises my stomach is making. We'll eat soon enough."

"Stay here," he says, laying her against the wall of the pool as he walks out. She shakes her head, smiling at the sight. She looks over when he returns. He takes a small rock, cleaning it in the ocean. She watches him lay a fish on it, carving it with his blade. He brings the pieces over. She looks up at him.

"Seriously?"

He laughs. "This is what we eat at home, just on finer dishes." He smiles, eating a bite.

She sighs as she looks it over. She takes a piece, nearly gagging at the thought. She shakes her head. "I can't. I'm sorry."

He sets the rock down, looking at her. "Are you sick?"

"No, I think I'm still upset. In my nightmare, the snakes… they killed me."

"Do you want tea and pastries? Isle Toro'pikar is not too far from here. I'll take you there."

"That would be really nice, if you want to. Please, don't feel like you have to make anything up to me."

He picks her up, carrying her into the ocean. They swim for the isle, going into a private cove to transform and dry off. He takes her to the market and smiles as she enjoys the sight of people walking around. She notices the women are in long, one-piece gowns while the men are in slacks and shirts. She looks at Dankin.

"Last time we were here, I was so lost in my grief, I didn't even notice how differently the people here dress!"

"I guess because men's clothing isn't so different, I didn't notice, either."

Sera catches a whiff from the market. "They're already smoking meats. It smells delicious."

"Okay, I must admit. That was one of the main reasons for me coming onto land."

"I beg your pardon?" she asks, stopping in her tracks.

"I would go for a swim to get away from the palace after…" He clears his throat. "Anyway, I would swim by here and smell the amazing foods! I had been on land a few times before, but I never really allowed myself to eat."

"Why not?" she asks.

"I was usually out on business."

They walk into the patisserie and select their pastries with honey tea, then sit at a table away from the market, and bask in the sun.

"Can I ask?"

"Ask anything," Dankin offers.

"What kind of business do you do on land?"

"I represent our kingdom, paying taxes and in return, the monarch or ruler of the land helps ensure our protection from fisherman. I also trade for weapons and armor, things we can't make under water."

"Wait—you mean there are people, like actual humans, who know about us? And you didn't tell me about this sooner?"

"It's for our own protection. Fishermen tell tall tales, so most people blow off hearing about a mermaid or a siren. However, as you well know, some want to try and hunt us. Now that Queen Kery'oto knows about us, I will speak to her, as well. I never really worked much with Isle Piscantur or H'ondo, because it is so far away from the merpeople kingdoms and clans. I have been on the mainland a few times for business, but I had never visited the isle. That's why I went there, knowing a few may have heard the name

Dankin, but no one would know who I am. At least, no one wandering around the small market."

"Well, I'm glad you didn't go to the mainland," she huffs.

He chuckles, sipping his tea. "Me, too." He sets his cup down, taking her hands. "Sera, will you talk to me now?"

"About what?" she asks.

"Whatever is bothering you. I've seen it in your eyes lately, but I was trying not to push."

She smiles, squeezing his hands. "Dankin, I assure you, I'm fine. We went through a lot together, but I'm all right now."

"Sera—"

She pulls away. "Do you think I'm lying to you?"

"No. Let's not ruin the morning."

She looks down, taking a sip of her tea. "You're right. I've ruined enough time with you."

He sighs. "That's not what I meant. Please, can we have a nice breakfast together? Like you said, after what we've went through?"

She nods, pushing down her tears as she finishes her pastry. "Would you get me another one? I really like the cherries."

He chuckles. "I'm glad your appetite is back. Give me just a moment."

As soon as he's gone, she wipes her tears away. *He's right. We've had enough fighting. I will talk to him when I am ready, not when he is.* She takes a deep breath, holding it in before letting it out. She shakes her head.

"What are you thinking about?"

She looks up and takes the pastry. "Thank you. Something as simple as breathing. Weird?" she asks with a small laugh.

"Not at all." He chuckles as he sits down.

"Having gills was weird for me. What was weird about turning human for you?"

"Using my legs for the first time."

"Really?"

"Yes. I sat on the beach, watching people walk. I bent my knees and moved them first, but I fell down when I tried to stand."

"I'm sorry. At least I had you to help me."

"Are we ready to go back?" Sera looks over, seeing a mother carrying her baby along the market. "Sera?"

"Yes, that's fine."

He sighs. "What's wrong?"

She looks at him as she gathers their trash. "I'm fine." Throwing the trash away, she returns to him and takes his hand. "Ready?"

She's confused when he takes her to the shore and sits with her. "We need to talk," he explains.

"Okay. What's going on?"

"That's what I should be asking you."

"Dankin—"

"No. Please, talk to me?" he asks.

She looks down at his arm wrapped around her, tracing her fingers over it. "I'm still grieving. I'm sorry, and I don't mean to—"

"Sera, take as long as you need to. Why haven't you said anything?"

"Please, promise you won't get mad at me?" she asks, her voice breaking.

"I swear it."

"I feel so alone."

He tightens his grip. "What can I do?" He buries his face into her hair, wrapping her tighter in his arm as she trembles from crying. "Why didn't you tell me sooner?" He strokes her hair, speaking quietly. "I'm sorry. Everything is okay now. I love you, so much."

She wipes her tears, pulling back. "You already have so much grief on your own, I didn't want you to carry mine as well."

"I understand, but I want to be here for you. I wasn't when you needed me. Will you let me now?"

She nods, clutching him tightly. "I feel... lost and empty."

"How can I help?"

She shakes her head. "I don't know. I've never felt like this before."

"I have," he says, pulling her back and caressing her face. "I'm here for you, whatever you need."

"Thank you," she replies. "I know we need to get back."

"Right now, this is what we need. Both of us."

She gasps softly. "I'm so sorry. I didn't think—" She hangs her head.

"Sera, you have been through so much, lost so much, it's understandable. I didn't mean to make you feel guilty, I swear. You have no reason to feel like that. Will you lay with me now, let me hold you here?"

She nods, climbing into his arms. "Thank you. I'm sorry for what we went through. I wish I could've done more..."

"It's okay. We're here now." She snuggles in, holding him tightly. He looks down, shaking his head when he realizes she fell asleep. "Why have you been carrying this on your own? I never meant for you to feel that way." He kisses the top of her head, letting her sleep an hour before waking her. "Ready to go home?"

"Yes. I miss the palace," she says, yawning.

He smiles at her words as he carries her into the water. They transform as they go under. At the palace, he takes her into his office. "I have to do some paperwork." He places her gently on the chaise.

"Can I help?" she offers.

"Rest. I just wanted us to be together while I work."

"Thank you."

She lies down and falls back to sleep. Dankin checks on her from time to time as he works, worried that she is sleeping so much. She's been through a lot. I'll give her a few days, and if she's still sleeping like this, I'll take her to the mainland for tests. I pray she is all right. He finishes and files his papers. He swims to her and sits on the edge of the chaise, taking her hand and kissing it.

"Sera?"

"Hmm?" She opens her eyes, sitting up. "I fell asleep?"

"Yes, you did. How are you feeling?"

"I'm okay. I think it was all the crying."

"Are we going to supper?"

"Yes, please." She smiles.

* * *

They've just sat down at their table when Ma'like approaches. "Majesty, Da'vae is requesting you come and speak with him."

"I'll be down shortly."

"Yes, Majesty." He bows and swims off.

"What could he want?" Dankin wonders aloud.

"I was thinking the same thing," she admits.

"We'll eat, then I'll talk to him. Do you want to be there?"

She looks up, surprised at his question. "Hmm. I don't think I do. I'm grateful you asked me, though."

"I have to remember, we're a team now. We are running this kingdom and overseeing things together. I forget that sometimes."

She brings her hand up, tracing his jawline with her fingertips. "We're both adjusting. It's a day-by-day process."

He takes her hand, kissing along her fingertips. "I've missed this."

"What?"

"Us. You're right, we have fought enough. I want you as my friend, my lover, my wife. Never again as my enemy."

"Hmm. Don't kidnap me, and I think we'll be okay." She grins up at him.

"Sera!" He laughs. "I may still kidnap you from time to time. Take you to the grotto…" he leans down, whispering in her ear. He chuckles when she blushes.

She shakes her head. "Most improper, Your Majesty!"

They both laugh. "A thousand apologies, Your Grace." They finish eating, then he escorts her back to their room. "I won't be too long."

"I'll wait up for you," she says, kissing him softly at the door. Once he's out of sight, she goes inside, shutting the door. She goes to the closet and gets out a pink nightgown. *I'd give anything for a shower before bed.* She sighs at the thought. She gets changed and sits at the vanity, looking over her notes, then swims about the room as she waits for him.

When Dankin returns, she swims to him and takes him in her arms. "Are you all right?" he asks, looking down at her.

"I missed you," she says, muffled into his shirt. She pulls back. "What did he say?"

"He sincerely apologized again for all that he did to you, stating that he wants to earn your forgiveness. He was angry and jealous, and he regrets what he did. I think I believe him. He seemed genuinely concerned when he asked how you were, after healing us both."

"Time will tell."

"For now, let's get some sleep."

She laughs as she pulls him with her. "Don't have to tell me twice."

"Sera!" he cries out, joining in the laughter. "I have to remove my dress shirt first."

She looks him over, sighing. "Fine," she says, slowly unbuttoning his shirt. He carries her to the bed. He's getting her settled in when she grabs his hands and pulls him onto her. He studies her face, wanting to kiss her but worrying over her. She smiles at him, nodding. He leans down and kisses her gently.

"Sleep, my sea nymph. You need your rest, after the past few days."

"I will. As long as you are here with me."

"I promise, I will be."

"I love you, Dankin."

"Sera, you know how much I love you." He kisses her again, pulling her into his arms and holding her tight. "I was cursed to find love, and I have never been so happy about being cursed."

She laughs softly. "Hmm. Me, too." She falls asleep to his breathing, his heartbeat, his love.

* * *

Dankin wakes up first, looking down and smiling at a sleeping Sera. He gently caresses her face and back as he holds her to him.

"Hmm. Morning," she says.

"Morning. How are you?"

"A little tired still, but I'll be okay. Let's get dressed and go to breakfast."

They go into the closet. He slips on a shirt then swims out as she's changing.

"Sera, we need to go over plans for—" He swims back in, freezing at the sight of her on the floor, unconscious. Ignoring the looks he gets, he rushes her to the infirmary. "I need help!" he yells as he bursts through the doors.

The doctor swims over and takes Sera to an exam room. "What happened?"

"I don't know. She passed out when she was getting dressed."

The doctor draws blood and checks her vitals. "How has she been before this happened?"

"Tired a lot, but you know she healed me and Da'vae."

They both lean in when Sera starts to come to. "Sera, it's okay. We're just running some tests. How do you feel?" the doctor asks.

"Stop!" Sera calls out. "No tests, nothing!"

Dankin gently grips her hand. "Sera, what's wrong?"

"No." She turns away.

The doctor looks at Dankin. "I have to abide by my—"

399

"I am the king, and I command you continue!"

"Yes, Your Majesty."

Sera looks at him. "Please, I—"

"What is going on?" he demands.

She sits up, looking at the doctor, then back to him. "I think I'm pregnant," she confesses.

The doctor nods and gives them a moment. "Why haven't you told me sooner?" he asks.

"I was waiting to be sure. I wanted to be… to be far enough along…"

"I understand. Still, I wish you had told me."

The doctor returns. "She is correct. Congratulations."

Sera hangs her head. "I can't transform again, can I? It's too much on my body, on the baby?"

"I wouldn't recommend it," the doctor confirms. "I'm sorry."

"We'll send word to your family," Dankin says, taking her hand.

"I'd give anything to tell them myself."

The doctor swims closer. "I think one more transformation will be okay, but then I wouldn't recommend it again until after the baby is born."

She looks at Dankin. "Today?"

He turns to the doctor. "She should be okay for that," she assures him.

He looks back at Sera. "Yes, we'll go today. Now, we need to talk about this."

She sighs. "Can we go to our quarters first?"

"Of course."

The doctor looks over her chart. "See me again in two weeks for an update, sooner if you need. Otherwise, you're free to go, Your Grace."

Dankin takes Sera's hand, leading her into their room. She swims inside and sits on the bed, looking over when Dankin sits with her.

"Sera—"

She looks down. "I'm sorry."

"I don't understand?"

"We never really talked about… about starting a family. You've been through so much, losing yours. I didn't want you to think I did this on purpose, to protect myself from you or as an attempt to save our marriage when we were still working through things."

Dankin sighs, taking her hand. "Look at me, please?"

She raises her head, worry in her eyes. "I'm so sorry."

"You have nothing to apologize for! I'm happy and excited for us." He smiles at her, squeezing her hand.

"Really?"

"I mean it. Aren't you?"

"I want to be," she says quietly. "I'm scared."

"I know. This is so different for you, and since you changed… I didn't think of any of this. At the time, I was focused only on breaking the curse."

"It's not your fault. You know I love you, and I am happy to be here, with you. It just—it scares me, what the future may hold."

"Do you want to see your mother now? Tell her the good news?"

"And have one last hot shower and cup of tea?"

He laughs. "Of course."

They leave the palace and swim in silence to the island, both of them thinking on their future. He gets her into the cove and helps her transform. "Dankin?"

"I thought it best to help."

"Of course." She walks on the beach, looking down at her feet as she walks. She turns to him. "I think we're dry enough now."

* * *

Rae'lin's eyes open wide when she opens the door and sees them standing before her. "Sera! Back so soon? Is everything okay?"

"We have news," she says.

Rae'lin gestures them to follow her. They sit in the parlor. "Well?"

Sera smiles at her. "We're pregnant."

Rae'lin's eyes go wide as a huge smile spreads across her face. "Oh, wonderful news!" She stands up and envelops Sera in her arms. "Wait, that means—"

"I won't be coming here for a while. We think it's best not to transform, as it is hard on my body."

Rae'lin sighs, pulling back. "I see." She looks at Dankin. "Then do it to me. Make me a mermaid."

He gets to his feet, shock on his face. "What?"

"Make me a ring like hers, so I can become a mermaid and visit her. I can't go that long without seeing her!"

Sera looks from Dankin to Rae'lin. "Are you sure? It's really painful the first time, then learning to use your tail—"

"Sera, this is what I want. If it's what I have to do, in order to see my family, I will do it."

Dankin nods. "Okay. Sera, stay and visit. I'll be back." He leans down and kisses her softly before leaving.

"It's really a process. Are you sure?"

"I am. I had already been thinking about it, and it's what I want. I want to be with you through this. I can't do that from here, can I?"

"And Na'ito? The estate?"

"He and Kye are doing very well. Chi'yo can oversee things. I'm not coming to live with you. I just want to be able to visit when I can."

"It's scary at first, trying to use your tail." She tells Rae'lin how it wouldn't respond to her, that she didn't swim right away, and Dankin had to teach her how to use it.

"I see. Still, it's what I want."

"All right."

They continue to visit until Dankin returns. "Now, where are we doing this? She'll need to get into water immediately after."

Sera sighs. "I can't go with you."

"Why not?" Rae'lin asks.

"When I transform back, it will be the last time until the baby comes. I'm not ready."

"Oh, right." She thinks a moment. "Let's visit some more, then we will all go to the ocean together."

"Actually, could I get a shower?" Sera asks.

Rae'lin laughs. "Of course! I'll talk with my son-in-law about swimming while you do."

Sera walks over and kisses Dankin. "Be nice!" She shakes her head when he answers with a laugh.

Once in the washtoire, she strips down and starts the tap. Stepping into the shower, the hot water rains down on her, soothing her as she pushes down her tears. *This will all be worth it. We're going to be a family.* She runs her fingers over her stomach. *What will you look like?* Reluctantly, she shuts off the water. She dries and dresses before joining Dankin and Rae'lin downstairs.

"Well?"

Rae'lin laughs. "What? I'm doing this."

"Okay. Go put on your favorite color," Dankin instructs.

She gives Sera a confused look. "Do as he says," Sera answers with a smile.

"All right." She steps out.

Sera walks over and sits on his lap, kissing him. He grips her tight. "Isn't this improper, Miss Sera?"

She laughs. "Well, since we won't be like this for a long time…" She leans in and kisses him again.

"Sera?" She pulls back, looking in his eyes. Biting her lip, she nods. He picks her up, stopping by the main quarters. "We'll be upstairs for a bit."

Rae'lin chuckles. "Of course. I need to do a few things, then we'll go," she responds, muffled through the door.

Dankin carries Sera into her room, shutting the door. He takes her to the bed and leans over her with his hand caressing her face and neck. "Please?" she asks.

He smiles, leaning down and kissing her. "I love you, my pregnant sea nymph."

"I love you, too."

* * *

Sera walks up to Rae'lin as she's leaving the main chambers. She gasps softly at the sight of her mother's gown, looking at Dankin. He nods in approval. They go to the private cove on the beach.

Sera sits in the shade, watching as Dankin helps Rae'lin sit down. "This might be a little easier." He gets out the ring and hands it to her. She slips it onto her right middle finger. Sera watches her body go tense, her back arching. Rae'lin closes her eyes as the pain radiates throughout her legs.

She opens her eyes to see her feet flatten out as the purple scales climb up her legs. As hard as she tries, she cannot keep her legs apart. She watches as they fuse together while her gown grows shorter. Lying down, her back arches as the transformation completes. Sera runs over, kneeling beside her and taking her hand.

"Mother? How do you feel?"

"I'm okay. I need water."

Dankin picks Rae'lin up and carries her in. Sera looks down at her legs one last time before walking into the sea and transforming. She follows

Dankin, watching him get Rae'lin settled onto a rock. Sera swims to her, showing Rae'lin how to use her tail.

"This is so weird!" Rae'lin laughs, swimming with Sera while they hold hands.

"I know. At least you knew what was coming. I woke up to this!"

She laughs again. "I can't imagine. Okay, I think I can try on my own."

Sera lets go, staying close. They swim around a while, as Rae'lin adapts to her tail. Dankin stays back, to let them have the time together as Rae'lin learns. "You're doing great!" Sera beams then swims over to Dankin. "She said she wants to be able to visit. How will that work? I don't want her swimming through the ocean by herself," Sera says.

He chuckles. "She and I discussed that. I told her how to send a message, then I will have someone from the palace meet her at the beach."

"Oh, good! I was worried."

He looks her over. "You need to rest."

"Dankin—"

"I'm not being overprotective, I promise. I can't say I won't be at times, but this isn't one of them."

She nods. "Okay." She swims to her mother. "We need to return to the palace so I can rest. When will you visit?"

"In the next week or so."

Dankin swims to them. "I'm going to escort her back to the beach to ensure she transforms back without any problems."

"I'll stay close by."

She follows them to the shore, watching as her mother and Dankin transform then walk onto the beach, Dankin speaking with Rae'lin to be sure she is okay. Sera wipes her tears, telling herself it's not that big of a deal. *I'll be human again soon enough. This isn't forever. I have to calm down.* She wraps her arms around herself, looking up when Dankin joins her.

"Sera?"

"Just thinking of how long…" she shakes her head.

"It will only be a few months."

She looks at him, confused. "What are you talking about? I'll be pregnant for seven to eight more months."

"Is that how long it is for a human?" he asks. She nods. "It's only five months for a mermaid. You are about two months along?" She nods again. "See? Not so bad, is it?"

"Oh, I didn't know! The chart showed some development, but it didn't really specify how long."

"This is why I told you to ask me anything you want," Dankin says.

She looks down, blushing. "I'm sorry."

He sighs, taking her hand. "Let's get back to the palace. You need to rest now."

"Thank you."

* * *

She sits on the bed, looking at the picture she had copied into her notes, smiling at it. It's a sketch of a merbaby in the womb, curled up and gripping its own fins. Dankin sits beside her.

"Are you excited?" he asks.

"I am," she answers quietly. "I'm also worried and scared."

He pulls her onto his lap. "I am with you through all of this. In about three months, we will meet our son or daughter. Can you imagine?"

She shakes her head. "Oh, their tail! What will that look like?"

He laughs. "You saw the picture of my family. It's luck of the draw, a complete surprise what they will get."

"Hmm. Rae'lin's tail is beautiful. Purple and black?"

He laughs. "Very unique. You'll start showing in the next week or so."

"Really? So soon?" She looks down, bringing her hand to her stomach. "It doesn't seem real."

"Can I remove your gown?"

When she nods, he unties the sash and gently pulls the gown off, bringing his hand to her stomach. She puts her hand on his. "We have a future as a family, don't we?" she asks.

"We do."

"We need to plan for a nursery, and make the announcement, and—we have so much to do."

"Sera, take a breath. I've been through this before, and your mother and I will help with whatever you need. When do you want to announce it?"

She gasps softly. "I don't know." She brings her hand up, trailing along the scales on her chest. "Wait, these scales cover me. How will I—" Dankin leans in, speaking softly. Her eyes go wide in surprise. "Really?"

"Really."

She pulls her gown back on, flushing. "I'm self-conscious now, and I—"

"You have no reason to be," he assures her as he wraps her in his arms. "This is wonderful news, and everything will be just fine. Now, you need to lay down and get some sleep."

"I'm not tired," she argues.

He chuckles. "Sera, you may not be yawning, but I can see how tired you are. Please, get some rest?"

She nods her head, laying back. He covers her with the blanket. "Are you staying with me?"

"I need to check on the kingdom."

"I understand. It's okay, I'll fall asleep soon."

He brings his hand up, caressing her face. He pushes her hair back and leans down to plant a gentle kiss on her mouth. "I won't be long, I promise."

She nods, watching him leave. Her hand caresses her stomach. "What are we going to name you, little one?" She thinks of names as she drifts off to sleep.

* * *

"You seem to be doing well," the doctor says, looking her over. "No pain, sickness, anything like that?"

"No. I know you said to come in two weeks, but—"

"It's all right. First pregnancy, I understand."

Sera looks away a moment. "Well, it's not—" She takes a breath.

"Now, you were concerned about how much you are already showing?"

"Where I came from, women were pregnant eight to nine months, so I'm surprised to already be getting so big. Especially since you just confirmed it a week ago."

The doctor lets out a soft chuckle. "I understand your concern. It may look big to you, but I assure you, it's perfectly normal. Now, you are taking it easy? No transformations, no strenuous activity?"

"To my husband's dismay."

They both laugh when he blushes. "Sera, really?" Dankin asks with a chuckle.

"Now, do you have any questions for me?" the doctor asks.

"What—" She looks down, squeezing Dankin's hand. "What will the delivery be like?"

"I've heard tales of human deliveries. It won't be like that. I'm not saying there isn't any pain, but it's much easier."

Sera nods her head. "That's what I was hoping for."

"Now, do you want to hear your baby's heartbeat?"

Sera sits up. "You can do that?" The doctor smiles, getting her trioscope. She places the pad on Sera's small baby bump. They each take one of the three earpieces, listening in. "It's so fast! Is that normal?"

"It is," the doctor assures her. "So far, everything is perfect."

"I'm relieved."

"I normally tell my pregnant patients to come every two weeks. However, given your… unique situation, come again next week?"

"We will," Dankin assures her.

"Yes, Your Majesty. I'll see you then."

"Thank you," Sera says, as she ties her gown on. Dankin helps her off the table and takes her towards their quarters. "Aren't we going for lunch?" she asks.

He laughs. "It's only a little after ten. I will get you food."

"I am eating for two."

He laughs. "Hmm, or three?"

She gasps. "Don't you dare! Don't jinx me, I'm not ready for two!" She laughs, hitting his shoulder. They are almost to their room, when a squire approaches. He hands Dankin a message, bows, and swims away. They go inside as he opens it.

"Your mother is ready for her first trip here."

"I know you don't want to leave me alone, but would you please accompany her? I don't really trust anyone else, and I worry over her."

"Promise to keep your handmaids nearby?"

"I do."

"I'll request them and get you food."

"I'm starving!"

He laughs as he goes into the corridor. She swims to the mirror, opens her gown, and rubs her hand over her belly. Dankin comes back in, concerned.

"Sera?"

She looks up at him, blushing. "I can't believe how fast I'm growing."

"Any movement yet?"

"I feel him moving about."

"Him?"

She laughs. "I don't know why, but I'm sure it's a boy. We need to come up with names."

"I know. I thought you might like your mother to help."

"Of course."

He goes to the door to let her handmaids in, Fai'mi carrying a plate. Sera ties her gown back on. "Ladies, I will be gone a little while. Stay with Her Grace until I return," Dankin commands.

"Yes, Your Majesty. We brought books," Ava'lei says to Sera.

Sera smiles. "And food!" The girls laugh, swimming to her. Sera takes the plate, sits down, and begins to eat. "I'm sorry."

"Whatever for, Your Grace?"

"Eating in front of you."

"We don't mind, really. Can I ask, how far along?" Fai'mi inquires.

Sera nearly drops the plate. "You can tell?" she asks, looking down.

"No. Um, we heard rumor. I apologize—"

"It's fine. We are going to announce it soon enough. I'm about eleven weeks along. Where I grew up, I would still be months away from showing. Here?" She opens her gown slightly, showing her small baby bump.

Fai'mi smiles. "We are so happy for you, Your Grace."

"Thank you." She closes her gown back up. "I'm nervous and happy, both."

She finishes her meal and tries to focus on the books Fai'mi and Ava'lei brought for her to learn from. "Your Grace, is everything all right?" Fai'mi asks.

"Sorry. My mother is coming and—"

"A land-dweller?"

"Yes. She asked Dankin to help her transform, like me, so she can help me through my pregnancy."

"Incredible!" Fai'mi smiles, then looks down. "Apologies—"

Sera laughs. "It's all right. I know this whole situation is unusual, to say the least. Oh!" She brings her hand up when the baby moves.

"Are you all right?" Ava'lei asks, worry in her voice.

"Yes. I think the baby moved. I've never experienced this before and— Oh!" she cries out again.

Fai'mi rises up, leaning over Sera. "Do we need to take you to the infirmary?"

"No, I'm okay. I think he's settled back down."

"He?" Ava'lei asks.

She laughs. "We're not sure, but I think it's a boy." She looks over as Dankin and Rae'lin come in. Rae'lin rushes to Sera, pulling her up and hugging her. "Mother, please! Are you all right?"

"I am. I've missed you, and I've been so worried." She looks over at the handmaids. "Sera, who are they?"

"Rae'lin, this is Fai'mi and Ava'lei, my handmaids and trusted friends."

The girls bow. "It's an honor to meet you, ma'am," Ava'lei offers.

"You as well. You're taking good care of my daughter, right?"

"Yes, ma'am," Fai'mi answers. "We are honored to serve her."

"For now, could we have a little privacy?" Sera asks.

"Of course. Call for us when you have need, Your Grace." They bow and swim out.

Sera looks at her mother. "Well? First time here, what do you think?"

"It's absolutely beautiful!"

Sera looks over at Dankin, blushing and looking down. He swims over. "Sera, are you all right?"

"Could we have lunch?"

He laughs. "Of course. Rae'lin?"

"I'll try it…" she looks at Sera, unsure.

"Here or the great hall?" Dankin asks.

"Well, mother?"

"Here, please. I would like to see the great hall, but I am still getting over how much everyone stared when I came in."

Sera laughs. "They don't even know who you are, just that you are new to the palace. I was very self-conscious my first few days here."

Rae'lin looks at the bed. "So, you woke up and realized you had a tail instead of legs?"

Sera laughs. "Yep! Completely freaked me out."

"I bet." She looks at Dankin. "You told me when we started discussing your engagement, that you would take her to a palace where she would be part of the court. You left a lot out!"

He laughs. "Like I asked her, what would you have said, if I had come to you and said, 'I am Dankin, king of the merpeople and undersea life. I would like to marry your daughter.' Hmm?"

She laughs harder than he does. "Yes, I see your point." She looks Sera up and down. "How are you feeling? Are you doing okay?"

"Yes, mother. I'm fine. The baby was moving earlier, and it felt… weird. I am not even three months, but I feel like I am further along."

"Technically, you are. It's just because you aren't used to this," Dankin interjects.

"Do you have a bump yet?" Rae'lin asks.

Sera laughs, opening her gown slightly. "Yes."

Rae'lin gasps, running her fingers over it. "Oh, this is incredible!" she cries.

Sera hugs her. "Mother, please. It's okay."

Dankin is smiling at them when he hears someone knocking. He goes to the door and retrieves the tray of food. He takes it to the table. "Ladies?"

"Of course! My daughter needs to eat."

They laugh as they sit. "I was looking at some names while waiting for you." She looks from Rae'lin to Dankin. "What do you think of Ami'rua for a boy?" Sera asks.

"Oh, I like that," Rae'lin says.

"As do I," Dankin agrees.

"What does it mean?" Rae'lin inquires.

Dankin thinks a moment. "Loose translation, rock of the sea. It relates to the foundation of the ocean, the creation of life."

"Oh, I do like it!"

Sera smiles at her. "Now you see why I do, too."

"So, a boy?"

"We don't know," Sera admits. "It's what I think…"

"Still, pick out a girl's name, just in case."

"We will." She watches her mother eat the fish and crab. "How is the food?"

"Hmm, it's different. I like it."

"Now you see why I like coming home for a hot meal."

Rae'lin laughs. "Sera, you and Dankin can still come. Stay in the cove, and he'll bring you food. I mean that."

"I wish I could. He insists on keeping me prisoner in here."

Dankin nearly chokes on his food. "Hey, I told you I wouldn't do that again, and I meant it!" He winks at Rae'lin.

They all three laugh. "Still, I am staying nearby. I don't want to swim too much or overexert myself," Sera explains.

"I understand."

"I really want to see my grotto," she says, looking intently at Dankin.

"Sera—" he starts.

"Please?" she begs.

He looks at Rae'lin. "How do I tell her no?"

"Is it far?" Rae'lin inquires.

"Far enough," he snips.

Sera sticks her tongue out at him. "It's really not."

"Both of you, behave!" Rae'lin laughs.

"I'll be back shortly. You two visit," Dankin offers as he takes the dishes.

Sera watches him leave then turns back to her mother. "He is being so protective of me."

"What else is new?"

Sera gets out her drawings and notes so she can show her mother everything. "The doctor said it's not near as bad for a mermaid as it is for a human, but I still worry how much everything will hurt," she confesses.

"I understand. You weren't too bad. Na'ito? I didn't know if I would ever walk again, it hurt so much. Still, I would go through it, if it meant having you both."

"How is he? Does he know about you?"

"No. I think one mermaid in the family is enough for him, at least for the moment."

They both laugh. "How do you feel? How does your tail feel?"

"I'm okay. I see now what you mean, about needing time to adjust."

Sera swims up, looking at her mother. "I still forget sometimes, wanting to take a step or sit with my legs crossed."

"Simple things we don't really think of at the time."

"I miss dancing," Sera admits, spinning in the water. "So much."

"I'm sorry. I never got to watch you dance. I was so jealous of you, how graceful you were, how beautiful. I'm sorry I wasn't the mother I should've been. I really hope to make that up to you, not just by being here for you, but for your child, as well."

Sera stops spinning, looking at her. "Thank you."

The afternoon wears on and Dankin returns, his advisor with him. "Rae'lin, this is Ma'like. Ma'like, this is Sera's mother."

Ma'like swims to Rae'lin, taking her hand and kissing it. "Pleasure to meet you."

She smiles at him, blushing. "You as well."

He backs up to Dankin, staring at Rae'lin. Dankin clears his throat. "Apologies, Your Majesty. I will retire now." He gives a small bow before leaving.

Rae'lin looks at Sera. "Who is he?"

"He is Dankin's advisor. I don't know much about him."

"What are we talking about?" Dankin asks, taking Sera into his arms. "I missed you, my little sea nymph."

"I missed you. I believe my mother is infatuated with your advisor."

"Sera!" Rae'lin yells as they all laugh. "I will admit, he is quite handsome."

"Well, he is unattached. Wait, you would court one of us?" Dankin asks.

"Possibly. I miss Tsuji, but I am lonely, as well. Na'ito and Kye spend all day at market then study after. I would like to court again."

"And if something comes of it?" Sera asks.

"It's worked out for you, hasn't it?"

Sera laughs. "It was a bit of a different situation, but yes, it has."

"Shall I see how he feels about you?" Dankin offers.

"Oh, one thing at a time. I am here for my daughter, not a man. Human or mer," she adds.

Sera gives Dankin a small nod, smiling. He winks back. "Are you staying the night?" Sera asks.

"Not yet. I want to do this a little at a time."

"I understand. I wasn't given such an option," she says, grinning at Dankin.

"Sera, are you going to be mean the whole time your mother is here?"

"I can't help it if it reminds me of my first transformation," she says with a laugh.

Rae'lin laughs. "It is tiring. I'm sorry, but I think I'm ready to return to the estate."

"We'll escort you," Sera offers.

Dankin grips her hand, gently pulling her back. "I'll take your mother home. You stay and rest. Eat some more."

"Now who is being mean?" Sera asks.

He leans down, kissing her. "I'll be back shortly."

"All right." She hugs her mother. "If you see a shark, offer him Dankin!"

Rae'lin laughs. "Oh, no. I see a shark, I am run— erm, swimming away as fast as I can!"

Sera watches them leave before going to bed and falling fast asleep.

* * *

Dankin swims over, leaning down, and kissing her softly. "Sera?"

"Hmm," she opens her eyes. She smiles at the sight of him and pulls him onto her, kissing him fiercely. "Love?"

"Yes?"

"Can we go to our grotto? Please?"

He sits beside her. "Sera—"

"You can carry me the whole way. I need the warm water, the sun, the sand. Please?" she pleads.

"The sun will be going down soon. I promise you, tomorrow after breakfast, we will go and spend the whole day there."

"Really?" she asks, sitting up.

"Really."

She climbs into his lap, kissing him passionately in response. "Thank you!"

"Sera!" He laughs. "You need to continue taking it easy. Rest while I get us supper."

"Could I have salad?"

"Hmm, okay. Is that all you want?"

"And some crab… with clams and shrimp."

He laughs as he swims out to the hall, requesting food then swimming back to her. She cries out in surprise when he pulls her to him. He looks down. "I'm sorry."

"For what?" she asks.

"I know you were partly kidding, but I didn't mean to make you feel trapped in here. I worry over you both."

She smiles at him. "I know, but I need a break." She caresses his face. "I need fresh air and sunshine. I haven't had that since we went to Isle Piscantur."

"I didn't realize. You're right, I was keeping you prisoner."

She laughs. "No, you're protecting us. I understand that."

"Tomorrow, you will get plenty of fresh air and sunshine."

"For now, I need plenty of food." She grins when he laughs.

"Hungry, are we?"

She leans up, her lips devouring his. "For food," she says, batting her eyelashes at him.

He chuckles. "It will be here any minute."

"I'm going to change for bed." She goes to the closet, removing her gown. She picks out a blue nightgown and slips it on. She looks herself over, her hand on her stomach. Dankin swims to her.

"Are you okay?"

"I am," she says, giving him a small smile. "Picturing what I'll look like in a month."

"As big as a house, the way you are growing."

"Dankin!" She laughs. "That's not nice."

He kneels before her, opening her gown at the stomach. He leans in and gently kisses her baby bump. "There's nothing wrong with that, either. It's the truth, you know."

She blushes, pulling him up. "Are we ready for this?" She looks away. "I never gave much thought to having a family. I thought whole my life would be spent caring for the estate."

"I didn't think of that. Plus, having a merchild instead of a human. I took so much from you—"

"No, Dankin. Stop." She looks up at him and gently places her hands on his shoulders. "You have given me everything. Is this the life I envisioned for myself when I was growing up? Obviously not," she laughs, "but I wouldn't want it any other way. We have each other, we have a family, and we have a wonderful life." She kisses him softly.

He pulls away when he hears knocking. He gets their food, sitting with her as she eats. He laughs. "Keep eating like that—"

"And what?"

He clears his throat. "Nothing, my little sea nymph."

She looks at her plate. "No, you're right. I don't mean to eat so much, but—"

"Sera, it's okay. You are growing and need it, I assure you."

"Thank you. Now, can we get some sleep? I'm excited about tomorrow."

He hands off their dishes and carries her to bed. "Me, too."

* * *

Sera wakes up, smiling at Dankin, who is still asleep. She wakes him up with kisses. "Koy'lei?"

He opens his eyes, smiling up at her. "Yes?"

"Are we going?"

He laughs, as he sits up and stretches. "You both need breakfast first."

"Hmph! We could eat there, you know."

"We'll eat lunch there."

They get dressed and go into the great hall, surprised to see it already busy. Dankin rises up, getting everyone's attention. "Good morning," he starts, as the room goes silent. "I have an important announcement to make. Queen Sereia and I are expecting our first child." Applause breaks out in the room. "Thank you for sharing in this joyous time with us." He sits back down.

She takes his hand, squeezing it. "I think they are excited for us."

They look over as a siren and merman approach. "Your Majesties, congratulations," they offer with a bow.

"Thank you," Dankin answers. A few others come by as they finish their meal. They leave the palace, with Dankin carrying her to the grotto. He helps her over the sandbar, chuckling when she moans at the warm water soothing her.

"Oh, I've missed this."

He laughs as he joins. "So I see and hear…"

She blushes, looking down. "Why are you being mean?"

"This isn't too warm, is it?"

"It's fine." She looks up, seeing the concern on his face. "Really, it's okay. I promise."

"All right."

They enjoy the warmth of the water, holding each other tight as they morning breezes by.

"Hmm," she snuggles into his chest, holding him tightly. "We needed time away, too. You've taken up all the responsibility again, while I am pregnant. It's not fair to you."

"I will do whatever I must for my family."

"Dankin, it's paperwork... I can help, really."

"Let's not argue."

She looks down. "I was trying to have a discussion—" she pulls away. "Why are you being like this? I thought we came here to get away?"

"You're the one talking about work."

She closes her eyes. "I just wanted to help." He carries her onto the beach, as she squirms in his arms. "Let me go!"

He sits on the sand and holds her tight in his arms. "You're right," he admits.

She stops struggling. "What?"

"I am so worried over the both of you. What I've been through, what we have been through—" His breath hitches. "I can't help it."

She clings to him as her tears are streaming down. "I wasn't thinking. I'm sorry. You have every right to worry, to be so protective."

"One of us has to."

Her eyes fly open as she pulls back, looking up at him. She laughs at the grin on his face. "I thought you were being serious!" She hits his shoulder. "Don't do that to me!"

"Sera, I know how worried you are. We both are. Everything will be okay. In a little less than two months, we'll welcome baby sea nymph into the world."

She giggles. "Really? It's going to be a boy!"

He laughs. "How do you know?"

"Just... a feeling."

"As long as he looks like me."

"Dankin! What about me?" she asks with a pout.

"What about you?" he asks, leaning down and kissing her before she can respond. He lies back on the sand, his legs wrapping around her.

"That's not fair! Why do you get to be human when I don't?"

"Jealous much?"

"Yes," she admits. She bites her lip, wrapping her arms around him. "Dankin, please?"

"We need lunch."

"I know what I need. Don't you?"

"Let me get us lunch, then we will relax on the beach." He looks down. "I really don't want to leave you, though."

"Put me in the grotto. I have my blade if I need it."

"Okay."

He carries her over, kissing her softly. "I won't be long."

She watches him dive into the water as she relaxes in the warmth of the pool. She closes her eyes, fighting sleep. I have to stay awake. I can't risk getting caught off-guard, not like before. Exhaustion washes over her as she continues swimming.

* * *

Dankin comes into the grotto, setting everything down on a smooth, flat rock. He looks over. "Sera?" When he looks down and sees her at the bottom, he dives in. "Sera?" he asks again urgently, pulling her up.

"I'm all right. I must've fallen asleep."

"Don't scare me like that," he says, clutching her to him.

"I didn't mean to. I'm sorry—"

"No, it was the safest place for you to be while I was gone. Honestly, I should've thought of that."

"Do we have food?"

He laughs. "I ate mine. Was I supposed to get you some?"

She gasps. "So mean!"

He picks her up, carrying her over to the beach. He lays her on the sand, then gets their food. "I would not make you eat alone."

"Thank you." They eat their lunch. She sips her tea. "Hot tea! Oh, I've missed this! And beef, and rice, and—"

Dankin laughs. "I know, your favorites."

"How did you bring this here?"

"Like when we went to Isle Piscantur, I stayed on the surface." He looks at her when she laughs. "What?"

"Picturing you swimming here with a bag above your head."

"Anything for my sea nymph. Speaking of which, I've been thinking about it, for when the baby is born. Visiting your family, I mean."

"What do you mean?"

"We could wrap him in a blanket, so no one would see his tail, then we would go to the estate. We can stay a night or two."

"Really?" she asks, her excitement flowing out.

"Really. I see no reason why that wouldn't work."

"Oh, that would be wonderful!" She finishes her meal, and he gathers their trash, putting it in the bag. He sits beside her when his tail grows back.

"I have missed the sun and sand, too."

She leans over him, looking down. She climbs on him and plants soft kisses on his face and neck. "Dankin—"

"You are supposed to be taking it easy."

She rolls away, lying next to him. "I'm sorry."

He leans over her and looks down while his hand softly caresses her face. "I love our time here. You know that, right?"

"I know," she says softly, looking away.

His hand lowers, gently gripping her chin. He brings her face to him, kissing her fiercely. "Are you sure?"

She nods, as she wraps her tail around his. "Please, koy'lei?"

He kisses her again, her hands gripping his hair. He smiles as she holds him tightly, the sun pounding down on his back. "Let's move somewhere a little cooler," he says, picking her up and taking her to a shady spot.

"I love you, Dankin."

"My sea nymph, you know I love you."

* * *

"Hmm," she snuggles into him. "Thank you for today. Getting fresh air, getting away from the palace, we really needed a day like this."

"You're right, but you aren't going to like what I have to say."

She pulls back, looking up at him. "What do you mean?"

"This is the last time, until after the baby comes. It's too dangerous and too strenuous for you."

"I love you, but you don't make decisions like that for me—"

"For him, too. For both of you."

She sighs. "I don't want to argue." She turns on her side, away from him. "I'll just enjoy this while I can." He scoops her up, getting to his feet. "No fair!" she cries out. "If I can't transform, you shouldn't either."

He laughs, kissing her. "Then how can I carry you like this?"

"You win," she says, holding him tightly. "I am exhausted again. You're right, about coming here. It's just—I miss this. I miss the sun, the sand. I miss my legs," she reluctantly adds, worried she will upset him.

"Sera—"

"No, I know. I'm not complaining. I'm so happy to be with you, to be carrying our child. I want you to understand, I will need to come here again at least once before he is born. I can't have my legs yet, I know. But I will need fresh air and sunshine again."

"I'll compromise. I'll bring you up to the surface above the palace. If you agree to that, we can do it a few times."

"Why can't I have both?"

"Sera—"

"No." She struggles to get down.

"We are not ending today in a fight!" He looks down as she stops struggling, trembling in his arms. "Sera?"

"I'm sorry. You're right. I won't argue."

"I didn't mean to scare you. I don't want our last day here to end on a bad note, is all. Please, can we discuss this later?" He sits down, running his fingers through her hair.

"That's fine," she says, keeping her head down.

He sighs. "All right. We will come back here one more time before the baby comes. I promise you here and now."

She looks up at him, as he wipes her tears. "You mean that?"

"I do."

She leans up, kissing him. "Thank you."

"I love coming here with you, I just worry over you."

"I know, but I needed the sun, and we needed this time alone. I needed you."

"I don't deserve you, Sera Rose. You are incredible, beautiful, and most of all, you put up with me."

"You have overcome more than I could ever imagine, on top of running a kingdom while dealing with war and loss. You are so amazing for all you do, while still keeping everything together."

"Sera, I hurt you and broke your trust, gave in to my anger. How can you possibly think that of me?"

"I was trying," she says softly.

He sighs. "Here I am, saying I wanted today to end on a good note, then I say that to you. You're right. I am pretty amazing."

She laughs as he gets her settled on the sand. "Thank you."

"Now, enjoy our time here. We'll be going back shortly."

"We can't have supper here?"

"We could. I don't want to leave you again."

"No, you're right." They share a gentle, loving kiss. "I'm ready to go back," Sera says, not wanting to leave but knowing how much he is worried over her and their baby.

"Are you sure?"

"As long as you mean it, that you'll bring me here again?"

"I will, before the baby comes."

"All right."

"I promise."

* * *

He takes her back to the palace, and when they reach their quarters, he gets her into the bed. He chuckles. "Sera, I can see how tired you are. You can barely keep your eyes open. I'll get food." He swims into the hall, and when he returns, she cries out. He rushes to her. "What's wrong?"

"Nothing," she says, taking his hand. She places it on her bump. "He's active!"

Dankin laughs. "So I feel." He sits on the edge of the bed, holding her hand as his other hand continues to feel the baby moving. "Is he usually more active this time of day?"

"No, it seems to be whenever."

"You're right about how fast you are growing. You've already grown since yesterday."

She sits up, pulling her gown opening and looking down. "Should I be concerned?"

"The doctor said this is normal. We'll see her again next week," Dankin assures her.

"You're right. I need to stop worrying so much."

"We are both adjusting to this. I went through this with my first wife, but she wasn't a human before. I am just as concerned over everything as you."

"I didn't realize it was a competition."

His head jerks up, shaking when he sees her smirking at him. "Sera!"

"Seriously, though. How big will I get?"

"We'll find out together." He gets their plates from a member of staff, then swims back to her. Sera takes her plate, smiling at him.

"Thank you. I'm sorry today didn't go exactly like we wanted, but I'm glad we cleared the air about some things."

"I am, too."

She sighs. "Will you—" she shakes her head, eating her salad.

"What?"

"No, I need to take it easy now."

"Sera?"

"I was going to ask if you would dance with me, after we eat."

"We can do that. I'll hold you, so I'm doing all of the work."

"Okay." When they finish eating, he takes her to the middle of the room. He picks her up, smiling as she brings her arms up around his neck. They spin around the room as she hums her favorite song. He holds her close to him, thinking of the future. Once she finishes humming, he takes her to the closet. "Get ready for bed, then I'll tuck you in. I need to check on things, but I won't be long."

"All right." She goes inside.

He looks around the room, thinking of when Ko'era was pregnant. He swims to where they had the bassinet, thinking of his daughters cooing and crying. Sera swims to him.

"What's wrong?" she asks.

He smiles, looking at her. "Nothing. Just thinking of when we put the bassinet in here for the baby."

"Dankin, please?"

"I was… I was thinking of my daughters, when they were babies in here. I would watch Ko'era swim over here, lifting them out and cradling them when they cried." He looks away. She gently pulls his head down to her shoulder, and he buries his face in the crook of her neck.

"I'm sorry for your loss," she whispers. "No one should suffer so much."

He clings to her, holding her tightly as he cries. "I'm grateful to have you with me."

"I want to be here for you. You have done so much for me, helping me back at the estate, loving me when I never thought anyone could. Please?"

"Sera, I love you, so much. My soul was a ship lost at sea. Your heart is the lighthouse that will always guide me home."

Her heart swells at his words. They leave her speechless, and all she can utter in response is a quiet, "I love you."

"For now, you need to rest," he says, picking her up and carrying her to bed. "Will you sleep now?"

"If you'll kiss me."

He leans down, his mouth an inch from hers. "Promise you'll rest—"

She smiles as she catches him off-guard, kissing him suddenly. "I promise."

"I'll be back shortly."

Chapter 24

Preparation

Two weeks later, they are in the infirmary for her check-up. "Everything looks good. No pain? No sickness?"

"I've had a little nausea. It's just in the morning and doesn't last long."

"Okay, that should be fine. Now, let's take a look."

Sera looks at Dankin when the doctor brings over some sort of screen, holding it above Sera. "What is this?"

"It's fairly new. We can see the baby."

"Yes, I want to look."

Ish'a turns the device on, and Sera watches in fascination as a small black and white image appears. She gasps when she starts to make out the tail. "There's your baby. Of course, we can't tell if it's a boy or girl until they are born," the doctor explains.

Sera reaches her hand down, tracing along the baby's head and face. "That's ours?"

"It is," the doctor answers.

She smiles up at Dankin. "Well?"

"This is incredible! Where did this come from?"

"The Mar'its'oto kingdom. Their technology is more advanced than ours, as you can see."

Sera gasps when she feels the baby move, watching him on the screen. "Oh, this is amazing!"

Dankin squeezes her hand. "Did you feel him move?"

"I did! And to see it…" She laughs.

The doctor turns it off, laying in on the table. "Now, any questions for me? Issues?"

"I don't think so."

"Sera?" Dankin gives her a knowing look.

She looks from Dankin to the doctor. "I want to go to the grotto one more time, but he is worried it might be too much for me."

"I don't want her to overdo it," he adds.

"I think if you carry her there and take it easy, one more trip would be fine. Just, not too much sun or heat?"

"All right. Thank you," Dankin says.

"I'll give you the room."

Sera gets dressed. "If you're really that concerned, we don't have to go. Just, take me up to the surface like you offered?"

He thinks a moment. "Okay. We need lunch, first, though."

"When am I going to turn down food?"

He laughs, taking her hand. They swim to the great hall and sit at their table. Fai'mi and Ava'lei swim over. "Your Grace," they say, bowing. "We want to see how you are feeling," Ava'lei inquires.

"I'm doing well, so far. We have plans today, but would you come to our quarters at nine in the morning? Bring books, and we'll study?" She looks at Dankin, who nods in approval.

"Yes, Your Grace." Fai'mi answers. They bow and swim off to gather the books for the next day.

"Thank you. While you are working on paperwork, I can at least do some reading."

"That should be fine. Plus, I don't want you alone now that you are getting further along."

She looks over, seeing a few pregnant sirens. "I wonder what it's like for them, since this isn't what they are used to?"

He shakes his head. "Everyone's adapting, it seems. Your mother is coming tomorrow afternoon, and she wants to stay one night, to see how it goes."

"Are we putting her in my room?"

"Sera?"

She laughs. "The smaller one next door. You know what I mean!"

He joins in the laughter. "I had to tease. Yes, she will be fine there."

Their food arrives. He smiles when she greedily eats her meal.

"What?" she asks with a piece of food caught on her lip.

"Watching you be ever so proper," he says as he leans forward, wiping her face and nibbling her lips playfully.

"Don't be mean," she says with a laugh. "You're right. I shouldn't—"

"It's okay. I think it's cute."

She shakes her head, finishing her meal. She eyes his crab. "Are you going to eat that?"

"I would not deny my wife food," he says, scooting the plate to her. He laughs again as she attacks it. "Sera?"

She looks down, blushing. "I'm sorry. I don't know what came over me."

"How are you feeling?"

"Okay, just really hungry!"

"Hmm, maybe we should slow down. I don't want you getting sick, either. Let's get some fresh air, and we'll see how you feel."

"Thank you."

They leave the palace and head towards the surface. As they draw near, she grabs his hand and pulls back. "What's wrong?" He looks as she points over. "A ship. Good catch!" They lower back down, watching as it passes. She trembles against him. "Sera?"

"Sorry. Bad memories."

"The merchants?"

"They were going to sell me for food."

"What?"

"They said mermaid tail is a delicacy."

"I can't imagine how scared you were. Are you okay now?"

"I am." They look around, making sure it's clear before continuing up. She relishes the breeze on her face when they break through the water's surface. Basking in the sun's warmth, she melts into Dankin when he kisses her. Closing her eyes, she wraps her arms around him.

"Well?" he asks, pulling back.

"I feel really good. Still hungry," she admits with a small laugh. "What else is new?"

"Come on," he says, taking her below the surface.

"Going back already?" she asks.

He takes her into his arms, carrying her as he swims to their island. He gets her to the beach. "We aren't staying long."

"I understand. Thank you for bringing me here." They lie on the sand. She looks over at him. "Does this island have a name?"

"No. It's relatively unknown, being so small. Why? Do you have a name for it?"

"Isle Solis."

"I like that. All right, Isle Solis it is."

"Great!" She says with a smile. He rolls over, leaning above her. His hand caresses along her baby bump. "Hmm," she moans softly, blushing. "Dankin!"

"What? I didn't do it on purpose."

"Everything is sensitive right now. I guess that's part of it."

He leans down and kisses her softly. "Are we ready to go back? The doctor said not too much heat."

Her shoulders slump. "We just got here, but I know you're right."

"We'll stay a few more minutes." He picks her up, carrying her over so she's mostly in the shade. "Better?"

"Yes, koy'lei. Thank you."

"We'll rest a moment then head back."

"I swear, I'm bigger than I was this morning," Sera comments as she gently rubs her pregnant belly.

He picks her up and carries her into the water. "Hmm. You are heavier."

She hits his shoulder. "Dankin! Why are you being so mean to me?"

He laughs, as they go into the water. "I'm sorry, my sea nymph."

"Be nice," Sera says as she laughs with him.

* * *

When they arrive at the palace, they find Rae'lin waiting for them inside the entrance. "I thought you were coming tomorrow," Dankin says.

"I was, but I had a bad feeling and needed to see her. I just arrived."

"By yourself?" Sera asks. Rae'lin nods. "Mother, it's not safe."

"I know, but I had to. Are you all right?"

"I am. I was having some pain earlier, but it stopped now. I'm sorry, I know you just got here, but I need sleep now."

"Of course."

"Come with us, and I'll show you to your room. It's right next to ours."

"Thank you."

Dankin gets Sera into their quarters and covers her with the blanket before he takes Rae'lin next door. "There are gowns in the closet, help yourself," he gestures.

"May I ask?"

"This was one of my daughter's rooms. I mean it, though. You are welcome to anything in here."

"Thank you. I'm sorry for your loss."

"You as well. I'll post a guard in the hall, so if you need anything he can get it for you."

"Thank you. I haven't eaten supper."

"Come to the great hall in an hour, if you're up for that."

"I am."

"Until then."

After he leaves, she swims around a bit, still trying to get used to having a tail. *Sera did this, with no warning or preparation. I can do this, too.*

She floats down onto the bed, thinking of the fact that she is completely underwater, in a bed, in a palace. She chuckles at the thought before drifting off to sleep.

* * *

Rae'lin wakes up, forgetting where she is. She tries to stand up but lowers to the floor instead. She sighs, looking over her tail. "Right." She swims over to the closet, and selects a lavender hanfu, slipping it on and fixing her hair. Outside the door, she finds the guard and asks to be escorted to the great hall.

When she arrives, she doesn't see Dankin anywhere. Ma'like approaches her, and she smiles. "Afternoon," he says.

"Good afternoon to you."

"Would you join me for supper?"

"It would be my pleasure," she says, her smile growing.

He helps her sit and orders their meal. Dankin swims in and notices them, smiling as he quickly leaves the room. He returns to their quarters, letting Rae'lin have time with his advisor. He swims over to Sera, gently waking her up.

"Hmm?"

"Supper will be here soon."

"Thank you."

"Also, your mother is dining with my advisor."

She sits up. "What?"

He laughs. "I saw it myself."

She shakes her head. "This will be interesting, to say the least."

"How are you feeling? Any more pain?"

"No, thankfully."

He gets their plates and sits with her. "You don't look well. Are you all right?"

"I don't know. I feel… heavy." She looks up. "I don't know how to describe it."

"Your tail or the baby?"

"All over. I feel… off again."

He takes her plate with his, setting them on the table behind him. He moves closer to her, takes her hand between his, and speaks softly, the blue magic streaking from his hand into her. She breathes in relief as a feeling of warmth overwhelms her, comforting her.

"Did that help?"

"Yes, thank you. I don't know what it was."

"You've changed and adapted to so much. Can you eat?"

"Yes."

He retrieves their plates, and they finish eating. As he's handing the plates off, Rae'lin comes in.

"So, how was your supper?" Sera asks, smiling at her.

"Well, word travels fast here, doesn't it?"

Sera laughs. "Dankin saw you."

"Hmm-hmm. We had a nice time. He would like to see me again, but I don't know. I like coming to visit you, but staying here? Leaving Na'ito and the estate? Sera, I don't know how you did it."

She looks down. "I didn't have a choice, at the time." She looks up at Rae'lin. "When I did have a choice, it was the easiest one I've ever made. I love Dankin more than I ever thought I could love someone, and I was willing to give up everything. Fortunately, you don't have to make a decision like that. Not yet, at least."

"I know. Ma'like is very sweet, and I have been so lonely since losing your father. I will think on it. For now, how are my babies?"

She laughs. "Mother, I am a grown woman," Sera argues.

Rae'lin sits on the bed, holding Sera in her arms. "I'm sorry it took me so long to see you for who you truly are. I made you think I was ashamed of how you looked, your skin, your ears, but I was truly envious of your beauty, and I took it out on you. Your father was so happy the day you were born, fawning over how beautiful you were."

"That's the past. You've proven yourself to me now, that's what matters."

"I don't deserve such kindness nor your forgiveness."

"That's what I said," Dankin admits. "When she forgave me for leaving her on the shore, I didn't see how she could possibly love me, after the things I did to her."

"You've both wronged me, hurt me in your anger. But you've also shown me love, patience, and kindness. That is what is important." She squeezes her mother's hand. "Thank you."

Sera cries out suddenly, clutching her stomach. Dankin rushes over. "Sera?"

"Ahh!" she cries out again, squeezing her mother's hands tightly. "It hurts! Ahh!"

Dankin rushes to get the doctor as Rae'lin lays her on the bed. "Sera, stay with me. Keep squeezing my hands," she instructs.

"It's too early! I know he's not ready!"

"Shh, it'll be all right. Focus on me, focus on my voice instead of the pain. Everything will be okay."

"Mother, please—" she cries out again.

Dankin and the doctor come in. She swims up to Sera, taking her vitals and looking her over. "Sera, where does it hurt? What does it feel like?"

"My—ahh! My stomach and chest—" she cries out again, nearly losing consciousness from the pain.

"Sera, stay with us. How badly do you hurt?"

"Horribly!" she answers through clenched teeth. "Please, do something!"

The doctor looks at Dankin. "I think it's false labor. Let's get her comfortable and see what happens."

Rae'lin and Dankin help Sera sit up against the pillows, watching her for any pain. Dankin takes her hand. "Sera?"

"That's a little better, but I'm still cramping."

"Let's wait a moment and see if it eases," the doctor suggests.

She squeezes Dankin's hand, breathing slowly out of habit. She looks at the doctor. "It is easing up. I think you're right."

Dankin sighs in relief. "What do you need?"

"I need sleep. I think I'm—" She falls unconscious.

He looks at the doctor. "Is she all right?"

She feels her pulse, looking her over. "She's resting now, after that. She should be okay."

"Thank you for coming," Rae'lin says.

"Yes, ma'am. Any time." She looks at Dankin. "I apologize if this comes across as abrupt, but it must be said. I am very concerned about her, since you took a human and turned her into one of us. This is… uncharted water, and I do not know what will happen with her pregnancy and labor."

"I know. We were cursed by Maren, and I did what I had to in order to save the people of this kingdom. I feel so guilty for what I have done to her, what I have put her through."

"Dankin!" Rae'lin swims over to him. "She loves you, and she is willing to go through all of this for you. You have no reason to feel guilty."

"I didn't just turn her into a mermaid, I turned her into an experiment! You're right, that we don't know how she will do with labor, with being a mother, with living the rest of her life down here." He looks at Rae'lin, who shakes her head.

"Don't even think of it! We are both staying right here. My daughter—"

"Wait, you were a human, too?" the doctor asks.

"Yes."

"Your Majesty, how many more—"

Rae'lin laughs. "No, no. I asked him to change me, so I could be here for my daughter. I knew the risks, and I agreed willingly to come. Please, do not chastise him for my decision. I do worry over her, though."

The doctor feels around Sera's chest and stomach, listening and checking her vitals again. "Everything seems okay now. Hmm," she says as she listens intently to her heart.

"What?" Dankin asks.

"Previously, when she had been attacked, her heart beat like a human. I didn't catch it before, but I realize her heart is beating like ours now."

"I take it that's a good thing?" Rae'lin asks.

"Ma'am, I can't say for sure, but I want to say yes."

"I truly hope so," Dankin says as he caresses Sera's face. "She has suffered enough."

"Whether she is immortal or not, I know she will want to spend the remainder of her life here, with you and her child," Rae'lin says. "Please, don't tell me you were thinking of taking that away from her?"

"No, I promised her I would never transform her without her consent again. I meant it, even if—" he looks away. "It'll be all right. We're all emotional right now, after seeing her like that. Let's get some rest."

"I agree," the doctor says, closing up her bag. "Please, call for me again as needed."

"Thank you."

Rae'lin looks around the room. "Is there a way to have a couch or chaise brought in here? I want to sleep here tonight, with my daughter."

"I'll take care of it." As he swims to the door, she takes Sera's hand, holding it tightly between hers.

"You'll be okay," she says, silently praying it's the truth.

* * *

Sera wakes up, looking over, and seeing Dankin still asleep. She reaches over for him, barely able to move with her enormous stomach, and startles him awake.

"Sera! What's wrong?"

She laughs softly. "No, no! I'm sorry. I was just trying to wake you up. I didn't mean to scare you."

He moves over to her, wrapping his arm around her. "Oh, my little sea nymph. You scared us enough last night!"

"But I'm okay? We're both okay?" she asks, rubbing her hand gently over her belly.

"You are. She said it was false labor, and that it may happen again. How do you feel this morning?"

"Starving and exhausted. I know, what else is new?" She gives him a small, reassuring smile. "I'm okay, really." She sees Rae'lin is asleep on a chaise. "Why is she in here?"

"She was worried about you and insisted."

Sera laughs. "I can imagine." She looks down at her stomach, her hand continuing to gently rub. "You scared us, little guy. Don't do that again."

"Is he active?"

"A little," she says, taking Dankin's hand and laying over her bump. "Feel for yourself."

He chuckles softly at the movement. "Don't rush, you'll be here soon enough." He kisses her forehead. "I'll get us breakfast and wake her up."

"Be nice!"

He laughs as he swims over and gently wakes up Rae'lin. She swims to Sera, looking at her in concern. "How do you feel?"

"Much better, tired is all," Sera assures her.

"I bet. Last night was… rough."

"How was it for you? First full night here?"

"Well, I rolled off the chaise at one point and landed on the floor." Rae'lin chuckles. "Otherwise, it was fine."

"How long are you staying?"

"I was going to leave after lunch, but with last night—"

"Please, I'm fine now. You know Dankin will send word if I need you. I don't want you overdoing it down here, either. Not while you are adapting to all of this."

"Have you picked out a girl name yet?"

"No," Sera admits, blushing. "I don't see the need for one."

Rae'lin laughs. "All right. If it's a girl, you name her after me. Problem solved."

Sera joins the laughter. "We'll see about that." She looks up at her. "What did you tell Na'ito? About where you are?"

"He thinks I am on the mainland, visiting with a friend who recently moved back. I couldn't tell him I was coming here, not only because he would know I am now a mermaid, but I was afraid he would beg to come with me." Rae'lin looks over at Dankin, who is speaking softly with Sera's handmaids. She leans down. "He feels so guilty about last night, about what he turned you into."

Sera shakes her head. "Why? He knows how much I love him and how happy I am to be here."

"Still, he feels responsible for your pain, and he worries about you going into labor."

Sera sighs. "I'm worried, too. Especially after last night."

"We'll both be with you when it happens. You'll get through it fine."

"Thank you."

Dankin swims to them. "Your handmaids are here. I didn't know if you felt up to studying or if you need more sleep after breakfast?"

"I can study a little. I'm sure Rae'lin would like to learn some of our history, too."

"Yes, I would. Then I will return home at lunch."

Dankin gestures them in. They come over, sitting beside her as they go through the books they brought. They stop long enough to eat breakfast, Sera and Rae'lin asking questions as they read. Dankin has his paperwork brought in and sits at her vanity as he fills everything out. He looks over from time to time, happy to see her surrounded by people who care for her.

At noon, Rae'lin swims to him. "I'm returning home now."

"I will escort you. It's too dangerous—"

"I don't want you away from her."

"Ma'like can escort you."

She gasps at the suggestion. "Does he know who I am? What I am?"

Dankin chuckles. "I haven't told him. I figured it was yours to tell you who choose, as long as it's not a human."

"Don't worry, that I will not do. Yes, he can escort me. Then we will see what he thinks."

"All right." He swims out and sends for his advisor. Rae'lin returns to Sera, hugging her fiercely.

"I am returning home, but I plan to come back soon. I will send word."

"Thank you for everything. I love you."

"Oh, Sera. I love you, too."

Sera watches Rae'lin swim to the door, then looks at her handmaids. "I believe I will need to rest after lunch."

"Yes, Your Grace. We will be in the hallway, if you need us," Ava'lei says.

"Girls, please. I'm sure there is something you could do? I hate the thought of you just standing—well, whatever you call it," she laughs softly, "hanging around the hallway. Please, I insist. If I need you, I will send for you."

"Thank you, Your Grace," Fai'mi says. They bow before they swim out.

Dankin joins her, taking her hand.

"Dismissed for the day?"

"I need rest after lunch. I can barely keep my eyes open."

"Take it easy and know that I am right here, too."

"Thank you, koy'lei."

He leans down, kissing her softly. "I love you, both of you."

Her smile grows. "Now, I need food."

"It's on the way."

* * *

The following week, Sera is at her appointment. "Everything appears to be on schedule," Ish'a says, pressing her hands gently on Sera's belly. "You should be due any time, and we have our plan in place for when it happens. Do you have any other questions for me?"

She looks up at Dankin then back at the doctor. "I am worried. It's going to hurt, isn't it? Like when I went into false labor?"

"I can't say anything for certain. I'm sorry."

Sera nods her head. "It's okay. Thank you." Dankin helps her back to their quarters, carrying her in his arms. "Dankin—"

"No, you need to rest. I'm okay to carry you."

He is getting her settled in when someone knocks frantically at the door. Dankin rushes over to find a squire. "You have an urgent message, Your Majesty," he says, handing it to him.

Dankin thanks him before shutting the door and swimming to Sera. He tears it open, reading quickly. "Your brother fell from a ladder and is gravely injured. Rae'lin is asking me to come help."

"Please, go!"

"I will. Sera, you need—"

"Dankin, he is dying as we speak. Go help him! Send for my handmaids, and I'll be fine until you get back. Please!"

He gives her a small nod, swimming quickly from the room. She lies back on the bed, consumed with worry over her brother. She looks up as her handmaids swim in.

"Your Grace, His Majesty asked us to stay with you," Fai'mi says.

"He had to leave on urgent business. Please, stay in here in case I need something? I'm sorry to bother you."

Ava'lei swims forward. "It's no bother, we wish to help you any way we can."

"Thank you. You both are so wonderful, and I am grateful to have you with me through all of this. I'm going to rest a bit, then we'll have lunch brought in."

"Of course."

Sera covers up with the blanket, praying over her brother and Dankin, before drifting off into a restless sleep.

Chapter 25

The Expected Meeting

A sudden cramp jerks Sera awake. "Ava'lei?" she calls out.

She swims to her side. "I'm right here. What do you need, Your Grace?"

"I… I don't know—" She cries out as her pain continues to grow. "Oh, I think this is it!" She grabs Ava'lei's hand, squeezing it. "Get the doctor! And send word to Dankin. He's on Isle Piscantur."

"Yes, Your Grace," Fai'mi says, swimming from the room.

Ava'lei looks at Sera, worried. "How can I help?"

"Just stay with me, please?"

"I promise, I'm right here."

"Thank you—Ahhh!" She cries, her back arching as her body writhes in pain. "Oh, it hurts! Maker, please!" Fai'mi and the doctor rush in. Ava'lei starts to back up, giving them room. "Don't leave me," Sera begs.

Ava'lei swims around to the other side and takes her hand. "Your Grace, the doctor has to be able to reach you. I'm right here."

"Sera, does this feel like last time?" the doctor asks.

"No. The cramps are coming faster, and the pain is worse." She screams, biting her lip as she falls back against the pillow. "Where is my husband? I need Dankin, please!"

"He's on his way," Fai'mi assures her, looking at Ava'lei, both of them clearly worried. "He'll be here soon."

Her back arches again, causing her stomach to roll. She screams out as she tries to turn onto her side. "No, Sera," the doctor says, holding her down. "You need to stay on your back for this."

"It hurts!"

"I know. It'll be all right." She checks her pulse, then lifts up her scales just below the waist. She feels around then looks at Sera. "This isn't false labor this time. The baby is coming."

"I'm not ready!"

"Sera, we both are."

She looks over as Dankin swims in. "Koy'lei!" she cries out. "Please!"

He rushes to her, taking her hand. "I'm right here." He closes his eyes, softly murmuring as he tries to ease her pain with his magic. The doctor says nothing as the blue light streaks from his hand into Sera. She grips his hand tighter, before the pain lessens.

"Oh, that's helping. Thank you," Sera says, panting.

"All right, Sera. You need to push," the doctor instructs.

"Wait, how is Na'ito?" she asks.

"He's fine. Your mother will be here soon."

"Okay." She holds her breath, giving everything she has to push. Dankin holds her hand, comforting her and reassuring her. The doctor continues to guide her through.

"We're almost there, Sera. I can see the head. I need one really good push from you. I know you're tired and hurting, but can you do that for me?"

"I can't!" she cries out.

Dankin leans forward, kissing her forehead. "You can do it, Sera. We are so close to seeing our baby boy. Don't you want to meet him?"

She nods her head. "I really do."

"Then push for us."

She rolls her head back onto the pillow, her back arching, as she screams with one final push. The doctor takes the baby and cuts the umbilical cord. Dankin brushes Sera's hair back, kissing her forehead again. "That's my girl." They look over, as the doctor examines the baby.

"You have a healthy baby boy," the doctor says with a smile.

"Oh!" Sera cries out in relief. "Welcome, little Ami'rua. We're so excited to have you with us," she says, looking up at Dankin. "I don't—" She falls unconscious. Dankin takes the baby from the doctor, who swims over to examine Sera.

"Her pulse is weak, thready—"

Dankin hands Ava'lei the baby. "I've got his." He sits with Sera, taking both of her hands and speaking his magic into her. He looks over when Rae'lin swims to them, worry apparent on her face. Dankin continues with Sera, giving her everything he can. He watches his magic flow into her, healing her completely. He looks at the doctor, exhausted. "I think she'll be okay."

The doctor examines Sera. "Her pulse is steady, and I think she's resting now. I've never had a labor be so intense."

"Neither have I," he says. "It was smooth for my first wife, with our three daughters." He looks at Sera. "Please, my little sea nymph, wake up."

Ava'lei hands Rae'lin the baby. She looks down at the bundle of joy in her arms, handsome with Dankin's blond hair, blue eyes, and blue tail.

"He looks like you," Rae'lin comments.

He chuckles softly. "Sera will be so mad."

She laughs in return. "I think she will just be happy to meet him."

Sera opens her eyes, moaning as she moves to sit up. Dankin helps her. "Slow down, Sera. We almost lost you back there."

"How do you feel?" Rae'lin asks.

"Okay, tired. How is my baby?"

"He's perfect," the doctor answers. "I'll give you all privacy now. I'll come by this evening to check on them both."

"Thank you," Dankin says, shaking her hand.

"Congratulations." She smiles at him, then swims out.

Rae'lin hands the baby over to Sera.

"It's a miniature Dankin!" she exclaims, as she takes him in her arms.

He laughs. "I'm sure there is some of you in there. Maybe he will love to drink hot tea in the sun."

Sera laughs. "He really is a child of land and sea, isn't he?"

Rae'lin nods, smiling. "What would your father think? Having a merchild for a grandchild?"

"He would love him as much as we do." Sera settles as he begins to cry. "I think he's hungry already."

"I'll help," Rae'lin offers, swimming closer as Dankin backs up to give her room.

"I'm going to finish getting things moved in here, for the baby," Dankin says.

"We will help," Fai'mi says, as they follow Dankin from the room.

Rae'lin helps Sera get comfortable. "Do you have any questions about this?"

"How will I know when he's full?"

"Well, if he's like you, he'll try to drink until there's none left." She laughs. "Otherwise, he'll ease up in your arms and probably fall asleep."

"Okay." She looks down, watching him feed. "Hmm, it hurts a little."

"It will take some getting used to. At least he's not teething, yet."

Sera groans. "I didn't think of that!" They both laugh. She watches as he slows down, his fists opening up. He falls back to sleep. "He's so beautiful, our Prince Ami'rua."

"It's a beautiful name."

"Could you hold him for a bit? I'm exhausted."

Rae'lin takes him into her arms. "I will always hold my grandson. He is absolutely precious." She looks at Sera. "It's funny."

"What's that?"

"Not that long ago, I asked if you wanted to be a wife and mother, and you were adamant in your response, telling me no, you did not."

Sera laughs. "At that time, my life belonged to the estate, to caring for everyone. I couldn't think of what I would want, but I focused instead on making sure Na'ito always had his medicine."

"You sacrificed everything taking care of us."

"I also never wanted to be a wife and mother," she looks up as Dankin returns, seeing the worry on his face at her words when she smiles at him, "as I only imagined being married off to those horrible men, never to someone whom I would love so dearly, who would love me in return." The worry leaves his face, replaced with a smile as he swims to her.

"The woman who saved our kingdom, saved our people, saved me."

She smiles up at him. "Oh, koy'lei. You saved me first. Thank you for all you have given me. I know you still feel guilty, but please, don't. You have given me a home, given me your heart, and now," she adds, looking at Ami'rua, "a family of our own. Thank you, for introducing me to your world, making me a part of this. I couldn't imagine being anywhere else."

He leans down, kissing her as she begins to fall asleep. He floats onto the bed, holding her in his arms, exhausted from using so much magic in one day. "Rest now, my little sea nymph. We have a life ahead of us, filled with joy and hope. When I first saw you, I never expected you would be the woman to break the curse and free my heart. I love you, Sera, my unexpected queen."

Epilogue

Sera laughs, watching Dankin, Da'vae, and Na'ito play with Ami'rua in the water. She stands on the beach, looking over when Kery'oto joins her.

"Sera, your family is beautiful," Kery'oto says.

"Thank you. Dankin told me he would speak to you about us, but I had no idea he was ready to expose merpeople to the human world."

"I think it's wonderful."

Sera returns her smile. "So do I." She turns back to her family, watching them play and splash around in the water. "How did the mainlanders react to the news?"

Kery'oto chuckles. "Shock, disbelief. Then fishermen came forward with their stories, and we even had a small festival. We released floating lanterns, celebrating the union of land and sea." Kery'oto looks at Sera when she laughs softly. "Sera?"

She shakes her head, looking at her hand. "He proposed to me, then turned me at a lantern festival. We both celebrated a union the same way."

Kery'oto smiles at the thought. "I did not know that. Now, I don't wish to bother you—"

Sera looks at her. "You want to see me in the water?"

She blushes. "Yes."

"Come in with me!" she says, taking her hand.

"Sera! I'm not dressed—" Splash! Kery'oto breaks into laughter when they land in the water. She looks down and sees Sera's tail. "I'm very envious." She takes a breath, meeting Sera's gaze. "I asked Dankin, you know."

"Asked him what?"

"To make me a mermaid."

"Your Grace!" Sera blushes. "Apologies, but I was not expecting that."

"He said for you and me to talk, first."

"It is very painful the first time, and there is a lot to adapt to. However, if that is what you wish, I will not stop you."

"Thank you!" She surprises Sera, hugging her. "I'm sorry—"

Sera laughs, pulling back. "Oh, no, it's fine. Now, would you like to meet our son?"

She nods in excitement. "Yes, I would."

They swim towards the others, and Na'ito freezes at the sight of Kery'oto. "Your—um—Your Grace," he says as he bows as best as he can in the water. "I am Sera's brother, Na'ito."

"It's an honor to meet you." She laughs at the surprise on his face. "May I?" she asks, nodding to the baby merchild in his arms.

"Oh, of course, Your Grace!" He hands him over.

Kery'oto holds Ami'rua tight, unable to believe she is holding a baby merchild. "He's beautiful, Sera."

"Thank you." Sera looks over, laughing as Da'vae and Na'ito swim around each other, playing tag.

"Oh, by the way, we are instituting a new type of medical setup. Patients only have to pay what they can, with an increase on the richer citizens to help make up the difference. Everyone now has equal access to the care they need."

Sera smiles, her eyes watering. "That is wonderful!" She looks over as Rae'lin approaches them. "Would you like to meet my mother?"

"I would be honored."

Rae'lin looks at Kery'oto in shock, seeing her swimming in her gown. Sera and Kery'oto laugh. "Mother, this is the Her Majesty, Queen Kery'oto."

"Your Grace," Rae'lin says, bowing. "It's a pleasure to meet you. Sera speaks so highly of you. I am Rae'lin."

"The pleasure is mine. Your daughter is an incredible woman for uniting the kingdoms in ways we never even knew were possible."

"And for giving me a grandson," Rae'lin adds, smiling at Kery'oto with Ami'rua.

Kery'oto chuckles. "You wish to hold him?"

"I will soon enough. Please, take your time with him."

"Thank you." She looks at Sera. "Does he need dipped in the water from time to time?"

"That is fine, yes."

Ami'rua grabs at her hair. Kery'oto throws her head back, chuckling. "Nice try, little one!" They all laugh as she gently dips him in the water. She holds him with his stomach down, watching him wriggle his tail and try to swim away.

"That, he gets from you." Rae'lin laughs. "I have never seen a human that took to water the way you did."

Sera smiles. "He truly is a child of two worlds, growing up where he can be part of both." She looks over at Dankin, smiling at him. "I never would've imagined it, either."

Dankin swims to her and kisses her softly. "Apologies," he says to Kery'oto.

She smiles. "Not necessary. Your son is very handsome."

"Like me!" Dankin declares.

They all laugh again as Sera shakes her head. "Where is Ma'like?" she asks Rae'lin.

"He'll be here soon," Rae'lin answers.

Sera turns back to Dankin. "Kery'oto has my blessing, if you are okay with it, too."

He thinks a moment, seeing the hope in Kery'oto's eyes. He chuckles softly. "All right. We will do that this afternoon. For now, let's play in the water and enjoy this time together."

"Thank you!" Kery'oto exclaims. "Oh, I am most excited!"

They spend the day together, Rae'lin swimming with Ma'like as Sera, Dankin, Kery'oto, and Na'ito play near the beach. Kery'oto and Na'ito play with a ball as Sera, Dankin, and Ami'rua watch. Da'vae flirts with the Ga'ishi on the shore. Sera turns to Dankin, smiling as Ami'rua nurses, covered by her towel.

"You have given me a future that I never, in a million years, in a million lifetimes, could've thought possible. How are you so incredible?"

He smiles, leaning down and kissing her. "Oh, no, my little sea nymph. You get all the credit, fighting for love, fighting for peace. You thanked me, now it's my turn. Sera, thank you, for making me part of your world."

Acknowledgements

To Emily, my editor: I took a chunk of marble, chiseled out a book, and you polished it, helping me make it into the work of art it deserves to be. Thank you for all you did to make this book into the polished, shining beauty it now is.

To Traci: You were my biggest cheerleader, answering questions (day or night), offering advice and words of encouragement even dealing with your own struggles. Thank you for your support in all of this. I am eternally grateful to have you in my corner.

To Amanda: Thank you for your time and input, as a beta reader.

To Gran: This book would not have happened without you. You introduced me to a world of books and stories, and because of you, I never saw the world the same way. Thank you.

To Marleen: Every Monday you had to listen to me for four hours as I rambled on about my book, whether I was writing, editing or working on covers, or whatever I happened to be doing at the time. You always listened with sincere interest, offering a friendly word from time to time. Thank you.

To mom and dad: Thank you for believing in me. Dad, I know you're looking down on me, proud of my accomplishment.

Thank you, God, for blessing me with the gift of writing and the desire to share my love of fiction and fantasy.

About the Author

A.R. Kaufer has dreamed of becoming a published author as long as she can remember. She lives in Indiana with her husband and furbabies. When she's not writing or reading, she enjoys playing video games, watching movies, and going for walks in the woods around her home. She has an eight book fantasy series premiering in December 2022.

Author Photo by: Kevin Kaufer